BLOOD
IN THE
DUST

Bill Swiggs was born in Victoria and brought up in Western Australia, where he still lives. He joined the Royal Australian Air Force as an aviation firefighter before becoming a police officer, and now works as a firefighter for a defence contractor. Bill divides his time between working, writing, flying and his grandchildren.

BLOOD
IN THE
DUST

BILL SWIGGS

ZAFFRE

First published in Great Britain in 2019 by
ZAFFRE
80–81 Wimpole St, London W1G 9RE

This is a work of fiction. Names, places, events and
incidents are either the products of the author's
imagination or used fictitiously.

A CIP catalogue record for this book is
available from the British Library.

ISBN: 978-1-78576-907-8

Also available as an ebook

1 3 5 7 9 10 8 6 4 2

Typeset by IDSUK (Data Connection) Ltd
Printed and bound in Great Britain by Clays Ltd, Elcograf S.p.A.

MIX
Paper from
responsible sources
FSC® C018072

Zaffre is an imprint of Bonnier Books UK
www.bonnierbooks.co.uk

This book is for my mother and father,
Joan and Robert Swiggs

The Colony of Victoria, Australia, 1853

The two boys came up along the spine of the spur where the last of the cleared land gave way to verdant bush. The older one carried the musket slung over his left shoulder and plodded along behind his brother who was armed with a long spear that he used to probe at the ground as they walked. On a patch of dirt among the dried grass he found what they were looking for.

'Here, Toby! He came this way.'

Toby O'Rourke squatted in the shadowed undergrowth and traced his fingers around the paw print. The marks left by the dog's claws were plain to see and Toby lifted his face in the direction the animal had gone, towards the rocky ridges below the first sweeping rise of the escarpment. He had been afraid of that, even though he suspected it all along.

'What do you reckon, Pad? Is this the bugger?'

'Could be,' Paddy murmured, glancing down for a moment. 'It's big enough to be him. Got a lair up among those rocks, I reckon.' He shifted the spear to his other hand as he spoke and looked to where the backbone of the ranges stood against a perfect sky.

Toby nodded and looked at the print again. Here in the shadows the dirt still held moisture from the night dew, but the edges of the print had dried enough to crack and crumble. He pressed his thumb into the soil and studied the outline it left, comparing it with the one left by the dingo.

'About three hours ago. We haven't come across any feathers since the chook pen. He's headed home for sure.' He stood and followed his brother's gaze, the Lovell musket heavy in his hand. 'Once he gets onto rocky ground it won't be easy to track him.'

'Ma will throw a blue fit if he gets any more of her chooks,' Paddy said. 'This is the fifth time this month he's raided the pen.'

'He's got a taste for chicken all right,' Toby agreed. He shouldered the musket and pointed uphill. 'Lead the way, Pad.'

Paddy moved off into the bush, his long spear held at the ready. Toby followed his brother's back and neither spoke for almost an hour, not until they had climbed to within fifty paces of the ridge line. Here, the bushland thinned out and a group of tumbledown boulders, as large as cottages, sat in the warm sun. Paddy stopped in the shade of one of the boulders and took the canteen from around his neck. He drank thirstily and then handed it to his brother.

Toby took several mouthfuls and wiped the back of his hand across his mouth. 'He must have come this way. Let's scout about a bit and see if we can pick up his spoor between the boulders.' He handed the canteen back to Paddy.

'Toby?'

'Yeah?'

Paddy pointed at the Lovell in his brother's hand. 'If we corner the bugger, do you think I could take the shot?'

Toby shook his head. 'You know how Pa feels about you using the Lovell. I wasn't allowed to touch it until I turned sixteen.'

'I'll be sixteen in a couple of months,' Paddy shot back. 'It's time I started learning how to shoot.'

'More like eight months. If Pa found out he'd skin us alive. It's one of his strictest rules.'

Paddy looked down at the ground, pouting. 'You've been using the gun for three years now and all I get is a spear. It's not fair.'

'But you're good with a spear, Paddy. Better than I ever was. We have to find the dingo before anyone gets to have a go at him anyway – with spear or gun.'

'Fine,' Paddy said. He shouldered his spear and moved away between the boulders.

Toby watched him go and shook his head, then turned to explore the ground in the opposite direction. He hadn't gone more than five paces before a low whistle stopped him. Turning, he doubled back and found his brother crouched between two rocks.

'This is the mongrel.' Paddy pointed at several paw prints in the dust between the boulders. Then he lifted a white feather from the ground and waved it under Toby's nose.

'He still has the chook in his mouth. I think you're right about his lair, Pad. Better let me take the lead.' Toby pulled the musket's hammer to full cock and moved off.

The tracks followed a well-worn path between the boulders, heading high along the ridge. They disappeared on rocky ground near the top, but Toby crossed the stony patch and found another print on the far side of the ridge. Here, the dingo had changed direction, traversing the high ground to their right.

Without ever really knowing how, Toby felt they were close to their quarry. He turned and held a finger to his lips. Paddy gave a curt nod and Toby started forward again, travelling more slowly, mindful of where he put his feet.

The backbone of the ridge ended abruptly at a twenty-foot drop. Fifty paces away it rose again in a series of giant steps and continued on. Toby looked down into the space between, into a mess of boulders and stunted vegetation. The dog had somehow found its way down and as Toby started to look for a way to do likewise, Paddy tapped his shoulder and pointed. Toby followed the direction of his finger and saw a small patch of vivid white, out of place amongst the earthy tones of granite and bushland. It took him a moment before he realised it was a mess of white feathers, the remains of his mother's chicken. Next to it was a flash of yellow and he could see the dingo, almost blending into the background. The dog stood in the shadow of an overhanging boulder, head held high as it sniffed the air. Paddy's fingers dug deep into Toby's shoulder.

As slowly as possible, Toby raised the Lovell and took aim. The dingo moved, turned, sniffed the wind. It sensed danger, but the boys were downwind and their scent had not carried to the animal. Toby tightened his finger on the trigger, but the dog moved behind a rock and was mostly hidden from view. Then it climbed onto the rock and turned in their direction, at last seeing the two brothers on the ridge.

Toby fired as the dog moved, the butt of the Lovell thudding into his shoulder as a cloud of gun smoke billowed. When it cleared the dingo was unhurt, twisting and turning around boulders as it sprinted in the opposite direction.

Paddy ran forward and let his spear fly in a high arc. It reached its zenith and plummeted towards the ground. A good throw, at least sixty yards, the distance helped by Paddy's vantage point on the ridge. The spear struck the ground two feet to the dog's right, the fire-hardened tip shattering against the rocks.

Toby dropped to one knee and opened the ammunition pouch slung around his neck. He pulled out a fresh cartridge, tore it open with his teeth, poured the fine grains of gunpowder into the barrel of the Lovell and followed it with a musket ball in a wad of cloth. With speed garnered through practice, he slid the loading rod from beneath the barrel and tamped the load. As he slid the rod back home with one hand, the other was already placing a cap onto the firing nipple. Then he had the hammer at full cock again and aimed at the yellow shadow dashing between the rocks.

The dingo reached the far rise and started its climb, leaping from boulder to boulder. The animal was tiring, but it still carried too much speed for Toby to have a clean shot.

'Take him, Toby,' Paddy urged. 'You can do it.'

Toby watched the dingo climb higher and higher, following every movement with the front sight.

'C'mon, Toby! Take the shot!'

There was such an edge of excitement in his brother's voice that Toby glanced up at him. Paddy's gaze followed the dingo intently and it took him several moments to realise Toby was holding the musket towards him.

'You take the shot, Pad.'

Paddy blinked uncertainly, not taking his eyes off the gun. 'But what about the rules?'

'You're nearly sixteen. C'mon, do you want to take the shot or not?'

Paddy hesitated for a heartbeat, then he took the Lovell from Toby and mimicked his posture, crouching down on one knee.

'Don't fire yet,' Toby warned. 'He's moving too fast.'

'U-huh!'

'Too many rocks in the way. Wait until he tops the ridge and exposes himself on the skyline.'

'U-huh!'

'The ball will drop about four inches at that distance, so aim a little high.'

'U-huh!'

The dingo was a yard beneath the ridgetop now. It paused briefly on a boulder and gathered itself for the final leap that would carry it out of the gully.

'When he lands after this jump. Take him, Pad!'

The dingo leaped gracefully through the air with its front legs outstretched, looking more like a cat than a dog. It gained the edge of the gully and paused to glance in the direction of the brothers, its outline silhouetted against the sky. At that instant, Paddy fired.

Toby heard his brother grunt from the force of the recoil. Another cloud of gun smoke obscured their vision before being snatched away on the breeze. The gunshot echoed off the ranges, coming at them again and again.

The dingo lay sprawled on the opposite ridge. The ball had struck the animal in the ribs and its hind legs twitched as it died.

'Nice shooting, Pad. You killed him. He won't be coming down to raid Ma's chooks any more, that's for sure.'

Paddy lowered the gun, a grin of triumph on his face. He held the musket out for Toby to take. 'That was the best thing I have ever done in my life, Toby.'

'Just make sure Pa doesn't find out I let you use the gun. He'll never let either of us near it again.'

'I won't, Toby. You can bet I won't.'

Toby could see in his brother's eyes that there was no way he would give either of them up. 'C'mon,' he said. 'Let's go skin the bugger to prove to Ma that we got him.'

Chilbi watched the smoke coming from the chimney of the little homestead on the valley floor and knew that soon they would kill again. The two Djarriba were excited, shifting in their saddles and chattering in that strange tongue of theirs, talking quickly so that he was only able to follow half the conversation.

'There'll be food down there. I can't eat too much more of that black fella shit,' the one called Tanner complained. No matter how good the hunt had been or the amount of food on offer, he would often study his meal with a disgusted look, push it away and eat some of the dried meat he carried in his saddlebags instead.

The other Djarriba, the big white man Chilbi's people had named Warrigal, was better accustomed to the food offered by the land, though he never hunted for it himself. That task he left to the three Jannjirra warriors.

'Chilbi?'

The white men had finished their discussion.

'Yes, Warrigal?'

'You heard the Djarriba thunder earlier?' the big man said, speaking the language of the people.

Chilbi nodded. The noise had caused Warrigal and Tanner to reach for their weapons and they had waited nervously in the shadows until the echoes died away.

'How far away?'

Chilbi pointed across the valley. 'Long way that way.'

Warrigal considered this information. 'Those shots were far enough apart to have come from the same gun.'

'Just a little homestead,' Tanner said. 'A ma and pa outfit, I reckon. Even if the hunter gets home before we get there, I don't think they'll give us too much trouble. We've been three weeks in the bush. I need a good feed, Warrigal.'

'Me too,' Warrigal nodded his big, scraggly head. 'Chilbi? Scout us a way down into the valley.' He pointed at the homestead. 'We will take our war to those below.'

'Yes, Warrigal.' Chilbi urged his mount forward, still feeling a little uncomfortable at the motion of the huge beast beneath him. His brothers, Yawong and Tarrat, fell in behind, their hands resting on their war clubs.

S tanding on the verandah of the homestead, Sean O'Rourke looked at the dingo pelt at his feet, then his two sons, and then the pelt again.

'So you got him, boys?' He towered over both his lads, his greying head almost brushing the bush poles that were the homestead's rafters.

'Sure did, Pa.' Paddy said, excited to tell the story of the hunt, the words gushing from his mouth. 'We tracked him right into that gully up beyond the ridge.'

'That so?' their father said. He picked up the raw pelt and poked his finger through the hole made by the musket ball. 'Only one hole in it. I heard two shots echo off the hills.'

'Missed with the first one,' Toby said quickly, before Paddy could respond. 'He made a run for higher ground. Gave me time to reload and take him down when he reached the skyline.'

'Ah! Nice work.' Their father nodded his head. 'Well, your mother will be pleased. This old dog won't be raiding her chooks any more.' He dropped the pelt onto the verandah boards. 'We can cure this later.' His hand shot out and gripped Toby's chin, the thumb rubbing his right cheek. 'The cap from the Lovell has left a little mark on your face, Toby. Best you go and wash it off.'

Toby felt the acid of despair in his stomach. As his father rubbed at his cheek, he turned his eyes towards Paddy. His brother still had that triumphant grin on his face, and the mark left by the flash of the firing cap was plain to see against his tanned skin.

'Paddy? You best wash yours off, too. Then you can come and help me take a hind quarter off a side of mutton for your mother to roast. Go now,' he barked, and Paddy turned and ran to where the washstand stood behind the homestead, his hand rubbing at his cheek.

Toby felt the grip tighten on his chin and he looked up at his father. Sean O'Rourke's eyes were fixed firmly on him. There was a hint of anger in the steel-blue depths, but his father's beard hid the set of his mouth.

'Who taught you to shoot, Toby?'

'You did, Pa.'

'Are you a good shot, boy?'

'I like to think so, Pa.'

'Oh, you do, do you?' The eyes lightened a little and creased at the corners. 'So, if you're such a good shot, then you must've had a good teacher.'

'Yes, Pa.'

'But not good enough to teach your brother how to shoot.'

Toby wanted to turn away, to look anywhere but at his father, but the grip on his chin was firm. 'Pa, he was pleading with me. I did it more to shut him up than anything else. You know what Paddy's like when he gets to whining about something.'

Sean ignored the tone in his son's voice. 'Toby, when I let you use the gun, I place it into your responsibility. My rules then become your rules.'

'Yes, Pa.'

'Oh, "Yes, Pa", is it now? It wasn't "Yes, Pa" when you let Paddy use the gun.'

'I'm sorry, Pa.'

The hand dropped and Toby rubbed at his chin as he waited for his father to decide what his punishment would be.

'Your mother is cooking a roast for tonight's dinner. She needs the wood box by the kitchen door kept topped up with a good supply. In between cutting wood, you can help her in the kitchen. Peeling potatoes, stripping cabbage, whatever she needs.'

'Yes, Pa.'

'And you won't be using the Lovell for a while. From now until Paddy turns sixteen. You can both wait.'

Toby drew breath to protest, but the look in his father's eyes made him think again. He was nineteen years old and his father was punishing him as if he were twelve, but he knew there was nothing he could do but accept the punishment and wait out his time.

'Go and wash your face, Toby. Then I want to hear that axe ringing for an hour or more.'

Toby nodded and turned away, but his father's voice brought him up short.

'So, the first time Paddy fires the gun, he drops a dingo with a chest shot. At what range?'

Toby turned to see his father holding the pelt again, his finger through the hole. 'Must've been all of eighty yards, Pa.'

'Eighty yards, hey?' Sean looked at his finger and shook his head in wonder. Then he gave Toby a look that said he had better get moving.

Toby was at the wood heap behind the tack shed when he first noticed the riders. They were still high on the ridge, but coming steadily along the outside of the house paddock. It was the direction they came from that made them a curiosity. The O'Rourke place was the last of a string of properties that followed a narrow valley into the maw of the mountains. There was nothing north until the settled areas of the Goulburn valley and the only paths through were east at the Kilmore Gap, or at the Mount Alexander road, a day's ride to the west.

The riders rounded the corner at the far side of the house paddock and paused beside the two-rut track that led into the settlement of Bunyong Creek, five miles down the valley. Toby saw an arm or two gesture back and forth as they discussed their options. After a few moments they turned towards the slip rails at the bottom of the paddock.

Toby gathered up an armload of wood and walked around the shed to the front of the homestead where he climbed the verandah steps and dropped the wood into a box beside the open kitchen door. Careful to shake any woodchips from his hair and clothing, he went inside.

The heat in the humble little home was stifling and sweat prickled the skin on his arms. His mother stood stirring a pot in the shimmering air around the oven. A pile of peeled potatoes sat on a plate on the table.

'I cut a good load, Ma. Enough for a couple of days at least.'

Ellen O'Rourke finished her stirring and tapped the wooden spoon on the brim of the pot a few times before setting it down. 'You're a good lad to be sure,' she said in her bubbling Irish brogue.

'Where's Pa?'

Ellen pointed with her chin towards the side of the house, in the direction of the little shed. 'He's still out there with Paddy, cutting a hock off last week's kill. Tell him to be quick about it. If it doesn't go in the oven soon we won't be eating till well after eight.'

'I will, Ma.' He turned for the door then remembered the horsemen. 'Might have a few guests. There's five coves down at the slip rails.'

'Five?' Ellen gave a startled look. Her free hand automatically went to her hair, brushing several sweaty strands into place. 'I shall have to put a bonnet on. Tell your father to make it a whole hind quarter if we are going to have guests for dinner.' She looked at the plate of peeled potatoes and shook her head. 'I shall be needing some more potatoes peeled, Toby.'

'I'll let Pa know and then I'll peel some right away, Ma.'

He found his father standing beside the carcass of a sheep that hung from a chain fixed to one of the shed's rafters. The damp hessian cloth had been removed and his father was running a knife back and forth across a steel, using rapid, well-practised strokes. Paddy stood nearby, waiting to help with the hock once his father cut it away.

'What's up with you, me boyo?' Sean said as he noticed Toby in the doorway. 'I don't hear that axe ringing.'

'There's five horsemen heading for the slip rails. They're planning on paying us a visit.'

'Geoff Smith and his boys, back from their stock camp?' Sean said.

Toby shook his head. 'Nah. These fellows rode down off the ridge. Looks like they've been up in the ranges.'

'Maybe they're prospectors,' Paddy offered.

'I don't think so.' Toby shook his head again. 'They look pretty ragged – like they've been living rough.'

'They might just be after a good feed.' Sean set the steel aside and traced his first cut with a finger.

'Ma says to make it a whole hind quarter. Just in case they're here for supper.'

'Good thinking.' Sean shifted his finger. He went at the carcass with the knife, using fluid strokes. 'Ready to take the weight, Pad?' Unlike the homestead, the shed had a dirt floor. To allow the cut of meat to fall would be a travesty.

Paddy stepped up and took hold of the leg. 'Ready, Pa.' Their father made the final cuts and Paddy stood back with the hind quarter in his hands.

'Get that to your mother. She'll be waiting for it,' Sean said, and Paddy turned for the homestead, brushing past Toby. Sean watched his son go and then wiped the knife clean on a piece of cloth before placing it in its leather sheath. 'Now, let's take a look at these fellows.'

Toby walked with his father to the homestead and they climbed the steps onto the verandah. The riders were at the slip rails, about three hundred paces off. As they watched, one of the men dismounted, walked to the rails and pushed them open.

'They don't look like diggers to me.' Ellen came out of the kitchen and stood beside her husband. She wiped her hands on her apron and Toby noticed she had tidied her hair and now wore a dark-blue bonnet. 'I can't see a pick or shovel anywhere on those horses.'

Paddy pushed his way in next to Toby, working his elbows to make room. 'Ma's right,' he said. 'Those miners that called in last month had two packhorses loaded with stuff.'

Squinting against the afternoon glare, Toby studied the horsemen. The two leading the little procession sat straight-backed, heels low in the stirrups in the English fashion, but the three trailing behind sat their mounts in a loose, undisciplined manner. Even at that distance his sharp eyes could pick out broad brows and deep-set eyes.

'I reckon the last three are Aborigines.'

'They could be native police,' Paddy said excitedly. 'Maybe they've been out chasing bushrangers.'

Toby elbowed his brother in the ribs. 'Don't be daft, Pad. They'd be in uniform if they were police. These blokes are in little more than rags.'

The men urged their horses through into the house paddock and Toby expected to see the dismounted man push the slip rails closed again, but he simply swung up onto his horse and followed the others towards the homestead, leaving them wide open. There was a herd of two hundred and fifty head in the paddock, waiting to be driven to the butchers' yards at the diggings. These visitors would cop hell when they arrived at the homestead.

Beside him, his father straightened, eyes narrowing with suspicion.

'Toby!' His voice came as a low growl.

'Yes, Pa?'

'Fetch the Lovell for me, boyo.'

Paddy gave a little chuckle at the thought of the drama as their father prepared to confront the men. Toby, on the other hand, felt uneasy. Sean O'Rourke was an emancipated convict and had survived the horrendous conditions of a prison hulk, had been worked to the point of exhaustion on a chain gang and still bore the scars of the punishment lash. There wasn't much in the world that frightened him, and yet Toby thought there had been a hint of fear in his voice.

He found the Lovell where it was always kept, behind his parents' bedroom door, along with the leather pouch containing powder, caps and shot. He knew the weapon was loaded. His father had seen to that after the boys' return, in case of a chance shot at fresh meat for the stew pot. It stayed that way, propped behind the door, unprimed until needed. With trembling fingers, Toby opened the bag and took out a small copper cap, fumbling as he placed it onto the nipple. He eased the hammer down and, keeping the muzzle pointed skywards, stepped back out onto the verandah, where he handed the musket and leather bag to his father.

'Here you are, Pa. Primed and ready.'

Sean pulled the hammer to full cock. 'Good lad!' He cradled the barrel of the musket across the crook of his left elbow. 'Ellen, take the boys inside and close the door. Looks like these men are planning on leaving us in a hell of a hurry.'

'Sean, are you sure this is the right way to go about things?' His mother's voice had lost its melodic quality, replaced instead with a quivering tension. 'Maybe your being armed will only provoke them if they mean us harm?'

Sean shook his head. 'If they mean us harm, then it won't hurt to show them we have the means to defend ourselves. They may just be in a hurry, but until we find out for sure, I want you and the boys inside.'

Ellen nodded and took Paddy by the arm, leading him into the kitchen. Toby hesitated, his nervous gaze flicking between the approaching men and his father. If there was going to be trouble, he wanted to be standing at his father's side.

'Inside, Toby!' Sean growled. Toby didn't move and his father gave him a wink. 'I'll be fine, son.' His voice softened and his hand reached out, giving his shoulder an affectionate squeeze. 'Do as I tell you.'

Toby hesitated a moment more then went inside and closed the door. He hurried to the window by the stove where his mother and brother were watching the horsemen ride up from the slip rails.

The riders were closer now and he could make out more detail. Two white men rode at the head of the little column. The man leading seemed too big for his horse, his large frame filling the saddle, the stirrup straps at full length to accommodate long legs. He had a cabbage-tree hat pulled low over his eyes and a full beard of black, matted hair that reached halfway down his chest. His head turned from side to side as he rode, examining the corners of outbuildings and shadows beneath the trees. When he saw the faces in the window, he paused and his cold stare filled Toby with fear.

The other white man was thin and short with sickly-yellow skin. He wore a seafarer's peaked cap pushed back on his head. A broad smile exposed a set of tobacco-stained teeth.

The other three men were Aborigines, dressed in a curious mixture of animal skins and European clothing. They kept a little distance between themselves and the two leaders, their eyes flicking left and right.

The white men eyed the musket in Sean's hands and said something to each other. They separated as they came on, heading for opposite ends of the verandah. Sean had to step back a little to keep them both in sight without turning his head too far. The little yellow man reined in on the left and lifted a hand in greeting.

'No cause for concern, sir,' he said, pointing at the musket. 'We're just after some directions.' He swept his gaze over the front of the homestead. 'Be glad of some food, too,' he added, his nostrils flaring as he sniffed the air. 'Happy to pay you.'

'Why the hell didn't you close the slip rails?' Toby heard his father snap. 'Can't you see I've got cattle in the paddock?'

'We don't expect to stay long,' the other man responded, his voice as deep as mountain thunder. 'We'll close them on the way out.'

'If you want anything from me, you'll ride back down and close them now.'

The little man lifted his chin defiantly. Toby saw the way his eyes narrowed and knew then that they meant trouble. His next words only served to confirm this.

'And if we don't?'

Sean lowered the musket's muzzle a little. 'Then you'll get nothing here.'

'Now, don't be rash, sir.' The large man fidgeted in the folds of his shirt, drawing Sean's attention. He produced a little leather purse and bounced it on the drawstring so the contents jangled. 'Like we said; we'll pay you.' The purse slipped from his fingers and fell into the dust beside his horse. 'Oops!'

'I don't want your money. You can turn around and ride away. There's nothing for you here.'

The big man raised his hands in resignation. 'Sorry to have caused you any concern. If you'll be kind enough to return my purse we'll be on our way. We'll close the slip rails as we go.'

Toby watched as his father stepped off the verandah and stooped towards the purse. A flash of movement drew his attention back to the little man as he pulled a single-shot pistol from beneath his shirt and aimed it at his father. There was a metallic click as the pistol cocked.

'Pa! Look out!'

His father was half turned away and had one hand out-stretched towards the purse, but at Toby's warning he straightened and raised the musket, levelling the barrel at the little man as a spurt of smoke erupted from the pistol. A wind snapped at his father's shirt and the concussion of the gunshot rattled the glass in the window. The musket fired a heartbeat later. His father's arm jerked with the recoil of the unbraced, one-handed shot. The little man took the musket ball in the centre of his chest and fell backwards off his horse. Even as the man fell, his father reversed the empty musket in his grip, holding it like a club as he turned towards the other rider. But the big man had a revolver in his grip and fired before Sean had halved the distance between them.

Toby's mother screamed as his father staggered backwards. Sean dropped the musket and clutched at his chest. The stranger extended his arm straight and paused, taking aim down the barrel. He fired again and Sean fell backwards onto the ground.

The echo of gunshots boomed about the valley, holding Toby in that brief, terrifying moment. Then, through the horror, he became aware of another noise. His mother was screaming again, a high-pitched, keening wail. She held her skirts bunched in both hands to free her legs as she ran across the kitchen. Too late, Toby realised what she was about to do.

'No, Ma!'

He moved to stop her.

Ellen reached the door and yanked it open, rushing out onto the verandah, screaming as she ran. The revolver fired again and her scream was cut off. Toby reached the doorway to see his mother on the boards, her skirts thrown up in disarray, her arms reaching for the steps and her husband. Blood pounded in Toby's ears, his stomach a knot of fear and panic. He moved to where his mother lay, but the sound of the revolver being cocked stopped him short.

The big man aimed the gun at Toby's head.

'Don't bloody move!'

Toby was torn between wanting to help his mother and fear. His indecision held him fast and probably saved his life.

The stranger swung off his horse. He tossed the reins to one of the Aborigines and walked calmly up the steps, barely glancing down at Ellen and the growing pool of blood.

'I thought she was you.'

He grabbed Toby by the arm and turned him back to the kitchen door.

'I thought she was you coming at me with another bloody gun.' There was no emotion in the voice, no hint of regret, just a simple statement of fact. He pushed Toby inside and turned to the three Aborigines.

'Search the other buildings. Make sure no one else is hiding.'

The Aborigines pulled clubs from beneath their cloaks and slid from their horses. They rushed between the homestead and the tack shed.

Paddy dropped to the floor and crawled under the table as the stranger stepped into the kitchen. The man let Toby go, shoving him towards the far wall.

'Sit!'

Toby lowered himself onto a kitchen chair and watched through tear-filled eyes as the man opened the door to his parents' bedroom and glanced inside. He then went to the back door and did the same with the boys' little lean-to room. Satisfied there was no one else in the house he moved to the stove where the remainder of the stew Ellen had prepared for lunch still simmered away. He ladled out a huge helping into a bowl, came back to the table, pushed the hind quarter of lamb aside and sat down, then shovelled stew into his mouth as fast as he could manage.

One of the Aborigines came to the doorway. 'No more people here, Warrigal.'

The man nodded and droplets of stew flew from his tangled beard. He pointed at the pot on the stove. 'Take it to the others, Chilbi. Eat while you can. The traps may not be far behind us.'

Without a glance at Toby or Paddy, the Aborigine went to the stove, picked up the pot and hurried back out into the yard.

The stranger emptied the bowl in moments and pushed it into the middle of the table. He stood and went to the kitchen cupboards where he rummaged around and found a flour bag that he began filling, tossing in bags of sugar and tea, a large tin of golden syrup and a loaf of bread. Then he went into their parents' bedroom and Toby could hear him pulling open drawers and cupboards. He came back into the kitchen and pointed the revolver at Toby.

'Where does Daddy hide his money?'

Toby knew his father had at least twenty pounds in a rawhide wallet hidden under the chest of drawers in the room. Beyond his grief and terror he felt a little spark of defiance flare. This man was not going to take everything from him. 'There isn't any.' His voice cracked and didn't sound as convincing as he'd hoped.

'Don't lie to me, boy.' The revolver barrel almost touched Toby's nose.

'We—we don't have any money. Not until we sell the cattle in the yard.'

'Is that so?' He lowered the revolver and shoved the table aside. Paddy tried to squirm away, but the stranger took a fistful of hair and yanked the boy to his feet. Paddy was a big lad for fifteen, but the stranger had no trouble holding him at full-stretch.

Paddy let out a squeal of terror and closed his eyes. 'Please, Toby! Make him stop.'

Toby stood and the man whirled, dragging Paddy by the hair like a child's doll.

'Sit!' he roared.

Toby shrank back onto the chair.

The man twisted Paddy around so he could look into the boy's face.

'Open your eyes, boy.'

Paddy kept his eyes firmly closed.

Infuriated, the stranger shook him by the hair and screamed, 'Where does Daddy hide his money?' He shook so hard that some of Paddy's hair came away in his fist and he lost his grip. Paddy cried out and fell to the floor. He scrambled for the door on all fours, reached the verandah and broke into a full run.

Toby ran after him, but the stranger grabbed him by the collar of his shirt and held him fast. He saw Paddy reach the rail and leap it in a clumsy lunge, landing in the dust beyond where he rolled to his feet and kept running.

The three Aborigines were crowded around the pot, using their hands to ladle stew into their mouths. The one who had come to the kitchen door saw Paddy land in the yard and gave chase.

'Run, Paddy!' But Toby could see that his brother wasn't going to make it. The Aborigine caught him in several paces and the club hissed through the air. The vicious knob of fire-hardened wood struck Paddy on the side of his head. His brother let out a grunt and sprawled in the dust where he lay still.

'You bastards!' Toby felt his stomach slide with terror and anger. He struggled to get free, but the stranger just chuckled under his breath and pushed him out onto the verandah.

Toby stopped struggling and stooped towards his mother, but a kick in the backside sent him tumbling down the steps.

'Stay down,' the deep voice warned.

He lay on the ground and watched as the stranger went to his horse. He was carrying the hind quarter from the kitchen table and tossed it to one of the Aborigines.

'Take this, Tarrat. If we get nothing else from this place, at least we will eat well for the next few days.' He then walked to where Toby lay sobbing on the ground and took hold of his shirt front, pulling him to his feet. The stranger held him so close Toby could smell stew on his rancid breath.

'Don't be fool enough to follow me, boy.' The dark eyes seemed to burn through him.

Toby's head lolled like a drunkard's as he was shoved backwards. The stranger swung up onto his horse and rounded on the Aborigines.

'On your horses, you black heathens.'

The Aborigines dropped the pot and ran for their animals, springing lithely onto their backs. One of them gathered up the reins of their dead companion's horse, ignoring his body on the ground. They followed the white man towards the slip rails.

Toby stood between the bodies of his mother and father and watched the men ride away. They reached the slip rails and did not pause or look back, riding on until the bush surrounded them and they were gone. He stared after them for a long time, too scared and shocked to move, his gaze fixed on the patch of bushland where they had disappeared.

His brother's low groan snapped him out of the trance-like state.

'My God, Paddy!'

Standing at the starboard rail of the *Charlotte Elizabeth*, Annie Hocking watched the low, green hills of Australia slip by. This was not her first glimpse of her new homeland, but with the ship on a long starboard tack past the battered headland of Cape Schanck, it was the closest she had come to that mysterious continent at the end of the world. For the past five days a gusting north wind had prevented the ship from entering Port Phillip Bay. After seven months at sea they were forced to tack back and forth across the choppy waters of Bass Strait, a mere sixty miles from their destination, as the captain waited for more favourable conditions.

Annie lifted her face and sniffed the air, delighting in the medicine-like smell of eucalyptus carried on the wind. There were other scents there as well, grasses and something earthy that she imagined was from the great inland deserts, the birthplace of the wind itself. Underneath her feeling of delight, the pang of disappointment grew, for it appeared today would be no different from any other and the *Charlotte Elizabeth* would not be attempting to cross the notorious bar guarding the bay. Holding the rail with one hand, the other firmly on her bonnet, Annie studied the hazy hills, longing to be among them.

'Do you think we will be able to see kangaroos when we enter the bay?' Betty asked.

Annie tore her gaze away from the shoreline and looked down at her sister. Betty had not been successful in keeping her own bonnet on and her hair fluttered behind her in long, auburn streamers. With her freckled face screwed up against the glare, she examined the distant shore.

'I don't know,' Annie said. 'Maybe.'

'I bet we do,' Betty said with certainty. 'I bet we see kangaroos and wombats and possums, but not snakes. I don't want to see any snakes. I think they are horrid creatures.' Among the ten-year-old's most treasured possessions was an almanac of Australian creatures that she studied every day with great intensity.

'I imagine there aren't many snakes in Melbourne itself,' Annie replied, turning back to the shoreline. 'Or any of those other animals either.' Then another thought occurred to her.

'Was Mama dressed when you left our berth, Betty?'

The little girl nodded. 'She was. Papa was most insistent that she come on deck and take the air. I think she will this time.'

'I hope so,' Annie said. 'She can't stay in her bunk forever.'

'She still misses Tom,' Betty said softly. 'I miss him, too.'

Annie placed an arm around her sister. 'We all miss Tom, but it's been four months nearly. He wouldn't want us to be so miserable.' As she spoke, she couldn't help but let her gaze drift to the port rail, to the place where the captain had spoken his kind words, where the crew had tilted the board, committing her brother's body to the deep, somewhere off Africa. Their mother had not been on deck since that moment.

Tears welled in the depths of Betty's hazel eyes. Their brother's mysterious illness and sudden passing had been a great shock to them all. Annie decided to change the subject.

'I read somewhere that in Ballarat you can pick gold nuggets from the ground just by kicking a few stones out of your way.'

'I'm going to find the biggest gold nugget ever,' Betty said, her mood brightening. 'And then I'm going to buy some land and build an enormous house with huge stables and have lots of horses. I really like horses, Annie.'

'I know,' Annie responded, pleased with herself for preventing another bout of tears.

'What are you two nattering about?'

The girls turned to find their parents behind them. Frank Hocking had an arm around his wife's shoulders and a smile on his freshly shaven face. Their mother wore a black shawl despite the warm wind. Her dark eyes and haunted face still showed a mother's grief.

'Come look, Mama,' Annie said, making room at the rail. 'Beyond those hills is Port Phillip Bay and Victoria.'

Maree moved beside her daughter and examined the distant shore. 'Then why are we sailing away from it?'

'The wind is blowing straight out of the entrance,' Annie said. 'We have to wait until it changes into the southern half.' Her months at sea had given her more than a smattering of nautical terms.

'Nearly there,' Maree said more to herself than anyone else. 'This horrid voyage will be over soon.'

'Yes, Mama, we're nearly there.' Annie took her mother's hand and gave it a squeeze. 'Why don't you and I take a turn around the deck?' Before her mother could protest, she turned her towards the bow and led her away. Groups of sailors stopped whatever they were doing and watched the women walk past. At forty-one years of age, Maree still possessed an hourglass figure of which most women would be envious. Annie had turned seventeen two months after sailing from Plymouth. With her button nose, raven hair and full-breasted figure, some of the sailors stared a little longer than would be considered polite.

'It's wonderful to see you up and about, Mama. There's no good to be served by lying in your bunk.'

'I've had little strength for much else, my girl. And I just couldn't bear to look down at that cold dark water. Tom should have been laid to rest in the cemetery back home in Hastings, but I suppose that just wasn't possible.'

'No, Mama,' Annie said, giving her hand a squeeze. 'But at least he's at rest and is suffering no more pain. For that we should be grateful.'

'Yes, grateful,' Maree said softly.

They paused close to the bow. The haze had cleared and the hills stood out in crisp contrast to the blue sky. Almost close enough to touch, Annie thought. Maree must have seen the direction of her gaze.

'Do you think there will be happiness for us beyond those hills, Annie?'

Annie considered the question for a moment. She knew it had been no mean feat for her parents to sell up everything they owned and head out to the colonies at the bottom of the world. They had bickered most nights in the weeks leading up to their departure. Back then, Tom had been the mediator. Good old dependable, quietly spoken Tom who had stepped in and made them both see sense when it seemed the situation was becoming impossible. He had wanted to come, to start a new life in a new world, away from the dirt and grime and poverty of England. A place where you never got ahead, no matter how hard you worked.

'I think everything we have ever wanted is waiting for us behind those hills, Mama.'

'I hope you are right, my girl. I hope you are right.'

Annie looked once more to the hills and felt the warm breeze on her face. She felt the wind drop and above her the sails slackened and fluttered fitfully. From behind them an officer yelled an order and sailors poured into the rigging to make adjustments. The ship lost headway until she wallowed in the troughs, pitching and rolling so that Annie and her mother had to grasp the rail to keep their feet.

'What is happening?' Maree asked as she stared aghast at the flurry of activity.

'It appears your coming on deck was a good omen for us, Mama. The wind is shifting at last.'

They returned down the pitching deck to where Frank and Betty watched the sailors at work. They seemed to be getting a grip on the ship. The sails snapped taut and the vessel let out an almost mortal groan as the masts and rigging took the strain. The deck surged beneath their feet as the *Charlotte Elizabeth* gained headway. Annie was delighted to see the bow swing towards those distant hills.

The Hocking family stood together at the rail for an hour or more and watched their progress along the shoreline. Soon they were close enough to see waves crashing onto a white beach. Looking ahead, Annie could see a rocky headland, steep-sided with stunted vegetation clinging to the heights.

'That must be Point Nepean,' she said, remembering the name of the eastern headland that guarded the bay. 'We are nearly there.' She felt the excitement building inside her.

'Begging your pardon, sir, ladies.' A sailor Annie knew as Bosun Miggins addressed them from the port rail. 'Cap'n says there's enough light left in the day to attempt the bar. He'd like all passengers below decks until we make the bay.'

'Certainly,' Frank said. He spread his arms wide and herded his family towards the companionway.

They found the way to their berth and Annie climbed onto the bunk she shared with her sister. There were no portholes, so she sat in silence and imagined their progress by the motion of the ship. The bow rose and plunged as they beat into a heavy swell. From forward came a steady slap and splash as the ship cut through the waves. Some time later she heard orders shouted on the deck above her and the familiar creak from the rigging as they changed tack. The *Charlotte Elizabeth* moved with a new motion now, rolling and surging, as if the waves came from all directions at once. Betty let out a shriek of delight as they were lifted high on a crest, then plunged suddenly into a trough. The sound of retching came from the next berth and the stench of bile filled the air. Soon, others were vomiting as well, but Annie and Betty just smiled and hugged each other in the gloom. Nothing would spoil their mood. They were nearly there.

This crazy ride went on for twenty minutes or more before the motion of the ship settled as she pushed into a moderate sea.

'I think we are through,' Annie said to no one in particular, and beside her Betty clapped her hands. To confirm this, a sailor came down between the berths announcing that they were free to go on deck. Annie and Betty were the first to the companionway, but Betty beat Annie onto the steps.

'Look how close the land is!' Betty paused at the top step. 'You can almost touch it. Come and look, Annie.'

'I will if you get your backside out of my way.' Annie gave her sister a push on the rump and Betty stepped out of the companionway and onto the deck, allowing her through.

Patches of windswept vegetation and sand dunes as white as virgin snow drifted past. Off the starboard beam waves crashed onto a rocky headland. The sun sat low on the western horizon and the ship appeared to be sailing on a sea of liquid gold that made both girls gasp with delight.

'Excuse me, miss,' someone said from behind, and Annie realised she was now blocking the companionway. She apologised and climbed onto the deck.

The warmth was gone from the wind. It pushed out of the south-east now and carried a chill that made Annie wish she had brought a shawl up with her. She needn't have worried. Her parents appeared on deck a few minutes later and Maree carried shawls for both girls, insisting that they put them on immediately. Then together they made their way forward and stood near the capstan to watch the setting sun.

'Such a display of colour,' Maree said, and Annie could sense the delight in her voice, the first in months.

'Tomorrow,' said Annie. 'Tomorrow we will stand on Australia.' She pulled her sister to her and they hugged each other with excitement as they watched a golden sky above a golden sea.

'Everything in this country is gold,' her father remarked, his family standing around him. 'We just have to work at getting our share now.'

The horse's flanks were a lather of foaming sweat as Toby wheeled the wagonette in a tight circle around the Bunyong Creek Hotel. The sun had set while he'd been on the road and he used the waning light of dusk to find his way. Crossing the track that was also the main street, he headed for the creek where a string of tents marked the camps of travellers who had stopped to rest and slake their thirst before continuing northwards to the diggings at Mount Alexander and Bendigo Creek.

Two diggers sat beside a campfire outside the first tent in the row. Toby reined the horse to a stop and the men scowled up at him, waving their hands in front of their faces in annoyance at the cloud of dust that settled around them. One digger, his face a mass of ginger whiskers, spat a glob of dust-stained spittle onto the ground. 'What's the hurry, young fella?'

Toby ignored the dirty looks. 'My neighbour tells me there's a doctor camped along here somewhere.'

The other digger climbed to his feet. 'Someone better be hurt real bad to warrant driving into camp like a madman.'

'My brother,' Toby said, gesturing into the load space behind him.

The digger strode over and looked into the wagonette where Paddy lay on a makeshift mattress of saddle blankets. The depression in his skull still bled and had stained the blanket under his head. Only the shallow rise and fall of his chest gave any indication the boy was still alive.

'Bloody hell!' The digger gasped and crossed himself. 'What happened to him?'

'Bushrangers,' Toby snapped. 'Now tell me, is there a doctor camped along here or not?'

The digger came up level with the driving seat and pointed down the row of tents. 'That tall one near the end, that's the doc's tent.'

Toby didn't bother to thank the man. He whipped the reins and the panting horse started reluctantly forward. Outside the designated tent he reined in, applied the brake and jumped to the ground.

'Hello?' He rapped his knuckles against the support pole outside the flap. 'Hello the tent. Is the doctor here?'

The flap parted and a gaunt, bespectacled face appeared. 'I'm Doctor Collier.'

Toby grabbed the doctor's arm and pulled him towards the wagonette. 'Please, sir. It's my brother. He got clouted with a club. He's in a bad way.'

The doctor leaned over the sideboard and held his spectacles on his nose with one hand as he gave Paddy a cursory examination. Tut-tutting under his breath, he stepped back and rounded on the gathering crowd of diggers come to see what the commotion was all about.

'You and you.' The doctor singled out two burly men. 'Lift the boy out of the wagonette very carefully. Be mindful of his head. Don't let it twist or be bumped. Take him into my tent and lay him on the bed. Carefully,' he warned. 'Any rough handling might kill him.'

Toby stepped back and let the two diggers lift his brother out of the wagonette, relieved to see them handling him gently. The doctor held the flap of the tent open and they settled the boy onto a camp bed.

'He was hit by a club, you say?' the doctor asked.

Toby rattled through the events of that afternoon. A couple of diggers interrupted and tried to ask questions, but the doctor waved them into silence.

'Your parents were shot?' The doctor had a look of disbelief on his face as he took Toby's arm and led him outside.

'Both dead.' Toby tried hard to control his voice. He swallowed down the lump in his throat. 'I got Paddy into the wagonette and headed for town. I ran into a neighbour, Mrs Smith, on the way. She told me you were camped here. Thank God you were. I thought I was going to have to take him all the way to Bacchus Marsh. He never would have survived that journey.' Toby's lips started to tremble and the doctor placed a hand on his arm.

'I shall do what I can for your brother. It's best if you wait outside.'

The doctor slipped into the tent and Toby lowered himself onto a packing box beside a smouldering campfire. A digger came over and thrust a pannikin of hot tea into his hands. 'There you go, young fella.' Toby looked up and recognised the digger who had directed him to the doctor's tent. He nodded his thanks and looked down at the tea, but didn't take a sip.

The doctor muttered away to himself in the tent as he worked on Paddy. Toby had seen a skull with a depression like that once before when one of his father's horses had kicked a dog. The animal had lived through one agonising night of miserable whimpering. The next morning his father had taken the dog and the Lovell behind the tack shed and ended its suffering.

Not my brother. Please God, not my brother. He's the only person I have left in the world.

He thought of his parents, their bodies lying where they had fallen. He hadn't even taken the time to move or cover them. When he'd discovered Paddy was still alive he'd hooked the horse to the wagonette, bundled his brother in as best he could and headed for town. Colleen Smith and her daughter had been returning to their neighbouring property when Toby came across them on the track. She'd told him about the doctor camped in town and said she would go to the homestead and see what she could do, but his neighbour was a frail woman and Susie only nine years old. Toby doubted they would have been able to move the bodies.

Toby wasn't sure what time it was when the doctor finally emerged from the tent. The pannikin of tea had gone cold in his hands. He hadn't touched a drop.

'I've done what I can,' the doctor said, squatting on his haunches beside Toby. Someone had thrown wood onto the fire, though he couldn't remember when. By the light of the dancing flames he could see blood on the doctor's hands. 'I managed to lift the bone fragments. He's a strong boy. If he lives through tonight, he'll be through the worst of it.'

Toby thrust thoughts of the whimpering dog from his mind. 'He—he'll be all right?'

'I'll know more when he regains consciousness.' The doctor paused and Toby thought he was going to add, 'If he regains consciousness.' Instead, he adjusted his spectacles. 'But he's a fit lad. I think he'll pull through. There's nothing more you can do here. Have you reported the incident to the police?'

Toby shook his head. 'I brought Paddy straight here.'

'Rightly so,' the doctor said. 'Maybe you should go and find the local sergeant. He seems to spend a lot of time in the hotel. Don't worry about your brother. I'll take good care of him.'

A lantern burned on the verandah as Toby pushed open the slip rails, allowing Sergeant McTavish and a member of the native police named Barraworn into the house paddock. No moon showed, but the stars gave enough light to see the way. The Southern Cross sat just above the horizon, lopsided at this late hour.

They reined in below the steps where the Smiths' sulky stood beside the homestead, the horse still in the traces. The bodies of Toby's mother, father and the bushranger lay on the ground where they had fallen, but someone had at least covered them with sheets. The horses whickered and shied at the smell of death, bringing Mrs Smith out onto the verandah, the Lovell tucked under one arm.

'Ah, Toby, it's you.' She uncocked the musket. 'How's Paddy?'

Toby ran a sweaty palm over his face. The preceding few hours had blurred into a confusion of events. 'Doc Collier says he'll live.' He shuddered as he recalled the depression in the side of his brother's skull. 'He's keeping him at his place for a while.'

'I'm sure he'll be fine,' McTavish cut in. He had a hawk-thin face with beaked nose and a huge walrus moustache that seemed to be constantly twitching. Heavily veined cheeks indicated the sergeant's penchant for hard liquor. Toby had been lucky enough to locate the policeman before the night's session could begin in earnest. 'I need you to explain to me everything that happened here.'

Toby took several breaths and began narrating the events of that afternoon, his voice a monotone in the darkness.

As he listened, McTavish squatted and lifted the sheet covering the bushranger's body. 'Little jaundiced-looking fellow,' he muttered. 'The other bugger was a big man, you say?' He dropped the sheet and looked at Toby who nodded. 'I've heard reports of these two getting into mischief over on the north road, usually with two or three natives.' He pointed at the lump under the sheet. 'This one your pa shot was Jack Tanner. He had a reputation for rolling drunk sailors outside waterfront pubs in Melbourne, but disappeared a year or two back when things got a little too warm for him. The one who murdered your parents is Anderson, the most evil bastard you never want to come across. He ran off from a convict work party around five years ago and is rumoured to have lived with the blacks for a while. Showed up last year with his little band of followers and started robbing folks on the roads to the diggings.'

The policeman moved towards the body of Sean O'Rourke. He lifted the sheet and Toby looked away, studying the stars over the hills.

'I'm sorry, laddie,' McTavish said on seeing him hold back. 'I'm no' a man to disturb the dead normally, but I'll have to write a report for my superiors and I need to be sure of the facts.'

Toby nodded his acceptance but kept his gaze turned away.

McTavish spent several minutes examining the bodies of Sean and Ellen O'Rourke by lantern light. When he was finished, he said, 'We'll get your folks inside. Why don't you go and see to the horses, laddie? Me and Barraworn can take care of your ma and pa. Then, if you can show me where these fellows rode into the bush, I won't bother you any more tonight.'

Toby nodded and hurried in the direction of the horse yard. He knew the horses were fine, but McTavish had noticed the look on his face and had given him an excuse to get away while his parents' bodies were moved into the homestead. Tears were welling in his eyes and he didn't want the policeman to see him cry. Seeing his parents, his once vibrant, happy, hopeful parents, reduced to two lifeless lumps under bed sheets, consumed his emotions. Six hours ago it had been a normal Sunday, like the one before it and the one before that. Right about now he should be helping his mother clean up after dinner, listening to his father tell a story from the wicker chair on the verandah. Six hours ago his life had been full. Now there was nothing but a hollowness growing inside him

Blinded by tears, he ran headlong into the rails of the horse yard, hitting them hard and sprawling onto the ground. Winded, he struggled to breathe and pushed his face into his arms. The warm night felt oppressively heavy. When he had his breathing back under control, he tried to climb to his feet, but the grief hit him fully and forced him back down. His knees sank into the dusty earth and he tilted his head back, discovering the stars as if for the first time in his life. The evening seemed to taunt him with its display of peacefulness.

Oh, Ma . . . Pa. What am I going to do now?

The stars dissolved behind a watery veil of tears and he slashed at them savagely. Somewhere off in the distance a sheep let out a mournful bleat. The sound of it steeled him. Through his grief he wondered if another dingo was out there, stalking one of his mother's lambs this time. The thought reminded him that he still had responsibilities.

Standing from the rail, Toby squared his shoulders and wiped the tears from his face. By the light of the verandah lantern he could see that McTavish and Barraworn had taken his father's body inside and were now carrying the dead bushranger to the tack shed. He glanced once more at the stars and started for the homestead.

With lantern in hand, he led McTavish and Barraworn down to the slip rails. They climbed through the gap between and he took them to where the bush overhung the track.

'About here I reckon. This is where I last saw them.'

Barraworn took the lantern from him and began to cast back and forth. He worked quickly, pausing every now and then to squat and study a piece of ground by the yellow light. Eventually his path brought him to the edge of the bush where he stopped and called McTavish over.

'Five horses. They went bush here.' He pointed at a hoof print in the dusty earth. 'This horse got a big fella on him.' Barraworn looked up and gave his sergeant a huge grin, his teeth brilliant in the lantern light. 'This the fella make the trouble, boss.'

Trouble, Toby thought. *My ma and pa are shot dead and he calls it trouble.*

McTavish looked at the hoof prints and then at the bushland, a wall of darkness beyond the light of the lantern. 'We'll sleep here tonight,' he said. 'At first light we'll see if we can't track these fellows down.'

T he *Charlotte Elizabeth* had dropped anchor three hundred yards offshore from a pristine white beach. Above the high-tide mark was a ramshackle hotel where Frank Hocking had paid an exorbitant price for lodgings for his family.

Annie stood with her sister and mother in the shade of the hotel verandah as they waited for her father to return from the ship. The crew had wanted fifteen shillings to bring their belongings ashore, but Frank had been advised by the hotel owner that his son could retrieve their two chests in the morning for no more than sixpence, as long as Frank was willing to lend a hand. It would cost a further shilling if he wanted the trunks and his family transported the three miles to the migrant camp on the south bank of the Yarra Yarra.

Her first footsteps on Australia had not been the romantic affair Annie had imagined. She and Betty had leaped from the rowboat the moment it grounded on the beach, both wanting to be the first to touch dry land. Their shoes had immediately filled with sand and their father forbade them from taking them off in public, insisting they wait until they were inside the hotel room. Now, both girls were content to wait on the boards of the verandah, not wanting to repeat the mistake of yesterday.

'I believe this is him now,' Maree said, pointing to where a small rowboat neared the beach. She spoke loudly enough to be heard over the rhythm of crashing surf.

'Yes, that's Father,' Annie said, using a fan to shield her eyes from the glare and to chase away the swarm of flies that seemed intent on getting up her nose.

At that moment a two-horse team pulling a wagon came from the far side of the hotel and made its way onto the beach. Annie watched as her father and a young man hauled two trunks out of the rowboat and up onto the load bed of the wagon.

'I do believe that is our transportation to Melbourne,' Annie decided, and wondered where they would all sit. The vehicle had only one seat across the front, and the driver occupied half of that. Once the trunks were in position the driver steered the wagon around in a loop and brought it alongside the hotel verandah. Frank came striding across the sand on his long legs, a sheen of sweat on his face from the growing heat of the day.

Maree cocked one eyebrow at the wagon and turned to Frank. He must have noticed the look of disdain on her face.

'You ride up on the seat with the driver, my love. The girls and I will make ourselves comfortable in the back.'

Maree drew a sharp breath and Annie thought her mother about to protest, but when she spoke, she said, 'I suppose this is the best we can do.' She held out a hand and Frank steadied her as she climbed onto the seat beside the grinning driver and settled her skirts around her legs.

It took them about an hour to reach the migrant camp. Here, a veritable city of tents had been erected on the south bank of the Yarra Yarra River. Annie could see no way into their midst and thought the driver would surely have to drop them off on the fringes, but the lad had obviously been here many times. He found a street of sorts that ran right up the middle of the settlement and steered the wagon onto it.

Children played on the street and in the labyrinth of lanes formed by thousands of tents. Some of them stopped to look up at the wagon and wave at the occupants. Annie and Betty waved back, hugging each other and giggling with delight as the children laughed and ran off, playing a game, the rules of which only they understood. Some of the tents had signs erected over them, advertising the trades of their occupants. There were butchers, laundries and storekeepers and quite a few coffee houses.

Near the centre of the camp their street met an even wider cross-street and it was here that the driver stopped. Annie looked down the street and saw that near the edge of the camp it crossed a bridge and entered the permanent structures of Melbourne town itself.

Their driver must have noticed the direction of her gaze. 'That's Prince's Bridge,' he said, then turned to her father. 'If I were you, sir, I'd buy my supplies on the other side. Prices on this side of the river can be a little hefty.'

Frank thanked the man and paid him for the journey. The driver helped him unload their trunks then wheeled the wagon around the square and headed back the way they had come without looking back.

'What do we do now?' Maree asked.

Frank stood between their trunks and pushed his hat back on his head. He pivoted in a circle, but could find nothing to answer her question. 'I really don't know,' he said.

'Here comes someone now,' Betty said, pulling at her father's sleeve. They all turned to see a portly man wearing a blue velvet waistcoat hurrying in their direction between the tents. With some difficulty, he climbed over several guy ropes and stood on the edge of the street panting heavily.

'Glad I got to you before someone else did,' he said between breaths. 'Saw you come in on that wagon. Allow me to introduce myself: I am Sylvester Styles. My partners and I are about to leave camp. Off to the diggings, you see, but we still have a week left on a tent in that direction.' He gestured vaguely over his shoulder. 'No refunds, you understand. A whole week would go to waste unless we can find someone to take it on and pay us out.'

Frank crossed to where the man stood and shook his hand. 'Francis Hocking, sir. Am I to understand that you have a tent for rent?'

The man shook Frank's hand for a long time. 'Ah! the lilt of southern England. Like music to my ears, sir. I'm a Devon man meself. Born and bred. Yes, I do have a tent. Well, not me exactly. The government has it. We were a bit rash and paid too much in advance, but the mayor of Canvas Town – that's what we calls the government official what collects the money – told us no refunds, even though we said we was off to the diggings today. He did say that we could find someone to take on our tent and pay us out the remaining week, though.'

Annie could see her father's head bobbing as he tried to keep up with the torrent of information. 'We could take on your tent? How much is the rent?'

'The government charges five shillings a week per tent. Tell you what. You take it on and you can have our remaining week for four and six. How's that sound?'

'Your generosity is too kind, sir,' Frank said. 'But I wouldn't hear of it. I shall pay you your entire five shillings. If you still want to be charitable, maybe you can find your friends and help me move our trunks to this tent of yours? Seeing as I only have the missus and my girls.'

The handshake became more vigorous and the man nodded. 'It's a deal.'

Sylvester Styles disappeared between the tents and reappeared several minutes later with five men. They greeted the newcomers by touching their fingers to the brims of their hats, then they slung the trunks between them and set off with the Hocking family in tow.

The tent was about a hundred yards in from the northern edge of Canvas Town, close by the banks of the river. Annie was delighted that she was able to look across the waters into the town proper. There were men and horses and vehicles hurrying in all directions, and even women in white dresses with parasols on their shoulders moving on the streets.

Frank paid Sylvester his five shillings. The men tipped their hats, took hold of the handles of a wheelbarrow, loaded high with a multitude of tools and belongings, and headed for the bridge. Children ran along beside the procession chanting:

'Off to the diggings! Off to the diggings!'

'I certainly hope we aren't pushing wheelbarrows to the diggings, Frank?' Maree sat on a trunk, one hand holding the tent flap open as she examined the space within. 'How on earth did six men and all that stuff fit in here? There's hardly room for the four of us.'

Frank rubbed a hand over his face, a sure sign of the stress he was feeling, but he drew himself together with a great deal of willpower and smiled.

'Let's get our things inside, Maree. We'll worry about how we are going to get to the diggings later. We have somewhere to stay. We'll settle in and learn a bit more about this place. We've just spent seven months on a ship. How about we enjoy some dry land for a while?'

L ate in the afternoon the Hocking family walked across the bridge and into Melbourne. The streets weren't as well formed as Annie had first thought. There were no boardwalks on most, and hoof-churned mud reached the edge of the buildings, but she wasn't to be deterred. Taking her sister's arm, they hurried along ahead of their parents, marvelling at each new sight and sound. When a clamorous screeching filled the air, Betty pointed at a flock of birds winging high over the buildings.

'Look, Annie! Sulphur-crested cockatoos. I recognise them from my book.'

'Yes, wonderful,' Annie said, but her eyes had found something far more interesting in a window across the street. She dragged her sister by the arm, guiding them both, for Betty was still watching the noisy birds as they settled into the trees by the river.

'Look, Betty! A dressmaker's. And they have dresses on display.' She hauled Betty up to the window and they both stood admiring the creations of crinoline, silk and lace adorning dressmaker's dummies until their parents caught up.

'Would you look at these, Mama. Aren't they simply beautiful?'

Maree had one arm looped through Frank's. She stopped in front of the window and a smile crossed her face. 'They are certainly things of beauty, my girl. I think the one on the right would be more suited to your figure though, Annie.'

'Do you think so, Mama?' Annie gave a small twirl in the street, flaring her skirts wide.

'What about me, Mama?' Betty tugged at her mother's sleeve. 'Which one would be best for me?'

Maree placed a hand on her daughter's head. 'For you, my girl, I think the green one in the middle. It has the colour to bring out the highlights in your hair.'

Betty blushed. 'Really, Mama? What do you think, Papa?'

Frank detached his wife's hand from his elbow and stepped away. 'I think I'll leave you girls to admire the dresses.'

Annie watched her father continue down the street, then turned back to the window. 'Well, we have Betty and I sorted, Mama. Which dress shall we pick out for you?'

They stood at the window for five minutes, admiring the dresses and inventing occasions to wear them to. When they moved on, they found Frank standing beside a window a few doors down.

'This place is not quite the backwater I expected it to be, Frank,' Maree called to him. He didn't respond, but kept his gaze fixed firmly on whatever was on display.

'Frank? I'm talking to you.'

He looked at her then, and at all of them, a smile on his face. 'It's true,' he said. 'The stories are all true.'

They came level with him and Annie could see into the building. It was a bank and there were iron bars inside the glass. Beyond the bars sat a table covered with a black velvet cloth. There was a rock on the table, shaped something like a peanut, but as long as her forearm. It seemed to catch the afternoon light and glittered like a fish seen in the depths of a stream. A printed card sat on the table in front of the rock. It read:

The Harrington Nugget
This large gold nugget was pulled from the soil of Canadian Flat at the Ballarat diggings.
It has been valued at £139,000.

As if the value of the nugget was not enough on its own, two stacks of gold sovereigns had been placed beside it. The sovereigns alone were more money than Annie had ever seen, yet they were only a fraction of the value of the nugget.

Frank stepped back from the window and kept walking until he was in the middle of the street. He looked about him, like a lost man looking for a familiar landmark.

'I have no idea where it is, but that's where we're going.'

'Where, Papa?' asked Annie.

Frank looked at her, the smile still on his face. 'Why, to Ballarat, of course.' Pointing at the nugget, he added, 'There has to be more where that came from. When we get our gear together and have a means of getting there that doesn't involve pushing a wheelbarrow; when we have everything ready, we're off to Ballarat.'

Paddy awoke in the cold chill of dawn and opened his eyes. At first he thought he was in his own bed in the little lean-to room behind the homestead that he shared with Toby. But, as the light strengthened and the walls and roof took on an ethereal glow, he realised he was in a tent, but he didn't know where. Panic started to well up inside him.

He turned his head to search for something or someone familiar, and a bolt of pain, like liquid fire, shot from the middle of his back to the top of his head. Bright sparks of light danced in his eyes and he wanted to cry out, but all that came from his mouth was a guttural grunt, and even that had the flames dancing in his head and sending him to the very edge of consciousness.

'Ah, you're awake!'

The voice came from somewhere to his left. It took a long time before the sparks faded and Paddy was able to pick out the owner of the voice. A man he had never seen before sat in a camp chair beside the bed, a blanket draped around his shoulders. He wore a pair of wire-framed spectacles that had been knocked crooked while he slept.

Paddy opened his mouth to speak, to ask, 'Who are you?', but the fire pooled into the middle of his head. He tried to fight through it, drew a breath and tensed his vocal chords, but the intensity forced him to close his mouth and eyes. Slowly, the agony withered to a dull ache until finally he was able to open his eyes again.

The man stood over him. He straightened the spectacles on his nose and squinted through bloodshot eyes.

'It was a close run thing, my boy. A few times there I thought I'd lost you.'

Paddy's eyes flicked about the tent, like a caged animal searching for a way out. He felt the panic rising again and tried to sit up, but the man pushed him gently back onto the bed.

'You're in no danger, Patrick. I'm Doctor Collier. Your brother Toby brought you to me the day before yesterday. You've had a severe blow to the head.'

Toby? Toby brought me here?

Paddy relaxed a little. He settled back onto the pillow and watched as the doctor examined his head then lifted the bedclothes to listen to his heart with a tube-like device.

'How are you feeling, Patrick?'

Paddy opened his mouth to respond and the glowing embers in his head flared into a raging inferno once again. The sheer intensity of the pain inside his head made him writhe in agony.

'What's wrong? What is it?' The doctor placed a calming hand on Paddy's shoulder. Eventually, the pain subsided and he stilled his wild thrashing.

'Can you tell me what's wrong?' the doctor asked, and Paddy shook his head. Keeping his mouth tightly shut was the only thing that would stop the pain from coming.

That evening Toby rode into Bunyong Creek and found Paddy sitting up in bed in the doctor's tent, slowly sipping at a bowl of broth, his head wrapped in a clean bandage. He wore a borrowed nightshirt and looked up and smiled as Toby stooped under the fly.

'Look at you, eating in bed like a lord,' Toby said. 'What a life.'

Paddy offered a weak grin and continued slurping from the spoon.

'What's the matter, Pad? Cat got your tongue?'

The smile slipped from Paddy's face. He shrugged and kept on eating.

Doctor Collier came and stood beside Toby. 'I'm very pleased with his progress. You can take him home in the morning.'

'That is good news,' Toby answered. 'We are burying Ma and Pa tomorrow.' He raised his voice to include Paddy in the conversation. 'I've found a priest who will consecrate a piece of ground at home. They will be buried on O'Rourke land, Paddy. I thought up on the ridge where we've already cleared. They liked walking up there. What do you think, Pad?'

His brother looked at him and nodded. Toby turned to the doctor.

'Why won't he answer me? Have you given him something for the pain that stops him from talking?'

Doctor Collier removed his spectacles and polished them on the tail of his shirt. He took his time, and Toby felt his spirits slide as he realised the doctor was gathering the right words for some bad news.

'He hasn't spoken a word since he regained his senses,' the doctor said, placing his glasses on his nose and hooking the frames over his ears. 'Oh, he's tried, but each time he opens his mouth to say something he clutches at the side of his head as if in great pain. That blow to the skull has unsettled something in your brother's brain – or his mind – something associated with the power of speech.'

Toby felt his chest constrict and shuffled uneasily on his feet. 'Will he get better?'

The doctor shook his head doubtfully. 'I can't say. The human brain is a strange organ. Science has only just begun to delve its mysteries. Whatever agony is preventing your brother from speaking may heal over time, or—' his voice trailed off.

'Or he may be mute for the rest of his life,' Toby finished for him, his voice barely a whisper.

'Young man, he is very lucky to be alive. That blow to the head might have killed him. He is able to function in all other respects. The fact that his power of speech is gone, or inhibited, is a small price to pay considering the circumstances.'

Toby realised the doctor was right. Paddy had been near death when he'd brought him into town. He *was* lucky to be alive, and Toby was lucky to have him. Paddy was the only person he had left in the world now.

'Will he be well enough to attend the service tomorrow?'

'Of course,' the doctor said. 'Just don't leave him standing for too long. And watch his head. That area will be very susceptible to injury until the bone knits. If he were to fall and knock it, well . . .'

'We'll be careful, won't we, Pad?'

Paddy looked up and nodded.

'I'll be back to fetch you first thing in the morning, matey.'

Paddy smiled at his brother. The silence grated at Toby and he hurried from the tent to where his horse, Moonlight, was tethered to a tree. He stood for several minutes, stroking the animal's neck and staring off into the distance as he contemplated how much his life had changed in just a few days.

Toby stood beside local storekeepers, Hans and Helga Gutten, who had driven out from Bunyong Creek in a buggy to attend the funeral. Geoff Smith and his three boys had come in from the stock camp. They wore black frock coats over their work clothes. Like himself, they possessed no other clothing for special occasions. They had helped him dig the double grave on the ridge and then donned the coats moments before the service got underway. Mrs Smith and Susie had somehow found enough flowers in the parched countryside to make a wreath that now sat at the head of the grave.

Much to Toby's surprise, their neighbour, Henry Pelham, also attended, accompanied by his head stockman, a swarthy fellow by the name of George Grey. The pair stood a little apart from the other mourners and seemed more interested in the surrounding land than the ceremony, leaning close and whispering quietly.

Toby paid no interest to the words of Father Dalgleish. Nor could he look at the two canvas-wrapped bodies in the grave. He settled his gaze on Paddy, who stood beyond the grave beside Mrs Smith, his head swathed in bandages. The woman had a motherly arm around Paddy. Tears streamed down his face and his mouth hung open as if he were about to wail in despair, but no sound came. Paddy had not uttered a single sound since Toby had fetched him at first light.

Toby had no tears himself. He hadn't cried since the night of the murders. A deep hollowness sat in his gut – a feeling as though part of him was missing. Though the crying had stopped, he doubted the emptiness would ever be gone.

Heat haze shimmered on the high ground. Father Dalgleish did not dwell on his words. He rattled through the service and finished with a hearty 'Amen', snapping his leather-bound Bible closed to signal the conclusion. As the little gathering turned to wander back down to the homestead Toby went to where the shovels stood waiting. Geoff Smith cut him off.

'Me and my boys will take care of this, Toby. You go and see to your guests.'

Toby nodded his thanks and followed the others.

Down at the homestead he wandered about aimlessly, uninterested in the food Helga Gutten and Mrs Smith had prepared for the wake. He accepted offered condolences with a humble nod of his head, but found it hard to maintain any sort of meaningful conversation. Geoff and his boys eventually wandered down from the grave and Toby found himself standing with his neighbour, leaning on the verandah rail, looking out over the pond and the valley.

'McTavish get on the job quick enough?' Geoff asked.

'Left at first light the very next morning,' Toby said.

'Not a bad fellow, McTavish,' Geoff said. 'Hits the grog a bit every now and then, but he has a good sense of duty.'

'He seemed keen to get on the trail. Barraworn had a good set of tracks to follow.'

'Here's to them catchin' the bastards.' Geoff raised his cup of tea in a toast, but before either of them could take a sip they were interrupted by a raised voice from the far end of the verandah.

'I asked you a question, young man. I would like an answer. I know you are grieving, but that is no reason to forget your manners.'

Toby turned to see Henry Pelham looming over Paddy. The boy stood before the grey-haired man, wide eyed with fear.

Toby hurried along the verandah and stood beside his brother. 'I'm sorry, Mr Pelham. Paddy was injured in the attack.' He gestured at the all too obvious bandages. 'He can't speak, but maybe I can answer your question?'

Pelham looked from Toby to Paddy and back again. He held his head tilted back, nose lifted high as if there were some sort of offensive smell in the air. His eyes flicked to the watching faces and his expression immediately softened a little, but there was no hint of apology in his voice when he spoke.

'Yes, I've read of cases like that happening after a blow to the head. Especially in children. But I think the instances I read about were in much younger children.' He gave Paddy a dismissive look before speaking to Toby. 'I merely asked the boy about your pond. It's fairly brimming with water. Does it ever dry up?'

'No, Mr Pelham, it has never dried up. Not in my lifetime.'

'I see,' Pelham said. 'Thank you. That is all I wanted to know.' He turned and walked down the steps to where his stockman, Grey stood beside the sulky. They discussed something for a minute or two, their heads inclined close together. Every now and then they glanced towards the pond. Grey turned away and walked towards the water and Pelham came to the bottom of the steps.

'I shall have to be going now, Toby. You have my deepest sympathy for your loss.' Without waiting for a response, he turned and walked to the sulky. Grey saw him standing by the vehicle and hurried back from his examination of the pond. Without looking back at the people on the verandah they drove away towards the slip rails.

'Thinks he's Lord Muck, that one,' Mrs Smith said, watching the sulky go.

Toby nodded slowly as he watched the pair at the slip rails where Grey climbed down and slid them open. He had an uneasy feeling in the pit of his stomach. Something more than the soul-wrenching grief eating into his guts.

Geoff Smith gestured at the pond with his teacup. 'He's jealous of that spring there,' he said. 'I can understand why. We've been in the grip of a drought for the past four years and that spring hasn't dropped an inch. I wish my place had permanent water like that. I think ol' Pelham is having the same problem. Even though he fronts onto the Coliban River, the ground is too steep to get his stock down to the water.'

'Pa was lucky with this place,' Toby said. 'The squatters have got all the good waterfront properties along the big rivers. Most of the creeks lower down are dry. If it wasn't for the spring feeding that pond we'd be in a spot of bother, especially this high in the ranges. What's the water like at your place?'

Geoff gave a little laugh. 'We've still got some. Mostly trapped in deeper pools, but the creek hasn't flowed for over a year. It's pretty mucky and the sheep have a hard time reaching it after the cattle have churned up the banks. We've been bucketing some into troughs.'

'That's certainly doing it the hard—' He was interrupted by someone tugging at his elbow and turned to see Father Dalgleish.

'Where shall we bury the other fellow?' the clergyman asked.

Toby stared dumbly at the man. He had forgotten all about the body of Jack Tanner wrapped in damp calico and lying in the tack shed. As far as he was concerned the bushranger did not deserve a decent burial. His body could be dumped out on the ranges for the dingos and crows to feed on for all Toby cared, but he doubted the good father would see it that way.

'You can bury him anywhere you like, Father,' Toby said. 'That is, anywhere but on O'Rourke land,' he added a little callously.

P addy hummed a tune in his head as he worked, careful not to enrage the fire in his mind. When he had a full load of white quartz stones, he returned to the grave and used them to add to a border he was making. He couldn't stand the fact that the grave was unmarked. There was nothing to distinguish it from a vegetable garden or a place where the kangaroos had dug for roots, churning the earth over in their efforts. This little patch on the ridge held special meaning for him and he wanted it defined as such.

He had nearly completed all four sides when he noticed Toby climbing towards him. A little shiver of dread ran through his body. He knew his brother would try and make him talk. Toby had tried to get him to say something almost every night in the week since the funeral, but Paddy was afraid of the fire.

He could understand why Toby wanted him to get his voice back. Before the murders the homestead had been filled with noise. Their mother had always sung while she cooked or cleaned, filling the humble structure with her lilting voice. Sometimes their father would join in and the boys would be given a duet that usually ended with all four of them erupting into fits of laughter.

The evenings were the worst. Where once their father had told stories of Ireland or his days on the chain gang as a convict, now he only had Toby's voice to listen to, while poor old Toby had no one.

Paddy wanted to talk and had tried to do so, if only to placate Toby's fears. But each time the fire had begun in his head, building as he tried to form words with his mouth. If he persisted, tried to fight through it, then the fire would engulf his mind and star his vision. Sometimes his wound ached for no reason, but if he tried to speak, the agony was almost enough to kill him. The only way to keep the pain in check was to stay silent.

'You've been busy.' Toby walked up and stood beside him.

Paddy smiled and nodded.

'Good job, too, matey. It needed doing. Maybe we should make a wooden cross, just to make do until we get the cattle to the diggings and some money in the purse. Then we'll find a stonemason and have a proper headstone made. What do you think, Pad?'

Paddy nodded again, a broad grin lighting his face. In the past few days Toby had learned to ask yes or no questions so that Paddy could answer with a simple nod or shake of his head. They were learning to communicate quite well, despite the one-sided conversations.

'Let's go down and find some boards. We can get the cross done before dinner time. Then we have to decide what to do about the cattle. We can't leave them penned up like this, they've eaten down all the grass. Soon they'll start to lose condition. We have to either take them to the diggings or down to the sale yards in Geelong.'

Paddy nodded again as they wandered down the hill together. Most evenings Toby spoke about his plans for the farm, which were really their parents' plans. As the eldest, he had taken on the mantle of responsibility, which suited Paddy fine. Since Toby had turned eighteen, Paddy noted that their father had been including him more and more in decisions about the running of the property. Though neither brother attended the little class Mrs Gutten ran in the back of the store any more, Toby had been the one who excelled at numbers and had often been called upon by their father to add up a bill of sale or calculate the value of a mob of cattle at the sale yards.

'You know, Pad,' Toby said as they descended the ridge, 'We can do this, you and me. We can run this place and make a good living, just the way Ma and Pa did.'

Paddy smiled and felt a little of the hollowness ease from his soul. His big brother had always been his hero. Since the moment he could walk he had followed Toby like a faithful puppy, wanting to be just like him. And Toby had always been there for him, to help him with an onerous chore or to convince their father that he wasn't a baby any more, that he could be trusted to chase down a bolter from a mob of cattle or was big enough to learn to shoot the Lovell. Paddy knew his inability to speak grated heavily on Toby. But he also knew his brother would stand beside him and help him through this problem – however long it lasted.

They reached the shed and rummaged around for a few minutes before they found a pair of boards. Paddy used some nails to hammer them together, then they carried their makeshift cross back up the ridge. They had forgotten to bring a shovel to dig a hole and the ground was far too hard to dig by hand so they collected more lumps of quartz and built a cairn of stones to support their creation. When they had finished they stood shoulder to shoulder at the foot of the grave to admire their hard work. The cross was a little lopsided and the arms weren't quite square, but it was better than nothing. Paddy decided that their parents' final resting place now looked like a proper grave. The late afternoon sun cast a shadow that extended across the hillside.

He felt his brother's hand on his shoulder. 'We'll get a proper headstone, Pad. I promise. Just as soon as we sell the cattle.'

They turned back towards the homestead. 'C'mon,' Toby said. 'I'll let you cook me dinner.' He punched Paddy in the arm and ran on ahead.

For a moment their grief and sorrow were forgotten. They were two boys again, looking for fun. Paddy let Toby get a few paces ahead then picked up a lump of dried manure that he hurled after him, hitting him between the shoulder blades.

'Good shot,' Toby yelled, and began searching the ground for ammunition of his own.

Paddy didn't want to jar his head by breaking into a run. Instead, he dodged Toby's missile with a short sidestep, and would have yelled, '*Hah, you missed me.*' But he didn't want to awaken the fire.

There was only light traffic as Henry Pelham turned into Collins Street, but even that had lifted a pall of dust into the air. He had been on the road for three days and nights. There was a hotel at the far end of the street that he always used when in Melbourne, but that would have to wait. The object of his journey was much closer. He waited for a laden dray to pass and guided his horse to the far side of the street, to a two-storey wooden structure with bars behind the window. A sign above the verandah proclaimed it to be The Colonial and Providence Bank of Victoria.

He reined in by the hitching rail, tied his horse and patted a little of the dust off his clothing before going inside.

A clerk sat on the far side of an expansive counter. He looked up as the bell over the door rang and immediately leaped to his feet.

'Mr Pelham, sir!'

The clerk hurried to the little trapdoor that closed off the counter and flung it open. Before Pelham had taken three steps he was at his side.

'Please, let me take your coat, sir. I had no idea you were calling on us today. It looks as if you've had a long journey. Can I offer you some refreshment?'

'That would be marvellous, thank you, Roger. A sherry, please. Make it two, for I am sure Mr Stratford will not have me drink alone. Is he available? I have a matter of some importance to discuss.'

Roger took Pelham's coat and hung it on a stand, ushering him through to the back of the counter area at the same time. 'I shall inform Mr Stratford that you are here, sir. I am sure he will receive you straight away.'

'Good man!' Pelham patted a little more dust from his clothing and watched the clerk's back as he practically ran towards a side door and gave a discreet knock.

'Mr Pelham to see you, sir.'

'Show him through, man. Show him through,' a voice bellowed.

Roger beckoned Pelham to the office and gestured him through the doorway. 'I shall see to those sherries right away, sir.'

A rotund man stood from behind the desk in the office and waddled towards Pelham, his hand held out. 'Henry! What an unexpected surprise.'

'Hello, Richard. How are Amelia and the children?' Pelham shook the offered hand.

'Oh, they are fine, fine.' Stratford beckoned for him to sit. 'I trust Mavis and your boys are well?'

'Ticking along just nicely.'

'Is she with you? Roger hasn't left her in the outer office? I'll tan his hide if he—' He cut off as Pelham waved a hand to quiet his concerns.

'No, she's not with me. I came alone. Rather urgently, I might add. I have a matter of some importance to discuss.'

'Intriguing. You must tell me.'

A knock sounded at the door and Roger entered bearing a tray with two glasses of sherry. He served them to Pelham and Stratford. 'Will that be all, sir?'

'Yes, yes.' Stratford waved him towards the door. 'Close it on your way out. There's a good chap.' He waited until the door snibbed closed before turning to Pelham. 'Now, Henry? What do you wish to discuss?'

Pelham sipped his sherry and let the warmth settle into the pit of his stomach before speaking. 'There has been somewhat of a tragedy near my property above the Coliban River.'

'Goodness, Henry. Whatever has happened?'

'To put it rather bluntly, Richard, murder has happened.'

'Murder!' Stratford's eyebrows shot up in surprise. 'Anyone I know?'

'Well, actually yes. Two of the bank's debtors. Mr Sean O'Rourke and his wife Ellen.'

'O'Rourke? O'Rourke?' His eyes searched the ceiling. 'Name doesn't ring a bell.' He walked to the door, opened it and bellowed, 'Roger? Bring me the file pertaining to—' He looked at Pelham for confirmation, 'Sean O'Rourke?'

'That's the chap,' Pelham confirmed.

They sipped their sherries and waited until Roger had deposited the file and left. Stratford opened it and delicately turned the pages. 'Initial loan amount of three hundred pounds. Offered up a property five miles north of a place called Bunyong Creek as collateral, as well as a few horses. Money was to be used to establish a herd of cattle, breeding bulls and cows from the sale yards in Geelong. Also for supplies and building materials to improve the said property.' He turned to another sheet of paper. 'Payments made are all regular and on time. Coinciding with the sale of cattle at various yards around Melbourne and Geelong. The principal has been knocked down by a third already. An amount of two hundred and five pounds, four shillings and sixpence outstanding, not taking into account interest, of course.' He looked up at Pelham. 'Would that all the bank's debtors were like this fellow O'Rourke.'

Pelham placed his glass on a side table. 'Alas, dear Richard, he is no more. All that is left behind are two young boys. I doubt they will be able to meet the repayments.'

'Then the bank will have no option but to foreclose and seize the property.'

'Yes, one more property to add to the bank's portfolio,' Pelham said. 'This one is so far back in the ranges it will be of little interest to any serious investor. New settlers won't want to pay over two hundred pounds for a partly-established property. Not when the governor is making land available for next to nothing.'

'I can see why you made the trip down here, Henry. Thank you for advising me of the situation.'

'I came to do more than advise you, Richard. I came to null the bank's loss.'

Stratford looked at him across the desk, his eyes narrowed. 'But how?'

Pelham smiled. 'The property borders my own and may be of some use to me. There is a spring there of sorts, a source of permanent water. If I can develop it, it may negate the need for me to keep herding my cattle down to the river each summer.'

'You want to buy this property after we foreclose? Is that it, Henry?'

Pelham waved a hand dismissively. 'Foreclosure is such a drawn-out and tedious process, Richard. I am proposing to buy out the debt owed by this O'Rourke fellow. The eldest boy is nineteen. The law dictates that I must offer him the chance to pay out his father's debt. If he fails, then I shall seize the property as my own. He gets his chance to carry on with the family property. If he succeeds, I get my money back. If he fails, I get a permanent water source in the mountains. Either way, the bank negates its loss.'

Stratford stood and moved towards the door. 'I shall have Roger draw up the necessary documents while we partake of another sherry.'

Chilbi stood in the shadows and watched the distant treeline across the valley. There was no sign of their pursuers, but he knew they were there. Two days ago, Warrigal had sent him back along their spoor to check for signs of pursuit, as he suspected the boy from the Djarriba settlement was following their trail, seeking revenge for the killings. Chilbi had found no boy, but instead one of the blue men Warrigal called a *trap*, along with a tracker from another tribe.

'Are they still there, Chilbi?' Warrigal Anderson spoke in Jannjirra from the back of his horse.

'Still there, Warrigal. They follow down the creek there. Soon they will cross and follow up here.' In the beginning, Chilbi used to marvel at the fact that Warrigal could not see the signs for himself, but he had learned to keep his mouth shut on such matters. To question the big white man often brought a fist or booted foot.

Anderson shook his head. 'Kill a man and they follow for a day or two. Kill a woman and they never give up. That tracker the trap has with him is good, but you are better, my little black heathen. We'll cross onto the ridge and make our way onto the escarpment.'

Chilbi turned towards the rising ground Warrigal had indicated and a smile crossed his face.

'That's right, Chilbi,' Anderson said, 'We're going back up to your tribal lands. The ground here is rocky and we aren't leaving much of a trail, but we can't afford to lead that trap bastard up there. I'll take the horses. Tell your brothers to hide the spoor until we are into the passage. Make sure nothing is left for the Djarriba tracker to follow. We'll hide out for a while then come back to continue the war.'

Chilbi passed the reins of his horse to Warrigal as Yawong and Tarrat slid from their saddles. They tied their horses into a string that the big bushranger led forward, then they moved back along their trail to erase all sign of their passing.

M cTavish held the reins of both mounts and let the horses drink their fill while Barraworn squatted in the trickle of water and topped up the canteens. He had his jacket undone, one hand resting on the handle of his horse pistol. Here the bush was thick and dark, the perfect place for an ambush, and his eyes flicked to every sound in the under-growth.

Barraworn finished filling the canteens and stood. He handed one to McTavish, and the sergeant took a long swig. 'It's no' a good malt whisky, laddie, but it slakes the thirst none the less.' He slapped the stopper in before looping the strap over the pommel of his saddle. 'Now, tell me. Where did these rogues get to?'

Barraworn turned and wandered down the creek bed. Every few paces the tracker stopped and squatted in the water. McTavish watched him work and marvelled at the tracking skills of Aboriginal people. Anderson and his gang had obvi-ously entered the water in an attempt to throw off pursuit. To McTavish, the creek and surrounding bush appeared untouched by the hand of man and he never would have thought four men and five horses had been anywhere near this place, but Barraworn found clues in out-of-place stones and bent grass stems that only he could see. These people certainly knew the land in which they had lived for thousands of years. At one place, Barraworn paused longer than the others and changed the direction of his meanderings, crossing to the other bank.

'Them fellas cross here, boss.' He pointed up along the ridge line. 'Gone up that way.'

It makes sense, McTavish thought. The spine of the ridge was sparsely wooded and would make for easier riding. 'How long ago?'

Barraworn examined the ground once more and came to a decision. 'Soon after sun-up, boss.'

McTavish tossed the reins to Barraworn. 'Lead the way.'

They crossed the creek and headed up the rising ground of the ridge line. McTavish left his hand on his pistol. He had a carbine in a leather bucket strapped to the saddle, but the weapon would be unwieldy in the closely pressing bush and hard to ride with. The thought kept crossing his mind that they were outnumbered. The O'Rourke laddie had said there were three natives with Anderson, though apparently only the white man carried firearms. The natives seemed to prefer clubs and spears. He had been in the colony long enough to know that these weapons were deadly in the right hands.

Around noon they reached a point where the ridge changed direction, switching back on itself and climbing into the north. Barraworn dismounted and searched for the spoor, so McTavish pushed his hat onto the back of his head and looked up along the ridge line. About a mile away the land rose steeply in a boulder-strewn escarpment, seemingly reaching the clouds. The ground looked impassable to a man on foot, let alone any-one on horseback.

Barraworn crossed the narrow piece of open ground and squatted by the scrub near the far side. He had a frown on his face as he traced a hand around a hoof print. He took a pace, looked at the ground again and shook his head.

'What's the matter?' McTavish asked.

'Tracks gone, boss.'

'What do you mean gone?' He could see the look of superstitious awe on Barraworn's face, the fear in his eyes.

'Plenty tracks back there, boss.' He pointed back in the direction they had come. 'Five horses. Four got fellas on them. Black fellas get off their horses here.' His arm shifted to a point some five yards ahead of McTavish. 'Tracks go here.' He pointed at the ground at his feet then looked up at the sergeant. 'No more tracks, boss.'

'What do you mean *no more tracks*? They have five horses with them. It's impossible to hide the tracks of five horses.'

Barraworn shook his head. 'No more tracks, boss.'

McTavish swung from the saddle and looped his reins over a branch. Pulling the carbine from its bucket, he crossed to where Barraworn waited.

'The ground here is stony and hard. They must have covered what little spoor they left. They've been following the back of this ridge up to now. Let's go forward on foot for a bit and see if we can't pick them up again.'

Barraworn shrugged and moved off with McTavish following. Every few paces the tracker squatted on his haunches and examined a piece of ground. But every time he would look up at McTavish and shake his head.

'No more tracks, boss.'

McTavish shouldered the carbine and pointed back towards their own horses. 'Let's head back and scout the sides of the ridge. They can't just vanish. There will be some sign of them somewhere.'

For three hours they tried every possible direction from the last trace of the spoor, but each time the search turned up nothing. McTavish was starting to feel a little of the dread that was evident on Barraworn's face. It seemed four men and five horses had vanished from the face of the earth.

The sun was well into the west by the time he admitted defeat. 'Okay, laddie. It would seem they have given us the slip.' He looked up at the escarpment, now a looming shadow to the north, like the ramparts of some giant castle. 'If they've gone up there, it will need more than the two of us to find them. Lead us back down to the creek. We'll camp there tonight. Tomorrow we'll head back to Bunyong Creek. My superiors can decide what to do about Mr Anderson and his band of thugs.'

'Hellooo the house.'

Toby and Paddy were cleaning up after dinner when they heard the hail from the yard outside. Paddy shrank back against the wall, a look of terror on his face. Toby eyed the Lovell leaning beside the kitchen door. The firearm was loaded, but not primed. He decided that if someone meant them harm they would not yell from the yard and announce their presence.

Walking to the door, he carefully pulled it open and peered out into the darkness. Two horsemen sat their mounts just below the verandah rail.

'Good evening, Toby,' a familiar voice said. 'Sorry to call so late.'

'Mr Pelham?'

The more portly of the two figures lifted a hand in greeting. 'Yes, Toby. George has escorted me over.' The hand gestured towards the other rider and Toby recognised the bulky figure of George Grey.

'Please, Mr Pelham, come in.' Toby pushed the door wide and waited while the men dismounted and looped their reins over the verandah rail. 'Paddy?' He turned to his brother. 'Boil the kettle. Some tea for our guests.'

Minutes later, Pelham and Grey sat at the kitchen table with steaming cups in front of them.

'I just got back from Melbourne a few hours ago.' Pelham shook his mane of silvery hair. 'I simply had to know if there is any word on the hunt for those scoundrels.'

'I haven't seen or heard from McTavish since the morning after the murders,' Toby admitted. 'Presumably he is still on Anderson's trail.'

Pelham shifted in his chair and gave a little cough.

'There is something I need to discuss with you both,' he said. 'It pains me to have to raise the matter, especially given the circumstances.' His eyes darted about the room, unable to settle on either brother. 'You see, boys, your father died owing a considerable amount of money. A little over two hundred pounds to be exact. I wasn't going to mention it now,' he went on hurriedly, 'but you boys need to be made aware of the facts.'

Toby slapped his hand onto the tabletop. 'I don't believe it,' he said out of shock.

Grey stood from his chair. 'Are you calling Mr Pelham a liar?' His hands came up, reaching for Toby.

'It's all right, George.' Pelham waved his stockman back into the chair. 'They are going to want proof whether they think I'm a liar or not. I know I would if I found myself in their position.' He reached into his frock coat and pulled out a sheaf of documents tied together with a red ribbon. Some of the papers were dog-eared and yellowed with age. Others appeared more recent, the parchment the colour of fine china and festooned with official-looking stamps.

'When your father and mother came down to the Port Phillip district from New South Wales they were emancipated convicts,' Pelham said. 'They were freed of their shackles, freed of their debt to society, freed of everything except the stigma of their convict past. Your father managed to obtain this land, to gain title by some means I'm not privy to. But that was all he had, just a piece of land so far back in the hills it had been overlooked by others. Certainly, it has much potential. You have good water here, some splendid pastures and fertile soil to plant in. But to work the land properly, to get good stock and the right seeds to plant takes money. Your father had none. There was nothing with which to buy decent cattle or build little more than a native hut.' Pelham shifted his weight in the chair.

'Your father was a very smart man,' he continued. 'He had the land and he could see the potential. All he needed was some money to start to build on that.'

Toby had an uneasy feeling building in the pit of his stomach. Why had Henry Pelham come to their homestead in the late evening to talk about money? He was, by far, the richest man in the district. Why was he concerned with their father's financial affairs?

Pelham shuffled through the documents and found what he was looking for, smoothing it out on the table in front of Toby.

'This is an original loan document for a sum of three hundred pounds.' He swept his hand towards the bottom of the page. 'As you can see it has been duly notarised and witnessed by a stipendiary magistrate. I'm sure you will recognise your own father's signature.'

Toby stared at the document. His father would not have been considered a literate man, but he could write a few words and was able to sign his own name. In sanded ink, scratched out in a familiar scrawl was the signature of Sean O'Rourke.

'You may have been old enough to remember when things started changing here, Toby? When your father had the money to improve this place?'

Toby remembered the little ramshackle hut with its dirt floor. He remembered the few unbranded wild cows his father had chased out of the scrub as he attempted to put together a herd, and how they had eaten possum stew and when flour and tea and sugar had been luxuries. And he remembered a time when it all suddenly changed. His father had taken him to Geelong and bought up a good herd of breeding cows they had driven back to the farm. There had also been sheep and a couple of milking cows and building materials for the homestead. Then had come the horses, including the mare that was the mother of his own beloved Moonlight. The pantry had gone from sparse to overflowing with food.

Yes, he could remember that time.

Pelham sipped at his tea. When he lowered the cup he said, 'Your father still has two thirds of the loan outstanding to the bank. With his unfortunate demise, the bank would have no choice but to foreclose.' He looked at Toby's frowning face over the teacup. 'You do know what foreclosure is, don't you, my boy?'

Toby shook his head.

'The bank would seize this land and sell it off to cover their loss.'

The uneasiness changed instantly into panic and Toby squirmed in his chair. 'They can't take our home, can they?'

'They can and they will,' Pelham shot back. Then a smile crossed his face. 'Well, they would. But I was in a position to see this coming and I have put things in place so that it will never happen.'

'So, the bank won't take our land?' The dread was still there, gnawing at his insides. Henry Pelham was not known for his generosity.

Pelham produced a new document and slid it towards Toby. He looked down at it and tried to read the words, but some were so long he got stuck while sounding them out, and didn't know what they meant anyway. He looked up at the old man opposite him.

'To put it into simple terms, Toby,' Pelham said, the smile gone from his face now, 'I have bought out your father's loan in order to stop the bank from seizing this property. What was owed to the bank is now owed to me.'

'You want us to honour this debt?'

'Oh, you will honour the debt all right, young Toby. As you can see from the original loan document, your father used this land as security for the loan. In the event of forfeiture, I am legally entitled to take this land to recover my losses.'

Toby wasn't sure what 'forfeiture' meant, but the thought of Pelham taking their farm was a worrying one. He studied the documents spread before him without really seeing them. All he could take in was the fact that his father owed two hundred pounds to the bank, and Pelham now owned that debt. If he and Paddy didn't pay the owing money back, Pelham could take the farm from them.

'We—we don't have that kind of money, Mr Pelham,' Toby stammered.

'Of course not. Don't look so worried, my boy,' Pelham said, the smile back on his face. 'I'm sure you'll have the money after you drive your herd up to the diggings. Prices are double at the sale yards in Bendigo Creek. That should certainly see you clear the debt.'

'You can count on it, Mr Pelham,' Toby said, his mood brightening. 'Pa, Paddy and me, we spent weeks putting that herd together for a drive to the diggings. That must have been Pa's plan all along. To clear his debt.'

'I'm sure it was.' Pelham scooped up the documents, retied them with the ribbon and slipped them into his pocket. 'George and I have taken up enough of your evening.' He stood and moved towards the door.

Toby and Paddy walked them out onto the verandah and watched as they swung onto their horses. Grey remained silent, but Pelham bid the brothers a good night before the pair turned their mounts away from the verandah. They didn't ride directly down to the slip rails, instead taking a more circuitous route that brought them out by the pond. Toby could hear their voices as they discussed something animatedly, Grey's arms waving about in the moonlight, but the men were too far away to make out their words.

As soon as Pelham and Grey reached the slip rails Toby took the lantern and hurried back inside to his parents' room. He went through all the drawers and cupboards, sifting through the contents. Looking up, he saw Paddy standing in the doorway, a look of horror on his face. Their father had strictly forbidden the boys from touching anything in this room.

'Don't worry, Pad. We can't get into trouble. This is our stuff now. Ol' Pelham is up to something for sure. He shouldn't give a toss whether the bank takes this farm or not. I don't trust him.'

He opened one drawer and discovered it was full of papers. Upending the contents onto the bedspread, Toby rummaged through them and found what he was looking for. He held the document up to the lantern. It was a duplicate of the original loan document showing the conditions for the loan and the amount borrowed. The next document in the pile was a duplicate of the repayments. Toby quickly scanned to the bottom of the page. Two hundred and five pounds four shillings and sixpence. All the amounts had been witnessed by both a clerk and his father.

Toby felt his anger rising. He wanted to yell and scream, to curse this bad hand fate had dealt him. Instead, he gathered up all the papers and stuffed them back into the drawer. He slammed the drawer closed and, as he strode past Paddy, he could see the questioning look on his brother's face, the worry in the depths of his eyes.

'Don't worry, Pad. If Pa was going to pay this back, then we can too,' he said determinedly. 'We'll brand the cattle and take them to the diggings for sale. Then old man Pelham can kiss my arse.'

enry Pelham sat on his mount quietly while Grey pulled the slip rails closed. He waited until the stockman was back in the saddle and urged his horse forward.

'That pond makes the O'Rourke farm practically drought-proof.'

'The spring is still pushing out, despite the lack of rain,' Grey said. 'If they extended the pond they could run another thousand head. Those two brats have no idea what they're sitting on.'

'No,' Pelham shook his head. 'No idea at all.'

'What do you suppose they'll do?'

Pelham was thoughtful for a moment. He had planted the right seeds in Toby O'Rourke's head and knew exactly what the young man would do. 'He'll brand his cattle and drive them to the diggings for sale.'

'But if he does that,' Grey's voice had taken on a questioning tone, 'then he'll be able to pay out the loan. You'll have no chance of forcing a foreclosure.'

Pelham chuckled in the darkness.

'Only if he succeeds, George.'

rank was relieved to see his information had been correct. He had ventured through the town and out onto the western fringes of Melbourne where the Ballarat road entered bushland. Under a canopy of gum trees sat a group of wheeled vehicles, from buggies and wagonettes to wagons of all sizes. Beyond them was a horse yard where prospective buyers were walking animals about while casting a critical eye.

While most diggers walked to Ballarat or Mount Alexander, usually pushing a wheelbarrow piled high with equipment, Frank knew he could not expect that of Maree and the girls. Those that could afford it purchased their own transportation, and he had learned of this sale yard of sorts from one of the men in the migrant camp.

The first wagonette he looked at had seen better days. Both axles were worn and all the rims in need of re-riveting. Some had missing spokes and the load bed was worn and weathered with a few planks gone. Frank eyed the vehicle doubtfully and was about to move on when a man with greasy hair and a thin moustache approached.

'Is it transportation to the diggings you are seeking, sir?'

'I have my wife and two daughters with me,' Frank pointed out. 'I can't expect them to walk to Ballarat, though I'm game to try myself.'

'Ah, Ballarat! Land of dreams.'

'You've been there?' Frank asked.

'Alas, no,' the man shook his head. He held out his hand. 'Thomas Cruikshank, at your service. This wagonette here is one of the better vehicles I have. Made the trip to Ballarat and back on several occasions, I do believe.'

Frank shook the offered hand then pointed out the wagonette's deficiencies and Cruikshank said, 'Yes, these tracks have taken their toll, but you'll not find a better vehicle anywhere.'

'That may be so,' Frank replied, 'but it will still need some work before it's fit for the task.'

'The planks are easy enough,' the man said. 'I can do that work myself. It is the wheels that are the problem. The only wheelwright for five hundred miles is in the employ of the government and they are loath to allow him to freelance, as it were.'

'That won't be a problem for me, sir,' Frank said. 'Wheels is my trade. Learnt it in the carriage works in Hastings, back in the mother country.'

Cruikshank's eyebrows rose a full two inches. 'A wheelwright?'

'Yes, sir,' Frank nodded.

He took Frank's hand again and shook it vigorously. 'Would you be interested in making a little money before you head off to the diggings? I will pay you handsomely for each wheel you fix.'

'I'm sure we can come to some sort of an arrangement,' Frank said. 'Maybe the terms could include my choice of vehicle from your stock when it comes time for me to leave.'

Cruikshank's eyebrows dropped back down and Frank thought him about to refuse the offer.

'You drive a hard bargain, sir. I tell you what. How about a shilling a wheel and your choice of wagonette when you leave, as long as you give me a month of service? That doesn't include the horse, mind. You'll have to pay for that yourself.'

Frank only hesitated briefly, just to show he was giving the offer some consideration.

'I find your terms acceptable,' he said.

'When can you start?' Cruikshank asked as he pumped Frank's hand.

'My tools are back in Canvas Town,' Frank admitted. 'How about I come back first thing in the morning and get stuck in?'

'Certainly,' Cruikshank said. He dropped Frank's hand and gave him a little salute. 'I'll see you then.'

Frank headed back to the migrant camp feeling rather pleased with himself. Things were certainly falling into place. They had somewhere to sleep, he had found paying work and, when that was completed, he would have money in his pocket and a means to take his family to Ballarat. As he crossed Prince's Bridge he wondered at his luck. Australia had so far proved to be the land of dreams everyone said it was. At the moment, they wanted for nothing.

He paused by the railing and looked down into the muddy waters of the Yarra Yarra River and thought about his son. Tom had been the one who had wanted to come. The lad had convinced them all that a better life could be had here.

'I'm sorry you never made it, my boy,' he told the rippling water. 'You were right. I know you would have loved it here.' Tears welled in his eyes and he wiped them away with a thumb. Seven people had died on the voyage out from England before the shipboard doctor's treatment and quarantine procedures had stemmed the spread of the disease. The doctor had called it diphtheria, or something like that. All he knew was that it had claimed the life of his son. He could feel a lump forming in his throat and quickly turned and continued on his way.

He was still feeling low as he entered the main north–south thoroughfare into Canvas Town and made his way towards the cross-street where their tent was. Thoughts of his son were still in his mind as he neared one of the tents bearing a painted sign that proclaimed it to be a coffee shop. Frank had quickly learned that most coffee shops in Canvas Town were actually fronts for sly grog shops and this one had a few patrons squeezed inside or seated on chairs out front.

He heard the *clink* of glass on glass and paused. All the men outside had drinks in their hands and were chatting amiably, some laughing loudly at a joke or ribald remark. Frank put his hand in his pocket and felt the couple of coins there, turning them over and over in his fingers as he watched the men drink.

No, Francis, me boy. Don't be starting that caper again. You've come a long way down the road since then.

He let go of the coins and turned for his tent, walking as quickly as he could.

S itting on the top rail of the paddock fence, the brothers watched the cattle mill about them in the twilight. Toby massaged a bruised shoulder, where he had been too slow to avoid the kick of a cow struggling under the sear of the branding iron.

'We'll go into town tomorrow,' he said, wincing at the pain. Over the past week they had worked hard, often finishing the day's chores by the light of the branding fire. He felt the work had been good for them. With their hands and minds occupied by day and their bodies yearning for sleep by night, they'd had little time to dwell on their grief or the farm's financial situation. Now they had completed the branding and most of the necessary preparations for the drive to Bendigo Creek.

'We can't manage a herd this size on our own,' Toby went on. 'We'll need to hire some help.'

Paddy frowned and held out his hand, rubbing his thumb and forefinger together.

'I found Pa's wallet while I was searching for those papers the other night. There's about twenty-one pounds in it. More than enough to hire a couple of drovers and pay for some supplies. I reckon it'll only take about five days, maybe a week at most to reach Bendigo Creek.'

I n the morning they hitched up the wagonette and drove into Bunyong Creek. Toby manoeuvred across the rutted main street and pulled up beside the store.

Helga Gutten fussed about the boys. Within minutes of climbing off the wagonette they each had a pastry in one hand and a glass of lemonade in the other.

'So good to see you boys,' Mrs Gutten said, with a huge smile.

Hans had been serving a customer when they arrived, but he soon came hurrying over to shake them both by the hand. 'Ah! Tobias und Patrick. I see Helga is filling your bellies. What brings you to town? You are needing supplies, *ja?*'

Toby hurried to swallow a mouthful of pastry so he could answer the affable German. 'Some flour, tea, sugar and baking powder, please, Mr Gutten,' he said. 'Oh, and some powder, shot and percussion caps. We'll also be needing a few medical items, some iodine and castor oil.' Toby rattled through his mental list.

'Come, come,' Hans gestured them forward. 'You can eat as we go.'

They spent the next twenty minutes going up and down aisles of mining and farm equipment, selecting what they needed and carrying it out to the wagonette. Hans had a pencil and piece of paper with him and he kept a tally of the boys' purchases. Finally, they found themselves standing in a little alcove at the side of the store where Hans kept the firearms and associated items.

Toby replenished the supply of powder, shot and caps for the Lovell and was turning to leave when he noticed the rack of firearms along the back wall. 'How much have we spent so far, Mr Gutten?'

Hans ran his pencil down the figures on his piece of paper, his lips moving as he added the column. 'Exactly three pounds two and six,' he said, looking up. 'But I can put it on your account if you wish.'

'No thanks, Mr Gutten. I'll be paying cash. I was wondering how much one of those guns will cost me?'

'For you?'

'For Paddy,' Toby said.

Paddy was examining a gold-washing cradle nearby, but at the mention of his name he wandered over.

'It won't hurt to have another gun around,' Toby explained. 'Things might have been different if we'd had two guns the day Anderson paid us a visit. We still have enough money for the supplies and to hire the hands,' he added.

'For Patrick, *ja*?' Hans asked.

Toby nodded.

Hans studied Paddy for a moment. 'You are big solid boy,' he said thoughtfully. 'There is much of your father in you.' Turning to the rack he selected a musket and took it down. 'This is a short sea-service musket. It was designed especially for use by the Royal Navy.' He passed the weapon to Toby.

'It is nine inches shorter than your father's musket and half a pound lighter,' he said, slipping easily into the role of sales-man. 'It takes a three-quarter inch ball the same as your father's weapon and has the same conversion to the Lovell percussion principle.'

Toby ran his fingers over the polished wood and cold metal then swung the musket up to the firing position, aiming down the barrel. The weapon felt firm and balanced. He pulled the hammer to full cock and felt the tension in the trigger, testing its resistance until the hammer flew forward and struck the nip-ple with a reassuring *thunk*.

'It is owing me four pounds,' Hans said, 'but to you I think maybe we can get away with three pounds and I shall be throwing in thirty cartridges and shot.' The German smiled. 'But you must be promising me you will come back soon and help me eat some of Helga's biscuits. God knows, I need the help,' he added, grab-bing his bulging paunch and laughing loudly.

Toby handed the musket to Paddy who imitated his brother, aiming, cocking and dry-firing the weapon.

'What do you think, Pad? You can carry it in a scabbard while riding Patch.'

Paddy nodded, holding the musket at arm's length to exam-ine it. He had never received such an expensive gift before and was not entirely sure they could afford it. Although he had lost his voice, he had not lost his boyish love of guns and the noise associated with them. He smiled a thank you at his brother and carried his new gun out to the wagonette.

Toby took out his father's wallet and counted out the bank-notes for Hans. When the account had been settled, he still had close to fifteen pounds, more than enough to procure the services of a couple of drovers for a week.

Leaving Paddy to watch the wagonette and their supplies, he crossed the track to the hotel and went inside. The air felt a little cooler, but Toby wrinkled his nose at the smell of tobacco smoke mingled with the pungent aroma of unwashed bodies. Bright sunlight on the calico walls gave the room an unnatural glow which illuminated several rough tables and a bar.

Dusty, dirty men crowded around the tables. Some were on their way to the diggings: hopeful, smiling, dreaming people who laughed and joked, the promise of instant riches uplifting their spirits. At the other end of the spectrum were the poor diggers who had laboured and toiled for weeks or months on a worthless square of land. These were the men who had ended up with 'shicer' claims – mines that didn't produce enough gold to cover the high cost of living which inevitably followed a rush. When their money ran out, they were left with nothing but callused, broken hands and a useless hole in the ground to be filled with water when the winter rains came.

The publican, Chris Stanton, shuffled backwards and forwards along the opposite side of the bar, filling pannikins and collecting empty bottles. He greeted Toby with a friendly smile.

'Sorry about your folks, Toby.' His voice had a softness that belied his size. 'If there's anything I can do, you be sure and let me know.'

'That's why I'm here, Chris.' Toby leaned on the bar. 'You get to meet just about everybody who passes through here. Do you know of any men looking for work?'

The barman put down a half-filled bottle and cocked his head towards Toby. 'What kind of work?'

'Droving a mob of cattle from here to the Bendigo diggings. Two hundred and thirty head to be exact.'

Stanton lifted his head towards the roof as he pondered the question. 'Pelham and Grey was in here yesterday asking the same question. I thought ol' man Pelham had all the workers he needed.'

'So did I,' Toby said. 'As far as I know, he does all his hiring from the sale yards?' He felt a nagging suspicion creep into his guts, the same one as from the night of Pelham's visit.

Chris nodded. 'Told him I hadn't heard of anyone looking for work, then the strangest thing happened.'

'What?'

'Two men wandered in here yesterday evening and asked about work in the area. Funny-looking coves. Don't know if they will be any good to you, though. One was missing an eye and the other a hand. Maybe Pelham found 'em first but passed 'em up on account of their appearance. I don't even know if they're still around – haven't seen them in here today.'

'Did they say where they were camped?'

'Down by the creek along with everyone else. Up near the crossing I think they said.'

Toby thanked the barman and left the hotel. He crossed the track and walked down the side of the police horse yard towards the creek. There were about two dozen tents of all colours and sizes lining the banks, some snowy-white and new, others dirtied with age and hard use.

A small dog ran from a tent and barked ferociously about Toby's heels until a heavily bearded man yelled for it to be quiet. 'I'm looking for two men,' Toby told the man. 'One is missing an eye and the other a hand.' The man simply pointed towards the far end of the encampment and went back to whatever he had been doing.

Down near the crossing Toby found a camp consisting of two bedrolls on either side of a fire. A man sat poking at the coals with a stick while another lay on a bedroll and watched. Two horses were tethered to a gum tree which shaded the camp. He wasn't sure he had found the right camp until the man at the fire turned and fixed him with an icy stare from a solitary eye.

'What do you want, boy?' One-eye stood up. He still held the stick and its end smouldered with a thin wisp of smoke. His thin frame loomed a good head and shoulders over Toby. A black patch covered his left eye.

'I heard you were looking for work.'

'Who told you that?' The man on the bedroll got to his feet. He was about Toby's height, but a little heavier and had a thick crop of blond hair and little, pig-like eyes that squinted from behind thick glasses. His right arm terminated at a large metal hook secured to his wrist by means of a leather bucket and straps.

Toby had to force himself to stop staring at the hook, deciding to look into the man's glasses. 'Er – Chris, the barman at the hotel. You told him you were looking for work in the area.'

One-eye threw the stick onto the fire and stepped forward, effectively establishing himself as spokesman for the pair. 'What sort of work you offering?'

'Droving,' Toby said flatly. 'A mob of cattle from here to Bendigo Creek.'

The one-eyed stranger seemed to ponder this. He rubbed his stubbly chin and glanced at Hook, who gave a noncommittal squint.

'How much your father payin'', boy?' One-eye asked.

'My father's dead. My brother and me are paying three shillings a day until the cattle are in the yards in Bendigo Creek. I expect the drive to take from five days to a week. No longer.'

'Me and Dundas are wantin' to head to the Bendigo diggings eventually. We ran out of money on the Ballarat fields and thought we'd try our luck up there, but we need to raise some more money first. Make it four shillings a day and we're your men.'

'I'll go to three and six, but that's it,' Toby retorted, feeling pleased with his bartering skills.

The two men looked at each other for several seconds. 'Agreed,' One-eye said. 'You drive a hard deal, boy.'

'If you're going to work for me then you'd better call me Toby.'

One-eye thrust his right hand forward and Toby took it, matching the man's grip as his arm was pumped up and down.

'I'm Scotchy,' the man said. 'My friend here is Dundas.'

Toby was tactful enough to change hands before shaking with the other man. The handshake felt awkward, but Dundas' grip was tight and wiry.

'You can ride back to our place with my brother and me if you like. We just came to town to grab some supplies at the store. We're about ready to leave.'

'Tell you what,' Scotchy said. 'We'll get ourselves packed up and meet you at the store in ten minutes.'

'Got any decent feed at your place, Toby?' Dundas asked as he lifted his saddle off the ground. 'For our horses I mean. They haven't had nothin' but dry grass and a few apples some brats were feedin' 'em yesterday.'

'I've got a few bags of chaff. I guess they'll need a good feed.' He eyed the tight stomachs on the horses. 'We'll fix 'em up.' He turned away and headed back up the creek towards the store.

There was no sign of Paddy at the wagonette. Toby climbed onto the footboard and spotted his brother standing by the horse yard at the police post. Two horsemen were in the yard and he felt his heart race as he realised it was McTavish and Barraworn.

He jumped from the wagonette and sprinted to the yard. The policemen were unsaddling their mounts. McTavish had many days of beard and he moved like an old man, saddle weary and bone tired. He saw Toby and Paddy standing by the rails and came over, dropping the saddle on a fencepost.

'I did no' expect to see you boys here,' the sergeant said. His uniform was covered in dust and his nose glowed with sunburn.

'We came to get some supplies.' The obvious question nagged at Toby, but he held his tongue. McTavish would tell them what had happened out in the ranges when he was ready.

McTavish brushed some of the dust from his jacket. As he worked he glanced about the cluster of buildings. His eyes seemed to be everywhere – everywhere except on the two anxious faces before him.

'We followed their trail for eight days,' the sergeant finally said. 'They made for the river and followed it upstream for a while before striking out east. Then they cut across the north road above the Kilmore Gap and headed into the ranges east of there. That's where we lost them. One moment the trail was there, easy to follow, the next it was gone. It was like it had never existed. Barraworn cast back and forth for a day without finding anything. Anderson and his gang just rode up to the mountains, their spoor plain to see, and when they got there they decided they weren't going to leave a trail any more.'

Toby slapped a hand onto the fence rail. 'They can't have vanished into thin air.'

'Barraworn thinks he did, laddie. He thinks there was some sort of magic involved. You know what his lot are like when they get the notion there has been magic at work. He was scared out of his wits.'

'Maybe he was too scared to find the trail, or didn't want to.'

'Unfair, laddie,' McTavish said, but his voice carried no tone of rebuke. 'Scared or no', Barraworn could track each individual horse around the course at Royal Ascot a week after the event. I wanted a different outcome for you boys. I really did. But there was nothing more we could do. The trail just stopped at the mountains and went no further.'

Toby and Paddy left the two policemen to their tasks and wandered back to the wagonette, heads hung low.

Scotchy and Dundas were nowhere to be seen. Toby looked up and down the row of tents along the creek bank, but apart from a few diggers sitting around a campfire, there was no one else about.

'Climb up, Pad,' he told his brother. 'Looks like we'll have to find the coves.'

He wheeled the wagonette around and headed along the creek. When they reached the spot where Scotchy and Dundas had been camped, the ground was empty, the bedrolls made up and the horses gone. Toby flicked the reins and guided them out onto the main road.

Scotchy and Dundas were standing on the hotel verandah. Dundas had a whisky bottle in his hand and the pair were talking to Henry Pelham and George Grey. He reined the wagonette to a stop alongside the verandah. Grey was his usual surly self, cocking his head to one side and studying the brothers with a sneer on his lips. Pelham looked up and smiled at them.

'Ah! The O'Rourke boys. I was just having a word with the two drovers you have taken on for the drive to the diggings. I knew you would get onto the matter as soon as possible, Toby.'

'Leaving the day after tomorrow, Mr Pelham. I'll have your money for you in a fortnight.'

Pelham waved a dismissive hand. 'No rush, my boy, no rush. I shan't detain your employees any longer. I just wanted to wish them well with the drive. They look a fine pair of fellows. I'm sure they will serve you well over the coming days.'

'Thank you, Mr Pelham.' Toby touched a finger to the brim of his hat then turned to the two drovers. 'I thought you two were going to meet us beside the store.'

Dundas lifted his face and Toby saw the contempt in the little pig eyes. He opened his mouth to say something, but Scotchy placed a hand on his arm and said, 'Sorry, Mr O'Rourke. We were on our way. Just grabbed a bottle of whisky to slip into my saddlebag. Then we got talking to these gents. Sorry to have caused you any delay.' There was such sincerity in his voice that Toby felt ashamed for snapping at him.

'No harm done. I just want to be off the track before dark.'

'Well, we had better get moving, then,' Scotchy said. He and Dundas walked to the end of the verandah where their horses were tied. Dundas slipped the whisky bottle into his saddlebag and the men mounted up, taking positions at either side of the wagonette.

'I shall pay you a visit in a fortnight, Mr Pelham, and settle the matter at hand.' Toby touched a finger to his hat again and flicked the reins. He heard Pelham's voice behind him.

'Safe travels, boys.'

P addy awoke to something shaking his bed. He opened his eyes and lifted his head from the pillow. Beyond the little window it was still dark outside, but light from a lantern flooded through the door, along with the aroma of frying bacon and eggs. Toby was silhouetted against the doorway.

'C'mon, lazybones.' The bed shook again and he realised Toby was kicking it. 'We've got a mob of cattle to drive to Bendigo Creek.'

The smell of cooking did more to spur Paddy along than his brother's words. Within moments, he was dressed and sitting at the kitchen table where Scotchy and Dundas were waiting.

They ate in silence by the light of an oil lamp and then washed down the meal with sweetened tea. When they stepped out onto the verandah, the eastern sky was aglow, but the stars still showed overhead.

'I'll get you to drive the wagonette,' Toby told Dundas as he shrugged his jacket on. 'I don't doubt your skills on a horse, but Paddy knows the countryside around here. If we have any bolters, he'll be able to chase them down without getting trapped in a blind gully.'

Dundas removed his glasses and polished the lenses on the tail of his shirt. 'Suits me fine,' he said, squinting at Toby. 'I'll do all the driving if you want?'

'We'll share it around,' Toby said. 'Everyone will get a break from horseback from time to time.' Dundas blinked and settled his glasses back on his nose, making a show of tucking the wire arms around his ears.

Knowing that he might be in for some hard riding today, Paddy took extra care when cinching down his saddle and adjusting the stirrups. This was not his first cattle drive. He had accompanied his father and Toby to the sale yards in Geelong on several occasions. Those mobs had been small enough for three riders to manage. On this drive, they had four times as many cattle and still only three riders, although the wagonette driver would be expected to mount up at a moment's notice if needed to lend a hand.

Toby walked Moonlight to the gate and swung into the saddle. He looked down at Paddy who was still fussing with the musket in its scabbard. 'How's your head, Pad? You sure you want to be on horseback? I can swap you onto the wagonette.'

Paddy looked up at Toby and shook his head. The headaches weren't so bad now, and the scar on the side of his scalp only hurt a little bit whenever he pressed it gently with a finger.

'You be careful, matey. Don't fall off, whatever you do. The doc said to be mindful of that wound.'

Paddy gave a thumbs up and took up Patch's reins as Toby spurred his mount forward.

'Get down to the slip rails and open 'em up, Pad,' Toby yelled over his shoulder. 'I'll get the mob moving. Make sure you and Scotchy are in a position to turn 'em down the track once the leaders come through.'

Paddy nodded that he understood and trotted Patch down to the slip rails with Scotchy following along behind. When he reached them, he dismounted, looped his reins over a post and pushed the rails wide open. Scotchy rode through the gap and took up a position to the left of the track.

Looking back to the homestead, Paddy could see his brother trotting Moonlight back and forth as he pushed the mob together. Toby had his stock whip in his hand. He twirled it about his head a couple of times and sent it snaking out to explode in a loud crack that echoed off the ranges. The cattle shied away from the noise and trotted towards the open slip rails, a river of black and tan bodies, gaining momentum with each passing second. Paddy mounted up and waited and watched, his whip twirling about his head. As the lead cattle came through, he flicked his arm and the tip cracked like a gunshot. The river of cattle changed course, turning down the track towards Scotchy. Already, a pall of dust that Paddy knew would be with them all the way to Bendigo Creek hung in the air.

When the last of the herd had passed through the slip rails, Toby waited until Dundas had guided the wagonette through then slid from the saddle and closed off the paddock. He paused to look up at the homestead and the ridge above it. Paddy followed the direction of his gaze and could see the shadow of the cross on their parents' grave extending along the ridge.

We'll be back, he thought to himself, the words directed to the little rectangle of stones just visible in the dawn light. *Then this place will be truly ours.*

He had no time for further melancholy. A shout from Scotchy warned him that something was happening, and he turned back to the mob to see that three beasts had broken away and were making a dash for the bush. He spurred Patch's flanks and the horse shot forward, breaking into a gallop. By the time he reached them, the three cattle were in the treeline and starting up the ridge. He ducked under a low branch and spurred his horse again, getting in ahead of them. He twirled his stock whip around once and sent the tip flying towards the lead beast, a huge black steer. The leather thong cracked an inch from the animal's nose. It baulked at the noise and turned along the ridge, leading its two companions with it.

Paddy was ready for them. He lay along Patch's neck, arms pumping hard like a jockey. As he drew beside them, he had the whip twirling again and let it fly towards the black steer. The tip cracked beside the steer's ear and it almost stumbled as it turned away. The two animals behind it had to head downhill. The steer regained its stride and followed its comrades back down the ridge towards the mob. Paddy trotted Patch at their side until they joined with the herd. His heart pumped fast and he was breathing heavily, but there was a huge grin on his face. This was the most fun he'd had in months.

At noon they reached the outskirts of Bunyong Creek. Toby was riding the left flank and he turned the herd to pass the settlement on the northern side. Scotchy was on the right and Paddy rode at the rear near where Dundas followed along with the wagonette. From this position he was able to cut back and forth, ready to lend a hand to either of the flank riders, should trouble develop on their side.

Patch had been bred to this work and enjoyed the chase just as much as his rider. Paddy could see his ears twitching towards every movement from the herd, the horse's muscles tensing as he anticipated another fast run to chase down a bolter. He let the horse have a loose rein and stroked the animal's neck. This was where he missed his voice the most. A soothing word could do more to calm his mount than anything else. On previous drives, he had chatted constantly. Patch was a good listener. Together, they had talked over the problems faced by a boy in the rural districts of the colony, the one-sided banter eating up the miles. Now, the talk was gone, and Paddy wondered if Patch missed it as well. He patted his mount's neck affection-ately and hoped he would understand.

'Be needing to stop for a bite to eat soon.'

Paddy looked across to where Dundas sat on the driver's seat of the wagonette.

'I hope your brother ain't gonna keep us going all day?'

Paddy knew that the country opened up once they crossed the creek. There was a large waterhole about a mile on the other side, and he guessed this was where Toby planned to stop. He tried to mime this out to Dundas by pretending that one arm was a creek and his other hand the mob of cattle. He swept his hand across his arm and made a fist on the other side, then looked at Dundas expectantly.

The drover squinted up at him for a moment and then dropped the reins and waved his arms about like a lunatic, the hook at the end of his right arm slashing savagely through the air. 'What the bloody hell does this mean?' he growled at Paddy. 'It don't mean nothing.' He shook his head as he took up the reins and steered the wagonette away to the far side of the herd.

As expected, Toby guided them around the northern edge of the settlement. Here, the creek wasn't much deeper than a horse's fetlock and had a stony bottom. With a few well-placed whip cracks, the lead cattle plodded down the bank and into the water.

As Paddy waited for the herd to cross, he looked to where a cluster of tents were pitched by the water at the northern end of Bunyong Creek. There were six or seven children playing among the guy ropes, running and yelling and squealing. They saw the cattle and drovers making the crossing a little upstream and ran towards them, a small terrier dog yapping at their heels. They reached the trundling wagonette and ran beside it, squealing so loudly that the draught horse shied and bucked. Dundas fought to control the horse as he yelled at the children.

'Clear off, ya brats! Go on, get out of it.'

The children continued their game, oblivious to the abuse being screamed at them by the driver. Dundas let go of the reins and picked up a stock whip from the seat beside him. The wagonette bucked and jerked as the horse continued to panic, but Dundas ignored it.

'Clear off, ya little bastards, or you'll get a taste of this.' He waved the coiled stock whip over his head and the children thought better of staying. They scattered like flies and headed back towards the cluster of tents, all except the dog, which continued to run and yap and snap at the legs of the draught horse.

Dundas dropped the coils of the whip and gave the handle one quick twirl. The leather thong flicked towards the dog. The terrier didn't see it coming and took the full strike across its back. It let out a yelp of agony and fell to the ground, whimpering and trying to regain its feet. Paddy thought it was all over, but Dundas twirled the whip again and, with a gasp of horror, he realised the stockman was not finished with the dog. The tip came singing out and the terrier squealed as the leather thong clipped hair from its silvery back.

Paddy spurred Patch in beside the wagonette and yanked the whip from Dundas's hand.

'What the hell, young fella?'

Paddy coiled the whip and threw it into the load space behind the drover, then pointed at the backs of the last cattle crossing the creek.

'Yeah, all right.' Dundas had a sneer on his face as he gathered up the reins and gave them a flick. 'Don't be telling me what to do. They shouldn't have come running at me like that.' The wagonette started forward and Paddy could hear the drover still talking to himself as he descended the creek bank. 'Ha! That's a good one. A mute *telling* me what to do.'

Paddy watched the drover for a moment then swung from Patch's back. The dog still lay squirming in the grass and he went and picked it up. The little terrier struggled feebly and Paddy stroked it behind the ears. There was a raw welt on the silver-haired back.

'Is Bobby all right, mister?

A boy of about seven stood a few paces away. He wore a pair of trousers about four sizes too big for him that were held up by twine braces. The other children weren't so brave and waited near the camp, watching intently.

Paddy nodded and carried the dog to the boy.

'You all right, Bobby?' He took the dog from Paddy and cradled it gently, and the tongue came out, long and pink, licking at the boy's grubby face. Without another word, the boy turned and carried the dog back to where the other children waited.

Paddy collected Patch's reins and remounted. All the cattle were across the creek now, along with Dundas and the wagonette. Toby was waiting on the other side.

'Where have you been, Pad? What the hell happened?'

Paddy pointed at the wagonette and shook his head severely.

'Something happen with Dundas?'

Paddy nodded and shifted his finger to Scotchy, just visible on the right flank. He shook his head again.

'Yeah, they're a strange pair of coves. I don't like them much either, matey. As soon as we get to Bendigo Creek, we pay them off and never see them again. We just need them for a few days more. I need to get back on the flank. Are you all right back here?'

Paddy nodded and Toby spun Moonlight on the spot and trotted back towards the herd. He watched his brother for a moment and then let his gaze slip back to Dundas on the wagonette. Paddy had always thought of himself as an easy-going, friendly sort of person who got along well with everyone he met. As he watched the drover guide the wagonette through the pall of dust, he decided that he didn't like Dundas at all. The sooner this drive was over the better.

By Toby's estimation, they were covering a good ten to twelve miles a day. With six days behind them, Bendigo Creek couldn't be too far away. An hour before moving the herd off the track and making camp, he had spoken to two southbound riders who had informed him they had left the Bendigo diggings at noon that day.

Tomorrow, Toby thought. *Tomorrow we reach the diggings and I get ol' man Pelham off my back.*

He looked to where Scotchy and Dundas rode the flanks. Tomorrow he would be able to pay them out and see them ride away, a thought that brought a smile to his lips. The pair of drovers had been difficult to manage. They argued with him at every opportunity. Toby had done his best to divide the chores equally among them all, but Scotchy and Dundas found fault in nearly every task he gave out. In the end, he'd found it easier to do whatever needed doing himself, rather than get into an argument with the two men. Paddy had tried to take up some of the slack as well, offering to cook the meals each night and morning, tend to the horses and collect firewood. Toby was thankful for his brother's support. Even with the two drovers, he would not have made it this far without Paddy.

They made camp inside the sweeping bend of a creek. The far bank had been severely undercut and was impassable to the cattle, making it easy to keep them herded on the near side. One man could easily patrol the narrow neck of land and chase any strays back to the mob.

'Whatcha gonna cook for dinner, young fella?' Scotchy stood with his saddle in his arms as he watched Paddy build a campfire.

Paddy pointed at a skinned possum that Toby had shot out of a gum tree earlier that day.

'Possum stew *again*?' Scotchy screwed up his face in disgust.

Paddy nodded and went back to feeding the fire from a pile of sticks.

'Put a bit more salt in this time eh, Chatterbox? Help mask the taste. The one you did last night was bloody horrible. Me guts is still churning.'

Toby had rebuked Scotchy on several occasions for the names he called Paddy. The one-eyed drover always apologised profusely and then went on to call Paddy a different name. Toby opened his mouth to tell the drover off, but Paddy looked up from where he worked and gave a slight shake of his head. Toby took the hint and kept his mouth shut.

Tomorrow, he reminded himself. *I only have to put up with him until tomorrow.*

Dundas was left to patrol the cattle while the other three ate. Toby enjoyed the stew, but Scotchy complained at every mouthful and talked up the meal he was going to enjoy when they reached the diggings tomorrow and were paid out.

They finished eating and Toby sent Paddy out to relieve Dundas. Not wanting to get into an argument with Scotchy, he gathered up the dirty plates himself, placed them in the wash tub and waited for the big iron kettle to boil. While he washed the dishes, Scotchy rolled a cigarette and sprawled on his bedroll.

'So, Mr O'Rourke, how much do you figure your mob of cattle will be worth when we push them into the butcher's yards tomorrow?'

Toby dropped the tattered and stained dishcloth into the suds and looked at Scotchy. The drover had asked this question a few times over the past week, and Toby had always fobbed him off with a vague answer. His finances were none of Scotchy's business.

'Like I said the last time you asked, several hundred pounds.'

Scotchy grunted and drew on his cigarette. 'A good beast would be worth quite a few pounds, I would think, Mr O'Rourke. I hear a meal on the diggings can cost close to one and a half pounds. And that's for mutton. No, I reckon you've got a fortune wandering about in them trees over there.'

There was a strange edge to the drover's voice. Toby wasn't sure if it was admiration or greed. He looked down at Scotchy and found the drover studying him intently, his one good eye reflecting the firelight. A little chill ran down his spine.

'Anyways,' Scotchy added. 'Dundas and me are looking forward to getting paid. Been a pleasure working for you, Mr O'Rourke. An absolute pleasure.' He turned to place another stick on the fire, but not so fast that Toby missed the smile on his tanned face.

Toby had given himself the midnight-to-two o'clock shift, but he had trouble sleeping and was already awake when Paddy wandered out of the darkness and unsaddled Patch at the horse line, a hitching rope tied between two gum trees some twenty paces from the camp.

'All quiet, Pad?' Toby whispered. Across the fire, the two drovers were wrapped in their bedrolls, Dundas snoring so loudly he sounded like a bow saw cutting through a well-seasoned piece of gum tree.

Paddy nodded and gave Toby the fob watch that had been their father's. The youngster slipped into his bedroll as Toby threw his saddle onto Moonlight and he heard his brother start up a duet of snoring with Dundas. He swung onto the horse's back and headed for the creek.

Looking back towards the campsite, he could see the wagonette, horses and the shadowy lumps of the three sleeping figures. He had thrown a piece of wood on the fire before saddling Moonlight and it now flared brightly, throwing a large circle of light over the camp and into the scattered trees.

As he watched, a figure rose from beside the fire. Judging by the long silhouette it could only be Scotchy. He crossed the camp and relieved himself against a tree then went back to his bedroll, pausing briefly beside the prone form of Dundas before settling down once more. Toby was too far away to hear what was said – maybe Scotchy was ragging on Dundas for his loud snoring.

He found the cattle bunched together and tried to count them, but the task was nearly impossible in the darkness, so he wandered back and forth across the narrow neck of land, sometimes in the saddle and sometimes on foot with the reins looped over the pommel and Moonlight following behind like a faithful puppy. Once, when they reached the bank of the creek, Toby let the horse step down into the water to drink while he sat on the loose gravel and looked up at the stars. The Southern Cross had passed the vertical and now leaned drunkenly to the right as it continued its never-ending journey around the south celestial pole. A quarter moon stood in the eastern sky. Moonlight came up from the water and pushed gently at his shoulder. He took the reins and swung into the saddle, setting off once more to patrol the cattle.

After crossing the neck of land, Toby pulled his father's fob watch from his pocket. He had to twist it carefully to catch enough light to read the face.

Three minutes to two.

He walked Moonlight back to the camp and unsaddled him before waking Scotchy. The drover arose almost immediately, which was strange given the usual stream of oaths he'd let fly when woken for his shift.

'You're pretty eager to get at it tonight,' Toby whispered as he slipped into his bedroll.

'Last night out, isn't it, Mr O'Rourke? Tomorrow is pay day, and we'll have money to spend and nuggets to pick off the ground.' He poured himself a lukewarm cup of tea from the billy before saddling his horse and riding into the darkness. Despite his misgivings, Toby fell asleep before the drover was out of sight.

He awoke to something cold and hard pushing against his upper lip. He struggled to blink sleep from his eyes and tried to move away from whatever it was, but it followed his movements. His eyes finally focused enough to reveal Scotchy pressing a large single-shot pistol into his face.

'What the hell!' Toby tried to bring his hands up. A low growl from Scotchy warned him to be still. Across the dying embers of the campfire Dundas had Paddy's hands tied behind his back and was leading him by the trailing end of rope, jerking it savagely so that Paddy stumbled as he walked.

Despite the gun in his face, Toby felt his anger flare. 'Don't hurt him, or I'll –'

'You'll be doing nothing, Mr O'Rourke.' Scotchy's voice carried a promise of violence. 'Your brother and you will wait right here while Dundas and me take your cattle into Bendigo Creek.'

'You're duffing our cattle? You can't.'

'We can and we are,' Scotchy said. 'Tie him and his brother to the tree,' he added. Dundas used the tail of rope attached to Paddy to tie Toby's hands behind his back. When he finished, Scotchy uncocked the pistol and stood up.

'You can't take our cattle.'

'Me heart strings is pulling for you, but it won't do you no good. We've spent the last two year's scratching around in the dust, trying to make an honest living, only stealing when we had to. Fortune took the liberty never to smile on us, so we decided we'd just have to take someone else's.'

In the east the sky was beginning to lighten and Toby could see that the cattle had been moved close to the campsite. Scotchy and Dundas made up their bedrolls, strapping them to their saddled horses. He had been so tired he'd slept through the men's preparations.

'You can't just ride off and leave us here. We'll die.'

Both men swung into their saddles. 'I'll get the horses,' Dundas said, ignoring the plea. He rode over to where

Moonlight and Patch were tethered, cut the lines and used a stick to whip their rumps and send both animals galloping into the darkness. Then he went to the draught horse for the wagonette and did the same.

'Let's get a move on,' Scotchy said. 'By the time they get free and find one of them horses we'll be counting money in a sly grog shop and buying the bar.'

They urged their mounts off without looking back. Toby heard a whip crack and the cattle, used to the routine after a week on the road, turned as one and moved onto the track.

'Wait,' Toby called after them. 'Please, wait!' He yelled until they disappeared into the bush and the dust.

Paddy began to cry, snuffling softly, but Toby felt too angry to offer any comfort. He stared at the place where Scotchy and Dundas had disappeared and cursed softly under his breath. He kicked his bedroll away from his feet and tugged at the ropes binding his wrists. Paddy let out a whimper of pain as his hands were pulled up hard against the tree.

'Dundas tied these knots with one hand, Pad. How good can they be? See if you can get free.'

Toby wasn't sure how long they worked at the rope. Dundas's one-handed knot-tying proved to be better than first thought. Toby was almost ready to give up and try something else when Paddy was able to work a hand loose. He quickly untied himself then freed Toby.

'Stay here,' Toby said. 'Get the guns and load them.' He left Paddy and ran to the creek. Their horses were nowhere in sight. He searched up and down both sides of the narrow watercourse for an hour and finally found both Moonlight and Patch standing beneath the spreading branches of a stringybark. Moonlight wore a halter and the end of the cut lead rope trailed between his front legs. Toby took hold of the rope and headed back to camp. He threw his saddle on, pulled the bridle into place, then slipped the Lovell into its scabbard.

'See if you can catch your horse,' he told Paddy over his shoulder. 'He was over near the creek. Find the one for the wagonette as well, but stay around here. Keep your gun with you. I'll be back for you before dark.' Paddy nodded in understanding and Toby spurred the horse's flanks.

Scotchy and Dundas had about two hours start on him. If he rode hard, he might be able to catch them before they could sell the cattle. He urged Moonlight into a gallop the moment he found the track. A few minutes later he charged between two southbound riders who yelled and cursed at him as their startled mounts reared and plunged.

On the outskirts of Bendigo Creek Toby reined down to a trot. Foaming sweat had blown back from his horse's chest, soaking the legs of his trousers. He had never pushed Moonlight so hard before and felt guilty, though the horse had given everything Toby had asked of him. He glanced at the butt of the Lovell protruding from the scabbard and wondered what else he might be capable of if he caught up with Scotchy and Dundas.

A small boy stood at the edge of the road, throwing stones at a half-breed dingo.

'Did two men drive some cattle through here this morning?' Toby called.

The boy looked up and nodded.

'Did you see where they took them?'

A grubby finger pointed over tents and mullock heaps. 'The butcher yards on the other side.'

Toby found his cattle penned in a yard beyond a dry creek that divided the diggings from the commercial enterprises. He reined in at the rail and made his way towards a shack built from bush timber and calico. Near one of the yards, several men were setting up a gibbet in preparation for the coming slaughter.

A short, heavily built man sat at a makeshift desk inside the shack. He looked up curiously as Toby burst through the entrance.

'Those cattle in the yard,' he shouted. 'They were brought in early this morning by two men; one had a patch over his eye and the other had one hand.'

The man rose from his seat and matched Toby's aggressive stance. 'Mr O'Rourke and his brother. They drove the cattle up from Geelong. Apparently the prices are not so good on the Ballarat diggings.'

'They were two thieves named Scotchy and Dundas,' Toby blurted. 'I'm Toby O'Rourke. I hired them to help drive my cattle up from the Coliban. They jumped me and my brother before dawn and stole the cattle you have in your yard.'

'Those cattle bear the O'Rourke brand.' The butcher swept his arm in the direction of the yards. 'Mr O'Rourke had all the correct paperwork—'

'He's not an O'Rourke,' Toby screamed. 'Me and my brother spent weeks putting that herd together, and those bastards stole it from us.' He banged his fist on the desk.

The butcher came around the desk, fists held in front of him. 'You can't just barge in here and start throwing wild accusations around.'

Toby widened his stance and lifted his own fists, prepared to meet the butcher's advance. 'You're as bad as those thieving mongrels,' he yelled. 'Do you just let anyone offload cattle into your yards without checking their story?'

The butcher's right fist shot out and struck Toby squarely on the chin. He staggered back and came up against the wall, braced himself and then launched forward. The butcher tried another jab, but Toby rolled his head and the fist grazed past his ear. Inside the strike of those iron-hard fists, he swept the butcher up and carried him into the back wall. The calico parted like a pair of theatre curtains and they crashed through onto the ground outside. Toby managed to get his knee up and struck hard for the butcher's groin. The man let out a howl of pain and Toby lowered his knee to strike again, but rough hands pulled him away. Two workmen hauled him to his feet and held him between them.

'You all right, Mr Hatherway?'

Another worker helped the butcher to his feet, but the man couldn't stand straight. He rubbed at his groin and panted hard, doubled over. Finally, he gasped, 'One of you fetch the constable.'

The man who had assisted the butcher ran off to do his boss's bidding. Hatherway managed to pull himself up straight, but stood with his legs splayed. 'Get the little bastard into the hut. The traps can sort him out.'

The two workmen dragged Toby inside. Hatherway straightened his desk and placed a horseshoe on some loose papers. He glared at Toby, but said nothing.

A constable, a man named Gillies, arrived ten minutes later. After listening to the versions of the story he spent a few minutes examining the cattle and a few more with the papers Hatherway had drawn up for the sale. Finally, he pushed his spectacles back onto the bridge of his huge hooked nose and announced that everything was in order.

'The hell it is!' The two workmen had released Toby, but remained close at hand. 'Those duffers stole our cattle at gunpoint and you say everything's in order?'

The constable scowled at Toby, obviously not used to being spoken to in such a manner, especially by someone who was little more than a boy. 'The cattle are branded and the paperwork is in order. You have no right accosting Mr Hatherway. He runs a respectable business. You may be facing charges here, young man. I have your descriptions of Mr O'Rourke and his brother or Scotchy and Dundas or whatever they're called. Very distinctive-looking gentlemen. If they're still around here I'll find and question them. A report will go to Melbourne with the next mail and someone will check your story from that end. I can do little more than that.'

'That could take weeks,' Toby pleaded with the policeman. 'We need to find them before they get too far.'

'I can't have boys running around here taking the law into their own hands. The good Lord knows I have enough trouble just keeping the peace among the miners. Justice will eventually be served, young man, but you will have no part in it.'

Toby opened his mouth to protest, but the policeman got in first. 'Now, let's discuss the matter of your assault on the person of Mr Hatherway.'

'But he hit me first,' Toby protested.

'In self-defence I would say,' Gillies offered, turning to the butcher.

Hatherway nodded. He came around the desk and perched on the edge gingerly. 'It's all right, Constable. I don't want to press charges. If he's telling the truth, then he has every right to be worked up.'

'Consider yourself lucky, young fellow. If I were you, I'd thank Mr Hatherway for his kind gesture. As for this matter of the stolen cattle, I'll begin my enquiries immediately. Now, get out of here and stay out of trouble. If I have any more dealings with you then you'll find yourself chained to a tree and awaiting the magistrate.'

Without saying another word, Toby turned and walked back out to where he'd left Moonlight tied up. Not wanting anyone to see, he led the horse into a shallow gully behind the yards before pulling the Lovell from its scabbard to check it was loaded and primed.

Moonlight sensed the tension in him and whickered softly as Toby mounted up.

'So, I'm a mongrel cattle duffer who's just made a pile of money,' he said to the horse. 'Where do I go to spend it?'

Moonlight's ears twitched back and forth at the sound of his voice.

'Yeah, you're right,' Toby answered himself. 'I would celebrate with a nobbler or two of rum.'

He urged the horse forward and they climbed out of the gully. Two diggers were working a nearby claim.

'Where could a fellow get a drink at this time of the day?'

One of the miners looked up and studied him from beneath the brim of his cabbage-tree hat. 'Little early for drinking, young fella, but if you're in desperate need to slake your thirst, you might try O'Shaunessy's coffee shop.' He gestured over his shoulder with a thumb. 'It's over beyond the blacksmith shop by the creek.'

Toby thanked the man and urged Moonlight forward. He found O'Shaunessy's where the digger had indicated. Two horses were tied to a rail outside a grubby white tent and he could hear the low rumble of voices from inside. Neither horse belonged to Scotchy and Dundas, but Toby dismounted, pulled the Lovell from its scabbard and went inside.

There were three men in the tent, but he had never seen them before. The conversation stopped abruptly as he stooped beneath the fly and all eyes were on the musket. One man was polishing a glass with a piece of rag. He stepped nervously forward.

'Can—can I help you?'

'I'm looking for two men,' Toby said, wondering if stepping into the tent while armed was a good idea. 'One is missing an eye and the other a hand.' He held up his own hand to show them, but was dismayed as all three shook their heads.

'Ain't seen no one like that,' the shopkeeper said.

'Where else would a man get a hard drink at this time of day?'

The three men pointed in three different directions and Toby made a mental note of the names they gave him. He thanked them and went back out to Moonlight.

By mid-afternoon Toby had visited every coffee house and grog shop on the diggings. The closest he had come to finding Scotchy and Dundas had been when one patron had said he'd seen them riding out on the north road. Toby galloped along the road for six miles before he came across someone heading south. The weary digger shook his head and told him he hadn't passed anyone on the road since daybreak.

With disappointment weighing heavily in his heart Toby decided it was time to go back and find Paddy. As he walked Moonlight south along the track, he wondered what this meant for the farm. Would Henry Pelham give them more time to pay the debt? Even as the thought crossed his mind a niggling feeling of doubt started to eat through the worry he already felt. Pelham had a motive behind buying out his father's debt. Toby wasn't sure what it was, but he knew he couldn't trust Henry Pelham.

'I'll fetch Paddy and we'll make camp here at the diggings,' he told the horse. Hearing his own voice gave him some small comfort now that he'd decided on a course of action, but it did little to ease the worry. 'We'll scour the countryside every day until we find those two bastards.'

'This is it, my sweet,' Frank said. 'She was once battered and scarred by the colony's roads and the axles were so worn the wheels wobbled like a drunkard. I've spent many a day working on her and she's right to take us to Ballarat.'

Maree eyed the wagonette. The vehicle still bore many gouges and there was more raw wood showing than the original blue paint, but, as far as wagons and carriages went, she trusted her husband fully. She knew Frank had worked long into the nights to get it ready, and he was good at his craft.

'What about a horse to pull it?' she asked.

'Already taken care of,' Frank said, pointing to a roan gelding tethered to a nearby tree, grazing hungrily from the limited grass.

Betty squealed delightedly and ran ahead of the little group. By the time they caught up she was stroking the horse's muzzle and smiling up at him. 'Oh, Papa, he's beautiful. Does he have a name?'

Frank scratched the back of his head. 'I didn't think to ask. Tell you what, Betty, why don't you name him? Make it a good one. He has a lot of hard work ahead of him.'

Betty took a step back and studied the animal, looking for all the world like a seasoned horse trader. 'He looks strong. I think he is the strongest horse ever. We should call him Samson.'

'That's a wonderful name,' Annie said. 'Samson, the horse that will take us to Ballarat to make our fortune.'

Maree listened to the excitement in the voices of her daughters. The second part of their great adventure was about to begin. She turned to the west. Ballarat was out that way, she had learned. The sun felt warm on her face. Despite her original misgivings, she was coming to like this strange land. The days were not so hot now and the air was pure and clean, especially in the mornings. The long voyage out from England had taken its toll. Tom's death had nearly destroyed her, but her family needed her. It had taken all her strength to fight her way back. Now they were on the cusp of the last leg of their journey.

You were right, my boy. This will be a far better life than anything we could have had in England.

'When shall we leave, Frank?'

'The tent is paid up till the end of the month and I still have some work to finish up here. While I'm doing that, you and the girls can start getting our gear together. We should make a list, but we'll be needing a tent of our own, mining and panning equipment. I'm told you can buy that stuff on the diggings, but the prices are high. Far better that we buy it here and take it with us. Flour, sugar, pots and pans. Everything we'll need for a permanent camp.'

'The end of the month? We go to the diggings at the end of the month?' Annie said, squeezing her father's hand.

'Yes, my girl.' Frank gave her a brilliant smile. 'Then we're going to dig up a gold nugget like the one in the window of the bank.'

'Samson will have the best stable ever,' said Betty, kissing the horse's muzzle. 'Pride of place.'

Listening to her family, a smile played on Maree's lips and her gaze turned westwards again. A breeze made the trees sound like they were whispering to each other and she lifted her face to the sun. In the distance there were hilltops. The track led off into the forest until it disappeared in shadow. Annie's words spoken on the deck of the ship came back to her then:

'Everything we have ever wanted is waiting for us behind those hills.'

She wanted to be happy, like her family. They laughed and joked and made their plans for the future. Her husband and daughters relished the adventure that lay ahead of them. But this adventure had already claimed the life of her son. What more would it claim before it was over?

Toby sat his mount in a loose manner as Paddy drove the wagonette, Patch tied to the tailgate. He tried not to think too much about what lay ahead of them as they neared home. They had stayed on the diggings for two weeks, searching from sunrise until dark, but Scotchy and Dundas had vanished. Toby would have stayed longer, but their money had quickly run out and he was left with no choice. He could only hope Pelham had truly bought out their father's loan to hold the bank off, then he might give them some more time to get another herd together.

They rounded the last bend in the track and Toby felt his pulse quicken. Smoke curled away from the homestead's chimney and there were unfamiliar horses in the yard. A sulky sat beside the verandah. Swinging off Moonlight, he pushed open the slip rails and yelled to Paddy, 'Bring the wagonette up to the shed. I'm going to the house. We have visitors.' He swung back onto the horse and galloped towards the homestead. As he drew up to the verandah he recognised the sulky as the same one Pelham had used to attend his parents' funeral.

Henry Pelham sat at the far side of the table, as far as possible from anyone coming through the door. He nursed one of their mother's bone china cups and George Grey stood behind his boss with his back to the stove. He too had a cup in his hand that he used to salute Toby as he came through the doorway. Two men, Pelham's stockmen, sat on chairs facing the door.

'Ah! Young Toby,' Pelham announced, absently turning the teacup with his fingertips. His expression reminded Toby of a dingo that had found its way among the lambs.

'What the hell are you and your men doing in our house? You have no right to be in here.'

'That's what you think.' Grey took a step forward. 'It's Mr Pelham's house now. The magistrate has said so.' He went to take another step, but Pelham held up a bony hand, stopping him mid-stride.

'I don't give a tinker's toss what the bloody magistrate has said. You can't just march in here and take over the place like this.'

Pelham turned his hand towards Toby in a pacifying gesture. 'I'm terribly sorry, my boy. I gave you a way to pay off your debt. It's a downright shame you fell victim to the many rogues and scoundrels preying on unsuspecting people, but I can't be expected to do any more.'

'How do you know about that?'

'I should think the entire Colony of Victoria has heard of your unfortunate incident. Word travels fast, my boy.'

'Not as fast as you travelled to the bloody magistrate when you heard, I bet.'

The smile slipped from Pelham's face.

Paddy came up to the doorway behind Toby and looked into the crowded kitchen, a bewildered look on his face.

'Pelham's come to kick us off our land,' Toby spat. 'He's just as much a thief as those two bastards that stole our cattle.'

One of the stockmen leaped to his feet and slapped Toby across the face with the back of his hand. Toby staggered and tripped over Paddy. Both boys sprawled onto the floor of the verandah amidst a chorus of chuckles from the watching men. Rolling to his feet, Toby launched himself at the stockman's legs and took him above the knees with enough force to carry both of them back into the kitchen. They came up against the far wall with a thump that rattled the crockery on the sideboard. Toby was the first to his feet and landed a punch to the stockman's midriff. The man let out a bellow of pain and Toby cocked his fist, aiming for the whiskered face. Someone grabbed him by both shoulders and pulled him away.

The other stockman spun him about and held him against the bedroom door by the throat. His free hand went back, knuckles bunching into a fist. Toby braced for the blow, but before the punch came the stockman was swept sideways by Paddy's wild charge. They crashed into the boys' bedroom door and it gave way under the onslaught, slamming back on its hinges. Paddy laid into the stockman, fists and boots flying in a mad frenzy.

The first man forgot about Toby and tried to go to the aid of his friend. Toby stepped in behind and punched him in the kidneys. He howled with agony and tried to back away from the fight. Toby wasn't prepared to let him go so easily. He drew his fist back again, but rough hands seized his arm and he was spun back against the wall and pinned there by Grey's considerable bulk.

'Take it easy, boy,' Grey snarled, his mouth mere inches from Toby's ear. 'If it wouldn't upset Mr Pelham so, I'd knock the daylights out of you right here and now.' Toby struggled to shake free, but Grey's strength was too great.

The two stockmen managed to get a grip on Paddy's thrashing arms and legs. They held him against the floor, cursing under their breath.

Pelham rose from the table. He crossed the room and laid a hand on Toby's shoulder, then nodded to Grey and the other stockmen. They released the brothers and stepped back, but not too far.

'I'm not the sort of man who would turn two boys out into the cold, Toby. You and Patrick are welcome to stay in this very house in my employ. You will do the things you did before and be paid well to do them.' He dropped his hand from Toby's shoulder and stood back. 'The only change will be on the title of the papers concerning this land. You will have men to help you. I will even make you a foreman so you will never have to do any of the cooking or wood chopping or other menial tasks. Surely that must sound good to you?'

Toby scowled and Pelham turned to Paddy, who had climbed up from the floor.

'What about you, young Patrick? Do you want to remain living in this house?'

Paddy came to his brother's side. He looked up at Pelham and shook his head.

'We can still pay you back, Mr Pelham.' His Irish temper abating, Toby switched tack and tried to reason his way out of the godawful mess. 'There are scores of wild cattle in the hills. We can get another herd together and raise the money. All we need is time.'

Pelham shook his mane of grey hair. 'I'm sorry, my boy, but time is not a luxury I can afford. With the gold rush the colony is growing fast. The time for expansion is now and I can't wait any longer. I have an agent in Portland negotiating a herd of prime beef I plan to run on this land. The wheels are turning and I couldn't stop them even if I wanted to.'

'You didn't waste any time, did you? To have someone in Portland you must have sent him weeks ago. How did you know we wouldn't get our mob into Bendigo Creek?'

'You have to stay a jump ahead if you want to make it in this world, my boy. If you had managed to raise the money I would have simply taken that mob to Bendigo, where the prices are somewhat inflated as you know, and shown a tidy little return for my investment. However, I would rather work that herd into the best quality beef in the colony. You can still be part of it – both of you.'

The next words almost stuck in Toby's throat. It took a great force of will to spit them at Pelham, each one tearing out a little piece of his soul. 'If it's not our land or our cattle we want no part of it. We'll take what's rightfully ours and go.' Toby pushed himself away from the wall. 'What are we left with?'

Pelham pulled a folded sheaf of papers from his vest pocket. He smoothed them open on the kitchen table and gave two of the sheets to Toby.

'This is the magistrate's order authorising me to take possession of your land and releasing you from your father's debt.' He passed his hand over the document as he spoke. 'This is a copy of the land commissioner's registration of change of title for this land.'

Toby took the papers without inspecting them and pushed them into his pocket. 'What are we left with?' he asked again.

'Your personal possessions, of course,' Pelham stated flatly, businesslike. 'You can take your wagonette as well as your own horses. You can also take anything of your dear departed parents you feel attached to. I'm not an evil man,' he added. 'I have no wish for you to leave, but if you feel you must, then who am I to stop you?' He swept his hand around the room. 'Take whatever you want.'

At first light the brothers climbed the hill to their parents' grave. Paddy tidied the lines of rocks and Toby straightened the cross. He tested it by wriggling it back and forth, satisfied it would stand for at least a few weeks. There were many emotions bubbling inside him that made him want to cry, to yell and scream at this fate the world had cast upon them. He looked down at the homestead, at the wagonette loaded with their few meagre possessions, ready to head off to God-only-knew-where.

Paddy let out a sob and Toby placed an arm around him. 'We'll be back, matey,' he said. 'I don't know where we're going or what we're going to do, but I know we'll be back. And then this land will be ours once again. I promise you that.' He spoke the words for Paddy's benefit, but his eyes were fixed on the small patch of earth in the rectangle of stones. 'If it's greed that drives old man Pelham, then we'll use it to get our land back. We'll make enough money to buy it back. More money than he'll be able to refuse.'

Reluctantly, they walked down to the homestead. Grey stood at the end of the verandah with one of the stockmen. They had stayed the night under the pretence of helping load the wagonette, but Toby knew they were there to make sure nothing happened to the property. *Probably a good move*, Toby thought. More than once during the night he had considered burning all the buildings to the ground, leaving Pelham with nothing but a pile of ashes. But Toby knew he would be destroying more than a few simple structures; he would be destroying something his parents had built, a testimony to their very existence.

'Final goodbyes?' Grey asked, a cheeky smile on his face.

Toby ignored the stockman and sent Paddy to fetch Moonlight and Patch from the yard. They tied the lead ropes to the tailgate of the wagonette and climbed onto the seat. Toby took the reins and flicked the horse into motion.

Neither of them looked back as they trundled away from the homestead. When they reached the slip rails Paddy jumped down and pushed them open. Toby guided the wagonette through and Paddy was about to push them closed again, but Toby called him up onto the wagonette and they started down the track with Grey cursing loudly in the distance.

Toby toyed with the idea of calling to say goodbye to the Smiths and Guttens, but the hollowness in the pit of his stomach, combined with Irish pride, wouldn't let him. They would only offer sympathy, and sympathy wouldn't get their home back. He had failed this particular test of manhood and all he wanted to do was get as far away from the bitter memories as he could. Paddy made no sign of wanting to stop as they passed the turnoff to the Smith farm. He sat motionless, eyes fixed on the track ahead, so Toby urged the team onto the southbound fork. They circled the settlement of Bunyong Creek and travelled on.

That night they made camp in a grove of tall stringybarks. The cattle drive had given them both a routine to follow, and Toby set about unhitching the draught horse and tending to their animals while Paddy collected firewood and started on the meal. They had no fresh meat, so he baked a large damper filled with raisins. They sat on opposite sides of the campfire and ate the simple fare with golden syrup and sweetened tea.

As Toby sat staring into the flames he tried not to dwell on their misfortune. He didn't want to think about tomorrow or any of the days ahead, for he had no idea what they held for them and that scared him more than he wanted to admit. Paddy clapped his hands to get Toby's attention and then opened and closed his thumb and fingers on one hand the same way a person would make the mouth work on a sock puppet.

'Talking?'

Paddy nodded.

'Sorry, matey. I don't feel much like talking at the moment.'

Paddy nodded and pointed towards the south, the direction the track was taking them.

'I don't know where we're going, Pad. That direction is as good as any.'

Toby lapsed into silence and Paddy sat perfectly still on the other side of the fire. He could see the worry on his brother's face, but he had no words of comfort to offer. They were homeless. Everything they owned was within a few paces of the flickering flames of the campfire. He wanted to tell Paddy that they would be all right, that something would turn up, but he only felt a gnawing sense of hopelessness. The mental wall he had built suddenly crumbled and a tear rolled down his cheek.

Paddy got up and came around the fire to him. He sat down and poked a finger, first in Toby's chest and then his own. Then he placed an arm across Toby's shoulders.

'Yeah, Pad. Whatever happens, we are together.' The arm squeezed him gently and he felt a little of the hopelessness dissolve.

At noon on the second day, Paddy took a turn at driving the wagonette. Toby sat on the end of the seat, barely watching the scenery unfold about him. His mood remained dark and he brooded over the future that awaited them. They had their horses and would certainly find employment as stockmen, but Toby wondered if he would be able to put hard work into someone else's dream.

Late that afternoon they reached the Ballarat road. The well-travelled track stretched out on either hand, one path leading east to Melbourne, the other towards the diggings in Ballarat. Paddy stopped the wagonette and cast a quizzical eye at his brother that said, '*Which way?*'

Toby was quiet for a moment as he pondered the intersection in front of them. In Melbourne, the seat of government for the Colony of Victoria, they would certainly find work. The gold rush had deprived many larger towns of much-needed labour. But a labourer's wages were a mere pittance. It would take them years to scrape enough money together to make Pelham an offer on the farm.

He glanced down the road to the right. Two diggers struggled to manhandle a barrow across rutted ground. The barrow was piled high with their possessions, picks and shovels and a gold-washing cradle. The men were on their way to the diggings to seek their fortune. Toby wasn't sure how many fortunes were being made at the diggings. From what he had seen at Bendigo Creek, the goldfields looked more like a place of poverty and despair than a path to riches. But gold was coming out of the ground. Of that he was sure. Newspapers carried accounts of shipments of the precious yellow metal being taken under escort to Melbourne. There were fortunes out there to be found.

Toby gestured to the right with his thumb, towards the diggings and the gold. 'That way,' he grunted.

They travelled towards Ballarat for two days, making camp each evening by the side of the track. Sometimes other people camped with them. Toby hardly spoke to them, but he welcomed their closeness. Bushrangers were known to hold up travellers on the roads and there was safety in numbers. Before they went to sleep each night he made sure both muskets were loaded with a fresh charge and ready to hand.

On the afternoon of the third day they reached a river. Another wagonette sat low in the water, bogged to the axles in mud. It had almost made it across. The horse stood on firm ground, almost into the cutting of the riverbank, its legs caked with mud. A woman and two girls huddled on the bank, watching as a man unloaded the wagonette in an attempt to lighten it, piling their belongings on high ground.

Toby reined to a stop and studied the banks of the river in both directions. He cursed softly under his breath as he realised this was the only place where they could cross, and it was now blocked by the other travellers.

'I suppose we'll have to help the cove out if we want to get any further today,' he said to Paddy. He climbed off the seat and unhooked the trace from the drawbar of the wagonette. 'We'll help him out of the bog and then he can help us get across to the other bank.'

He took the horse by the halter and led it down to the riverbank, the chains of the trace rattling and clanging. The water felt cool against his legs as he waded out into it and crossed to midstream.

'Can you unhook your horse, move it further up the cutting?' Toby called to the misfortunate stranger. 'I'll move mine in behind. With two horses we might be able to pull you free.'

The man stopped what he was doing and looked at Toby. 'Much obliged, young sir,' he said in a southern English accent and moved towards the trace of his horse.

'Go and give him a hand,' Toby told Paddy. 'We don't want to be here for the rest of the day.'

Toby had to swing wide to get around the wagonette. He waded through waist-deep water, but the riverbed dropped away and he sank instantly out of his depth. For one panicked moment he had visions of being swept back under the thrashing hoofs of the horse, now swimming awkwardly in its harness. His boot touched bottom and he pushed himself out to the side, using the horse's momentum to carry him to the river's edge. Water streamed down his face and he pushed his hair out of his eyes with his free hand. He found his hat floating a few feet away, snatched it up and pulled it hard down onto his head. The women were standing above the cutting, their faces lit with smiles, but no one dared laugh at this stranger who was offering to help free them from the mud.

The man crossed over to him and offered a steadying hand as Toby climbed out of the water. Angry and embarrassed at his untimely dunking, and even more so by the smiles on the river-bank, Toby was about to shrug the hand away, but the man said, 'Sorry, young sir. I should have warned you about that deep water there. Took an unwanted swim myself a little while ago. Got ten pounds of flour wet in the process, more's the pity.'

Toby took the stranger's hand, the grip hard and strong, the roughness of heavy calluses evident. He was in his late forties with grey hair curling away from the temples in snowy wisps.

The man deposited Toby on firm ground and kept his grip, pumping his arm up and down. 'Francis Hocking. Pleased to make your acquaintance and thankful for your help.'

'Toby O'Rourke. This is my brother Paddy.'

Hocking dropped Toby's arm and strode to where Paddy waited in the cutting with the horse. 'Pleased to meet you, Paddy.' He took the boy's right hand and pumped it heartily. Toby was aware of the awkward pause as Hocking waited for Paddy to reply.

'Paddy's mute, Mr Hocking.'

'His handshake speaks volumes,' Hocking responded without pause. 'A man of character indeed,' and Paddy beamed a smile. 'But, please! Call me Frank.'

'Well, Frank, we can save the formalities for after we get you out of the bog,' Toby said. He climbed to his feet and led his horse to the front of the wagonette. Frank helped him hook up the trace. They then hooked Frank's horse to the rig and gathered logs and branches from amongst the trees lining the bank and laid them ahead of the wheels to prevent any further sinking.

'If you'd like to drive the team, Frank, Paddy and me can push from the back. Once we get the wheels up on the logs and the axles clear, we should be right, but don't stop until you get to the top of the cutting.'

If Frank had any reservations about taking instructions from Toby, he didn't show it. He gathered the reins of the team and positioned himself off to the side of the wagonette as Toby and Paddy waded in behind the rear wheels.

'Ready, Frank.'

Toby took up the strain, squishing his feet into the mud to find purchase. He heard Frank yell at the horses. The wagonette creaked and groaned as the slack was taken up. Under the combined strength of both horses the wheels came up onto the ramp. The wagonette shot forward out of the river and into the cutting.

Paddy and Toby climbed out of the mud and onto the riverbank. Frank's face appeared in the cutting above them.

'That was easy enough. Do you want to have a rest, or should we bring your wagonette straight across?' he asked, smiling down at the brothers.

'Might as well keep on while the going's good,' Toby said.

They unhitched the horses from Hocking's wagonette and Toby took them back across the river where he hitched them to their own vehicle. Then he climbed onto the seat and whipped the horses into motion. The wagonette bucked and rocked like a wild animal as it lurched across the riverbed, bouncing over rocks and dropping into ruts. The horses were up to their bellies in water and blowing hard as they pulled across midstream. They splashed up onto the log ramp. The front horse stumbled and Toby saw one of the logs rise up on end and rake its flank. He was almost thrown from the wagonette as the front wheels hit the ramp with a sickening crunch and was forced to grip the edge of the seat with one hand to prevent himself being launched into the river. The wagonette bucked again, but came out of the water, climbing up through the cutting. He reined in beside Frank's wagonette and climbed down to inspect the damage.

One horse had a graze along its flank where the end of the log had scraped its skin. The wound hardly bled at all and Toby knew the animal wasn't hurt too badly. The wagonette was in poorer shape. One spoke of the right front wheel had cracked through and the raw end stuck out at an angle.

'A fine piece of driving, young sir,' Frank said as he trotted up with Paddy at his side. 'Did you break anything? I heard a bit of a crunch.'

'A spoke,' Toby informed him. 'And one of the horses has a graze down its flank.'

Frank inspected the wheel and shook his head. 'You won't get too far on that.' He slapped the iron rim with the palm of his hand. 'I didn't have time to mention before, but I'm a wheelwright by trade. I would appreciate it if you would let me fix this for you. It's the least I can do after you gentlemen so kindly helped me out of the bog.'

'That's very kind of you, Frank. I'm not much good at woodcraft. Not good enough to fix a spoke, anyway. Besides, I'd like to give the horse a rest before we continue on our—' His voice trailed off as the women wandered over.

'My wife, Maree,' Frank said as the older woman slipped her hand into his.

'Toby O'Rourke, ma'am,' Toby said, touching a grubby finger to the brim of his hat. 'This fellow here is my brother Patrick.'

'Hello, Toby and Patrick,' the woman said. 'I'm so glad you came along to help us, otherwise I think Frank would still be wallowing about in the mud.'

'You're welcome, Mrs Hocking,' Toby said, scraping a cake of mud from his arm and flinging it into the grass.

The older girl tugged urgently at Maree's hand. 'I am so sorry. Toby and Patrick? Our daughters, Anne and Beatrice.'

Beatrice was about ten or eleven years of age with a mop of curly red hair making a massive breakout from beneath a green bonnet. A light cotton dress hung awkwardly from her shoulders and she shuffled her feet in lace-up boots while studying the boys with cat-like green eyes. Toby smiled at the girl and she blushed and hid behind her mother.

Anne Hocking was maybe a year younger than Toby. She wore no bonnet and had her dark hair tied back, emphasising every movement of her head by swishing back and forth like a horse's tail. Her face was broad and fine-featured, her eyes green. She wore a cotton dress also, but unlike the younger sister, this dress held shape at her breast and hips. She extended a hand towards him. Toby took it in his own hand and shook it gently, marvelling at the softness of her skin.

'Pleased to meet you, Mr O'Rourke.'

Under Frank's direction, the boys used a long bough to lever the front axle of their wagonette until the wheel was off the ground. They then supported it on several large rocks collected from the river.

'You boys get the wheel off and I'll see if I can find a piece of wood to make a spoke from,' Frank said.

Toby watched him move off into a grove of trees by the river, examining fallen branches as he went.

'Seems like a nice fellow, doesn't he, Pad?' Toby said as he removed the axle pin.

Frank returned a few minutes later with a piece of river gum in his hands. 'This feels a good solid piece of timber,' he said, testing its weight. He climbed onto his wagonette and rummaged about for a moment, producing a canvas satchel that he passed down to Toby. 'Tools of the trade,' he explained.

'How about some lunch before you get started?' Maree called. 'Toby and Paddy, you are quite welcome to join us. It's just a little salted pork on bread, I'm afraid, but there is plenty for everyone.'

'Thank you, Mrs Hocking,' Toby said. 'You are too kind.'

The girls had a blanket spread on the ground and Anne busily cut slices of bread from a crusty loaf while Maree sliced pork from a hindquarter. They had a small fire going and a large iron kettle sitting amidst the flames.

'A nice cup of tea. Just the thing,' Frank said.

'You haven't spent much time in the bush, have you, Frank?' Toby said.

'Only the past few days on the road out here. Why? What are we doing wrong?'

'It's nothing really—' Toby began.

'Go on, lad. It's all right. If you have some advice to offer, spit it out. I won't take offence. The good Lord knows we need all the help we can get.'

Toby shuffled his feet in the dust, a little embarrassed at picking holes while the Hockings were so accommodating. 'The kettle,' he finally said. 'It's great if you're setting up camp for a while. It'll give you lots of hot water once it eventually boils. But if you want a quick cuppa it takes forever. Didn't you bring a billy with you?'

'No. What's a billy?'

Toby climbed up onto his wagonette and rummaged around. He jumped to the ground with a soot-blackened tin in his hands that he swung back and forth by a wire handle. 'This is a billy. Nice thin sides. It will boil the water in a few minutes. We have a kettle like that as well to heat water for washing up when we camp of a night, but a billy is the best thing for a quick cup of tea.'

Annie came over and examined the billy. 'I remember seeing these in the store in Melbourne, Papa. Mama and I thought they were for storing water, not boiling it.'

'They can be used for both,' Toby said, pleased the girl was standing so close to him. 'Here, give it a try.' He passed the billy to Annie and she went to the fire, filled it from the kettle and set it amongst the coals.

'Am I doing this right, Mr O'Rourke?'

Toby wandered closer to the fire. 'That looks fine to me. You can scrape a few burning embers around it to help it on its way.' He picked up a stick and leaned over the girl to flick some wood around the billy. As he did so he caught a whiff of lilac and lavender from her hair.

'I wonder what else we're doing wrong, Frank?' Maree said. She carried a plate of pork slices and set it on the blanket. 'Help yourselves.' As everyone munched away she added, 'I have all the normal pots and pans one might find in a kitchen, Toby. Are they going to be suitable for the diggings?' She had a worried look on her face.

'For a permanent camp, yes, ma'am. You can make a good little fireplace with a tripod and a stone hearth. But don't use river stones. Get some rocks from higher ground. River stones have been known to explode when used around a campfire.'

'Explode!' Maree threw a hand to her mouth. 'Goodness. How are we ever to survive? This land has more dangers than I ever thought possible.'

'I dare say we'll pick it up as we go along,' Frank muttered as he chewed his food. 'You boys are obviously off to the diggings. Do you know much about it?'

'Paddy and me spent a bit of time up at Bendigo Creek recently, but we weren't there to look for gold. We pushed a herd of cattle up there to sell. We've seen how the miners work their claims, but that's about it. As far as life on the diggings goes, we're just as much new chums as you are.'

'Mama, what's a new chum,' Betty asked, tugging at her mother's sleeve.

'I think Toby means beginner or someone new to the colony.' She looked to Toby for confirmation and received a nod.

'Is that what you do?' Annie asked. 'Raise cattle I mean.'

'We used to, but we've had a run of really bad luck lately. Paddy and me are starting out anew. But we hope to make enough money on the diggings to buy our land back.'

'What about your folks?' Frank asked. 'You'll have to excuse me for saying so, but you fellows seem to be a little too young to be making your own way in the world.'

Toby looked down into the embers of the fire. 'Our ma and pa were murdered a few weeks ago.'

Frank shifted uncomfortably. 'I'm sorry.'

'No. It's all right. You seem like decent people. You didn't have to fix our wheel or offer us some of your food, but you did it anyway, because that's the decent thing to do. We haven't come across too many decent people lately.' Toby looked up from the fire and found Frank's piercing gaze on him. His father had looked at him that way whenever Toby had to tell him something important, something that mattered and required a man's full attention. He began to speak, not stopping until their whole sad story was told. When he finished, the Hocking family stood staring at him in stunned silence. Beside him, Paddy cried, his shoulders shaking in silent grief. Maree swept the boy into her arms and hugged him tightly.

'It's all right, pet,' she soothed, stroking Paddy's hair with her hand. 'You cry now. You let it all out. You have every right to.'

Paddy threw his arms around the woman and sobbed uncontrollably. Toby felt a little embarrassed for his brother, but when he looked at the faces of the Hocking family, he found no contempt, only concern for an orphaned and grieving boy.

Frank worked into the late afternoon and Toby and Paddy stood nearby, ready to lend a hand whenever needed. They were amazed at how Frank shaped the piece of river gum into a new spoke. It fitted perfectly into the space vacated by the damaged one. They replaced the wheel and lowered the wagonette back onto the ground.

'Good as new,' Frank said, taking a moment to admire his own handiwork before returning his tools to the canvas satchel. 'Should last you a few years. I don't have much of an idea about this Australian wood, but that seemed to be a good solid piece of timber. Well cured in this climate.'

'That spoke will probably outlast all the others,' Toby said, then turned his face to the sun. 'Too late to be getting back on the road today.' He turned to Paddy. 'What do you reckon we camp here tonight?'

Paddy nodded.

'That settles it, then,' Toby said. 'We'll get a good night's sleep and head off in the morning.'

'Sounds like a good plan,' Frank said as he climbed onto the wagonette to stow his tools. 'You can give us a few more pointers on living in the bush.'

'My pleasure,' Toby said, his gaze already casting about the campsite in search of Annie.

They ate an early dinner seated about the campfire on make-shift chairs of logs and packing boxes. Frank held the boys in awe as he told the story of their voyage out from England and the days they had spent being tossed about in storms. Whenever a detail slipped his mind, he was quickly reminded of the omission by one of his daughters.

'I tell you,' he said loudly, leaning close to Paddy for effect, 'by the time we sailed out into blue skies the bilges were awash with vomit.'

'Ooh, Papa!' the girls chorused together, screwing up their faces.

'I don't think that is very good talk to be had at the dinner table,' Maree chided.

'Except, my sweet pea, we don't have a dinner table here, do we? Therefore any talk is acceptable.' He smiled at his own cleverness until his eyes settled on his daughters. 'Within reason, of course,' he added quickly.

Toby was sorry the story had ended. Frank was such a good narrator his story had filled his mind, driving out the anguish, if only for a little while.

Maree was filling a large tub with water from the kettle. Toby climbed to his feet and went to her. 'If that's for the washing-up, Mrs Hocking, you can leave it for Paddy and me. It's the least we can do after such a fine meal.

'Thank you, Tom.' She paused and gasped at her mistake. 'I'm so sorry – Toby, I meant to say. Forgive me. It's just that you remind me so much of someone else.' She turned away, but not so quickly that Toby missed the look of grief on her face.

Toby and Paddy scrubbed the pots and pans and Annie and Betty hovered close by, asking an incessant stream of questions about Australia and some of the bushland creatures they had seen on their trek out from Melbourne.

'Sounds to me that what you saw by the track was a wallaby, Beatrice, not a baby kangaroo. What do you reckon, Pad?' And the younger brother nodded his head.

'*Betty*,' the young girl stamped her foot.

'Huh?'

'My name is Betty. Mama only calls me Beatrice when I'm in trouble.'

'Betty it is, then,' Toby said, and was rewarded with a broad smile.

'While we're on the subject of names, you had better start calling me Annie. Anne sounds far too formal. What do you think, Mr O'Rourke?'

'Fine by me,' Toby said. 'As long as you call me Toby.'

Annie gave a little laugh.

Toby inverted the tub over one of the sideboards to drain before taking a seat at the campfire. He was pleased when Annie came and took the seat beside him. She began to ask a question about the horses, but was interrupted by her sister, who managed to squeeze in between them.

'Toby, do you think that was a baby kangaroo I saw and not a wobalee?' Betty asked.

'Wallaby,' Annie corrected and received a stern look for her trouble.

'You know what, Betty? I do believe that was a baby kangaroo you saw,' Toby admitted, and the girl clapped her hands with glee.

'Are you boys pitching a tent?' Frank called from where he stood at the back of his wagonette.

'Paddy and I will sleep in our bedrolls by the fire,' Toby said.

'But what if it rains?' Annie's voice carried a tone of concern that Toby found somewhat pleasing.

'Then we drag our bedrolls under the wagonette and go back to sleep.'

'That certainly is doing it rough,' Maree remarked. 'I don't think I could sleep out in the open like that.'

'Paddy and me have always done it that way when out on the road. We don't even have a tent, but I suppose we will have to buy one when we reach the diggings. I can give you a hand to pitch yours though, Mr Hocking.'

Toby and Paddy climbed from their seats and helped Frank pull a large bundle of white canvas from the back of his wagonette. Then he retrieved the support poles and a longer piece of timber that would hold up the ridge. They picked a suitable piece of ground and Toby held one pole, Paddy the other, while Frank fitted the ridge pole and pulled the tent into position over the top. With a little hammering of pegs and adjusting of guy ropes, the tent was ready. Maree and the girls immediately busied themselves carting in bedding from the wagonette.

Despite their tiredness, they sat around the fire for another two hours, drinking tea and discussing the countryside, the weather or the prospect of finding gold. Annie sat on the same log as Toby, with just enough distance separating them to allow for propriety.

Frank yawned and leaned back, a fist covering his mouth. He stared up at the night sky and remarked, 'Such a strange pattern of stars. I don't think I'll ever get used to it.'

'What do you mean? Are the stars different where you come from?' Toby glanced heavenwards to confirm that nothing had changed.

'They certainly are, lad,' Frank said. He got to his feet and wandered about the clearing as he studied the sky. 'There's no Polaris or Cassiopeia here. How do you colonials know which direction you're facing when out and about at night?'

'It's quite easy,' Toby said. He climbed to his feet and walked to Frank's side. 'See those two bright stars there, just above the horizon?'

Frank followed the direction of Toby's finger. 'I see 'em.'

'Those are the Pointers. They point to the Southern Cross.' Toby lifted his arm a little higher.

'I was wondering if that was the Southern Cross. They certainly are bright.' Annie had wandered over and stood at Toby's side.

Toby's finger described a line through the sky. 'If you follow the longest line through the base of the cross for about four lengths of its height and drop your finger to the horizon, that's south.'

All the Hocking family were at his side now, staring up at the stars and practising finding south.

'You know, I don't feel like I'm standing at the ends of the earth now,' Frank said. 'From now on, I'll always know which direction I'm facing. Thanks, lad.' He placed his arm around

Maree's waist and they started back towards the campfire. 'It's getting late. Come, girls. Time for bed. Goodnight, Toby and Paddy. Sleep well, boys.'

Annie lingered at his side for a moment longer. 'Thank you for the lesson on finding south.' Her smile was brilliant, even in the starlight, and Toby felt his breath catch a little as she squeezed his arm. 'Goodnight.'

'Goodnight,' Toby squeaked. He watched her walk towards the tent, very conscious of the swishing noise her skirts made around her legs.

'What do you suppose that one is, Mama?'

Maree followed the point of Betty's arm. A little black bird with a ruby-red breast flitted through the branches at the side of the track, seemingly keeping pace with them as they trundled along, four abreast on their wagonette.

'I don't know, my dear. Is it not listed in your book?'

Betty opened the almanac on her lap and flipped the pages furiously. 'I can't decide if it's a scarlet robin or a flame robin. Do you think its wings are closer to black than grey, Mama?'

'It's hard to say. Why don't you ask your sister? What do you think, Annie? You've been unusually quiet this morning.'

Annie had her gaze fixed on her lap, but she looked up when her mother addressed her. 'I was just thinking about Toby and Paddy. What a horrible time they have had, what with their parents being murdered and their farm taken from them.'

'We've all had our tragedies,' Maree said. 'Or have you forgotten about your brother?'

'I could never forget Tom, Mama. I think he is on my mind at least once every hour of the day.'

'I think that bird is more black than grey, Betty,' Frank cut in. 'What does your book say about that one?'

Maree knew that the sudden change of subject meant that Tom's death was not to be discussed further.

'I think that one is a scarlet robin, Papa, but I am unsure. I shall have to ask Toby when we stop. Are they still behind us?'

Frank was the only one who sat high enough to see over the mound of their possessions packed into the load bed behind them. He turned his head and said, 'Still there. Though they are a bit behind. Probably trying to stay out of our dust.'

'That's good,' Betty said, and gave a little clap of her hands. 'I like Toby and Paddy. They are nice boys.'

'They are that,' Maree said. There was something about the older boy that reminded her so much of Tom.

They travelled on into the late morning, occasionally over-taking a solitary digger pushing a wheelbarrow in the same direction. Some moved off the track to allow the wagonette past and would offer a quick exchange of small talk and a smile. Others looked longingly at the vehicle, their faces shining with sweat. Maree was glad they were not on foot.

A little before noon, they rounded a sharp bend where the track turned back on itself as it climbed out of a hollow. Here, the bush crowded in close on each side and Maree realised that if another vehicle were to come from the other direction, there would be an impasse.

'Allo,' she heard Frank remark. 'Here comes a couple of riders from the other way. They might be able to tell us how far it is to Ballarat.'

She looked up to see two horsemen on the track ahead of them. They each had their mounts in the wheel ruts and plodded along slowly. They saw the wagonette approaching and swung their horses across the track so that Frank was forced to rein to a stop.

'Morning.' The rider on the left touched a finger to the brim of his hat. He was a young man, maybe in his early twenties. A thin beard sprouted from his chin and he had an acne-scarred face and lopsided smile. His companion was a little younger and offered no greeting. He eyed the family on the wagonette, one hand tucked beneath a grubby waistcoat in a way that made Maree feel uneasy.

'Morning,' Frank replied. Maree detected a hint of tension in his voice.

'Where are you folks from?' the first man asked.

'Melbourne,' Frank responded.

The rider gave a little laugh and glanced at his friend. 'No, I mean before that. Where did you come from?'

'England,' Frank said sharply. 'Now, will you move your horses off the track so we can be on our way?' He lifted the reins to give them a flick and start their horse forward, but the other rider reached down and took hold of Samson's halter, holding him fast.

'What are you doing?' Frank's voice had gone up in pitch. 'Let go of our bloody horse.'

Maree felt her pulse quicken and pulled Betty hard against her side.

The first rider continued as if Frank hadn't spoken. 'Ah! Being new to the Colony of Victoria, you won't have heard about the toll.'

'What toll?' Frank dropped the reins and rubbed the palms of his hands up and down the legs of his trousers, a sure sign he was nervous.

'This here is a toll road.' He gestured at his friend. 'Davey and me are toll collectors. Before you can continue on your way, you'll need to pay us.'

'I don't know anything about a bloody toll. This is an open road,' Frank snapped.

'Please, Frank,' Maree pleaded. 'Let's just pay them and be on our way.'

'I'm not paying them a penny. They aren't bloody toll collectors, just a couple of louts looking to make some easy money.'

'Please, Frank. We don't want trouble.

'Trouble is what you're going to get,' the rider said. 'No toll, no passage.' He reached into the folds of his jacket and pulled out a vicious-looking long-barrelled pistol. 'We're done talking nice, like.' He pointed the pistol at Frank. 'All your money. Put it in your hat.' He gestured at his companion. 'See what they have in the way of food, Davey. I'm hungry enough to eat the leg off a wooden chair.'

The other rider let go of Samson's halter and edged his mount down the side of the wagonette. He had a pistol in his hand as well, although Maree could not recall seeing him produce it. He leaned over the sideboard and pulled up the tarpaulin covering the load bed.

'They've got a whole heap of stuff, Rob. Flour, rice, sugar, tea. We won't be able to carry it all.'

'You won't be taking any of it,' a gentle voice said from the bushes beside the track. All faces turned to the voice. It was Toby, with a musket aimed up at the rider called Davey. Davey made to raise his pistol, but Toby shook his head. 'Drop it, or you are a dead man.' The rider opened his hand and the pistol fell into the grass beside the track.

The one named Rob let out a little chuckle. 'You can't keep us both covered, you stupid cove. You drop your gun, or I'll put a hole in the head of this pretty little miss here.' He aimed his pistol at Betty. The girl let out a whimper and pushed in against her mother.

'Please, no,' Maree said. Frank was half standing on the footboard, trying to push past Annie to place himself between his daughter and the gun. He paused when Rob cocked the pistol.

'I don't need to keep you both covered,' Toby said. 'That's what my brother is for.' He pointed up the track. Paddy stepped from the bushes with another musket aimed at the back of Rob's head. 'Your pistol, mate. Uncock it and drop it.' The gentleness was gone from Toby's voice.

Maree could see the man named Rob turning his head back and forth as he considered his position. He must have realised the hopelessness of it, for he uncocked the pistol and tossed it sideways. The moment it landed in the grass, Frank threw himself off the wagonette and swept Rob off his horse in a flying tackle that carried him over his horse's rump. The horse panicked and tried to run, but Rob's foot was caught in the stirrup and the animal wheeled about, rearing and plunging until Paddy managed to get hold of a rein.

Frank wasn't done yet. He climbed to his feet and kicked Rob in the side so hard that the youth let out a scream of pain. Then Frank leaned down, cocked a fist and punched him hard in the face.

'Point a bloody gun at my daughter, you little shite.' The fist came back again and again, striking hard until Rob's face was a bleeding mess. Frank would have kept going, but Maree could hear her daughter's give a little squeal each time their father's fist connected.

'Please, Frank. He's had enough. The girls have witnessed enough violence for one day.'

Frank paused, the youth's shirt gripped in one fist and the other poised. He looked up at Maree and then at the bloody mess of Rob's face.

'Bloody hell, mister! You didn't have to do that.' Davey was off his horse. He pushed past Frank and crouched at his friend's side.

Frank let go of Rob's shirt. The youth collapsed backwards onto the ground. 'The bastard was going to shoot my daughter.'

'He wasn't going to shoot anyone. Our guns aren't loaded. We haven't had any powder or shot for a week.'

'What do you mean?' Toby was there at Frank's side.

'They aren't bloody loaded. We weren't going to hurt anyone. We're hungry and after some money, that's all.'

Toby walked to where Rob's pistol lay in the grass and picked it up. 'No cap on the firing nipple.' He picked up a twig and poked it down the barrel, gauging the depth. 'He's telling the truth. It's not loaded.'

Frank took a step back, but still held his fists at the ready. 'I didn't bloody know that. He said he was going to shoot Betty in the head and he had a gun aimed at her.'

'Don't feel bad about it, Frank,' Toby said. 'The cove got what he deserved.'

Frank lowered his fists. 'What do we do with the mongrels?'

'We should fetch a police constable,' Maree said.

Toby shook his head. 'There's not one for miles. We'd have to take them with us into Ballarat, and I don't fancy that.'

'Me neither,' Frank responded, and Maree was glad. She had no desire to be anywhere near the would-be robbers.

'If we let them go, they'll come after us. Papa gave that one such a beating, they're sure to come looking for revenge,' Annie said, the fear evident in her voice.

Toby prodded the one named Davey with the toe of his boot. 'Is that what you're gonna do, matey? You gonna come looking for a little payback if we let you go?'

Davey looked up at Toby and shook his head. 'We won't. I promise. Besides, I think Rob's nose is broken. You did a good job on him, mister. I need to get him to a doctor.'

'The only doctor I know of is in Bacchus Marsh. That's about a day's ride back towards Melbourne,' Toby said. 'You take your friend here to the doctor and we continue on our way. You don't come looking for us and we don't report you two to the police. How does that sound?'

'Fine by me,' Davey said. 'Help me get him to his feet and on his horse, will ya?'

Toby and Frank took an arm each and, with Davey pushing Rob's backside, they managed to get him up on his horse. Rob swayed a little and his breath hissed through his open mouth, but he didn't look like he was going to fall off.

Toby went and collected both bandits' guns. He found a stick lying on the ground and forced it into the muzzle of the big pistol, hammering it home against the sideboard of the wagonette. Then he snapped the stick off so that the barrel was plugged with wood. He repeated the process with Davey's weapon. 'You'll get the wood out of the barrel eventually,' he told Davey as he handed the weapons to him.

Davey tucked the pistols into his belt and took up the reins of Rob's horse. He touched a finger to the brim of his hat as he led his friend back down the track. Maree watched the pair until they rounded the bend and were out of sight, the knot of panic in her stomach slowly unwinding.

'Paddy?' Toby looked to where his brother stood with his musket in his hand. 'Cut back through the bush, matey. Make sure they don't get any ideas as they pass our wagonette.'

Paddy nodded, shouldered his musket and trotted into the bush at the side of the track.

'Thank you, Toby,' Maree said. 'I don't like to think what would have happened if you and Paddy hadn't shown up. It seems you boys are making a habit of rescuing us.'

'Yes,' Frank said. He stepped over and shook Toby's hand. 'Thank you. But how did you know?'

Toby pointed through the bush in the direction Paddy had gone. 'We were hanging back a little so we didn't have to travel in your dust. You can see right through the trees from where the track switches back on itself. Paddy noticed those two coves had you waylaid. We grabbed our guns and ran up here as fast as we could.'

'It's a good thing you did,' Annie said from her seat on the wagonette. 'Those rogues would have taken all Papa's money. We didn't know their guns weren't loaded.'

'No one would have, Annie,' Toby replied.

Maree looked down at Toby standing by her husband. He was closer to man than boy, with a few straggly whiskers sprouting from his chin and shadowing his upper lip. He had lost his hat somewhere and a lock of black hair hung over one eye. Like Paddy, his hair hadn't been cut in a long time and Maree supposed their mother had done it for them when she had been alive. Toby had a strong, square jaw that made him quite handsome and she could see why both her daughters, Annie in particular, were rather smitten with this colonial youth.

'Toby?'

He looked up at her. 'Yes, Mrs Hocking?'

'Would you and Paddy join us for dinner tonight when we make camp? I don't have much in the way of special ingredients, but I think I can throw something together. Just to say thank you to you both.'

'That's a wonderful idea, Mama,' Annie said, and clapped her hands. 'I want to learn more about the southern stars.'

Toby pursed his lips as he gave the question a little thought. Maree saw his gaze drift to Annie and knew what the answer would be.

'We'd be delighted to join you. Thank you, Mrs Hocking.'

P addy grimaced as the scissors snipped close to his ear. Maree had a hand on his head to steady it as she squinted through one eye to judge her work.

'Hold still, Paddy. Just a couple more cuts.'

He would have nodded to show he understood, but that might mean losing an ear. He'd hated having his hair cut, even when his mother had done it, lining up their father, Toby and himself on the verandah once a month. Without a voice, it had been hard to object. It had been even harder when his brother had surrendered to his haircut so readily and was now standing by the campfire talking to Annie while she stirred the cooking pot that sat bubbling over the fire. The meal smelled wonderful. Paddy doubted he had eaten anything that smelled this good since the death of his mother.

'There you go. All done, my boy.' Maree pulled away the bed sheet from around his shoulders and gave it a flick to rid it of loose hair. She produced a pocket mirror and gave it to him.

Paddy looked at his reflection for a moment, but he didn't care about his haircut, he was just glad it was over. He handed the mirror back to Maree and gave her a smile of thanks.

'You're welcome,' she said, and began packing away the scissors.

Paddy wandered over to the fire where Toby stopped his conversation and ran a critical eye over him.

'You look rather respectable now, Pad.'

Paddy nodded and picked up a stick to poke at the coals. His stomach growled and he wondered how long it would be before supper was served up.

They ate sitting in a circle around the fire. There was no wind and the smoke rose straight up through the darkening canopy of trees.

'Of course, leaf springs make for a better ride for a gig or coach,' Frank responded to one of Toby's questions. 'But, for a heavy load, like a wagon or dray, it's far better to have the weight bear straight down on a good, solid axle.'

Paddy ate ravenously as he listened. A few questions of his own popped into his mind, but he had no way to ask them without putting down his plate and miming. Usually, this would frustrate him a little. Toby often picked up on this and would take the time to understand what he wanted, but tonight his brother was preoccupied with Frank's account of wagon construction and with Annie.

He was the first to finish his meal and went to the back of the Hockings' wagonette to place his plate in the washing tub. He knew Toby would offer to wash the dishes, so he filled the big kettle from a water bag and carried it back to the fire.

'That for the dishes, Pad?'

He gave his brother a nod and then mimed drinking from a mug.

'And a cuppa, too. Good work.' Toby turned to Frank and Maree. 'Paddy and me will do the dishes, Mrs Hocking.'

'Thank you, Toby, but please, call me Maree.'

'All right. Maree it is.'

Paddy scrubbed the pots and plates while his brother dried and placed them on the tailboard of the wagonette. When they had finished, they slung the tub between them and carried it out of the circle of firelight, emptying it into the darkness. When they turned back to the campsite, Frank and Maree were in earnest discussion on the far side of the fire, their heads close together. Annie had mugs of steaming tea waiting for them. As they settled onto their seats, Frank looked up.

'Maree and I have been talking, boys. You have shown yourselves to be very resourceful and helpful and I am sure your dear departed parents would be proud of you both. This country and its dangers are new to us, and my family is grateful we made your acquaintance and have your friendship. You boys know how to look after yourselves, and we—' he swept his hand to encompass Maree, Annie and Betty, '—we feel there is strength in numbers. Would you like to join forces with us? We can go to the diggings together. Work our claims as one. Share the work, the expenses and the profits – look after each other.'

'I—I don't know what to say.' Toby stammered.

'You and Paddy talk it over,' Maree said. 'There's no pressing rush for an answer.'

Toby and Paddy stood from the fire and went into the semi-darkness beyond the wagonettes.

'You understand what they're asking, Pad? They want us to join with them.'

Paddy moved his head in a slow nod.

'We'd share everything, the costs and the profits – the hard work. That could have its benefits.'

He nodded again and recalled the way Maree had embraced him when he burst into tears. His mind then jumped to Frank and the story of the ship in the storm. Their parents' deaths and the loss of the farm had consumed his and Toby's every waking moment. But, for a short time, while Frank told that story, he had forgotten all about his troubles and the problems ahead. It was a good feeling, and he hoped there could be more like that.

'What do you reckon, Pad?'

Paddy pointed at his own chest and then at Toby's. He pushed his index fingers together and looked at his brother's face, barely visible in the semi-darkness.

'You and me together?'

Paddy nodded.

'We'll always be together, Pad. Nothing will change that. After the shootings and Scotchy and Dundas and the business with 'ol man Pelham, I didn't think there were any decent people left in the world. That family over there have had their fair share of troubles, too. They need us, but I reckon we need them, too. What do you think, Pad?'

Paddy gave Toby a thumbs up and nodded.

'Well, let's go and tell them,' Toby said.

They walked back into the circle of light and found four anxious faces watching them.

'Paddy and me would like to accept your kind offer. Equal partners?'

'Equal partners,' Frank confirmed. He stepped forward and shook both brothers' hands in turn. 'May the gods of fortune have the good grace to smile on us all.'

'Amen to that,' said Toby.

Barramat came to Chilbi in the hours before dawn. Normally, the young warrior would be pleased to see his father through the mists of his mind, for the hand of guidance had not been taken by death. As the oldest of the three survivors, it was only right that he should be the one to whom the tribal elders gave counsel to. At times Barramat offered words of encouragement and Chilbi would feel his spirits uplifted. But this time his father's voice was wrought with anger. The season had changed and no sacred ceremony had been performed to appease the spirits of their ancestors.

The dream woke him and he sat alone for a while by the remains of the campfire. Around him, the others slept on, but the weight in Chilbi's heart would not let sleep come for him, so he gathered his war club and spear and climbed the hill behind their camp. As he climbed, the wind picked up and brought with it a cold chill out of the north-east. His kangaroo-skin cloak flapped about his legs as he stood on the boulder-strewn hilltop. Out to the east the sky was beginning to pale, but overhead the stars still glittered. The young Aborigine lifted his face to follow the great arc of light stretching from one horizon to another.

It was told in the tribal legends of the Jannjirra that during the Dreaming, Currabin, the great eagle, had swooped down into a mountain stream and seized a fish in his fearsome talons. When he flew back across the sky, droplets of water were thrown from his feathers and had stuck to the heavens to become the stars. The great arc over Chilbi's head was the path the eagle had taken back to his eyrie.

As with most tales, he had first been told this one by his mother, and he thought of her disease-ravaged corpse lying in the burial caves in the distant mountains. He turned his face towards those mountains and a deep longing clutched at his soul. He had been too long away from his tribal lands. The homesickness hung in his belly like the dead weight of a mountain boulder.

A faint noise sounded behind him and he turned to see Yawong and Tarrat climbing to where he stood. As soon as they reached Chilbi's side they too turned to those same mountains.

'When can we go home, Chilbi?' Yawong asked. The young warrior had asked this question many times since they had ventured out onto the lowlands.

'We must punish the Djarriba for what they have done to our people. They have taken from us, so we must take from them.'

'What does the Djarriba have that we want?' Tarrat asked.

Chilbi pondered the question. The Djarriba possessed many wonderful marvels he had never imagined existed: the thunder-weapons that kill men and animals from afar; the metal-bladed tools with which a man could cut open a kangaroo in but a few moments; even small fire sticks that were kept in a wooden container and could be lit by rubbing the small heads of the sticks on the side. These things fascinated Chilbi, but he had no answer to Tarrat's question. It was only Warrigal's desire to kill and take from the Djarriba that kept them from returning home.

'Soon we will go home,' he said in a non-committal tone. 'We will find wives from among the surrounding tribes and take them back to the land. From we three will come the seeds to grow a new people of the Jannjirra.'

'Will the Djarriba sickness not come again?' Yawong asked. 'It destroyed our whole tribe. There is powerful magic in everything the Djarriba does.'

'Warrigal has said the sickness only comes to a person once. We have survived its evil and it cannot harm us again.'

Both Tarrat and Yawong were unwilling to take Warrigal's word on that. They had both watched the terrible coughing sickness spread through their entire people. They had seen the pustules on the childrens' skin, obviously the mark of evil spirits. They had felt the touch of the terrible disease itself. Of a whole tribe of people, only Chilbi, Tarrat and Yawong survived.

'Why does Warrigal take the little yellow grains from the Djarriba we stop on the tracks?' Tarrat asked. 'We can't eat it or use it. He is very happy when he finds little pouches of the yellow grains – and the small pieces of skin with the strange symbols. He takes all that he finds.'

Chilbi had asked the same question of Warrigal. He had been told that the little grains were called 'gold' and the skins were 'money' and they could be used to trade for anything the Djarriba possessed. Chilbi did not understand why Warrigal would want to trade when he could take anything he wanted at spear or gunpoint. But the lands below the mountains were strange to him. It was Warrigal who understood the Djarriba ways, so Chilbi was willing to be led over this unknown ground with its strange inhabitants – until they returned to the lands of the Jannjirra. Then he would take his place as a tribal elder and guide them through the rebuilding of the tribe.

Toby reined the wagonette to a stop beside the track. 'Bloody hell, Pad. Would you look at that?' He swept his arm over the vista before them.

Toiling, sweating men seemed to fill every hill, every hollow and every gully. The clatter of pick and shovel on rock and the coarse voices of thousands of hopeful miners buzzed like a swarm of bees. There hardly seemed to be a piece of ground off the side of the road that did not have a hole sunk into it or a mullock heap piled on it.

The road twisted its way down into a shallow valley between sparsely wooded hillocks. In places tents were pitched at the very road edge, some with signs proclaiming professional services such as blacksmithing or doctoring could be obtained from within. Side tracks disappeared in every direction, twisting and turning around holes and piles of earth.

Near the floor of the valley another road crossed from north to south. Here, the buildings were more substantial, built to last longer than the ramshackle huts and tents littering the countryside. Some were finished in weatherboard and painted with whitewash. People moved around like ants. Miners in cabbage-tree hats carried washing cradles and spades and stepped nimbly around buggies and men on horseback, all with looks of determination on their faces as they went about their business.

Frank manoeuvred his wagonette alongside. His family sat four abreast on the seat with him, incredulous expressions on their faces. They craned their heads in every direction, trying to take it all in. Frank pushed his hat back and shook his head with amazement.

'Sweet lavender in the springtime! Where do we start?'

'We need to find the gold commissioner and get a licence before we peg a claim,' Toby said. 'And we need to know where our claims will be before we go to the trouble of setting up camp. No use in camping on this side of the valley if our claims are going to be miles away.'

'It's hard to imagine there's a piece of land out there not already being dug up by someone,' Maree said. She sat stiffly on the seat with her daughters on either side of her, arms placed protectively around them.

A heavily bearded man in dirt-stained clothes rounded a tent and made to walk past them. 'Excuse me, sir,' Toby said. 'Could you point us in the direction of the Gold Commissioner's office?'

The grubby man stopped and leaned against the nearside front wheel of Toby's wagonette. He opened his mouth into a broad grin and pushed his hat back on his head, leaving a dusty red smear above his eyebrows.

'The gold commissioner, you say?'

With one sweeping glance he surveyed the people on the wagonettes, taking in the fresh faces, neatly stacked belongings and shiny new equipment. His eyes lingered on Maree and Annie for a moment before he turned back to Toby.

'The Gold Commissioner's got a tent on the edge of Government Camp,' he said, pointing in the direction they were facing. 'If you're looking to set up a claim, I hear they're taking nuggets the size of chook eggs out of Canadian Flat. Me mates and me is thinking of moving over there from Golden Point. Ain't got nothing out of there 'cept calluses and aching joints.'

Toby touched a finger to the brim of his hat. 'Thanks, sir.'

Government Camp stood out as an island of orderliness in a sea of mayhem. The tents were pitched in neat rows, all evenly spaced, and a horse yard stretched across the back of the camp, leaving the front area free as a parade ground. A flagpole stood at the end of the open square, the Union Jack fluttering in the breeze. To one side of the flagpole sat a tent. A queue of thirty or so men stretched away from the tent and wound its way to the edge of the track.

They parked the wagonettes, and Toby and Frank wandered over to join the queue, leaving Paddy with Maree and the girls to tend the horses and find something for a midday meal.

'I hope to God I have done the right thing,' Frank said, as they waited in line.

'What do you mean?' Toby lifted his hat and pushed sweat-soaked hair out of his eyes.

Frank shuffled his feet in the dust, watching the marks his boots left as he trailed them back and forth. 'Ten thousand miles I've dragged them, away from the only home they knew,' he murmured, inclining his head towards the wagonettes. 'The stories we heard in England of this place: riches lying on the ground for the taking; land enough for every man just for the asking; a place where a man can be his own master. I knew they were mostly stories, but I hoped there was just an ounce of truth in them. Have I brought my family to the ends of the earth just to live in a tent beside a hole in the ground?'

'Pa used to say that for every man who finds gold, a hundred will run for home with their tails between their legs. This is where the riches are, Frank. We just have to figure out how to get our share.'

Frank looked him straight in the eyes and Toby could see the worry and pain behind the steely depths. 'I hope you're right, Toby. We don't have a home to run back to. Like you and Paddy, everything we have is over there on that wagonette.'

The gold commissioner handled proceedings efficiently and they moved steadily down the queue. Toby and Frank soon entered the small tent to find two men sitting behind a makeshift desk. Uniform jackets hung loosely from the backs of chairs, and the rear of the tent had been opened to allow what little breeze there was to drift through. One man, sitting straight-backed and military-like with his hands clasped on the table in front of him, asked the questions necessary to complete the licence forms while the other, short and overweight and sweating profusely, wrote the details down. Toby and Frank each paid one pound, ten shillings licence fee.

'You will need to renew your licence every month,' the straight-backed man informed them. 'You can peg out an area of twelve feet square each. You must carry out some form of work on each claim for it to be honoured. Try not to jump the claim of someone else. I do not have the stomach for another cut throat. Good day, gentlemen.'

'll take the first shift down the hole if you don't mind, lad. The air's still cool down there,' Frank said.

Toby didn't mind at all. Alternating their duties four times a day meant Frank would also have the first shift of the afternoon when the bottom of the shaft would be hot and airless. Frank knew this too, but he liked getting the best shift along with the worst. He dropped a shovel to the bottom of the pit and grabbed a pick before swinging onto the ladder and disappearing down the mine.

They had pegged two claims close to the floor of a gully, a little above the muddied waters of a creek. Under the terms of their licence each claim had to show some sign of being worked or that claim would become forfeit and could be pegged by another digger without any recourse to the gold commissioner. Shepherding a claim was a well-established practice on the diggings. If a party had two claims, but wanted to concentrate their attention on one at a time, they would show a token amount of work at the second claim, thereby honouring the terms of the licence and preventing others from taking over. Frank, Toby and Paddy had sunk their shepherd claim to a depth of three feet before turning all their efforts to this claim.

They had managed to sink a shaft almost fifteen feet into the hard, quartz-rich dirt of Ballarat. The sides of the shaft were roughly six feet by six, leaving a further three feet between their claim and those surrounding it. The formed trails and tracks were off-limits. Under the terms of the gold licence these had to be left clear. However, this didn't stop the more greedy diggers from staking a claim on a track if the area showed promise. The tracks and paths were formed by the diggers themselves and the gold commissioner and his troopers could not hope to be familiar with even half of them. The result was a lot of dead-end paths and trails that criss-crossed through and around the diggings. Care was required when walking, especially at night. One wrong turn could lead to a fatal fall down a shaft.

Paddy trundled the barrow and cradle a short distance down to the creek and returned a few minutes later with the empty barrow for Toby.

'All set, Paddy?' Toby asked and received a nod in reply.

'This could be the day we strike it rich. Then we go and buy our farm back off Pelham.'

Paddy picked up a shovel and scurried away towards the creek. Toby started every morning with that statement. He watched Paddy go, and wanted to share in his brother's enthusiasm, but the reality was all around him. Only a lucky few ever made a fortune on the goldfields. The road back to Melbourne was full of diggers who, having run out of money and luck, were forced to pack up and head back to town to find work. Toby wondered how long they could last. Everything on the goldfields was expensive. Everyone wanted to make a fortune, from the storekeepers and sly grog shop operators to the government themselves with their monthly licence fee. He hated to admit it, but if they didn't find some gold in the next few weeks, they wouldn't be able to afford a licence. If they were caught mining without one it would mean a fine or, if unable to pay, imprisonment.

'Bucket.'

Frank's voice snapped him out of his thoughts and he lowered the bucket into the shaft.

'Pull away.'

Toby braced his feet and pulled the rope hand over hand until the laden bucket reached the surface. He poured the contents into the barrow and then lowered the bucket again. Nine times this was repeated before the barrow was full.

Toby leaned out over the shaft and called to Frank, barely visible in the shadowy depths. 'Taking the barrow down to the creek, Frank.'

'Aye, lad.'

Toby took hold of the barrow's handles and headed down the path to the creek, the little wooden wheel wobbling and bouncing over rocks and bumps. Paddy saw him coming and was waiting with a bucket of water in hand. With a grunt Toby tipped the contents of the barrow onto the bank of the creek for Paddy to wash through the cradle.

With Paddy started on his task, Toby headed back to the shaft with the barrow. The lack of noise from below told him Frank was ready for the bucket again. 'Below,' he warned, and the bucket descended into the shaft.

The process went on like that until mid-morning when Annie and Betty appeared. Annie carried a billy of steaming tea and Betty carefully picked her way over the ground holding in her hands three mugs which already contained the sugar each of them took. This mid-morning ritual also signalled a change of shift for Frank and Toby.

'Frank, the girls are here,' he called down the shaft, and then climbed the mound of dirt to call Paddy up from the creek.

'Mama says lunch will be a little late today. She had a terrible row with the butcher over the price of beef,' Annie said, as she poured. Betty passed the full mugs to each of them.

'Mama says the price goes up every few days,' Betty added. 'She says we won't be able to eat beef soon the way things are going. And mutton isn't far behind either.'

Annie reached into her apron pocket and took out a carefully folded tea towel. She laid it gently on the ground and unfolded it to reveal three thick slices of damper coated in plum jam. She passed one each to her father and the boys.

Toby attacked the slice of damper and washed it down with a mouthful of tea. 'Very nice,' he said. 'Tell your mama thank you very much.'

'Oh, Mama didn't make the damper,' Annie beamed. 'I did. I'm glad you like it.'

Toby felt self-conscious as Annie continued smiling at him. 'Well, it's very nice indeed,' he managed to squeak out.

'I'll second that,' Frank added.

'This hole sure is getting deep,' Betty said from near the ladder.

Frank leaped to his feet and took his daughter by the hand. 'Come away from there, sweetheart,' he said, leading her back from the shaft. 'That hole is getting too deep to go leaning over like that.'

'But, Papa, I was just looking,' Betty said, a hurt look in her big eyes, her bottom lip pouting.

'In the first days it was okay to lean out over the mine, but not now. The hole is far too deep for that. Do you understand? Both of you?' He looked to Annie as well.

'Yes, Papa.' Betty and Annie chorused together.

Toby was in a position to see Annie roll her eyes and caught the slight smile at the corners of her mouth. But when she went to take her father's empty cup her face was expressionless. She gathered the remaining cups and, taking Betty by the hand, led her away up the path towards their camp.

'Tell your mama we'll leave it a little later to come up for lunch,' Frank called after them.

'Well, I guess it's my turn down the hole,' Toby said, and swung out onto the ladder. Although the sun held warmth, the hole was cool and smelled of the dirt they were busily digging away. He estimated they had started digging about twenty feet above the level of the creek bed. Other diggers had said any gold in the area would likely be at creek level or lower.

'C'mon, gold,' he told the coarse gravel as he swung the pick into it. 'Reveal yourself. Just one big nugget will do, something the size of a loaf of bread. Is that too much to ask?'

ight spilled from every window of the homestead and flooded across manicured lawns and rose gardens. From where he stood in the shadows, Anderson could see a hut some distance from the main building. This too had lighted windows. Raucous laughter erupted from that direction and he turned to the three Jannjirra warriors.

'The building behind this one. It is the hut of men. Kill them all.'

Chilbi, Tarrat and Yawong pulled war clubs from their cloaks and stole away into the darkness. Anderson turned his attention back to the homestead. A pair of French doors opened onto a wide verandah. Above the steps, a lantern burned, throwing light along a stone path. This was no squalid settlers' home, he realised. The owner must be a wealthy grazier, a person of stature.

A few frantic shouts drifted down from the stockmen's quarters. If anyone from the house heard the commotion and tried to go to their aid, he was in the perfect position to ambush them. But the Jannjirra worked swiftly and without mercy. One stockman made it as far as the doorway, but a fleeting shape materialised behind him. Anderson heard the strike of the club from where he stood.

Satisfied the workers had been dealt with, he pulled the revolver from his belt and strode up the path. He reached the French doors and kicked them open, shattering several panes in the process. The hallway beyond was carpeted, a regal-looking red pattern that stretched past several doorways.

A man came through the first door on the right wearing a dressing gown and carrying a shotgun. He opened his mouth to speak, but before he could say anything, Anderson raised the revolver and shot him in the head. The man fell to the floor and a woman screamed somewhere in the distance. He followed the screams to a bedroom and found a woman sitting up in bed. She saw him in the doorway and the scream rose in pitch. He placed his finger to his lips and the woman shut up, but she couldn't stop the trembling spasms of fear that wracked her body. Pulling the bedclothes up to her chin, she watched him through fear-filled eyes.

Deciding the woman was no threat, Anderson went from room to room. He found no one else before returning to the bedroom and pulled the woman from beneath the covers. She wore only a thin cotton nightdress and Anderson grunted with approval as he let his gaze roam over her body.

'What have you done with Cornelius?' the woman pleaded.

'Nothing, milady,' Anderson said and hooked a finger into the neck of the nightdress, tearing it halfway to the hem.

The woman struggled to get free and screamed again. Anderson reversed the revolver in his grip and struck her temple so hard she collapsed onto the bed, not out cold, but too dazed to scream. He loosened his trousers and let them fall to the floor. Then he completed the tear to the nightdress. It fell away, leaving the woman naked.

'Cornelius says for you to look after my every need, milady.' Anderson pulled her knees apart. 'And look after my every need you shall.'

Some minutes later he was aware of movement behind him. Chilbi stood in the doorway, his war club covered in hair and blood.

'Are all the men dead?'

'Yes, Warrigal,' Chilbi nodded. 'We have sent them to their ancestors.'

'Good.' He could see Chilbi's gaze on the woman. 'Do you want a turn at this one?'

'I will never lie with a Djarriba woman.'

'Suit yourself. Give me your war club. She'll be good for nothing now I'm finished with her.' He took the club from Chilbi's hands and stood back from the bed, his trousers around his ankles. The woman did not move or cry out as Anderson raised the club. The fire-hardened knob whistled through the air and struck her in the side of the head. Her legs twitched and blood pulsed from the wound at first, then slowed to a trickle. Anderson handed the club back to Chilbi.

'Take all that we can use,' he said, stooping to pull up his trousers. 'Take food as well. I'll gather up the weapons and gunpowder – and see what they have in the way of valuables.'

Chilbi turned from the room and strode down the hallway towards the front doors. As he passed one of the other rooms he heard a muffled cry from behind a closed door. Reaching for the door, he pushed it open, the club ready in his hand.

A lantern hung from the ceiling hook, lighting a small cot. A table near the window contained a pile of clean swaddling clothes, oils and powders. There was a large wardrobe against the far wall, one door hanging slightly ajar. Chilbi crossed the space in two quick strides and used the club to push the door wide.

A young girl of maybe fifteen or sixteen years crouched in the wardrobe holding an infant to her chest. The baby squirmed in her grip and the girl had a hand over its mouth, trying to stifle the cries. She looked up at Chilbi and her eyes flew wide. A whimper of terror escaped her mouth and Chilbi glanced over his shoulder at the doorway.

The girl began sobbing, huge wracking gasps that shook her body. She forgot about trying to keep the baby quiet and lifted her hand. The infant squealed in wild indignation.

Chilbi reached out to quiet the girl, but she mistook his actions and let fly a blood-curdling scream. He tried again to quiet her, but it was too late. He could hear Anderson thumping down the hallway.

'What the hell do we have here?'

Chilbi turned as Anderson's bulk filled the doorway. The bushranger eyed the girl in the wardrobe.

'Ah! Another little filly for my pleasure.'

He stepped forward, but Chilbi blocked his path.

'No, Warrigal. This one is mine.'

The bushranger paused, unused to having any of the Jannjirra oppose him. He eyed the war club in Chilbi's hand, but did not step back. 'Don't be stupid. She's a Djarriba woman. I'll have my fun with her and then send her to her ancestors – the bairn too.'

Chilbi lifted the club slightly, all too aware that Anderson's hand had started for the revolver in his belt. Chilbi tensed, ready to strike. He held the bushranger's cold stare, knowing that at any moment Anderson could erupt into deadly violence – he had seen it often before when the bushranger didn't get his way. His pulse raced, but he held his ground, not sure if he would be quick enough with the club.

They stayed that way for many moments. Finally, Anderson spoke.

'She is Djarriba. We must kill her.'

'Warriors of the Jannjirra do not harm women or children.'

Anderson's eyebrows knitted together as he contemplated this new turn of events. His eyes flicked again to the war club. Blood dripped from the weapon onto the floor and formed a small puddle on the carpet.

'Fine! She's yours! The bairn too. Hurry up and do whatever you are going to do. We ride out soon.' He turned and strode off down the hallway. Chilbi heard him haranguing Tarrat and Yawong, venting his anger on them.

Turning to the girl and baby, Chilbi found her studying him, wide eyed. His exchange with Warrigal had been in the language of the Jannjirra, so she could not have understood what was said. But she had recognised the way Chilbi placed himself between her and Warrigal. He went to her and tried to place a hand on her shoulder to placate her fears, but he was a stranger and a wild native. She slunk back into the corner of the wardrobe.

Turning, he went to the doorway and waited there while Warrigal and the others prepared to ride out. At the last possible moment, when he knew it was too late for Warrigal to come back into the homestead, he left this position and went to join the others.

A s he picked at his breakfast one chilly morning, Toby noticed Maree frowning at the tailboard of the wagonette where they kept their provisions.

'What's the matter?' he asked.

'We'll have to buy some more provisions before too long. We're running low on everything.'

'We'll need money for that,' Frank threw in. 'There's only sixpence in the kitty.'

Annie looked over from where she was filling a washing tub with hot water from the big iron kettle. 'Sixpence won't buy much in the way of food. I thought the prices at Canvas Town were high, but this place—'

Toby kicked the ground with the toe of his boot. 'I hate to do it, but I guess we'll have to sell some of our gold. We can reprovision and then get stuck back into working the claim.'

'I'll do the honours,' Frank said. He looked about to make sure no one from the other campsites was watching, then went to the nearest wagonette and crawled beneath it. When he came back out, he carried a tobacco tin and brushed away some of the dirt from its hiding place in the ground.

Frank pried the lid off. 'How much do you reckon, lad?'

'I don't know.' Toby said as he eyed the contents. The tin was as wide as Frank's hand span and two inches deep. Coarse grains of yellow-red gold covered the bottom to a depth of about a quarter-inch. 'It looks like a lot, but I suppose it isn't much really, not for three months' work.'

'I was really excited when the first streaks of colour showed in the cradle,' Frank said. 'But there's hardly any showing now. I think we're through the seam.'

Toby nodded. 'I reckon you're right. The shepherd claim is a little lower in the gully. It won't take as long to dig down to that level. We know what we're doing now.'

'We need to eat in the meantime,' Maree reminded them.

'Toby's right.' Frank shook the tin and watched the little grains slide about. 'We'll have to sell this gold to buy supplies. Toby and me will go find a gold buyer before we start work this morning.'

They finished their breakfasts and, as Toby pulled on his jacket, he gave some instructions to Paddy.

'Since we're not digging this morning, why don't you take the horses out into the scrub and see if you can find some new grass for them. They've both got their ribs showing.' To ease the strain on their purse strings, Toby and Frank had sold the two draught horses. It had taken Betty a month to forgive her father for parting with Samson. They'd built a small yard for Moonlight and Patch on the hillside above their camp.

'Can I go with Paddy, please, Papa?' Betty asked.

'Aye, lass. But only if your sister goes with you. There are too many dodgy characters lurking about. If Paddy is busy with the horses, he won't be able to keep a proper eye on you.'

Betty turned to her sister, a pleading look on her face. Annie nodded and she clapped her hands.

'Both of you stay close to Paddy and do whatever he tells— whatever he wants you to do. Mind you don't talk to anyone.' Frank pointed a finger at each of his girls in turn.

Toby hardly noticed the ring of pick and shovel or buzz of voices as he and Frank walked to what could loosely be described as Ballarat's commercial area. They had become part of the countryside, as natural to his ears as the warbling of a magpie or the call of a crow.

They discovered a sign above a hut proclaiming the occupant to be a gold buyer and merchant. The surrounds of the hut were littered with all manner of items. Spades and pans had been stacked against a wall, above which twenty or so hurricane lanterns were strung on a piece of rope running from the hut to a nearby gum tree. Washing tubs and frying pans sat on a trestle table with candles and other items scattered in the spaces between.

A large, yellow-haired dog, mangy and thin, skulked back and forth at the limit of its chain. Toby gave the dog a wide berth as he and Frank approached the open front door of the hut and stooped into the gloomy interior.

The only light came through the open door and spilled onto a makeshift counter and a set of balance scales. Counterweights were lined up neatly to one side. Behind the counter, a calico curtain divided off the back of the hut. It was from behind this curtain that the proprietor of the store appeared, a stocky man in his mid-forties with a pair of pince-nez glasses perched on the bridge of his crooked nose. He greeted them with a heavy Slavic accent.

'Good morning, gentlemen. What can we be doing for you?'

Frank pulled the tin from his pocket, but kept it in his hand. 'Your sign says you're a gold buyer. That right?'

The storekeeper eyed the tobacco tin in Frank's hand and his face broke into a smile. 'Yes, yes. That's what the sign says. Hugo Marcevic, buyer of gold. I will give you a good price – far better than Campbell.'

'What price is that?' Toby asked.

Marcevic adjusted his glasses and pushed a wayward strand of hair back onto his head. He looked at Toby through eyes as brown as the muddy water in the creek. 'You do not have an accent like your father.'

'Frank's not my father,' Toby said. 'We're partners in a claim.'

'Yes, yes,' Marcevic said excitedly. 'Partners in a claim – and now you have found gold to sell. I can give you a good price.'

Toby smiled thinly. 'And what price is that?' he asked again.

'Twenty-five shillings and sixpence an ounce.' The buyer touched his glasses again as he spoke.

Toby and Frank had taken the precaution of asking the other diggers around their claim what they were getting for their gold. Most had agreed that a fair price on the diggings would be a little below the going rate in Melbourne of thirty shillings an ounce.

Frank slipped the tobacco tin back into his pocket and touched the brim of his hat in farewell. 'Word on the diggings is that Campbell is the man to see. They say he's buying gold at twenty-nine shillings and throwing in a nobbler of rum to boot. We'll bid you good day, sir. Thought we could save ourselves a walk, but for a few shillings extra it'll sure be worth it.'

'Gentlemen, don't be in a big hurry. I can match the price of Campbell.'

'I don't know, Frank, a nobbler of rum sounds pretty good to keep the chill out on this cold morning,' added Toby.

'I can give you a drink,' Marcevic announced and pulled a half-gallon earthenware jug from beneath the counter, followed by three grubby tumblers. He pushed some of the merchandise aside and lined the tumblers up before pulling the cork from the jug. 'That is, if we are doing business, gentlemen?'

'Twenty-nine shillings?' Frank asked, his eyes fixed on the jug. Toby noticed the way Frank's tongue came out from between his lips for a brief moment.

'Twenty-nine shillings,' agreed Marcevic, 'and a glass of ouzo.'

'You can put the liquor away, sir,' Frank snapped, shaking his head like a man coming out of a deep sleep. 'We're just here to sell our gold.'

Marcevic nodded and took the empty glasses and placed them under the counter with the jug. 'So,' he said with a smile, 'we are doing business, no? Is it dust or nuggets?'

Frank twisted the lid off the tobacco tin and set it on the counter. Marcevic peered at the contents while holding his spectacles in place with one hand. 'Very fine dust. Excellent quality. I will be needing a funnel to pour it onto the balance. I have one at the back.' Marcevic turned and ducked behind the curtain. A few moments later he reappeared carrying a small tin funnel. Both Toby and Frank watched carefully as Marcevic poured their gold dust into the funnel and made a neat mound on one platform of the balance scales. He tapped the bottom of the upended tin a couple of times with his forefinger and handed the tin back to Frank. He then began placing small counterweights on the opposite side of the scale and counted aloud. All eyes in the hut were fixed on the needle in the middle of the scale as it swung back and forth before finally settling on the balance mark.

Marcevic adjusted his spectacles yet again. 'Just shy of four ounces,' he announced. 'We'll call it four.'

'Good enough for me,' Frank said. 'What do you reckon, lad?' He turned to Toby, but Toby wasn't watching the balance. He had his eyes fixed on the tin funnel still in Marcevic's hand. At the bottom of the funnel one of the coarse grains of gold had stuck to the tin at the edge of the outlet. As Marcevic moved his hand Toby could see more golden grains stuck inside the narrow end of the funnel.

'I reckon this bastard is trying to rob us blind,' he said through clenched teeth. He snatched the funnel from Marcevic's hand. The storekeeper jumped back with surprising agility.

'What's going on?' Frank asked, keeping a wary eye on Marcevic as he backed through the curtain. Toby held the funnel up for Frank. The inside of the funnel was coated with grains of gold.

'He smeared the inside of the funnel with honey,' Toby spat. 'There's got to be half an ounce stuck inside the bloody thing.'

Frank's face reddened. He shoved his way to the back of the hut. 'We've been scratching in this bloody earth for weeks to scrape together that little pile of gold.' Frank pulled the tobacco tin from his pocket and handed it to Toby. 'Put our gold back in here. I'm going to have a word with our friend.'

Toby quickly tipped the gold from the balance back into the tin as Frank ripped aside the curtain. There was a small cot, a table and chair in the space behind. At the far end was a small window covered by a flap of animal hide that Marcevic was trying to climb through, his backside wriggling and legs kicking.

'No you don't, you thieving bastard.' Frank's voice was a low growl. He reached out with a sinewy arm and grabbed Marcevic's belt, pulling him back into the hut with enough force to send him crashing through the curtain and into the counter.

'No. I'm sorry.' Marcevic tried to disentangle himself from the curtain, but only succeeded in pulling it down on top of him. 'I used the funnel to bottle some honey earlier. I forgot to clean it,' he pleaded. He kicked the curtain free of his legs and scampered past Toby on all fours as he made a break for the door, with Frank a pace behind.

The storekeeper managed to crawl out the door, but as he tried to stand up Frank kicked his feet out from beneath him and he landed hard on his back. 'Ten thousand miles in a stinking tub of a boat. Lost my only son on the voyage. Seasick for flaming months on end. Weeks in an immigrant camp in Melbourne before we finally get on the road to this hell-on-earth.'

Marcevic edged away on his backside.

The dog pulled at its chain, barking furiously. Toby could see the storekeeper was trying to reach the safety of the dog. He stepped over and placed himself between Marcevic and the animal. The storekeeper backed into Toby's legs and sank against the ground, resigned to his fate.

'More weeks breaking my bloody back, trying to scratch a pitiful amount of gold out of a hole in the ground. And then what?' Frank stooped and grabbed Marcevic by the front of his shirt. 'I'll bloody well tell you what.' He lifted Marcevic until his face was only an inch from his. 'So a little, thieving weasel like you could trick us out of some of our hard-earned gold.' Frank's right arm came back and he slapped the storekeeper hard across the face with a crack.

Marcevic let out a yelp and renewed his efforts to escape. A trickle of blood ran from the storekeeper's nose and into his moustache.

'Bloody hell, Frank. Don't kill the cove.' A few onlookers started to gather along the path, murmuring among themselves. 'C'mon. We've got our gold back. Let's go.'

Frank looked at Toby and then at the gathering crowd. He let go of the trembling man. Marcevic made no attempt to move. He lay on his back and looked up at Frank with pleading eyes.

'What'd he do?' a voice called.

Without thinking, Frank blurted out, 'Smeared honey inside the funnel so that it trapped some of our gold dust. The bastard was going to take us for about half an ounce.'

'That right?' The owner of the voice stepped forward. He was a big man with tattoos on his bare forearms and a huge, bushy beard that hid most of his face. 'I sold some gold to this cove a few days ago and he used a funnel then as well.'

Another voice piped up from the back, 'Yeah, me too. I thought it looked a little short.' More angry voices rose from the crowd. It seemed a lot of diggers had done business with Marcevic recently. The crowd surged forward.

'Now, gentlemen,' Frank said. 'Let's fetch a constable and let the law deal with him.'

'Like hell,' the big miner yelled. 'You've had your go. Now it's my turn.' He stepped towards Marcevic on legs like tree trunks.

Marcevic knew where his best chances lay. He rolled onto all fours and scurried behind Frank.

Frank stood fast. 'Now, matey, don't be doing nothing you'll regret later.'

Toby knew the words were futile. This mob was going to have their way with the storekeeper. He could hear the big dog barking madly behind him and chanced a quick look. Now focused on the most immediate threat to its master, it reared on its back legs, at the limit of its chain, teeth bared and foamy saliva dripping from its chin. It barked crazily, not taking its eyes off the big man. The animal ignored Toby as he found the catch on the chain and released it.

It took a moment for the dog to realise it was free. It let out a rumbling snarl as it raced towards the miner, who was pushing Frank aside in an effort to reach Marcevic. The miner stooped to pull the cowering storekeeper off the ground as the dog latched onto his leg. He let out a howl of pain and swung his free leg at the dog in an attempt to get it off. The dog saw the kick coming and twisted away, but kept its grip on the leg. It snarled and growled through clenched jaws, worrying the leg muscle. Screaming in pain, the miner reached down and slapped the dog hard across the neck. It let go and backed away with a piece of bloody linen hanging from its jaws. The miner took a step towards the dog and let fly with another kick, but the dog was too fast. It jumped backwards into the legs of the advancing crowd, which immediately scattered, giving the snarling beast a wide berth.

The miner looked down at his bloodied leg and bellowed a scream of rage. He stooped and chose a pick handle from amongst the storekeeper's wares. Gripping the handle in his huge hands, he took two practice swings, the wooden handle singing through the air like a cutlass. Then he advanced on the dog.

'Come to Ivan, poochie. I have something for you.'

The dog sensed the sudden change of advantage and backed away with hackles raised, growling fiercely. Each time the animal moved, the crowd parted like the Red Sea, staying far enough away to keep safe, but close enough to watch the sport unfolding before them.

'Come, poochie, poochie.' The miner feinted left and swung the pick handle in a swooping arc. The dog fell into the trap. It tried to twist away and almost succeeded, letting out a yelp as the handle grazed its flank, knocking it down for one fatal moment. Seizing his chance, the miner reversed his swing and the pick handle sailed towards the animal's head.

Without thinking, Toby leaped towards the miner and threw the full weight of his body against the man's arms as they came down in the swing. It was like throwing himself against the branches of a river gum, but the force was enough to spoil the miner's aim. The pick handle slammed into the ground a hair's breadth from the dog's head. The animal sprang to its feet and ran off between the tents.

'You little bastard. I'll kill you for that.' Ivan took a step towards Toby and raised the handle. Before he could swing, a loud voice erupted from near the storekeeper's hut.

'That man there! Stand fast in the Queen's name.'

A policeman sat on horseback looking down the barrel of a muzzle-loader pistol levelled at the big miner's chest. Off to his right a native policeman covered the crowd with a carbine.

Toby recognised them instantly.

'Drop the lumber. There's a good laddie.' McTavish used his free hand to point at the pick handle and then at the ground.

Ivan let the pick handle slide from his fingers and it clattered on the rocky earth.

McTavish swung from the saddle and stepped towards the group of men.

'Not very nice, was it?' he said to the big miner.

'What?' Ivan sneered, making it obvious he had more respect for the pistol than the office of the man holding it.

'Trying to clout young Mr O'Rourke after he stopped you from murdering a poor defenceless animal.' He touched the brim of his cap to Toby. 'Mind telling me what started this little fracas?'

Toby pulled the funnel from his jacket and showed it to the sergeant as he explained about the gathering crowd, Ivan, and the storekeeper's dog.

McTavish looked up at Ivan. 'If Mr O'Rourke doesn't want to press assault charges, you're free to go.'

Toby shook his head. Ivan went to walk away, but stopped and gestured at the storekeeper. 'What about the gold he stole from me?'

'Just hearsay, isn't it?' the sergeant mused. 'You have no proof, unlike Mr O'Rourke. Now, go away. I'm sure you don't want to spend two weeks chained to the tree at Government Camp waiting for the magistrate to pay us a visit.' That was enough for Ivan. No miner could afford two weeks without working his claim. He turned and strode down the path towards Golden Point.

'Good to see you again, laddie.' McTavish stepped forward and shook Toby's hand.

Toby pushed his hat back on his head and grinned at the policeman. He turned to the native policeman, now standing beside the sergeant. Barraworn shifted the carbine to his left hand so that Toby could shake it, then hesitated, his right hand half offered and the grin slipping from his face.

'Sorry, boss. Some fellas don't like to shake a black fella's hand.'

Toby grasped Barraworn's hand and pumped it heartily. 'I'll shake your hand anytime, Barraworn,' he said, then noticed the bewildered look on Frank's face. 'I'm sorry, Frank. This is Sergeant McTavish and Barraworn. They were at the police post in Bunyong Creek. They tried to chase down the cove that killed my ma and pa.'

'Pleased to meet you, gentlemen,' Frank said, shaking both their hands. 'I don't like to think what would've happened if you two hadn't shown up.'

'How come you're here?' Toby asked. 'I thought you'd be back at Bunyong Creek.'

'The police post at Bunyong Creek is no more.' McTavish shook his head. 'They decided to close it down. Like a lot of other small places. Police presence at all the major diggings needed to be increased. We were ordered to report here for duties as directed by the gold commissioner.' He looked Toby up and down. 'So, this is where you ended up, laddie? I heard about Henry Pelham's dealings. I'm so sorry. There was nothing I could do for you.'

'I don't suppose there was, Sergeant,' Toby said. 'He had everything in place. When our cattle got duffed, he made his move.'

McTavish nodded. 'Sly old fox, that one. Still, I feel pretty bad.' He pointed at the funnel in Toby's hand. 'I'll need to take that and the gold dust inside it to show the magistrate. I'm sure this laddie won't mind compensating you for the loss of your gold, hey!' He prodded Marcevic with the toe of his boot and the storekeeper nodded vigorously. 'Take what you feel is fair compensation from his wares. I'll leave Barraworn to guard the rest of it until I get this gentleman secured to the tree at Government Camp.'

Toby and Frank turned towards the store, both grinning like village idiots. They selected a couple of gold washing pans, two gallons of paraffin oil and a new lantern. Then they gathered up some foodstuffs, sacks of flour, sugar, tea and twenty pounds of rice.

Toby kept a running tally of the price in his head, but McTavish called out, 'Don't be shy, gentlemen. I'm sure Mr Marcevic is offering wholesale prices to compensate for the trouble he has caused.'

When they shook the sergeant's hand and left for their camp, they each pushed a wheelbarrow piled high with equipment and stores. Toby topped his load off with a bag of chaff for the horses.

Lieutenant Governor La Trobe sat stiff-backed behind his desk as he perused the latest reports from various outposts dotted about his domain. He rubbed his chin nervously as he anticipated the reaction to his next dispatch to Earl Grey, the Secretary of State for the Colonies. The fledgling colony was almost two years old, having separated from New South Wales in 1851, and the way to a bright and golden future lay before them, and yet it seemed he was unable to include a modicum of good news in any of his reports.

The present is certainly golden, he thought. The Victorian goldfields were showing enough promise to far outstrip their counterparts in New South Wales. It hardly seemed a day went by without news of a new find filtering in from the bushlands. To any other person this would come as good news, but to the lieutenant governor it was another reason for the thinning of his limited resources. A new goldfield meant a new rush of humanity to an otherwise wild piece of land and, wherever humanity gathered in his colony, he was expected – nay, it was his duty – to ensure a government presence in sufficient numbers to enforce the laws and regulations of the Crown.

And therein lay the problem. It seemed every able-bodied man with enough strength to turn over a shovelful of dirt was abandoning his station and setting off to make his fortune on one of the diggings. Gold fever had created a labour short-age the likes of which had never been known before – and it was hardly restricted to the government. He had invited several prominent businessmen to dine with him on the previous Saturday evening, and they had all complained in one way or another that they were hard put to find manpower.

He could do little but sympathise with them. He had raised the gold licence fee as high as he dared in an effort to quell the bush-bound migration. He had made it known that every labourer or hired hand should be indentured to his employer for a given period of time. But if the fellow chose to ignore that indenture and head off to make his fortune, there was little the law could do about it.

He shuffled through the reports to find one that backed up his line of thought. It seemed every brigand and cut-throat with darkness in his heart had found his way to the colony. Reports came in daily of highway robbery and murder taking place somewhere on the colony's roads or in the diggings. He found the report he was looking for and smoothed it out.

That's right, he reminded himself as he scanned the report. It seems this fellow Anderson has enlisted the help of a group of natives and is holding up travellers on the roads between the diggings, raping and murdering as he goes. The writer of the report, a captain currently stationed at the Bendigo diggings, went on to describe several attempts to hunt down this Anderson and his band of rogues, but the chap seemed well versed in using rough country to aide his escape, as one could well expect from a man consorting with natives.

He pushed the pile of reports out into the middle of his desk and called for his aide.

'Childers?'

The large door across from his desk swung open. A tall man in an immaculate military uniform entered.

'Your Excellency?'

'What is the current reward posted on this fellow Anderson?' The lieutenant governor tapped the topmost report as he spoke.

'Two hundred and fifty pounds, Excellency.'

'Have it doubled immediately.'

'I shall have the clerk draft a request to the printers before the day is out, sir.'

'Good man.' He waved Childers away with a casual flick of his hand. As his aide pulled the door closed, La Trobe leaned well back in his chair, lacing his fingers behind his head.

'We shall see if that doesn't encourage someone to rat the rascal out,' he said aloud, allowing himself a brief moment of relaxation. In his mind he had already begun to compose his next report to Earl Grey.

As Annie stepped from the tent into the cool of pre-dawn, she immediately noted the blanket of mist in the bottom of the gully and was glad of the heavy, woollen jumper she had pulled on when she dressed. The jumper had once been Tom's, one he had worn while working as a labourer, and she imagined she could still smell the musky odour of his sweat. Sometimes, when she was in a melancholy mood, she would bury her face in the sleeve of the garment and take in a huge breath. For the briefest of moments, while she held that breath, her brother was there with her.

As she did every morning, she immediately searched the campsite for Toby. No one else had emerged yet, but the sound of movement from the boys' tent beyond the wagon-ette told her she would not have long to wait, so she went to the fire and examined the bed of coals. There was still a faint glow among the embers and a fistful of dry grass soon had the flames building.

Betty was the next to emerge and Annie sent her to fetch the lamb chops from where they hung in a damp calico bag tied to the branch of a tree by the wagonette. She added wood to the fire and began heating the big frying pan. By the time everyone was up and gathering around the campfire, she had breakfast sizzling away.

'That smells marvellous,' Toby said as he knocked dirt out of his boots and sat on his favourite log by the fire to pull them on.

'It won't be too long, Toby,' Annie said, giving him a bright smile. 'Would you like coffee this morning? I can grind the last of the beans you and Papa got from that storekeeper if you like. The billy's almost on the boil.'

'Yes, please,' Toby answered quickly.

Annie knew that Toby had developed a liking for coffee and had secreted away a little stash of beans so she could surprise him.

Paddy took his usual place on the log beside Toby as Annie dished up the chops onto plates and Betty carried them to each person in turn. They ate in relative silence as around them the diggings came to life. Some men were already on the move towards their claims with tools slung over their shoulders or piled into barrows. Others were still eating breakfast around their own campfires.

'Want first shift in the hole today, Toby?' Frank asked.

Toby looked at him across the top of his cup of coffee. 'Actually, I'd like to check on Moonlight first. I think he has a shoe working loose. If I don't do something about it, he may hurt himself.'

'Ooh! Poor Moonlight,' Annie cooed.

'As soon as I finish breakfast, I'll go and check on him.'

'I'll help you,' Betty stated from across the fire.

'You'll finish your breakfast first, girl,' Maree said firmly, and Betty hurriedly cut at her chop.

When everyone had eaten, Annie gathered their plates and placed them in the wash tub while she waited for the big kettle to boil. Toby and Betty wandered up the path to the horse yard and Frank and Paddy loaded the cradle and digging equipment into the barrow. Maree helped Annie wash the dishes and they were nearly finished when Toby came back down the hillside, a glum look on his face.

'He has a loose shoe, all right. I'm sorry, Frank, but I need to do something about it before I get started.'

Frank was knocking his pipe out on the handle of the barrow. 'Best you see to it, then, lad. I know how important that animal is to you. Paddy and me can make a start at the claim.'

'I'll have to take him down to Blacky Pete's,' Toby said. 'He's the closest thing to a farrier around here. He'll probably relish the change from sharpening picks. Betty can come with me if she likes.'

'Oh, yes please! Mama, Papa, can I? Please?' The young girl danced beside Toby.

'If it's fine with Toby, then it's fine with me,' Maree said as she stacked clean plates on the tailboard of the wagonette.

'You mind your manners while you're out and about, young lady,' Frank added. 'Do exactly as Toby tells you, without any backchat. Understand?'

Betty clasped her hands in front of her pinafore and gave her father an angelic look. 'I will, Papa.'

Toby retrieved a halter from the ridge pole of his tent. 'I'll be as quick as I can, Frank.' Betty took the halter out of Toby's hand.

'I know how to put the halter on. I'll do it for you. Can I ride on Moonlight's back while you take him down to Blacky Pete's?'

'I don't see why not,' Toby said, and the girl squealed with delight.

Annie watched them go up the hillside, her sister holding Toby's sleeve and trying to urge him to greater speed.

'She's full of beans now,' her mother remarked.

'Toby will keep her occupied for a while. At least you and I can get some work done in peace.' She turned to her father and Paddy as they started away towards the claim. 'I shall bring morning tea down at the usual time, Papa.'

Frank waved and he and Paddy headed out.

'It looks as if we are in for a bit of sun today, my girl. I should like to bring the bedding out and give it an air. What do you think?'

'It could certainly do with it, Mama,' Annie replied. 'I'll strip the boys' cots if you want to do our tents.'

Annie went to Toby and Paddy's tent and tied the flaps back to allow a little air through. The cots were at either side with the space in between covered with loose boards so that they might stay out of the dust and mud. Paddy's cot was on the left, the bedclothes all bunched up at the foot where he had kicked them off before climbing out of bed. In contrast, Toby had pulled his blankets up and smoothed them out before leaving the tent. Annie quickly stripped both beds and carried the blankets and linen to where her father and Toby had tied a long rope between two gum trees to make a clothes line, hanging them to air in the sunshine and growing breeze.

The two women fussed about the campsite for an hour, cleaning and neatening as best they could. The sides of the tents were stained with dust and mud. Dust seemed to be on everything and Annie wondered if her mother missed the little stone cottage in Hastings that had been their home before coming to Australia. She dared not ask and risk bringing on a bout of tears. Maree seemed happy enough, humming as she worked, a smile on her face.

'Shall I make a damper for morning tea, Mama?' she asked instead.

'I think everyone would like that, Annie. Toby especially.' Her mother gave her a knowing look. 'He seems to have developed a great fondness for your cooking.'

Annie went to the tailboard of the wagonette that served as the camp's kitchen bench and began pouring flour into a large enamel basin. She had made damper bread often enough that she didn't need to measure out the flour.

'What do you think of Toby, Mama?'

Maree looked up from where she was sweeping in front of the boys' tent with a straw broom. 'He seems a good, kind lad who picks his words carefully before he speaks. He reminds me so much of Tom.'

'Me too, Mama. He's not the rough colonial one would expect,' Annie said as she worked. 'I think he is a fine man.'

'Definitely husband material.'

'Mama!' Annie was so startled by her mother's remark, she nearly dropped the egg she was holding. She looked to Maree and saw the cheeky smile on her face.

'You could do a lot worse, Annie. A lot worse.'

'I don't think Toby sees himself as husband material, Mama. And sometimes his mood is a little too dark.'

Maree came over and propped the broom against the tailboard. 'Given what has happened, he is certainly entitled to be a little moody from time to time. Paddy too. Toby is still fighting the demons of his past, but I've seen one smile from you chase those demons away, if only for a little while.'

Annie turned her face towards the trail to the horse yard. It was empty. She enjoyed Toby's company. He could be so serious and funny and caring, sometimes all at the same time. Looking about the camp, she wondered just what life in this strange place would be like if Toby and his brother weren't in it.

She was still thinking about Toby as she kneaded the dough and waited for the camp oven to heat.

S tanding at the edge of the mineshaft, Frank looked down into the darkness and lifted the lantern out of the barrow. He drew hard on his pipe until the tobacco in the bowl glowed, then used it to light a gum leaf that he in turn used to light the wick of the lantern.

'We're about eight feet below the bottom of the shoring,' he said, more to himself than for Paddy's benefit. 'Once I get the shaft down to ten feet we'll need to scrounge some more timber and brace that last bit. The gravel down there is too loose to trust to providence.' Beside him, Paddy nodded his understanding.

'Maybe four or five barrowloads to put through the cradle, Pad. Then I'll need you here to help with the timber work.'

Paddy nodded again and Frank pulled two picks and one of the shovels out of the barrow. In the early days, when the shaft was still shallow, they had simply used a length of rope to haul tools and the bucket up and down, hand over hand. As their skills had improved, and the shaft grew deeper, they had followed the example of other diggers and built a simple windlass over the pit. He tied the tools to the rope and turned the windlass handle, lowering them into the opening, unwinding steadily until the rope went slack. Then, with lantern in hand, he climbed onto the ladder and descended into the dark square.

They had dug to a depth of about sixty feet and had lined the sides of the shaft with timber to prevent it from caving in. Frank had used his carpentry skills to fashion a ladder that was better than most on the diggings. This was tied to the shoring at intervals with pieces of rope that could be undone when the time came to lower the ladder further into the mine. About halfway down, Frank noticed that one of these ropes had come undone and he placed the handle of the lantern between his teeth to free his hands while he tied it off, one arm looped through a rung.

The lantern swung about as he moved his head and the pool of light it cast washed about the walls of the shaft as he worked. Near his left shoulder, a trickle of dirt and stones spilled between a gap in the shoring where one of the boards had worked loose and Frank made a mental note to repair the shoring here when they added more bracing near the bottom.

Continuing down the ladder, the ring of lantern light travelled with him until it finally lit the bottom. Toby had been the last digger in the mine yesterday and Frank could see a pile of wash-dirt the lad had left piled in one corner. He quickly untied the tools and yelled up the shaft to where Paddy's head and shoulders were silhouetted against the sky.

'Your brother has left us some wash-dirt, lad. Send the bucket straight down.'

He heard Paddy clap his hands twice to signal he had understood. Moments later the creaking of the windlass filled the mine and the rope retreated upwards. A minute later he heard three claps and stood aside as the bucket descended towards him, tied to the rope.

Five shovelfuls of dirt filled the bucket and he yelled again. 'Pull away, lad.' Paddy gave two hand claps and the bucket rose towards the square of sky sixty feet above him. Frank watched it go, standing to one side to avoid being hit by any dirt that fell out of the brimming bucket. It developed a swing as it ascended and bumped the side of the shaft twice before Paddy grabbed it and pulled it out of Frank's sight.

He spent a few moments scraping the rest of the wash-dirt into a pile, then three handclaps warned him the bucket was on its way back down. He filled the bucket with the remaining dirt and waited until it was on its way to the surface again, then attacked the ground at his feet with the pick. The quartz-rich gravel was hard-packed and the point of the pick hardly penetrated more than an inch at each strike.

Something hit Frank's back and he glanced up to see the bucket had developed that swing again and had struck the shoring, either dislodging a stone from between the boards or losing part of its load. He pressed himself against the far side of the shaft and waited until Paddy retrieved the bucket before returning to digging.

Four more buckets of dirt made the ascent and then Paddy gave four handclaps to signal he was taking the loaded barrow down to the creek where their washing cradle sat ready to sluice the dirt and separate out any gold it contained.

'Right you are, lad,' Frank called up at Paddy's silhouette. The boy disappeared from sight and Frank turned his attention back to digging. Over the past weeks he had developed a technique of creating a small hole about a foot square and then using the pick to lever out the sides of this hole, expanding it until it covered the entire floor of the shaft and became the new bottom, a foot deeper than where he had started, stockpiling the wash-dirt in one corner until the bucket came back down to him.

As he levered at the sides of the hole, a large lump of quartz came free. The rock was striated with bands of colour and Frank felt his pulse quicken. He snatched it up and held it to the lantern, rubbing at it with his thumbs to scrub away the dirt. The lines glittered in the feeble glow, and Frank scrubbed harder, spitting on the rock to try and get enough moisture to wash it clean. The narrow seam glittered more brightly in the lantern light and he twisted the rock to examine it.

The striations were angular and looked like tiny cubes encased in quartz. The flat edges had an almost mirror-like shine to them and Frank felt his excitement ebb. He had seen enough iron pyrite over the past weeks to know that was what he held in his hand.

'Fool's gold!' He flicked the rock away in disgust, took up the pick and went back to digging.

He worked methodically, alternating between pick and shovel until three claps from overhead told him that Paddy had returned from the creek and the bucket was on its way back down. He waited until it settled on the bottom then filled it from the pile of dirt he had dug away. Filling the bucket was easier than digging and, while the bucket was in transit, Frank used this time to have a rest of sorts. He piled the last of the dirt into the bucket and discovered the lump of quartz containing the fool's gold. He placed the rock on top of the pile.

'Haul away, lad.'

The bucket rose out of the cylinder of lantern light.

Frank took up the pick and adjusted his hands on the handle. He raised the pick in a backswing, but a loud bump from above warned him that the bucket had struck the side of the shaft. He looked up to see a small, black dot against the sky, growing rapidly in size. With only a fraction of a second to spare, Frank stepped aside and the quartz rock from the bucket thudded into the dirt at his feet.

'Bloody hell! That was close.'

Frank kicked the rock into a corner, but there were more bumping noises from above. He looked up to see the bucket crash against the side of the shaft and catch its rim under the edge of one of the boards forming the shoring. The rope creaked as Paddy added more tension at the windlass. The bucket tilted to one side and emptied a little of its contents into the shaft, forcing Frank to stand back and shield his eyes. Something let out a snapping noise from above him and he risked looking up, holding his hand in front of his eyes and peering through parted fingers.

The bucket was now free and continued its ascent, but the board it had caught on had pulled partly loose. A trickle of gravel ran from the gap and rattled down the mineshaft. Frank put a hand to the ladder, ready to climb from the shaft, but the trickle slowed until only one or two stones landed at his feet.

He stood motionless, watching the loose board, but no more dirt poured through the gap. He lowered his gaze and studied the bottom of the shaft, judging that he had reached a point ten feet below the lowest shoring.

'I'll square off the bottom of the hole,' he said aloud to himself, his voice sounding hollow in the bottom of the mine. 'Then we'll need to do some more shoring. And fix that loose bit halfway up.'

Four handclaps echoed down from above, signalling that the last bucketful of dirt had filled the barrow.

'Take it down to the creek, lad. I'll do a little bit of squaring off down here, then we'd better get on with the shoring before we dig any deeper.'

Frank heard two handclaps of acknowledgement and then took up the pick. He only had a small amount of digging left to finish the level he was working on. The ground here was a little easier, and he was able to break out large chunks, using the shovel to scrape them to the side.

He became aware of a sound, something like hailstones hitting a slate roof. Looking up, he could see that gravel was pouring through the gap in the shoring and he paused his work, waiting for it to stop as it had before, but the gravel continued to pour through, coming faster and faster. Frank stood and lifted the lantern, holding it as high as he could to better illuminate the gap in the shoring.

His heart raced as he realised a whole ten-foot section of the shoring now hung loose, like an open gate. Dirt and rocks came through the gap and rattled down the shaft, bouncing off the rungs of the ladder. Even as he watched, the dirt came faster and he dropped the lantern and raced to the ladder. He got one hand to the rung when there was a crack like a gunshot and the whole section of loose shoring broke free and plummeted towards him. Frank jumped back, his movements hampered by the growing pile of dirt around his feet. The section of shoring, dropping like a guillotine blade, hit the ladder and twisted at the last moment, catching Frank across the chest and knocking him on his backside against the far wall of the shaft. It landed across his legs and he tried to push it off and get to the ladder, but gravel now thundered down into the shaft like a waterfall. He only managed to shift the heavy boards an inch or two before the gravel piled up over his legs, pressing against the shoring and making the task impossible.

The thundering sound continued and the hole went dark as the gravel slide buried the lantern. Through the gaps between the boards he could see the square of sky, sixty feet above him. He managed to squeeze his right arm through the gap at the side and grasped for the light, as if he could reach its safety simply by pulling it towards him. He tried to yell, to scream for help. Paddy was at the creek, but maybe some miners at a neighbouring claim would hear him and come to help. He drew a breath, but the dust was thick and sent him into a spasm of coughing. The weight on his legs increased and he could feel the boards pressing against him as dirt built up on the far side of the piece of shoring. Far above, the square of sky vanished.

Annie picked her way carefully down the gully holding a steaming billy of tea in one hand and two tin pannikins in the other. In her apron pocket she carried two thick slices of damper, hot from the camp oven and layered with a thick coating of plum jam.

Toby and Betty had not yet returned with Moonlight from their trip to Blacky Pete's. Normally, she would send her sister down to the creek to fetch Paddy if he wasn't at the mine, but this morning her father would just have to yell for him from the top of the mullock heap.

Rounding the final twist in the narrow path, she discovered the claim was deserted. The bucket sat at the side of the hole, a loop of slack rope connecting it to the windlass, a shovel lying on the ground beside it. Paddy was nowhere in sight and she guessed he was down at the creek, putting a barrowload of wash-dirt through the cradle. She placed the billy and pannikins on the ground and then stepped carefully to the edge of the shaft.

'Papa? I've brought morning tea.'

There was no answer, so she leaned over the pit.

'Papa?'

The shaft was filled with a smoky haze and the bottom was barely visible. It was empty except for a few boards that seemed to be poking out of the dirt. She gathered her skirts in her hands and climbed the mullock heap, her feet slipping on loose gravel. From the top, Annie could see all the way down to the creek, about two hundred yards away. Paddy was on the bank, working the handle of the cradle as he sluiced the wash-dirt, but her father was nowhere in sight. She did a slow pirouette on the summit, looking for him among the other miners on surrounding claims, maybe sharing a smoke. When she didn't find him, she slipped carefully down the side of the mullock heap and walked back to the mineshaft.

The haze had cleared somewhat, and the sun was now high enough in the sky to chase back the shadows. About halfway down she noticed some boards missing from the shoring and guessed they were the ones she could see at the bottom. Perhaps her father had gone off to find more timber to add to the bracing.

As she looked, she wondered if her eyes were playing tricks on her. The boards seemed to move slightly. The movement happened again, and she squinted into the gloom. There was other movement down there beside the boards. Something clawed its way upwards out of the dirt and she screamed in horror as a hand grasped the rough-sawn edges of the shoring.

Without thinking, Annie swung onto the head of the ladder and descended as quickly as she could. The heel of her boot caught on her petticoats, but she ignored the ripping noise and kept going, hand over hand until she stepped off at the bottom. She sank to her ankles in loose gravel and half walked, half waded to where the hand gripped the broken shoring.

'Papa? My God, Papa?'

Annie touched the hand and it let go of the boards and gripped her fingers, squeezing so hard it hurt.

'I'll get you out, Papa. I'll get you out.' The words came as a sob. She didn't let go of her father's hand, not wanting to break that one tenuous bond. Frantically, she pulled at the gravel, scraping it towards the far corner. More gravel slid back into the hole she had made, but Annie could see she was making headway. The hole deepened, and she could see her father's wrist and then his elbow where it curved around the edge of the shoring. Annie leaned in to the gap behind the boards.

'Papa? Can you hear me? Hold on, Papa. I'll get you out.'

'Can't breathe.' Frank's voice was little more than a whisper.

'Hold on, Papa. Please hold on.'

'Are you all right, miss? What's going on? We heard a scream.'

Annie looked up to see several heads silhouetted against the sky.

'There's been a collapse,' she shouted up the shaft. 'My father is trapped. Please, help me.'

'I'm bloody well not going down there,' a different voice said. 'A death trap if ever I saw one.'

'I suppose it's not your sorry arse that's trapped down there, Tomkins. Hang on, miss. I'm coming down.'

Annie heard boots on the ladder, but didn't dare stop her one-handed digging. She managed to open the gap behind the boards a little more, but it was too dark to see her father's face.

'Hold on, Papa,' she told the sliver of darkness. 'Help is coming.'

The sound of gravel crunching at the bottom of the ladder told her that the miner had arrived. 'Can you see him, miss?'

'I've got his hand. He's trapped behind the loose shoring. I think it's the only thing that saved him, but he can't breathe. We need to get the weight off him. Quickly.'

'Tomkins?' The miner yelled upwards. 'As many men with ropes and buckets as you can get. Quickly, now! The gravel is loose. We can shovel it in by hand.'

'Right you are,' a voice echoed down.

'I'll take over, miss. You get yourself to safety.'

Annie shook her head. 'I'm not leaving him.'

The miner didn't argue with her. He dropped to his knees and began pulling dirt away from the boards as fast as he could manage. Annie used her one free hand to help as best she could. The pile in the far corner was almost two feet high when they heard a voice from above.

'Two buckets coming down, Jack. More men on their way. Do you need any help down there?'

'Nah, Davo. Not much room anyway. Just keep them buckets coming.'

Something thudded into the ground beside Annie and she glanced over to see a bucket tied to a rope. The miner, Jack, snatched it up and used it to scoop up a pile of dirt.

'Pull away!' he shouted, and the bucket of dirt rocketed skywards as another landed in the bottom.

Jack worked quickly, filling buckets with loose gravel and sending them skywards. Annie kept up her one-handed scraping, adding her efforts to the pile until she heard a series of frantic claps from overhead. A familiar shape was visible on the skyline.

'Paddy? There's been a collapse. Papa is buried under some boards and dirt.'

Paddy immediately climbed onto the ladder and descended towards her, dropping six or seven rungs at a time.

'Careful, young fella,' Jack warned. 'Don't bring more dirt down on us.'

Paddy landed in the bottom of the mine and moved to Annie's side. His hand came up and closed over hers and her father's. She felt his fingers tighten their grip, a show of reassurance. Then he stood and caught the next bucket out of mid-air and set to filling it.

Paddy and the Samaritan, Jack, worked hard and fast. In moments, they developed a rhythm of catching buckets and filling them, sending them upwards again.

Annie kept her grip on her father's hand and felt herself getting lower and lower as the gravel resettled at a new level. When about five feet of the loose shoring showed, the men paused.

'How far below the top of the gravel is his face, miss?'

Annie reached in behind the shoring and felt her father's head. The gravel was up to his chin here, but on her side it was six inches higher.

'We're level with the top of his head.' She rubbed the back of her hand on Frank's cheek. 'Hold on, Papa. We're getting you out.' There was no response from her father and Annie felt the bite of despair in her stomach. 'Please, hurry,' she said to Jack and Paddy.

They kept on digging for three minutes, maybe four, maybe ten. Annie wasn't sure. Every few moments she was forced to adjust her position as the gravel shifted beneath her, settling lower and lower.

'What about now, miss?'

Annie reached in and checked the depth of gravel. 'You've got it down level with his chest. Both sides of the boards.'

'What do you say we try and lift the shoring off him, young fella?'

Paddy nodded and they grasped the top of the boards and pulled with all their strength. The shoring moved a quarter of an inch, but wouldn't budge further.

'It's no use,' Jack said. 'We'll have to keep digging.'

Paddy slapped the miner's shoulder and shook his head. He mimed tying a rope around the shoring and then winding a windlass handle.

'Good thinking,' Jack said. He lifted his face to the square of sky. 'Davo? Are any of the buckets still attached to the windlass?'

'Yeah, this one.' One of the buckets jiggled as Davo jerked the rope. 'But we haven't been using the windlass. Too slow. Hand over hand is much quicker.'

'This bloke's got part of the shoring lying on him. We think we can get it off with the windlass. Give us a minute to get the rope tied on.'

'Righto, Jack.'

Paddy untied the bucket and then moved in beside Annie, passing the loose end of rope behind the shoring where Jack took it and tied it back on itself. He gave the running end a couple of jerks to test his knot and then looked down at Annie.

'I think you should get out of the way for this, miss. If that rope snaps, it could be dangerous.'

Annie opened her mouth to protest, but Paddy knelt beside her and unfolded her fingers from her father's hand. She was horrified to see her father's arm flop lifelessly to the ground. Paddy led her to the far corner of the shaft and pressed her into it, placing his protective bulk in front of her. Then he gave Jack a nod.

'Haul away,' Jack yelled.

The rope went tight and let out a creak that reminded Annie of her time on the *Charlotte Elizabeth*. From high above, she could hear men grunting as they put all their strength to the windlass handle. The shoring shifted, raising to the vertical and her father groaned, causing Annie a mixture of elation and dread.

'Stop it. You're hurting him.' She tried to push past Paddy, but he barred her way, as solid as a granite boulder.

'He's nearly free. We can't stop now.'

The rope groaned and thrummed like a plucked guitar string. High above, she heard the squeak of the windlass as it turned. Then the section of shoring pulled free from the gravel and swung towards the anxious watchers until Paddy put a hand out to steady it.

'It's loose,' Jack yelled, but he kept them against the side until the heavy timbers had been hauled to the top and swung clear of the opening.

Annie and Paddy rushed to Frank, who sat with his back to the wall, buried in gravel to his midriff. His head had lolled forward and he looked dead.

'We're too late,' Annie sobbed and bit down on a dirty fist as tears welled into her eyes.

'He was groaning only a few moments ago. Let's get him out of the gravel,' Jack said. He and Paddy took hold of an arm each and pulled Frank to his feet so that he hung between them. Annie clasped her father's face in her hands and rubbed his cheeks. They felt cold and waxen.

'Papa? Please, wake up. Please, Papa.'

She placed her cheek to his nose and mouth, but there was no trace of breath. 'He's not breathing.'

'What's the matter with him?' a voice called from above.

'We think he's stopped breathing,' Jack called up.

'Get him up here as quick as you can. I might be able to help.'

Jack looked up at the patch of sky and Annie could tell he was wondering just how they were going to get her father to the surface.

'We can get the rope back down. Haul him up with the windlass.'

Paddy shook his head and bent his knees so that Frank draped across his shoulders. He locked one leg and arm against his chest and then stood, supporting Frank's full weight.

'You sure, young fella? That's a hell of a climb with a man on your back.'

Paddy gave no response, he stepped up to the ladder and began to climb, his legs powering him upwards. Annie held her breath until Paddy was halfway up and she realised he was going to make it, but she stood stock still until Paddy reached the top of the ladder and stepped out of sight.

'Never seen such a feat of strength,' the miner muttered. He looked over at Annie.

'I'd climb the ladder ahead of you, miss, but I can't leave you to be the last person out of the mine.'

'What do you mean?' Annie said.

Jack pointed at her clothing. 'Your skirts. If you're above me on the ladder, well—'

Annie realised that Jack was now concerned with her modesty. 'Not to worry, sir.' She reached between her legs and grabbed the back of her skirts, pulling them through and tucking them into the belt of her apron so that it looked like she was wearing a pair of pantaloons. Then she went to the ladder and began to climb.

As soon as she reached the surface she could see that they had placed her father face up on the ground. Six men crowded around while a man had Frank's arms in his hands and was folding them across his chest and then opening them out repeatedly. She stepped off the ladder and rushed to his side, shouldering her way through the watching men.

'What are you doing?' Annie asked. She wanted to hug her father and beg him to wake up, but the miner working Frank's arms was taking up all the room. She saw Paddy near the front of the throng and clung to him instead.

'Saw this done to a sailor what fell overboard once,' the miner answered, not breaking his rhythm. 'He wasn't breathing neither, but the bugger came back. Sure enough he did. Right as rain.'

Frank's lips were tinged with blue and his skin had taken on the colour of old wax that has dripped down the candlestick.

His head lolled with the motion of his arms and Annie thought him surely gone. She held tight to Paddy and watched the miner work, dread building in the pit of her stomach.

Frank gave a little cough and bile ran from the corner of his mouth. The miner kept up his ministrations and Frank coughed again, this time with enough force to spray spittle into the air. The miner stopped his efforts and Frank coughed once more. His chest rose and fell of its own accord and the crowd let out a gasp of wonder.

Annie let go of Paddy and rushed to her father's side. 'Oh, Papa! Thank God.' She lifted his head and cradled it in her lap, using her apron to wipe bile from his lips.

Frank opened his eyes. He seemed to have trouble focusing.

'I'm here, Papa.' Annie rubbed his cheek with her hand and the eyes settled on her at last.

'My girl.' His voice was a hoarse croak. 'You got me out.'

'Yes, Papa. Me and Paddy and all these men here. All these wonderful men helped to get you out. You're safe now.'

O n Sunday, when mining wasn't allowed, the men busied themselves with repairing any broken equipment. Toby was using a file to put a point back on one of the partly-blunted picks and Paddy was fixing a cracked handle on a shovel by binding it with a length of cord. Maree and Betty cleaned and tidied the camp while Annie busied herself at the cooking fire, adding wood so that she would have a good bed of embers for the camp oven.

Frank was sitting on a log by the fire, a blanket draped around his shoulders and a steaming pannikin of tea in his hands. By unanimous consensus, it was agreed that he would rest up today, as he had done for three days since the mine collapse, and look to returning to work tomorrow, at the beginning of a new week.

'All right, Papa?' Annie asked as she went to the tailboard of the wagonette and poured flour into an enamel bowl.

'Yes, girl, I'm fine. Stop fussing.'

Annie gave him her best smile and added more ingredients to the bowl. Then she kneaded the dough for ten minutes, floured the camp oven and placed it inside. Over the past weeks, she had learned to judge the temperature to perfection. When the damper came out half an hour later, it was crisp and golden on the outside and as light as a feather. She wrapped it in a tea towel.

'Toby?'

'Yes, Annie?' He looked at her expectantly and Annie realised he was waiting for her to offer him the first slice, as she usually did.

'Would you be kind enough to escort me through the diggings?'

Toby's hungry look changed to one of surprise. 'Where are you going?'

'It's not far. About five minutes' walk. It won't take long.'

Toby's brow knotted for a moment, then he dropped the pick and took the file back to Frank's tool satchel.

Annie gathered up the damper loaf in its tea towel and tucked her free arm through Toby's. 'A bit further up the gully,' she said, and led him away.

They found a meandering path that made its way along the lead. Toby was quiet for a little while, but when they were close to the creek, he could hold his tongue no longer.

'Where are we going, Annie?'

'To repay a kindness,' she responded cryptically and tugged at his arm.

Toby must have realised he wasn't going to get a straight answer from her, so he remained quiet as they walked on.

'Here it is,' Annie broke the silence some minutes later. 'The tent by that tall gum tree.'

'Whose camp is that?'

'You'll see.'

A man was sitting by the fire with his back to them as they approached. Annie cleared her throat and said, 'Excuse me, sir? Is this the camp of Jack Burton?'

The man by the fire turned around. As soon as he saw them, he climbed to his feet and rushed over.

'Miss? What are you doing here?'

Jack never once looked at her escort, and Annie felt Toby's free hand come up and cover hers in a show of possession. The thought of his jealousy made her smile.

'My mother and I would like to show our appreciation for your help in rescuing Papa. We've baked you a damper.' She offered the bundled tea towel. 'You do like damper, don't you?'

'Why, yes, I do.' Jack took the damper loaf. 'It's a beauty. Still warm, too. You shouldn't have gone to that trouble, miss. But tell me, how do you know my last name?'

'Oh, I asked around,' Annie said. 'You were so brave to climb down into that mine and help me with Papa.' She felt Toby's fingers tighten around her hand.

'I'm sure your papa would have done the same for me, had the roles been reversed.'

'Oh, how rude of me. Mr Burton, this is Toby O'Rourke.' She gestured at Toby.

Jack held out his hand and Toby shook it. 'Your brother?' There was just a hint of hopefulness in his voice.

Annie gave a little giggle. 'Goodness, no. Mr O'Rourke is a friend. He would have helped to rescue Papa, but he was across the diggings having a shoe put on his horse.'

'That I was,' Toby said. 'Missed all the excitement. But I'm glad my brother was there to help.'

'The quiet young fella?'

Annie nodded.

'Strong as an ox, that one. Never seen such an amazing feat of strength.' He dropped Toby's hand and held the damper up. 'Thank you very much, miss.'

'You're welcome, sir. I should have liked to bake one for everyone who helped, but we can't afford all the flour.'

They bid their goodbyes and Toby led her back towards the camp.

'Seems a nice man, Mr Burton. Doesn't he, Toby?'

Beside her, she heard Toby give a noncommittal grunt and his fingers tightened on her hand once again.

At the camp, Annie went straight to the wagonette and began mixing more dough.

'Another thank you?' Toby asked.

'As a matter of fact, yes,' Annie replied and turned back to her task. This time, when the damper came out of the oven, she cut it open while still hot and smothered a huge piece with butter and plum jam.

'Paddy? This one is for you.' She stepped up to the boy where he sat beside the fire and handed him the piece of damper. 'For the strongest boy in all the world.'

F rank sat perfectly still on his log by the fire, his attention fixed firmly on the flickering flames. Maree sat beside him on a folded saddle blanket darning a pair of Paddy's socks, humming softly while she worked. The others had gone to bed over an hour ago and the couple were enjoying a little rare solitude.

Across the gully, a fight broke out at another camp. Frank tried to distract his mind by listening to the shouted argument. Someone wanted to pull up stakes and move to the Creswell diggings. Someone else insisted that their fortune was waiting for them, just a few feet further down. All they had to do was dig a little more.

The thought of returning to the claim and climbing back down into that mineshaft made Frank shiver. Maree must have felt it for she put down her darning and threw another piece of wood onto the fire. Then she leaned over and pulled the blanket tight around his shoulders.

'We don't want you catching a chill, Frank.'

'Don't fuss, woman,' he grumbled, but clutched the edges of the blanket together under his chin.

Maree picked up the socks and darning needle again and Frank returned to staring into the flames. He could feel the darkness beyond the circle of firelight. It was a malignant thing, prowling around in the trees, stalking him, waiting, and all he had to keep it at bay was the flickering flames of the campfire. He had never known such darkness before, had never known it existed, not the way he knew it now. As the gravel poured into the mineshaft, burying him behind the piece of shoring and blocking out the light, he had discovered the darkness for the first time in his life. It had reached out and touched him, wrapping him in its cloying cloak so that the world beyond the darkness had ceased to exist.

He shivered again and leaned forward to grab another piece of wood and throw it on the fire.

'Leave some wood to cook breakfast with in the morning, Frank.'

He grunted an acknowledgement and settled back onto the log. Beside him, Maree placed the socks and darning equipment back into her sewing kit and stood up.

'That's me done. I'm off to bed. You coming?'

He shook his head. 'I just want to sit up a bit longer and enjoy the evening air. You go on, love. I won't be long.'

Maree nodded and went to their tent. He watched her untie the flap and stoop inside, then turned back to the flames. A few minutes later he heard the creak of the ropes beneath their cot as Maree settled herself into it.

Frank sat for a long time with only the dancing flames of the campfire for company. He ignored Maree's warning and fed another stick of wood onto the fire, then another. It was Betty's job to ensure a good supply of firewood, and the girl had a pile a foot high stacked beside Frank's log seat. As soon as the fire began to ebb, he would feed it again, until his hand reached for a piece of wood and there was no more to be had.

He dropped the blanket from his shoulders and stood up, searching the camp for more fuel, but Maree and Annie kept the place swept clean. There wasn't so much as a gum leaf left around the fire. Frank lifted his head and looked at the surrounding bushland.

A lantern hung from the end of the ridge pole of their tent and he went to it. As he took it down, he could hear Maree's soft snores from inside. He took the lantern back to the fire and used a burning twig to light the wick, adjusting it so that it burned at its brightest. With his shield of light about him, he turned and walked into the night.

The immediate surrounds of the camp had been picked clean of firewood, but Frank knew that more could be found among a dense grove of trees further up the gully. He made his way there, lantern held high. Somewhere in the distance he could hear men laughing. Probably a group of late drinkers at one of the sly grog shops that dotted the diggings.

He entered the grove and hooked the lantern to a convenient branch, then began picking up sticks, loading them into the crook of his elbow and always staying within the circle of yellow light. Once he had a good load, he went back and took up the lantern, but as he moved it, the flame inside the glass began to gutter and dim.

'No. No. No.' Frank dropped his load of wood and gave the lantern a gentle shake. The noise told him the oil reservoir was almost dry. A cold sweat broke out on his face and he looked about frantically. He needed light, any light. To his right, beyond the trunks of the trees, he could see the glow of a lantern through the wall of a tent. Frank started towards it and almost made it to the edge of the grove when the lantern in his hand went out.

The darkness rushed in and he was back in the mine with the gravel crushing down on him. He ran as fast as he could towards the distant light, and the darkness was a savage beast, chasing him. He could hear men's voices at the tent as he reached it and flung the flap open to allow the light to flood outside. He had beaten the beast. He was safe, for now.

The tent was larger than those normally used for shelter by the diggers. This one was tall enough to stand in and covered four times the ground area. A bar of rough-sawn timber had been built along the back wall where a publican shuffled back and forth, filling the glasses of five men who were leaning against the near side. Another man lay prone across the threshold, out cold.

One of the drinkers turned and saw Frank at the entrance. 'Don't mind Templeton,' he said. 'Never could hold his liquor. Just step over him and come and have a drink.' He moved sideways, pushing his fellow drinkers along to make room at the bar for Frank.

Frank stepped over the unconscious Templeton and moved into the space provided. The barman, a squat man with slicked down, greasy hair, placed a glass in front of him.

'House special is rum at tuppence a glass,' the barman said. 'Sixpence if you want whisky.'

Frank reached into his pocket and felt the few coins there, not having to look at them to count their worth.

'Rum will be fine,' he told the barman and slipped a coin onto the bar.

The barman reached under the bar and produced an earthenware jug, pulled the stopper and filled Frank's glass. He stared at it, his hands flat on the bar. He was conscious of the other men watching him, but he ignored them. The contents of the glass settled and the liquid was perfectly still, refracting the lantern light into a tiny rainbow that washed across the back of his left hand.

Somewhere in the distance a dog barked, drawing his mind outside to where the darkness waited. He took up the glass and watched the liquid slosh about.

'Please, forgive me,' he said under his breath and threw the contents of the glass into his mouth.

Toby sat beside Paddy at the campfire and surveyed the glum faces sitting across from him. Maree was propped against Frank's shoulder, one arm draped across his lap, the other clutching her woollen shawl closed against the night chill. Betty prodded at the fire with a stick and, as usual, Annie sat beside Toby on another log. Even though two feet of distance separated them, he imagined he could feel the heat of her body.

'It's going to take some time to sink that shaft down to where the pay dirt is,' Frank pointed out. 'Judging by the first shaft we'll have to dig to about thirty feet before we start getting any sort of return.'

'What about trying somewhere else?' Maree offered. 'The butcher's wife told me they're taking good-sized nuggets right off the ground over on Pennyweight Hill.' She instantly regretted the remark. She'd been on the diggings long enough to know that rumours far outnumbered the amount of gold and put her hand up in front of her face to silence any rebuke.

'We need to bring in a few extra quid and still be able to work the claim,' Frank said. 'I can always throw up a sign and do a bit o' work fixing wheels and such. God knows, the roads and tracks around here will give me plenty of work. Toby and Paddy will still be able to do some digging. Now the girls are washing dirt it will free me up to do something else.' He used the stem of his pipe to point at each of them in turn as he spoke.

'Sounds like a good start,' Toby nodded, wishing he had some sort of trade to offer their small syndicate.

'Toby, are there lots of possums around here?' Maree asked. 'In the bush I mean.'

'Plenty. Why?'

'There were some native women over near the Melbourne road yesterday selling possum-skin rugs. The diggers were buying them up for five pounds apiece. With the cold nights here, everyone is trying to get a warm night's sleep. I hate to cut those women out of their meagre earnings, but the girls and I could sew together some rugs of our own and sell them – if we could get the possum skins, that is.'

Toby's face broke into a broad smile. 'Paddy and me can bring in plenty of possums. We'll go out on a Sunday when we aren't allowed to dig. After work tomorrow, I'll get started on some curing racks. They can smell a bit while they're drying, so it's probably best if we build 'em up near the horse yard. You can sew them together as they're ready. We should do all right. I've heard plenty of complaints about the cold nights.'

Now that a plan of action had been decided on, everyone's mood brightened a little. Toby was too excited to sleep. He sat by the fire long after the others had gone to bed and stared into the flames, adding a stick every now and then to prevent it from dying down and to chase away the chill he could feel building on the wind.

He thought about the coming Sunday. It would be great to saddle Moonlight and head off into the countryside, to escape the diggings for a while. He missed the bush. He missed the wild country where a man could be miles and miles from anyone. He missed working with cattle and sheep and building things for the future, like chook pens and vegetable gardens. As he sat staring into the flames, he realised that he was homesick.

Was Henry Pelham looking after the home he had taken from them?

Toby felt his anger building and quickly tried to think of something else. He looked to the Hocking tent and realised that he and Paddy had been lucky to join up with such a loving family. Maree reminded him so much of his own mother, and he wondered at the friendship that might have developed had the two women had the chance to meet. The Englishwoman was certainly a caring soul. She mothered Paddy to the point where he could see his brother finding the attention annoying.

Frank had developed a soft spot for Paddy as well. Last Sunday the pair had spent three hours with Frank's tools, shaping a piece of red gum into a new handle for the spade rather than waste money buying a new one. Toby could remember his own father taking the time to teach him new skills, and he was glad that Paddy could still experience something like that. He didn't suppose that anyone could ever take the place of their father. Sean O'Rourke had been a big man, larger than life in Toby's eyes, where Frank was tall, but slender with it and more mild-mannered. He wasn't trying to be a father to him and Paddy, he was just being the father he had always been and including them as well. Frank was a good man, but something had changed in him since the cave in.

It had taken a week to repair the damage to the shoring in the mineshaft. Frank was reluctant to go back down the hole that had nearly claimed his life, so Toby and Paddy had completed the work themselves. It had been a wasted effort. Four days after digging resumed, they had bottomed out on shale. The claim had become what the diggers referred to as a shicer, a worthless pit. They had salvaged what timber they could and started working the shepherd claim. He knew Frank kept a hip flask with him now. Whenever they rotated duties in the shaft, Toby often caught the biting smell of liquor. He had never known the man to take a drink before and Frank certainly kept his drinking out of sight of the rest of his family.

A rustling noise sounded behind him and he turned to see Annie slipping between the flies of the tent. She saw that Toby had noticed her and held a finger to her lips to quiet any greeting. She had pulled on that old woollen jumper she often wore on chilly mornings. Crossing to the fire, she took Toby's hand and led him across the camp to where the second wagonette sat a little distance away. They climbed onto the seat and Toby was very aware of her body pressed against his side.

'I couldn't sleep,' she whispered, her lips close to his ear. 'I thought we could talk up here.'

Toby inclined his head to respond. 'What do you want to talk about?'

'Oh, I don't know. Why are you sitting up so late? You usually go to bed with the chooks.'

'I was thinking,' Toby whispered.

'About what?' Her breath was warm against his cheek and Toby struggled to keep his mind on topic.

'About Frank.'

'Papa?' There was a hint of surprise in her voice. 'But why? I had hoped you might have been thinking about—well, someone else.'

'He seems a little out of sorts since the mine collapse, Annie.'

'He nearly died, Toby. I should think that would be enough to shake anyone.'

'Do you know he can't go down the mineshaft without taking a drink?'

'He's been drinking?' She blurted it out so loudly that Toby held a finger to his own lips.

'I think he's afraid, afraid of the mineshaft and the dark, but he won't admit it.'

Annie didn't answer, and when Toby looked at her there were tears in her eyes. She saw him looking and shook her head sadly.

'Papa used to have trouble with the drink. It looks as if those troubles have come back.'

'I never would've thought. He seems such a dependable bloke.'

'Papa is a wonderful man,' she shot back. 'He provides for us quite well.'

'Yes,' Toby agreed.

'It was when Grandpapa died,' Annie said, and Toby sensed her need to explain.

'What happened?'

'Papa was Grandpapa's apprentice. He was taken on when he was just fourteen and he and Grandpapa were hardly ever apart. About five years ago they were in the yard outside the carriage works in Hastings when a stack of timber fell and startled some horses harnessed to a loaded wagon. Grandpapa went to settle the horses, but they bolted and the wheels ran right over him. They say he didn't suffer, that he died instantly. Papa saw the whole thing.'

'It must have been terrible,' Toby said.

'Papa wasn't much for liquor before that, but he seemed to find some sort of peace in the bottle. It got worse and worse. One day, he and Mama had a terrible argument over it, yelling and screaming at each other. That was the same night Tom brought up his idea of us all coming out to the colonies.'

'Your brother?'

'Yes. He was my rock back when Papa was at his worst. Coming here had been a dream of his for some time, but that was the first he told Mama and Papa about it. Mama thought it a terrible idea, but Papa was keen from the outset. I think he saw it as an opportunity to escape the bad memories. He had to go to the carriage works every day and walk right over the spot where his father was killed. He gave up his drinking and started saving all the money he could. He and Tom. When

Mama saw the change that had come over him, she relented as well.'

'I'm glad you came,' Toby said. He was about to add something else, but a cough sounded from behind them. Maree stood by the opening of her tent, holding the flap wide. She locked eyes with Annie and inclined her head towards the tent.

'I've enjoyed talking with you, Toby. Please don't tell Mama about the drinking.'

Maree coughed again, louder this time, and Annie scampered down off the wagonette and hurried towards the tent.

Only a few lights showed from the Djarriba settlement. At the far end of the street three saddled horses were tied to a rail outside the largest building. From his place of concealment on the edge of town, Chilbi could hear men laughing and talking loudly, although the street appeared deserted.

'We'll leave the horses here,' Warrigal said. He had on a dark jacket, taken from one of the travellers they had stopped, and had combed out his hair and beard.

The Jannjirra warriors pulled their war clubs, but Warrigal held up a hand. 'No killing tonight. I'm going down to that pub at the end of the street for a few quiet drinks. I can't be seen with you. People will know who I am if I'm seen with a group of blacks. You boys stay out of sight. Have a bit of a forage around the backs of the houses and buildings. Maybe you can lay your hands on a chicken or two.' He slipped his revolver into his belt and adjusted the jacket to cover it. 'If you hear any trouble, we'll meet back here, grab our horses and head back to camp.'

Chilbi watched Warrigal step out of the bushes and head down the middle of the street, then he turned to his brothers.

'Scout behind the buildings on this side of the settlement. I will go to the far side.'

He waited until they slipped into the shadows and then checked the street. Except for Warrigal walking to the far end, it was empty, so he crossed over as quick as a wraith and rounded the end building, the first of a string of cottages.

Most of the buildings had yards behind them, fenced with pieces of bush timber, built to keep animals and fowls in rather than people out. At the first yard, he paused and sniffed the air, detecting a musty odour. He waited in the shadows, searching with his eyes until he spotted the dog lying on the back step, a dark lump silhouetted against the door. Carefully, he backed away from the fence and moved on.

A crude wooden structure stood in the far corner of the next yard. Chilbi placed his eye to a gap in the wall, but it was too dark to see what the pen contained, so he stood in the shadows for a long time, watching the back of the building and searching for another dog that might raise the alarm. Satisfied that nothing and no one could see him, he crossed to the door of the pen. It was held shut by a loop of rope thrown over a piece of wood and he carefully lifted it and swung the door open. Enough light flooded in to let him see the nesting boxes at the far end where a pair of fat ducks were huddled together. In three quick strides he was at the boxes and grabbed the first duck. Before the bird knew what was happening, he twisted its head, snapping the neck. The other duck awoke and let out a single squawk before Chilbi grabbed it and snapped its neck too.

The noise the duck made was enough to rouse the dog on the back step of the neighbouring cottage. It let out a single bark and came to the corner of its yard, where it growled in the darkness. Chilbi stood motionless with the carcass of a duck in each hand and listened to the dog as it patrolled up and down the fence line. After a while, the dog gave up, and he heard it padding across the yard back to the step.

Moving as slowly as possible, he left the pen and climbed over the fence. The next yard had some clothes hanging on a line near the back door. There was a box-like container suspended from a pole near the door. Chilbi recognised it as a meat safe the Djarriba used to store their kills. For a moment he considered checking it for food, but the safe was so close to the back door of the cottage, he decided not to risk it.

The next building wasn't a dwelling. There were wheels from Djarriba vehicles leaning against a post. Near the wall was a bench, littered with tools. Chilbi moved on and made to round a large gum tree when someone stepped from behind it. He dropped the ducks and prepared to defend himself with bare hands.

The man looked up as he noticed Chilbi and took an involuntary step back. 'Who are you?'

The startled words weren't those of the Djarriba. They weren't quite Jannjirra either, but they were close enough that Chilbi understood.

'Just a hunter,' Chilbi replied in his own tongue.

The man stepped closer, swaying a little on his feet. He had dark skin, a broad nose and wore only a pair of Djarriba trousers. There was a trickle of blood at the corner of his mouth and across his chest were three raised welts, the initiation scars of a warrior. He had a bottle clutched in his hand that he used to point at the ducks at Chilbi's feet. 'Your hunt has been fruitful. I see you have two fat Djarriba ducks.' The man's breath carried the unmistakable stench of whisky, a drink that Warrigal sometimes enjoyed, and Chilbi found repugnant.

'Very successful, but I feel there is more the Djarriba can provide for my needs.'

'You speak the language of my father's people. I haven't heard it spoken for years. Where are you from?'

Chilbi looked to the stars to orient himself and pointed into the north-east. 'My country is in the mountains. Long way that way. My people are the Jannjirra.'

'The Jannjirra? I know of your people. My tribe, the Wad-dirawong, once traded for Jannjirra ochre for the ceremonies. I am Madagurrie. What is your name?'

'I am Chilbi.'

'Come, Chilbi. My family is camped near the river.' He ges-tured vaguely over his shoulder. 'If the Djarriba find us here, they will punish us. Especially since you have two of their ducks. I only came out to beg a bottle from the pub man. Some white fellas found me before I got out of there and sent me away with a beating.' He used a thumb to wipe at the blood in the corner of his mouth. 'They never got my bottle though.'

'You are a warrior of your people. You wear the scars of the initiated. Why did you not kill the Djarriba?'

'Keep your voice down.' Madagurrie glanced furtively at the alley between the buildings. 'Pick up your ducks and fol-low me.'

Chilbi retrieved his ducks and followed Madagurrie into the darkness, heading away from the little town. They crossed a grassy field and climbed through a fence. After a few minutes he could make out the glowing embers of a campfire in a grove of willows. There were about twenty people camped in the grove. They had built no gunyahs, dwellings of sticks and leaves, but instead sheltered themselves with blankets and scraps of canvas, the cast-offs of Djarriba society.

Madagurrie crossed to the fire and threw a couple of branches onto the coals. 'Come, Chilbi. Sit with me.'

Chilbi moved closer to the fire, but stumbled on a discarded bottle in the grass and had to be nimble to remain on his feet. His foot struck a sleeping form and an old woman sat up to stare at him.

'Forgive me, old mother.'

He went to step over the lubra's legs as the branches flared on the fire and lit her face. Chilbi drew in a sharp breath of fear as he saw the pustules on her skin. He jumped back, looking to

Madagurrie to see if he recognised what it was, but the warrior simply poked a stick at the coals and took a swig from his bottle, seemingly oblivious to this evil in his camp.

'The Djarriba sickness! The woman has it. They have sent the evil magic to destroy your people.'

Madagurrie looked up from the fire. 'The sickness comes and goes. Some recover and some die, but once it has touched you, it cannot come for you again. That woman is my aunt. She is the last of the elders, but I fear that she will succumb to the evil.'

'The Djarriba have sent it to destroy your people. They will take your country.'

Madagurrie chuckled. 'The Djarriba took my country a long time ago. When I was a young fella they only occupied a little piece of it. As I grew, they took more and more, spreading across the land.'

'What of the sacred grounds and ancestral places?' Chilbi looked at Madagurrie, his face aghast that such a tragedy could befall a noble people such as the Waddirrawong. To have lost their ancient lands, the spiritual home of their ancestors was a fate worse than death itself.

'They are denied us.' Madagurrie shook his head. 'Some we try to visit to perform the rituals, but the Djarriba run their animals there now. They chase us away with guns.' He raised the bottle in his hand and took a long pull. 'Now all we have is their poison.'

'But what of the sickness?' Chilbi gestured at the old lubra. 'Did they not send their magic first? Did they not use it to wipe out your people as they did the Jannjirra?'

The warrior had his eyes closed and seemed to have trouble sitting up straight, swaying back and using one arm to support himself. Chilbi thought him lost to the mists of the liquor, but his eyes opened and he spoke. 'The Djarriba have no magic beyond what they can touch. The sickness travels with them, they cannot send it ahead. If you have survived it, it cannot come for you again.' He lost his battle and fell backwards into the grass.

'Madagurrie? Madagurrie?' Chilbi prodded the warrior with his toe, but there was no response. He had seen the same thing happen to Warrigal after drinking from the Djarriba bottles and knew that there would be no more talk from Madagurrie that evening.

Chilbi climbed to his feet and looked about the campsite, at the remains of a once proud people. The warriors and hunters, the mothers and children had been reduced to these few poor wretches, huddled in blankets or sleeping drunk among the trees. He felt the anger building and turned his back on the campfire. Somewhere in the distance a dog barked and he thought about his brothers, the last of his people, sneaking about and taking their food from the Djarriba, forced to forage for it in the land of strangers instead of hunting in the country of their ancestors. He picked up the two ducks and made to head back to the settlement, but the old woman coughed and cried out, so that he paused at the edge of the firelight. Turning, Chilbi went to the prostrate form, shivering under her blanket. The lubra had returned to her tormented dreams and did not notice when Chilbi lifted the blanket and placed both ducks beside her.

'These will fill your belly and those of your family, old mother. Rest well until you go to your ancestors.'

He stood and walked off into the night.

That Sunday morning, while the night mists hung in the gullies, Toby and Paddy carried their saddles and tack up to the small horse yard on the hilltop. Slung on their backs were the muskets, freshly cleaned and oiled after an evening's preparation, and each of them carried a small leather satchel of shot and cartridges.

Moonlight whinnied softly when he saw Toby approaching out of the pre-dawn gloom. The animal enjoyed getting out of the yard and he was waiting at the slip rail as Toby and Paddy deposited their gear on one of the rails.

Patch pressed up to the rail and lowered his head to sniff at Paddy's pockets, correctly identifying which one contained the lump of sugar the boy had pressed together using a little water and the dregs from the bottom of the sugar bag. Paddy lifted the lump from his pocket and offered it to the pony. Then they set about the task of saddling the horses.

Toby led them north and they splashed across the ford at the Yarrowee River and on into Hit or Miss Gully, a narrow defile that eventually climbed into the heights of the Black Hills ranges. They continued into the north, passing the occasional prospector's camp and mining claim until, after several miles, all traces of civilisation were behind them and the bush closed in, dark green and grey, untouched by the hand of man.

It was almost dark when they returned to camp with twenty possums strung over the pommels of their saddles. Frank and his family had been busy while they were gone. A small spoked wheel from some discarded barrow hung from a pole above the camp. Under the wheel, a sign, painted in blue on a rough wooden slab read:

Hocking & O'Rourke
Wainwrights & Furriers
All Types of Wheel Repairs
Possum-skin Rugs

'As soon as the sign went up, some chap came wandering up and asked if Papa could fix a spoke on his gig,' Annie said. 'He took Betty along with him to keep her out of our hair for a while.'

'It looks as if we're in business,' Maree added. 'I've already had several men up here asking about the rugs. I told them to come back in a few days and we'd be able to fix them up.'

Toby and Paddy sat on a log by the fire and began skinning the possums. Maree and Annie busied themselves with salting the fresh hides as they came off the carcasses. Every so often Maree would stop what she was doing and look down the path, remarking Frank's absence and twisting her apron.

Darkness fell and they were just finishing the skinning by firelight when Frank wandered back into camp. A very sombre-looking Betty plodded along a few yards behind her father. Frank had his bag of tools in one hand and a bottle in the other. He dumped the tool bag by their tent and walked over to the pile of possum skins.

'You boysh were busy,' he slurred.

'Got enough for a couple of rugs and a good start on a third,' Toby said.

Frank nodded, a slow, forward motion of his head that almost brought his chin to his chest. He turned his attention to Maree. 'And you've been cooking a lovely meal, my raven-haired beauty. I shwear I could smell my dinner all the way down at the creek.'

Maree rounded on him like a featherweight boxer on an opponent. She had a large metal ladle in her hand that she waved under her husband's nose.

'Francis Hocking! You've been drinking. I thought we'd left this weakness for the bottle back in England.'

Toby thought she was going to lay the ladle across Frank's head. Instead, with what appeared to be a great effort of will, she pulled herself together, wiped the ladle on her apron and calmly placed it on a cutting board beside the cooking fire. She stepped up to Frank, took the brandy bottle from his hand and tipped the last of its contents onto the ground.

Frank watched the golden liquid drain into the earth, a look of remorse on his face. He opened his mouth to protest, but the stony look from his wife quelled any complaint forming in his brandy-soaked mind. He let Maree walk him towards their tent.

'Come on, Frank. You can sleep it off,' she said, steering him through the flap. 'I'll save some supper for you to have later.'

Some mumblings came from inside the tent and then a few moments later Maree appeared and went back to the cooking pot. The sound of snoring told everyone that Frank had accepted his wife's offer.

Betty stood quietly at the edge of the firelight.

'I'm sorry, Mama,' she blurted. 'I couldn't stop Papa. The man with the gig wanted him to have a drink with him. I told him we should be getting back, but he stayed for another and another. When we finally left, he went to one of those grog shops and bought the bottle with the money the man gave him for fixing the wheel.' Betty burst into tears. 'It's not my fault, Mama.'

Maree placed the spoon down and walked calmly to her daughter, picking her up as if she were a much smaller child. 'It's all right, my little one.' She stroked the back of Betty's head as she carried her into the firelight.

Watching, Toby had a feeling this scene had been played out in the Hocking household a few times before. He glanced at Annie, surprised to find her staring at him, her brow creased with concern. As soon as their eyes met, she stood up and spoke.

'I suppose the horses will need a little attention after a long day. Did they have enough water, Toby?'

'I should check. We did ride pretty far today.' He stood and went to fetch the large canvas water bag from the end of the ridge pole, but Annie beat him to it. She lifted it down and turned towards the yard.

'I'll give you a hand,' she said, walking into the night.

Toby followed her up to the horse yard. Annie seemed in a hurry to escape the camp. Her skirts swished about her legs as she tackled the slope in long strides. Halfway up the path she swapped the heavy water bag to her other hand, but her pace never slowed. She reached the rails and pulled the stopper from the water bag before Toby caught up, pouring the contents into the trough, which still brimmed with water. Toby let her empty the water bag, knowing she just wanted to be away from the emotion in the camp.

Moonlight wandered out of the darkness and pressed up to the rail to have his muzzle stroked. When Annie had finished topping up the trough, she replaced the stopper, hung the water bag over a post, then moved beside Toby to pat Moonlight's neck.

'He's a fine horse,' she said absently.

'Yes, he is,' Toby murmured.

'You ride well. You look good together.'

'We've had a bit of practice.' Toby waited for her to say something else. The silence drew on as they stood in the darkness patting the horse.

'He can't help it, you know.'

'Your pa?'

'Mama says it's a kind of sickness. She says that once a soul gets taken with the bottle it's a sickness that stays with them for the rest of their days – even if they never touch another drop of the stuff, the sickness is always there, waiting for a moment of weakness.' She spoke the words in a rapid, well-rehearsed stream.

Toby had seen his fair share of drunks at the hotel in Bunyong Creek and at various sly grog shops dotting the diggings. He did not know the words to comfort her. His own father had not been much of a drinker except for the odd nobbler on special occasions. He couldn't understand the pain and torment of having a family member blighted by the bottle. Annie took his silence for something else.

'Please, don't hate him, Toby.'

'I don't hate him,' he blurted. 'It was just a shock to see him in such a state.'

'You don't have to leave. Papa will stop now. He stopped before for such a long time, long enough for him and Mama to save the money to come to Australia. He never touched a drop for two years. Not on the ship, and not in the whole time we were in Melbourne and the journey out here.' She began to cry and dropped her hands to the rail. She didn't hang her head or hide her face, but stood holding the rail, staring off into the darkness as the tears rolled down her cheeks.

Toby wanted to hold her to him and comfort her, tell her that everything would be fine. Instead, he took her hand in his and gave it a gentle squeeze. Her skin felt warm and smooth. 'I'm not going to leave,' he said.

'Please don't,' she whispered. 'We need you and Paddy. We can't do this on our own. Mama and Betty need you, so does Papa—' Her voice trailed off, as she considered her next words.

'I need you,' she said suddenly. 'I don't ever want you to leave.' She squeezed his hand and Toby felt his pulse quicken.

No other words were spoken. They stood at the rail looking into the dark of night, content just to be near each other. Their hands still touched, neither wanting to let the moment end by breaking that one small piece of intimate contact. It wasn't until a rustling noise sounded on the path and Betty emerged from the gloom that the spell broke.

'Mama says you should both come back now. She's dishing up supper.'

A nnie had a large pot of stew bubbling on the fire when the camp assembled for lunch. Maree and Betty were the first to arrive, strolling up from the creek where they had been washing dirt through the cradle. The women chatted idly for a few minutes until the men turned up and took their places around the fire. Annie ladled stew into bowls and handed them around. She scowled at her father as he took the choice piece of bread – the one she had been saving for Toby.

'The pick is worn blunt again,' Frank said. 'It's rounded too much to fix with a file. We still have the other one, but we'll need to get Blacky Pete to put a point back on this one so we can start tomorrow with one sharp pick,' he added, using his boot to kick the pick he had carried up from the claim.

'I'll take it over,' Annie said, before anyone else could offer. 'I've got dinner almost ready to go into the pot, so I've a little time on my hands this afternoon. It'll be a good chance to stretch my legs.'

Frank glanced up from his plate. Annie looked at him expectantly. Depending on his mood, the decision could swing either way.

'All right,' Frank said.

After the others wandered back to work, Annie spent a little time cleaning up, then went to her tent. She combed out and retied her hair into a tight bun then pulled on a pair of white cotton socks and a stout pair of shoes inherited from her mother. Finally, she put on a fresh, clean bonnet and tied it neatly under her chin, before checking her image in a mirror hanging from the ridge pole.

'Presentable, Miss Hocking,' she smiled at her reflection. 'Presentable.'

Blacky Pete had his blacksmith shop in a gully behind the hill on which they camped. Annie walked up past the horse yard and tossed a greeting to Moonlight and Patch then descended the narrow path into the gully. She revelled in the sunshine on her back and marvelled at a flock of bright-green parakeets that flitted and squawked in the branches over her head.

At the bottom of the gully the bushland gave way to the unrelenting push of humanity. This gully was identical to the one they were camped in. The trail picked its way through a maze of tents and other dwellings.

Blacky Pete had set up his shop on the only piece of flat ground for five miles in any direction. His premises consisted of a large tent with the sides rolled up to dissipate the heat from the forge. Beside the forge, a huge iron anvil sat on a tree stump. Blacky Pete stood at the anvil hammering a point onto the glowing end of a pick. He wore a large leather apron over canvas trousers which had been scorched and holed a thousand times by hot sparks. Every few moments he used a neckerchief to mop the perspiration beading on his forehead.

A line of men talked quietly among themselves as they waited for the smithy's service, but when Annie joined the back of the queue the conversation died away and every head turned to look at her. The hammering stopped and a deep voice boomed, 'Good day, Miss Hocking.'

'Hello, sir,' Annie called to Blacky Pete.

'Where's your pa?'

'Oh, he's at the claim. I had a little free time so I came down here myself with this pick for sharpening.' *And you won't be sharing a nobbler of rum with him today*, Annie thought.

Blacky Pete went back to his work and Annie waited patiently in the shortening queue, content to watch the sparks fly from the forge.

'Hello, Flower.' A red-bearded miner joined the queue behind her. 'Don't often see a piece of fluff like you hangin' round the blacksmith shop.' Before Annie realised what he was about to do, the miner leaned close and sniffed her hair.

'That's enough, Simpson.' Blacky Pete rounded the anvil, the hammer cocked over his shoulder. 'I'll not have a lady treated like that. Not on my premises, or anywhere else.' He pointed the hammer at Simpson's head. 'I don't want your business here, you can clear out,' he said, pointing off up the gully with the hammer. 'Go on. Piss off.' He looked to Annie and added quickly, 'Beggin' your pardon, miss.'

The digger looked as if he were about to argue with the blacksmith, but several men stepped up beside Blacky Pete, showing where their allegiance would lie if trouble developed. Simpson cursed loudly and stormed off through the trees, a broken windlass handle in hand.

'I don't need your bloody services,' he shouted over his shoulder.

'Sorry about that, miss,' Blacky Pete said. He turned to the three men ahead of Annie in the queue. 'Thank you for the support, gents. You don't mind if Miss Hocking jumps to the front of the line, do you? I'm sure she is looking forward to getting back to her camp after such an awful display.'

The diggers nodded their agreement and stepped aside to let Annie move under the canvas.

With the resharpened pick in her hand, she wandered back up the hillside, the incident with the red-bearded miner all but forgotten. Her thoughts turned to preparing dinner and the time she would spend with Toby tonight as they sat together on the seat of the wagonette, their usual evening routine.

'I think I shall kiss him tonight,' she told the sky as she climbed the slope. 'I've waited and hoped that he would kiss me, but he's such a dunderhead. I think Papa has had one of his talks with him and scared him a little.'

Annie turned at a noise on the path behind her. Simpson was twenty paces away. He stopped as he realised his presence was known.

'Hello, Flower. I've come to finish what we started down at Blacky Pete's. Only this time there ain't no one to disturb us.' He advanced up the hill, leering wickedly.

Simpson closed the ground between them and Annie glanced about desperately. This side of the hill was as far as she could possibly be from any of the tents in this part of the diggings. Even if someone heard her scream, it would take them minutes to reach her. She adjusted her grip on the handle of the pick and widened her stance. Simpson saw her change in posture as she prepared to meet his advance and gave a little chuckle that made Annie's blood run cold.

'Get back!' she spat at him and raised the pick.

'Come, Flower. Be a good girl.' He glanced at the pick and then back at Annie's face, still grinning wickedly.

'Get back, or I'll have your head off.'

'A delicate little thing like you? I don't think so, Flower.'

Simpson took another step and Annie swung the pick as hard as she could. Even though he was ready for it, the speed of the swing surprised the miner. He managed to get a hand up and caught the handle in mid-flight, but the freshly sharpened point opened the sleeve of his shirt and went deep into his bicep.

'You little bitch!' He twisted the handle and Annie was powerless to resist. It came out of her hands and Simpson tossed the pick into the bushes. He took one glance at his bleeding arm, at the blood dripping from his elbow and closed the gap between them.

Annie screamed as loudly as she could and Simpson clasped a huge, dirty hand over her mouth as he grabbed her, stifling the scream to a muffled whimper. Simpson spun her about, pulling her back hard against his chest. The man's grip was like iron, holding her fast despite her frantic struggles. The hand smelled of dirt and tobacco. A mass of red whiskers pushed into the side of her face and he whispered in her ear.

'Don't struggle, Flower. We'll have a grand ol' time of it, you an' me.' He used his teeth to pull the bonnet from her head and her hair fell free. Then he placed his face into the raven strands and drew a deep breath. The arm that held her about the waist shot up to her neck. A finger hooked into the neck of her blouse and yanked down, ripping the garment to the waist.

Annie increased her struggles and kicked backwards with her legs, trying to deliver a telling blow. The miner was too quick and locked her legs between his own. They stood on the hillside, joined together like two performers in some brutal dance.

Again the hand shot to her throat and this time the cotton shift she wore beneath the blouse tore down to her navel. She felt a rough, callused hand grasp her exposed breast and was helpless in the big man's grasp as he rolled her nipple roughly between his fingers.

'Lovely little titties,' his voice rasped in her ear, husky with the force of his lust. 'Let's take a look at them.' Annie felt the pressure on her head and chest relax and she was spun about to stand facing the bearded man. He took a twist of her hair about his right hand to keep her restrained, but now her mouth was free and she filled her lungs and screamed as loudly as she could.

Simpson lifted his gaze from her breasts and scowled at the noise. He slapped her hard across the side of her face, snapping her head back.

Dazed by the blow, she hung suspended by her hair. Simpson raised his arm and hit her again with more force than before. Annie's vision starred and she felt her legs start to go from under her. Simpson let her fall to the ground and loosened his trousers. Dropping to his knees beside Annie he pulled her skirts up.

'Can't afford to have you off work with an infection, lad.' Toby held his right thumb firmly in his left fist, applying pressure to a cut from a sharp piece of shale.

'Go and have Annie treat the cut,' Frank added.

He nodded at Frank then picked his way through the mullock heaps and climbed the hill towards the camp. As he neared their tents he noticed the fire had died away to white ash. Annie was nowhere to be seen. Then he remembered she had gone to Blacky Pete's with the blunt pick.

He undid the flap to Frank and Maree's tent, removed the small wooden box of medical supplies and carried it to the tailboard of the wagonette. He found the bottle of iodine solution and poured some onto a clean rag. The biting sting caused him to hiss sharply and he looked about quickly to see if Annie had returned and witnessed this childish display. Replacing the bottle in the box, he used a strip of iodine-soaked rag to bind the cut. He pulled the knot tight using his teeth and was about to return the box to Frank and Maree's tent when he heard Annie scream.

The vagaries of distance masked the direction, but Toby knew Annie would have crossed the hill and gone down past the horse yard on her way to Blacky Pete's. He dropped the medical box back onto the tail-board and started up the hill. As he passed his tent Toby thought of the muskets lying under the cots, but they were unloaded and useless. Thinking fast, he ran to the wagonette and pulled the stock whip from under the seat.

Moonlight and Patch trotted nervously about the yard as he ran past and onto the head of the track that led down to Blacky Pete's.

He heard Annie scream again. This time the soul-wrenching sound was close, past a small spur of rock that hung above the track. Toby rounded the rock and came to a stop, breathing hard.

A large, red-bearded man knelt between Annie's exposed legs. He had her skirts lifted as he positioned himself, so engrossed in his actions that he failed to notice Toby.

Toby let the coils of the whip drop to his side, flung his arm back and flicked the handle past his ear. The tail of the whip shot out in a blur of speed that whistled shrilly as it parted the air. Despite being a little out of practice – he was once able to clip individual leaves from a tree while on horseback – the broad back of this man kneeling over his precious Annie posed no problem to his aim. The end of the whip flicked onto the miner's back with a sound like a gunshot. The shirt parted as if slashed by a razor and opened the skin beneath.

The miner screamed and arched his back with the agony of the whip's kiss. He spun from between Annie's legs and came to his feet in the same movement, a bone-handled knife in his hand.

'You little bastard,' he spat at Toby. 'I'll kill you for that.' He took a step forward before he realised his trousers were still around his ankles. As he stooped to hitch them up, Toby flicked the whip again. This time the flayed leather thong at the end of the whip whispered in between the miner's hands as he struggled with his trousers. The foreskin of the miner's penis took the full force of the strike. There was a moment of silence except for the echo of the whip crack as it died in the distance. Then the miner let fly a blood-curdling scream and fell to his knees. He dropped the knife, cupped his manhood with both hands and rolled onto his side, writhing in agony.

Now the miner's hairy buttocks were exposed to Toby and he sent the whip singing out once more. The miner's continuous scream rose in pitch as the whip raised a large red weal across his bare backside. He screamed for several breaths then looked up at Toby to see him re-coiling the whip for another strike.

'Please! No more!' Mud-streaked tears rolled down his whiskered cheeks.

'Run,' Toby said, the venom in his voice as harsh as the lash of the whip. 'Run, before I take your balls off.'

The miner struggled to his feet. With one hand still pressed against his damaged manhood and the other holding his trousers up, he started off down the hill, picking up speed with every pace.

Toby dropped the whip and ran to where Annie lay sprawled in the bushes. She had half pulled her skirts back down to cover her thighs, but her blouse and shift were torn beyond use and she struggled feebly to cover her breasts. Toby shrugged his shirt off, placing it over her shoulders and drawing it closed across her chest.

'Are you all right, Annie? Did he hurt you?'

Blood ran from the corner of her mouth and a bruise had begun to shade her right eye. 'No. You got here just in time,' she said between sobs and placed her head against his chest.

Toby held her tight as she cried. He stroked her hair and pulled twigs and leaves from the sable strands. It was several minutes before she had her crying under control. She lifted her head and looked up at Toby.

'My God! Do you know what he was going to do to me?' she whispered. The thought of it almost brought her back to tears and she fought bravely to control herself.

'It's over, Annie. He's gone. I sent him packing. Let's get you back to camp.' Toby stood and helped her to her feet, but her knees buckled and he swept her up in his arms. He carried her back to camp with her head on his shoulder. As they passed the horse yard she placed her lips against Toby's ear and kissed it softly.

'I love you, Toby O'Rourke,' she whispered.

Frank kicked things aside as he stormed about the camp. He clenched and unclenched his fists in quick succession then fronted Toby and took hold of him by the shirt.

'Are you sure you gave this piece of scum a good whipping, Toby? One he'll never forget in a hurry?'

'I damn near took his balls off, Frank.'

'You should have taken his bloody balls off,' Frank yelled and went back to pacing. 'Simpson, that's his name. Big red-bearded bastard. Wait till I see that piece of dung. I'll do more than take his balls off.'

'Frank. Your language. The girls.' Maree tried to restrain him.

'My language is the least of their problems,' he rounded on her. 'If they don't starve to death or catch some illness from the filth of this place, then some randy digger with a gleam in his eye will drag them off into the bush to have his way with them.'

Maree opened her hands, pleading. 'Annie's fine, Frank. Toby got there in time, thank the Lord. Please, let it be now. She doesn't need to be reminded of it every few minutes.'

Frank stopped and pointed a finger at his wife. He opened his mouth to say something but thought better of it. The finger curled back into his fist.

'Christ, I need a drink.' He dropped the fist to his side and strode out of the circle of firelight.

Toby got to his feet and went to go after him, but Maree stopped him with a hand on his arm.

'Let him go, Toby. He'll have a drink or two, or maybe more, but he'll be better to talk to tomorrow.'

Toby settled back onto the log that was his seat. 'I think we should make a rule, Maree.'

Maree was watching Frank's back as it disappeared into the darkness, a look of anguish on her face. 'What's that?

'You and the girls should not take any shortcuts that take you out of sight of regular folk on the diggings, especially down the back of this hill. It's just too far from any camps and the bush far too dense. An army could hide along that track.'

'I think that is a very good idea, Toby. We shall make it so.'

Frank came back into camp in the early hours of the morning, drunk and singing a bawdy song that woke Toby when he was only halfway up the gully. He heard a whispered exchange from Frank and Maree's tent, then all fell into silence.

Lying in his cot, Toby thought about the events of the day and their situation in general. Frank was turning to drink more often than not lately, and it was taking its toll on their finances. While they had been luckier than most in pulling good pay dirt from their claims, some months were pretty tight when it came to buying provisions and renewing the ever-important gold licence.

Something needs to change, he told himself as he lay staring up into the inky blackness above his head. *We certainly can't keep going like this.*

He closed his eyes and tried to clear his mind. A smile came across his face as he thought of those warm lips touching his ear and the words of endearment Annie had whispered to him as he carried her into camp. With the memory of that tender touch still filling his mind, Toby slept at last.

The white canvas of the tent was aglow with sunlight as dawn broke through the trees behind the camp. Paddy could hear something sizzling in the pan and the smell of frying bacon filled the air. He loved bacon for breakfast. It made such a change from the usual lamb chops, but today the aroma did little to rouse his appetite. He was usually hungry enough to beat his brother out to the cooking fire, but this morning a bone-weary ache had settled into his joints.

He heard Maree's voice from the campfire. 'Where's young Paddy this morning?'

'He was stirring when I got up,' answered Toby. 'I'll check on him.'

The tent flap opened and his brother appeared.

'Come on, lazybones. You gonna stay in bed all day?' Then the chiding expression on Toby's face changed to one of concern. 'You feeling crook, mate? You're as white as a sheet. It's not one of your headaches, is it?'

Paddy made to lift his head, but a spasm of shivers wracked his body and he fell back to the pillow, pulling the blankets tight about his neck.

Toby moved into the tent and placed the palm of his hand on Paddy's forehead. 'You've got a fever. Does it hurt anywhere else?'

Paddy extended a finger from beneath the blankets and pointed to his throat.

'Sore throat, hey? Got some aches and pains in the joints too, I suppose?'

Paddy nodded.

'What's the matter with him?' Maree stuck her head through the opening, a look of motherly concern on her face.

'Looks like he's got the flu,' Toby said.

'You poor darling.' She strode into the tent in a bustle of skirts, pushed Toby away and placed her hand on Paddy's forehead. Not satisfied with that, she pulled the blankets out of his grasp and felt about his throat and jawline with tender, probing fingers. Then she ordered Paddy to sit up in the bed and pulled his nightshirt up about his ears so she could examine his chest and back.

'No spots or blotches on his skin. It doesn't look like measles or mumps. I think your brother is right, Master O'Rourke. Well, we shall just have to take special care of you until you are well enough to go back to work,' she said with finality.

At midday Toby brought a pannikin of soup that Maree had made.

'How are you feeling?'

Paddy rocked the palm of his hand back and forth and took the pannikin.

'We'll be down to the shale shortly,' Toby said gloomily, and sat on the edge of his cot.

Paddy was well aware that once they had revealed the dark, slate-grey stone, the shaft had turned out a shicer, a claim that didn't pay.

'Frank is of the opinion that we should pull up stakes and try our luck on another lead, or move on to another diggings altogether,' Toby added. 'There's a bit of a move on to the Ovens district, but I think they're all the same if you ask me. One place is as good as another. It's the luck of the digger that changes the outcome.' He took the empty pannikin from Paddy.

'More?'

Paddy shook his head.

'Some of the other diggers along the gully are saying that the real gold is below the shale. They reckon that if a man could get through it there would be enough gold to fill a wheelbarrow. Hah!' He threw his hands up in a dismissive gesture as he realised what he was saying. The only thing there was plenty of on the diggings was stories about where there was plenty of gold. 'A man could blunt a hundred picks trying to dig his way through that stuff.'

Toby left the tent in a sombre mood. Paddy felt far too sick to care what was happening beyond the canvas walls of the tent. He let his thoughts drift to the pond below the homestead and wondered if the wild ducks were back this year.

On Sunday morning Toby pulled the muskets from beneath his cot and carried them to breakfast. Annie stood at the cooking fire, chops sizzling in the pan and the billy on the boil.

'Good morning.'

She smiled as Toby stepped under the tarpaulin shelter they had erected over the campfire during the last rainy day. Her parents sat on the far side. Maree sliced potatoes into the camp oven while Frank laced his boots. Annie never usually showed too much affection in front of her parents, but this morning she stepped up to Toby, kissed his cheek then took his hand and led him to his seat.

If Frank noticed the kiss he chose to ignore it. He finished lacing his boots and took up the plate of food waiting beside him.

'How's my patient this morning?' Maree asked.

'Still sleeping,' said Toby. 'He didn't stir much during the night. I think he'll be as right as rain in another day or two.'

'That's good, isn't it Frank?' she said and nudged her husband with an elbow to prompt an answer.

Frank muttered something unintelligible and didn't bother to look up.

'If you wouldn't go off drinking every Saturday night, I think you'd find the Sundays a little more tolerable,' Maree added.

'You going out alone?' Annie asked, pointing at the muskets.

'If I'm going to get some more skins for those rugs,' Toby said. 'Unless Frank wants to come along for the ride?' he inquired, knowing full well what the answer would be. Frank was not much of a horseman at the best of times, and in his self-induced state of illness, the thought of a day spent rocking and rolling on horseback was almost enough to cause his breakfast to reappear.

'Not bloody likely, lad,' he said, and belched as he stood and grabbed his tool bag. 'Anyway, I've got a wagon to repair over at Government Camp.'

'I could go with Toby,' Annie offered.

Frank spun about so fast he almost lost his balance. He took a little sidestep to stay on his feet and his pale face filled with colour. 'What? Have you two lovebirds ride off into the countryside alone? I don't think so. Anyway, you can't ride a horse, my girl,' he added, as if that took care of the matter.

'I certainly can ride a horse, Papa,' Annie said. 'I ride Patch and Moonlight all the time when we take them out for fresh grass. We have to ride them well out of the diggings to find good grazing.'

'But you'll still be unescorted. That's the part that concerns me, my girl. Boys and girls being what boys and girls are.'

Toby, a little awed by Annie's brazen proposal, realised his honour was in question.

'Frank, I can assure you that Annie and I—'

'You can assure me all you like, lad. But I know what happens to assurances when a man starts thinking with a different head than the one sitting on his shoulders.'

'Papa! Toby has shown himself to be nothing but a proper gentleman. He would never do anything—'

Frank held up a hand and Annie dutifully dropped into silence despite her rising temper.

'I know Toby is a good lad, Annie, and I know you will never be in safer hands than when you are with him. But can he protect you from himself? It's quite obvious the feelings you two have for each other, and I welcome the day when Toby will be my son-in-law, but it should be after a proper courtship that follows the normal custom.'

'Look around yourself, you daft beggar,' Maree shouted. 'Look at this place.' She climbed to her feet and pointed up the gully at the tents and mullock heaps stretching away into the distance. 'Does this look like a normal place to you? How can they follow normal custom when there is nothing normal about where we are? Here, we have to make our own kind of normal. Let them go off together, Frank. There's no shame in them wanting to spend a day alone. Whatever happens, I think their future together was ordained by the saints themselves.' She stopped, took a deep breath, then went on. 'Have you forgotten that time we snuck away to the Hastings Fair before we were betrothed?'

'And have *you* forgotten what we got up to under the mill-stream bridge on the way home?' Frank jumped in, then looked sheepishly at Annie and Toby, realising he had revealed a little too much.

'Exactly,' Maree blurted 'Our future together was meant to be. Otherwise I would never have let you get those rough hands of yours underneath my skirts.'

Toby, embarrassed by the direction the discussion had taken, tried to cut in. 'I don't think—'

'Quiet, Toby,' Maree snapped, holding the palm of her hand up. 'Let them have their time together, Frank,' she said, turning back to her husband. 'You know that they will end up together no matter what. You said yourself, Toby is a good lad. Our Annie is lucky to have him, and you know he will never hurt her.'

Frank stood as still as a river gum while he thought about his wife's words. Finally, he nodded his head in agreement. 'Fine,' he said. 'But I want you back before sunset.' He dropped his tool bag to the ground and stepped across to Toby. 'You look after my little girl,' he said, through unmoving lips.

Toby nodded his head. 'Yes, sir.'

Frank held his gaze for one lingering moment, then turned, gathered up his tool bag, and wandered off in the direction of Government Camp.

They found a pair of trousers for Annie so that she would be able to sit astride Patch without the worry of her skirts riding up. She borrowed one of Toby's chequered shirts, and when she stepped from her tent wearing the garb, he was shocked by the transformation in her appearance. With her mother's help she had tied her long dark hair up into a tight bun at the back of her head. Over this she had pulled down a broad-brimmed cabbage-tree hat. It was only the graceful lines of her face that revealed this was a woman standing before him.

'Ready,' she said, and giggled with excitement.

After leaving the camp, Toby led them across the creek and turned west, following it downstream for a mile or so before turning away again. They kept moving westwards, picking their way through clusters of tents and mullock heaps.

The sea of tents gradually thinned out as they climbed into the hills and left the cleared land behind. The bush closed around them, wrapping horses and riders in its verdant cloak.

Annie chatted away as they rode and Toby marvelled at the sound of her voice. She spoke about nothing and everything, all at once. The topic of conversation shifted from the height of the trees to the approaching summer.

In a grove of tall gum trees Toby dismounted and pulled the Lovell from its scabbard.

'I don't see any possums, Toby.' Annie had her face turned skywards, searching the branches. 'How do you know which tree to look up?'

'Come down here and I'll show you,' Toby said, and went to help her off the horse. He led her to the trunk of a nearby tree. 'Place your mouth close to the bark and breathe out in a heavy sigh.'

Annie looked at him and tried not to laugh. 'You're pulling my leg, Mr O'Rourke?'

'Not at all. I'll show you.' He leaned in close to the tree and exhaled onto the bark. Then he moved around the tree and repeated the action. 'Here! You try it.'

She moved to where Toby indicated and leaned in close, letting out a long breath onto the trunk.

'What did you see where you breathed?' Toby asked.

'The moisture from my breath is stuck to little tiny hairs on the tree.'

'That's the belly fur from a possum where it stuck to the bark as it clambered up the tree. There's one up there all right.' He stepped back and cocked the musket, searching the branches.

'There he is!'

Toby took aim and fired. Moments later a furry brown body fell to the ground.

'That's one,' Toby said. 'Paddy and I have already hunted this area out. 'There will be heaps more deeper into the bush. Let's move on. There's a place I want to show you.'

Toby helped her back onto Patch and then led them away through the trees.

At mid-morning they reined in beside a large pool below a waterfall that crashed down forty feet from a rocky overhang. He dismounted and went back to assist Annie out of the saddle, then they walked the horses down to the water's edge to drink. Annie found a place on one of the granite boulders rimming the pool where they could look down into the crystal depths as they ate scones that Maree had packed.

'It's very beautiful here,' Annie said, looking up at the high rock walls, at the overhanging trees and ferns.

'Yes,' Toby answered. 'We often stop here when I come out hunting with Paddy. It's one of my favourite places.'

Annie moved carefully down the rocks to the pool. She bent and scooped up a handful of water to drink, the droplets flying from her hand like sparks in the warm sunshine.

'Sweet,' she said, flicking the last drops into Toby's face with a mischievous grin. 'This is far better than the creek water upstream from the diggings. We should have brought the water casks to fill.'

'The poor horses would expire before we ever reached the diggings if we tried to carry those heavy casks all the way back from here.'

'It looks so cool and clean, Toby. Do you think we can spare a little time to bathe in the pool?'

The urge to get on with the possum hunt evaporated from Toby's mind. Everything seemed so perfect sitting beside the pool with Annie. He nodded his head eagerly and began to take his boots off.

Annie unlaced her boots and stuffed her socks into them. She turned to the water and picked her way carefully down the rocks before dipping one foot in up to her ankle. 'Chilly, but nice,' she grinned back at him, then stepped out into the pool. Water swirled up around her waist and she dipped both hands into it and splashed her face, giggling with exhilaration. Reaching back with one hand she untied the ribbon that held her hair up, shaking it out so that her tresses fell down between her shoulder blades. She sat down in the water, her hair floating about her shoulders like a dark halo. Only then did she turn back towards the rocks where Toby was standing, eyes fixed on her.

'C'mon, silly. Don't just stand there. Come in and have a wash. It won't hurt to get some of that miner's dirt out of your pores.'

Toby unbuttoned his shirt, shrugged it off and tossed it onto the rock. Then he stepped into the pool and waded out to Annie.

They stayed in the water for the rest of the morning, frolicking and splashing about. At noon they climbed onto the rock, their clothes dripping and clinging to their bodies. Annie unpacked some food from the saddlebags and they ate hungrily, sprawled in the sun. Toby gathered up some small sticks and lit a fire on the rock to boil a billy of water.

After their meal, they lay back in the sunshine, their clothes drying on their bodies. Annie talked while Toby idled beside her and wondered about the feel of her body in his arms as he let his eyes rove over her prone form. He had no desire to leave this wonderful place and the magical moments it held for them. He gave no thought to the consequences of their returning to camp with only one possum. He rolled onto his back, closed his eyes and listened to Annie's voice as she chatted, offering a grunt of acknowledgment every now and then.

'Toby? Do you think we could reach that rock in the pond where the rainbow is?'

Toby rolled onto an elbow and looked at her. Annie was sitting up and looking out across the pool to where the waterfall splashed down onto a jumble of boulders. The spray dissolved the sunlight into a broad arc of colour that terminated on a flat rock where the water thundered into the pool.

'All right.'

Annie clapped her hands with glee and sprang to her feet. Without the slightest show of modesty she undid the narrow leather belt that secured her borrowed trousers and let them fall to her feet. Underneath she wore a pair of frilly white bloomers that hung to her knees. She shrugged off the Crimea shirt and tossed it onto the rock beside her trousers as she stepped out of them. The white cotton shift she wore was still damp in places and clung to her narrow waist as she strode into the water.

Toby sprang to his feet, sprinted to the water's edge and launched into mid-air. He hit the water hard and flat, his momentum carrying him out to where Annie waded steadily towards the rock. A few strokes brought him up beside her.

Toby climbed onto the rock, then took Annie's hands and pulled her up beside him in one fluid movement. She sprawled back and Toby would have sat beside her, but he noticed the wet cotton of her shift was all but transparent. He could see the dark circles of areola surrounding her nipples which pushed up proudly against the thin cotton. He started guiltily as he realised she was watching the direction of his eyes.

'I'm sorry—' he began lamely, but she quieted his words with a press of her finger against his lips. Her hand moved to his and, taking it firmly in her own, guided it gently beneath the damp cotton. He could feel the coolness of the wet material on the back of his hand and the fire of her body against his palm. Then his hand enveloped her breast and he was surprised that something that looked so firm could be so soft and pliable.

Annie moaned softly at Toby's first tentative touches. She threw her arms about his neck and pulled him down to her. He opened his mouth and took her mouth on his, pressing so hard that their teeth touched. Toby was the first to break off the kiss. He lifted Annie up onto a higher rock and she gasped at the beauty of their surroundings. The sunlight refracted off the mist, splitting into a thousand rainbows.

She took a moment to take in the wonder. Then she pulled Toby to her and reached for the belt securing his trousers. Through the myopic mists of lust Toby had a vision of Frank Hocking standing before him.

'I can't. I promised your pa I would look after you.'

'You are looking after me,' she answered huskily. 'You are my man. You will look after me forever, and I you.'

With her words still echoing in his mind, Toby resisted no longer. He let Annie pull him down to her and he took her body against his own. Once more their lips met and Toby shut out all else from his mind.

I t was late in the afternoon when they climbed arm in arm up onto the rock where they had discarded their clothes and the saddlebags.

The horses were tethered to a nearby tree and Toby felt a pang of guilt that they had stood for hours still saddled and bridled. He gave Moonlight an apologetic rub down the flank as he re-secured the saddlebags.

'Sorry, fella,' he murmured. 'I got a little sidetracked.'

After they dressed, he helped Annie into the saddle, swung onto Moonlight and turned back the way they had come. The shadows were long and Toby had a look of concern on his face, which was echoed by Annie's words.

'Papa will have a fit if we come back with only one possum.'

'My thoughts exactly,' Toby grunted. He pulled the musket from its scabbard and searched the branches, but it was a vain hope. He and Paddy had hunted out this area over the past weeks.

'Maybe he will go off drinking. Your ma won't tell him we came back without any possums.'

Annie shook her head sharply. 'Papa had a bee in his bonnet about us going off together right from the start. He will be back in plenty of time to make sure we're home.'

They rode on, heading back towards Ballarat to meet the curfew Frank had given Toby.

'Where did you learn the trick with the possum fur on the tree trunk?' Annie's voice carried a hint of tension.

'It's an old Aborigine trick,' Toby said. 'They use it all the time when out hunting possums.' He was quiet for a moment and then added, 'Of course! I'm an idiot!'

Annie gave a mirthless laugh. 'You are not an idiot, Toby. What are you on about?'

'I know where we can get some possum skins.' And he turned his head to grin back at her.

F rank Hocking sat by the fire, strategically placed so that he faced the direction of the horse yard.

'G'day,' Toby said, as he deposited the riding tack on the wagonette and pulled a tarpaulin over it. He walked in under the tarpaulin shelter and dropped a bundle of possum skins on the ground.

Maree was stirring a pot that sat over the coals. Betty ran up to Annie, took her by the hand and fired a string of questions at her about riding the horses. Paddy was out of bed. He sat beside Frank, who was showing him how to sharpen the blade from a spokeshave on a whetstone.

'Have a good day, you two?' Maree stood up and placed both hands on the small of her back. 'I'd give my right eye for a proper stove,' she added. 'I don't know how much longer I can keep cooking at ground level.'

'It was wonderful, Mama. The countryside is so beautiful once you get away from all the mud and smell of the diggings.'

'You've been busy,' Frank said.

'What do you mean?' Toby shot a look at him.

Frank pulled his pipe from his mouth and used the stem to point at the skins. 'Must be at least twenty hides in that lot, already skinned an' all,' he said.

Toby patted the pile of skins, a broad grin on his face. 'We didn't muck around.'

After dinner, Paddy and Betty shuffled off to their beds, but the fire had died to glowing embers before Maree and Frank finally bid good night and wandered towards their tent.

'Don't sit up too late, you two. It's back to work tomorrow,' Maree warned as she ducked under the ridge pole and drew the flap closed.

Annie and Toby climbed up onto the wagonette seat, a nightly routine for the lovers. Toby placed his arm about Annie's shoulders and pulled her close. She seemed to melt into the side of his body and rested her head lightly on his shoulder. Neither of them spoke, lost in their own thoughts, relishing the closeness of the other. It was Annie who finally broke the silence.

'That was a wonderful idea to buy some skins off the Aborigines,' she whispered. 'Papa doesn't suspect a thing.'

'Don't talk too loudly. He might hear.'

She was silent for a moment and he let his thoughts wander, but she brought him back to her with her next statement.

'It's a big land, isn't it, Toby?'

'Yes,' he said.

'We will always be together, won't we?'

'Always.'

'I get so scared.'

'What are you scared of?'

'I'm scared this huge land will swallow you up one day. It will take you and keep you for itself and I will never see you again.'

'That will never happen.' Toby gave a little chuckle, but regretted it when he realised she was serious. 'I will always find my way back to you.'

'How will you do that if you are lost out in the wilderness?' Her words were almost a sob.

'Remember how I showed you to find south by using the Southern Cross?'

'Yes,' Annie said. She lifted her free hand to trace the outline of the constellation, drawing an imaginary line through its longest axis to meet a line from the Pointers and then dropping her finger to the horizon. 'South,' she said. Toby applauded her efforts.

'If we are ever apart, for any reason, I will use the Southern Cross to find my way back home.'

There was such conviction in his voice that Annie did not doubt a word of it. She placed her hand in his lap and let his rough, callused hand close about hers. They sat that way for some time, in silence once again. Then a brief but insistent cough from her parents' tent ended their time together.

t had once been a rather grand vehicle, painted gloss-black with yellow trim, but was now battered and scratched from years of service on ill-formed colonial roads. A four-horse team drew the carriage at a trot. The driver, a trooper, sat on the seat above the front wheels. Another trooper was perched beside him, his carbine held loosely across his lap. The windows of the carriage were obscured by canvas flaps, a barrier to the dust which swirled in the vehicle's wake, but Anderson knew there were at least four more armed men inside.

As the carriage straightened onto the incline, he signalled to Yawong and the warrior swung the axe into the tree where they had partly cut through already. He worked the handle back and forth, released the blade and then swung again, the muscles of his bare back knotted tight with effort. At the second swing the tree shuddered, but still remained upright. Anderson looked to the carriage, which would pass by in a matter of seconds.

'Put your back into it, you little black bastard, or they'll get clean away.'

Yawong worked frantically to free the axe. It came away with a jerk, and he continued the momentum into a back swing. If he grunted during the effort of the stroke it was lost amidst the yelling of the driver and the groan and snort of horses. The blade sunk a full two inches into the fibre of the tree. For a moment it appeared it still wouldn't fall. The trunk shuddered and a few leaves drifted down from the canopy. A loud 'pop' sounded and the angle of the trunk changed almost imperceptibly. Another 'pop' followed the first, then came a whole series of snapping reports like a string of Chinese crackers as the tree fell across the road barely forty paces in front of the rushing team.

The driver saw the tree coming down and pulled on the reins, his foot pushing on the brake to prevent the carriage from over-running the horses. The trooper beside him held tight to the back of the seat with one hand, the other keeping a tenuous grip on his carbine. The lead horses, left without enough room to pull up, turned across the road to where Anderson and Chilbi were concealed. Here, they finally stopped, tossing and rearing in the traces.

Anderson spurred his mount forward and cocked his revolver at the same time. He reined to a stop beside a pale-faced trooper, the muzzle of the weapon under the man's nose.

'Bail up!' he screamed at the top of his voice. 'Bail up, you bastards!'

Chilbi sprinted in behind Anderson and aimed his musket up at the door as one of the occupants swung it open. A walrus-moustached man with sergeant chevrons on his sleeves swung out onto the step. He had a single-shot pistol in his right hand, but the weapon was uncocked. The sergeant saw at a glance that he'd been too slow and reluctantly lowered the weapon as he stared down the barrel of Chilbi's musket. Yawong was behind Chilbi with his own weapon aimed up into the coach.

'Everyone out,' Anderson growled, climbing off his horse. 'If I see anything but open hands, it'll be a ball in the head.' He gestured at the ground beside the coach. 'You two as well.' He waved the pistol at the driver and trooper on the seat. The trooper placed his carbine on the footboard and followed the driver down. Four uniformed men climbed out of the coach and joined them. Chilbi and Yawong had been through this routine many times, and they shoved the men into a rough line without uttering a word.

One of the troopers glanced nervously back up the road. He turned to the sergeant and muttered, 'Sarge, what happened to—?'

'Shut up, you fool! Do you want to be shot?' the sergeant snapped.

'Inside the coach.' Anderson pointed with the revolver. 'The large box – drag it out.'

Chilbi and Yawong climbed through the open door and emerged a few moments later with an iron-bound, hardwood box slung between them. They struggled to lift it from the floor of the coach and onto the ground. It dropped into the dust with a thump and Anderson was unable to prevent his gaze flicking towards it as he wondered at the treasure it might contain.

'You seem to be the senior man here, Sergeant. I'll thank you for the key.'

'I don't have the key. There is one key with the gold commissioner in Mount Alexander and another in Melbourne.' The barest hint of a smile crossed the sergeant's face.

'I'll put a ball in your brain and have one of my men search your body.' The menace in Anderson's tone made the sergeant flinch. He nodded and opened his jacket, fumbling through an inner pocket on first the left side, then the right. The sergeant shrugged apologetically and then set about searching the pockets of his trousers.

'I know I put it here some—'

The barrel of the revolver came down hard, splitting his scalp open to the bone and knocking him to the ground. Anderson stooped and grabbed the sergeant's tunic, lifting him to his feet. Holding the man's face barely an inch from his own he said, 'If I don't see that key in two seconds I'm going to kill you.'

Before he could make good his threat an urgent shout came from where Tarrat kept lookout. The young warrior yelled something in Jannjirra.

Anderson glanced at Chilbi. 'What the hell is he yelling about?'

Chilbi cocked his head and listened to the excited words. 'Many blue men on horses. Coming fast.'

'I should hazard a guess your lookout has spotted a detachment of mounted police,' the sergeant said, confirming Anderson's fears. Blood ran down the side of the sergeant's face and into his right eye, but the man managed a smile. 'They were right with us all the way from the diggings. I don't know how the blighters got so far behind.'

Anderson cursed, shoved the sergeant to the ground and took aim at the man's head.

'I wouldn't waste a shot on me, old boy. I dare say you'll need every one you have in the next few moments.'

Anderson could see the sergeant was right. He swung back into the saddle. 'Leave the strongbox. Recall Tarrat and get into the bush, get away from here,' he told Chilbi and Yawong.

Chilbi cupped a hand to his mouth and mimicked the warbling of a magpie, the recall signal. Down at a grove of trees overlooking the approach, Tarrat heard the recall and broke cover. He sprinted towards the coach, his musket held loosely in his right hand.

Anderson caught a flash of movement in the trees behind the running warrior and six uniformed horsemen galloped into view. They saw the coach pulled up, the escort party lined up on the side of the road, and each pulled a pistol. Spurring their horses into a gallop, they charged up the hill, yelling and screaming as they came.

Tarrat had covered half the distance from the grove to the coach. He looked back at the fast-approaching riders and realised he wasn't going to make it. Turning to face his enemy, he lifted the musket to his shoulder as the mounted police thundered towards him, six dark shapes running ahead of their own column of dust. A spurt of gun smoke erupted from the weapon of the lead rider and Tarrat was flung backwards as the ball hit him. The musket flew from his hands and the young warrior was lost from view as the riders galloped past.

Anderson fired three shots in quick succession. It was extreme range for his weapon, and all missed their mark. However, the riders checked their reckless charge. They reined to a halt and pulled carbines from scabbards, prepared to shoot it out from a distance.

'Shoot,' Anderson yelled at Chilbi and Yawong. 'Then get into the bush. Reload when you can.' He emptied his revolver in the direction of the riders. The Aborigines flung their muskets up and fired without taking aim, then ran for the trees. Anderson spurred his horse after them.

The mounted police opened fire and a volley of shot crashed through the bushes, snapping branches and bringing down a rain of leaves and twigs. A white smear of wood appeared on a tree a yard from Anderson's head as the carbine ball stripped away bark and whined off in ricochet. He flinched and lowered himself along the horse's neck, pushing the animal faster.

The first volley faded into echoes as the police reloaded. Only the puffing, grunting warriors at his sides and the horse beneath him made any sound as they climbed. They were thirty or so paces short of the hilltop when the next gunshots boomed out from behind. The police had entered the trees and spotted the remnants of the gang on the slope above. One or two balls whistled close by, but the rest were wide of the mark. The thunder of the gunshots had not yet died away in the gullies when Anderson and his men topped the ridge and dropped into cover beyond.

'Reload. Reload, now,' Anderson urged them. He still had the revolver in his hand, but the weapon would take too long to reload. He tucked it into his belt and pulled a musket from the scabbard strapped to the saddle.

Chilbi finished reloading and crawled to the skyline. 'Six come on horses,' he called over his shoulder. 'Another three on foot.'

'Keep moving,' Anderson screamed at them. 'To the next ridge line. Run, you little bastards.'

With reloaded weapons in hand, Chilbi and Yawong slipped into the trees. Anderson raked his heels down the horse's flanks and descended into the gully. He heard shouting from behind and knew the police had reached the ridgetop. Someone called on him to halt and when he didn't, they fired. The ball whispered past his ear, ripping leaves from bushes as it tore into the under-growth. He spurred the gelding to greater speed, ducking and weaving in the saddle to avoid being knocked from his mount by a low branch or tangle of foliage. Another shot sounded as he reached the gully floor, but he couldn't tell how close the ball had come. He spurred the horse and headed up the ridge, not daring to look back for his pursuers, knowing they would be close.

As he topped the next ridge he saw Chilbi far to his left, crouched behind a small cluster of boulders. Yawong was lying prone beneath a fallen tree. They fired, and when the thunder died away, Anderson thought he could hear a man screaming in the gully behind him.

'Don't waste time reloading,' he called to Chilbi. 'There are too many of them for us to fight. Don't try and get back to your horses. We need to get deeper into the bush. Take a stirrup.'

Chilbi and Yawong each grabbed a stirrup strap and Anderson spurred the horse forward. He brought the animal into a trot, the natives half-running, half being dragged along at his side. They crossed the next ridge and he changed direction, angling north-west, away from the road. After two miles, he changed direction again, back to the south. The police had no native trackers with them, but he wasn't taking a chance on them returning to the area with one and hunting him down. The sun had set when he finally called a halt to the mad run. They were in a tangle of bracken fern beside a stream. The two Aborigines staggered to the water, dropped to their bellies and drank thirstily.

Chilbi was the first to stand. His chest still heaved from the exertion of his run and perspiration poured down his face and chest. 'Tarrat has fallen,' he said.

'A warrior's death,' Anderson said. All afternoon he had cursed himself for losing the strongbox. The thought of failure hung heavily in his belly and brought a hint of anger to his voice. There would be other chances. Gold escorts ran weekly from the various diggings dotted about the colony.

Next time, he thought. *Next time I will be better prepared. One of those strongboxes will be mine.*

'The audacity of the man!'

The governor slammed the report down onto his desk and looked to his aide. 'He's gone too far this time, Childers.'

'Yes, Your Excellency.' Childers knew exactly which report had sent his master into a rage.

'Robbing a few miners is one thing. But to try to take a gold shipment under escort is quite another. That gold belongs to Her Majesty. We can't have any old Tom, Dick or Harry thinking he can just seize it and run off into the wilds. Thank God his plans were foiled.'

'The escort party did well, Your Excellency. One of the brigands was shot dead.'

'One of the natives.' La Trobe stabbed his index finger onto the report. 'Pity it wasn't this scoundrel Anderson. What is the current reward posted against him?'

Childers, having known this question would come after preparing the governor's daily correspondence, had already checked the records. 'Five hundred pounds, sir.'

'Five hundred, you say?'

'Yes, sir. It was doubled from two hundred and fifty some months ago.'

The governor seemed to consider his next words carefully. 'Double it again.'

'Sir?'

'You heard me, man, damn your ears. Double it immediately. And Childers?'

'Sir?'

'Have the superintendent of police report to me at once. I want to hear from him just what is being done to bring this rogue to heel.'

'I shall dispatch a messenger at once, Your Excellency.'

The governor dismissed his aide and turned to the next report, hoping for good news, something to lighten his sombre mood. He was disappointed. It seemed another ship had been lost while attempting to cross the treacherous bar across the narrow entrance to Port Phillip Bay.

'This colony will be quite the death of me,' he muttered under his breath.

The sun had rimmed the horizon by the time Annie gathered enough strength to climb from her bed and begin dressing. She had tried to rise earlier, when the movements of her sister had woken her, but the nausea had only subsided when she lay back and closed her eyes tightly. This time she managed to fasten three buttons of her blouse before she was forced to quickly pull the chamber pot from beneath her cot and vomit into it.

The sound of her distress brought her mother to the flap of the tent. Maree stooped under the ridge pole and raised one eyebrow as she watched Annie use a handkerchief to wipe bile from her lips.

Annie carefully folded the handkerchief into her pocket. She noticed her mother's concerned gaze had drifted to the last buttons of her blouse, to the bulge of material where her once flat stomach now showed a slight curve. Maree said nothing as Annie turned with tears in her eyes.

'Oh, Mama.' She stumbled towards her and Maree stepped into the tent, embracing her tightly.

'How long have you known, child?'

'Three weeks, maybe four,' she said between snuffles. Annie felt the security a child feels in a mother's arms and clung to Maree with all her strength. 'What are we going to tell Papa?'

'Don't you worry about Papa.' Maree's voice was unwavering, reassuring. 'Have you told Toby?'

'No, not yet. Oh, Mama, I don't know what to do. Papa will be so angry when he finds out.'

Her mother broke the embrace and held her at arm's length so that she could look into her eyes.

'I'll deal with him. You need to tell Toby so the two of you can make plans. Some arrangements will need to be made over the coming months.'

'Mama, I'm so sorry.' Annie pushed in against her mother.

Maree stroked her long, dark hair. 'You have nothing to be sorry about, my dear. You are going to make me a grandmother, and that makes me very happy indeed.'

'I only hope Toby and Papa are happy too,' Annie whispered.

'Toby loves you, child. I see it in his eyes every time he looks at you. He will be surprised, and a little scared at first. I've never seen your father look so pale as when I told him I was carrying Tom inside me.'

Toby and Frank sat in their usual places, chewing busily on their breakfasts as Maree led Annie out of the tent. Betty was among the trees, poking a stick at something on the ground. Paddy sat beside a wagonette, knocking dirt out of his boots.

Toby saw her and smiled broadly. Annie was usually delighted by this silent greeting she received from him every morning. Toby had a way of making her feel so special and beautiful with just a look, but his beaming grin did little to loosen the knot of panic in her stomach. Toby's smile slipped from his face. He placed his plate on the log beside him and stood, rushing to her side.

'Annie, what's the matter? Are you ill?'

'She's fine, lad,' Maree answered for her. Then she stepped over to Frank and held her hand out to him.

'Walk with me, Frank.'

Frank cast a glance at Annie and Toby as he stood. He took the proffered hand cautiously before allowing himself to be led away towards the horse yard.

'What's going on, Annie? What's the matter?'

Annie slipped her hand into Toby's and pivoted on the balls of her feet so she could look into his eyes and gauge his reaction.

'I'm pregnant.'

She held his gaze.

'We're going to have a baby,' she added simply.

Annie saw the words dawn on him. Toby's head went back as if they had hit him square in the forehead. Her mother's words came back to her. She saw the initial shock transform into a look of sheer terror as his eyes flew wide and the jaw went slack. Then his eyes dropped and Annie self-consciously placed her hands over her belly.

'A baby?' There was a tremor in his voice and the look of terror remained, but his hands came up and he placed them over hers, carefully, protectively.

'Yes, a baby,' Annie agreed, the feeling of isolation dissolving with his touch. She stepped through his arms, and they closed around her, shielding her from all the doubts and worries she had harboured over the past weeks. He had accepted the news, if not with joy, then with the sense of togetherness and duty he applied to everything he did. For the first time in many days she began to feel everything was going to be all right.

Then she heard her father's yell of rage.

Frank came bounding down the path on his long legs, his face a deep purple. Maree was close behind him, skirts held high in both hands as she stumbled after her husband.

Frank hurdled the log at the far side of the fire and landed a pace away from Annie and Toby. She felt Toby's arms release her and he pushed her gently behind him, placing himself between her and her father. Frank stood staring at them, motionless except for his fists, which were clenching and unclenching.

'Frank, I want you to know that I will do the right thing by Annie.'

'Do the right thing,' he yelled in Toby's face. 'The right bloody thing would've been not to get her up the duff in the first bloody place.' He stepped towards Toby and waved a fist under his nose. 'I trusted you, O'Rourke. I placed my daughter in your care and you betrayed that trust. But what could I expect from a bloody colonial?'

At hearing her man insulted so, Annie tried to intervene. 'Papa, it wasn't a betrayal of your trust. Toby is an honourable man. We just—'

'I know what you were just doing, young lady. I see the way you look at him whenever he's around. Then you go off into the countryside with him, rutting like a common harlot.'

'Frank!' Maree went to place a restraining hand on her husband's arm, but he shrugged it off.

Toby waved his fist under Frank's nose. 'She is no such thing, Frank. We're in love.'

'Love?' Frank spat at him. 'Love doesn't put food in a baby's mouth or protect it from the cold and the dust. Take a look around you. Is this the kind of place where you want a baby to be brought into the world? What kind of father are you?' He pushed Toby backwards with enough force to send him crashing into Annie. Toby managed to keep his feet, but Annie fell backwards. Maree rushed past Frank and between her and Toby they lifted Annie to her feet.

'Are you all right?' Toby asked as he dusted the back of her skirts. Annie nodded, and then he rounded on Frank.

'At least I don't stagger back into camp drunk every other night. I don't spend our precious money on sly grog when it would be better spent putting food on our plates.'

Frank swayed as if he had been struck a physical blow. Annie could see the words had shocked him as only the truth can. He looked at Toby across the arm's length that separated them and drew in a sharp breath.

'You insolent little puppy.' His right fist came up in a swinging punch that whistled through the air.

Toby was ready for it. He swung his arm up in an effort to deflect the punch and only partially succeeded. Frank's fist glanced off the side of his face with a sound like a falling log hitting the ground. Toby's head snapped over to the right and he buckled at the knees. Annie thought he was going to drop to the ground, but then his knees straightened with a driving force and Toby's right fist came up in a swing that started at his belt buckle and came up past his chest and face with the speed of a striking snake. Months of hard labour had toned his body into a mass of muscle and sinew that was concentrated into the force of that single punch. The fist made contact with her father's chin and kept going up, snapping Frank's head back and sending him backwards so he collapsed in a heap beside the fire.

Maree ran to Frank's side and knelt to cradle his head. Frank's eyes had rolled back in their sockets and it was only the rise and fall of his chest that gave any sign he was alive.

Annie and Paddy rushed to Toby and each grabbed an arm to restrain him, but Toby had spent his rage and he dropped his arms to his sides and stepped back from the campfire.

Betty stood by the wagonette, tears rolling down her face. 'Please don't fight. Papa, Toby, please don't fight.'

Annie went to her sister. 'Don't cry, Betty.' Annie had tears of her own. 'Don't cry. It's all my fault. They won't fight any more. Will you, Toby?'

Toby shook his head. He looked to Frank and Maree and shook his head again. Frank sat up and rubbed his chin. He looked as though he was having trouble focusing. He squinted at the people around him, but never once looked at Toby.

Toby strode past the campfire and stooped into his tent. When he came out he was carrying the Lovell musket and his saddle roll. He went to the wagonette, uncovered his saddle and tack and threw them onto his shoulder. As he turned, he locked eyes with Annie and gestured in the direction of the horse yard.

'You stay here with Paddy,' Annie told her sister and detached herself from Betty's arms. She followed Toby up the path and caught up with him as he struggled under his burden.

'Where are you going, Toby?' she asked, taking the musket from his hand so he could adjust the load on his shoulder. He didn't slow his pace, but kept on up the hill in long, determined strides. 'Are you running out on us?'

He stopped, and Annie could see her words had hurt him. He turned towards her and she could see the beginning of a dark bruise growing on the side of his head. She reached out and touched it tenderly. Toby dropped the saddle, grasped her wrist and pulled her hand to his mouth, kissing it gently.

'No, I'm not running out,' he said. 'Your father is right about one thing: we can't bring the baby into this place. I need to find paying work with a regular wage so we can afford a proper home, not some scrap of canvas stretched over our heads.' He picked up the saddle and began walking again. Annie had to hurry to keep up with him.

'But—what will you do?'

'Plenty of work out there for a stockman,' he said without looking at her. 'It's high time I got my arse out of that hole in the ground and did something towards our future. I was stupid to think we would find enough gold to buy our place back.'

Annie caught his arm and dragged him to a stop, turning him to face her. 'You are many things, Toby O'Rourke, but you are not stupid. You are the most wonderful man I have ever met and I love you. As for your place at Bunyong Creek, if it is meant to be, you will get it back.'

'I love you too, but your father is right when he says love won't put food in the baby's mouth.' He turned back up the hill, but this time his pace was slower. Side by side they went to the horse yard. Toby threw the saddle over the rail and unslung the bridle from his shoulder. When his hands were free, he turned to Annie and pulled her to him.

'I said I would never leave you, and I'm not. When I find work I'll come back and let you know.'

Tears welled in her eyes and she sniffled softly. He wiped them away with the back of his hand and then hugged her tightly. 'You have an important job to do as well.'

'What's that?' she said, her voice broken.

'You have to stay strong and well so that our child is born fit and healthy. You also have to look after Paddy for me. You're the only one apart from me who understands his signs and grunts.'

He released her, kissed her softly on the lips and then Annie felt herself being turned around to face the camp.

'Go back to the camp,' he said, 'I'll see you tonight.' Annie started away before her heart could break. His voice stopped her at the head of the path.

'I need you to do one more thing, Annie.'

'Yes?' she said without turning back.

'Tell your papa I'm sorry for hitting him.'

'Yes,' she said again, and started down the hill as fresh tears ran down her face.

The foreman at the cattle yards across from Pennyweight Hill scratched the back of his head as he pondered Toby's question.

'I've got all the workers I need here,' he said, shaking his balding pate. He pulled a crumpled piece of paper and a pencil from his pocket. 'If you leave your name and where you can be found, I'll ask among the drovers who bring in the cattle.'

Toby wrote down his name and the location of the camp and handed it to the foreman. The foreman shoved the piece of paper into his pocket without looking at it. Toby thanked the man and walked back to where he had tethered Moonlight at the rails.

'Hang on a moment.'

He turned to see the foreman scratching his chin thoughtfully. 'I was putting away a few nobblers in O'Malley's last week. Fellow I got talking to said he was starting up a sawmill. Poor cove was complaining about not having enough workers.'

'Did he say where this sawmill is?' Toby asked.

'About four miles west of here, just off the main track.'

'Thanks,' Toby said, and swung into the saddle.

A whooshing, clanking rhythm led Toby the last mile to the sawmill. A steam engine puffed away in a pit beneath a crude bark shelter, running a huge saw blade. Two men were feeding a log onto the blade, sawdust flying in every direction. Toby looped Moonlight's reins over a branch and watched them work. One of the men noticed Toby standing by the engine and pointed him out to the other. They completed their cut, then the older man climbed out of the pit.

'If you're after timber, young fella, we won't have any to spare till after we fill this order for the Tudor Rose Hotel.'

'Actually, I'm looking for a job,' Toby said. 'The foreman at the yards by Pennyweight Hill said you were looking for workers.'

'Am I ever?' The man's face broke into a grin. 'There's only me an' Horrie at the moment. I put the word out, but everyone wants to dig up their fortune, not work for it.' He held out his hand and Toby shook it.

'Jim Clark.'

'Toby O'Rourke. Pleased to meet you, Jim. I'll give you a good day's work for fair pay.'

'You look a fit lad. You'll get plenty of splinters workin' for me, but I'll give you fifteen shillings a week plus bed and board.' He gestured over his shoulder at one of two huts sitting in the trees. 'You can bunk in with Horrie. Hope you're a better cook than he is. He's bloody atrocious. Sundays are your own to do with as you will. When can you start?'

'How about Monday?'

'I was hopin' you'd say today, but Monday will have to do. We have a big order in to supply timber for a new hotel in Ballarat.'

'I have a few things to sort out before I can get away.'

'Well you'd better get to it. We'll see you on Monday.'

Wanting as much time as possible to think, Toby walked Moonlight slowly up the trail on the reverse side of the hill. He was pleased to see the horse yard deserted. Only Patch was there to greet them.

His mind was in turmoil. Was he ready to become a father? What kind of father would he make at twenty years of age? If Frank's words were anything to go on, he was off to a bad start. Maybe Frank was right, that this was not a place to be bringing a child into the world. Toby prayed fervently that he would not be adding one more tiny grave to the many already dotted about the Ballarat cemetery. Then his thoughts drifted to Annie and he realised the love he had for this woman. He felt that together they would be an unstoppable force, able to overcome any of life's problems, no matter what was thrown at them.

He took his time unsaddling and tending to Moonlight's needs before he shouldered the equipment and wandered down to the camp.

Maree was peeling an onion on the tailboard of the wagon-ette as Betty stacked kindling by the fire. It was a scene Toby had wandered into a hundred times before and he felt a growing regret at the news he was bringing.

'Hello, Toby.' Maree looked over from her task. A small smile played at the corners of her mouth, but her brow was creased with concern. 'We were wondering when you were coming back.'

Toby nodded and offered an apologetic smile. 'Looks like a good stack of firewood you've got there, Betty,' he said as he placed the tack into the back of the wagonette and tousled the girl's hair. 'Where's Annie?'

Maree placed the knife down and turned, wiping her hands on her apron.

'She's been crying her eyes out all morning, Toby. I think the poor lass has finally drifted off to sleep.' She inclined her head in the direction of her tent. 'Shall I wake her?'

'No, let her sleep,' he said quickly 'Is Frank down at the claim?'

'Yes,' Maree said carefully. 'He and Paddy went down there after noon. Please, Toby, I don't want any trouble like this morning. I don't think I could stand it.'

'No trouble, Maree. I just need to talk with him. I need to put things right.'

Paddy was at the windlass raising a bucketful of dirt as Toby climbed the mullock heap. His brother looked up and smiled, hooked the bucket over the handle of the windlass and took Toby in a bear-like embrace, lifting him off his feet. Toby felt the pressure release and Paddy stood back with a scowl on his face. He pointed to the bruise on Toby's face and shook his head.

'No more fighting, Paddy. I need to talk to Frank. You take the barrow down to the cradle. Go on, it'll be all right.'

Paddy stepped back, looking unsure, but Toby held his gaze and smiled, flushing any fears away. He waited until Paddy had manhandled the barrow over the mullock heap, then stuck his head over the top of the pit.

'Frank? Got a minute?'

There was silence for a few moments, then Frank's head appeared at the top of the ladder. He squinted in the bright sunshine and the layer of dirt on his face only partly concealed the bruise on his chin.

'So,' he said softly. 'Finally come to do some work, have we? I thought you'd cleared out for good.'

'I'm sorry about this morning, Frank.' Toby ignored the jibe. Frank opened his mouth to speak and Toby continued before he could draw breath.

'I know I betrayed the trust you had in me and I'm deeply sorry for that.' Toby had rehearsed what he'd planned to say for over two hours, but nothing he had prepared came out. He lapsed into silence and Frank used the opportunity to have his say.

'I'm not angry that it happened, Toby. I'm just angry that it happened now, in this of all places. I always knew you and Annie would be together. I just wanted it to be later, after we found our big nugget and could live in some place without tents or bloody great holes in the ground.'

He climbed from the ladder and stood opposite Toby. His arms hung limply at his side, all aggression gone from his body, replaced by a deep tiredness.

'She's my child, Toby, and I need to protect her. It's a father's duty.' He held up his hand as Toby made to speak. 'I know I have a weakness for the bottle. And I know that money I spend on grog could be better used for other things. You made me see that this morning. I won't be touching another drop of the stuff ever again.' He went to where his jacket was draped over the windlass handle and pulled out the hip flask Toby had seen him drinking from in the past.

'Since that cave-in, the dark has been scaring me silly, Toby.' He pulled the stopper from the flask and upended it. They both watched the contents drain onto the earth at Frank's feet. 'I haven't touched any of that today.' He pointed at the shaft with his thumb. 'I've got two lanterns burning down there. I still get jittery, but I can work. Hell, I'll use three lanterns if that's what it takes.' He pushed the stopper into the flask and threw it down the hillside. 'No more grog, Toby. We'll need that money for my grandchild.' His voice almost broke and Toby wanted to reach out and place a hand on the man's shoulder.

'Frank, I've been offered a job at a sawmill to the west of here.'

Frank took a step back. 'So, you *are* running out. I was right.' The anger flared in his eyes and Toby continued quickly.

'No, Frank, I'm not running out. I took the job so I can get a wage and provisions. More money than we can scrape out of this bloody hole.' He used the toe of his boot to kick a few loose stones into the dark opening.

'And Annie?' Frank asked. 'Where does she fit into these new plans of yours, a woman with child?'

'Frank—' Toby had been looking into the other man's eyes, but as he spoke his gaze dropped to Frank's feet. 'Sir, I have come to ask for your daughter's hand in marriage.'

The silence dragged on and Toby lifted his eyes, expecting to see the rage building in Frank's face, but there was only a blank, expressionless stare. Suddenly a light winked on in the depths of his eyes that Toby had not seen for some months.

Frank said, at last. 'Every father with a daughter knows he will lose her to another man one day. I never expected to be asked for the hand of my daughter in such a place, in such circumstances,' Frank drew out his response, prolonging Toby's agony. 'Well, lad, you can have her with my blessing if she's daft enough to want you.' He laughed then, for the first time in ages, and Toby turned and scrambled up the side of the mullock heap in an effort to reach the camp as quickly as possible.

T oby turned to look back down the aisle at the vision of beauty being led towards him on Frank's arm. Annie wore a wedding dress her mother had sewn from a bolt of cloth purchased at considerable expense from one of the storekeepers. Maree had spent many long hours on the garment after Toby went to bed each night, for she had guarded it from his sight with a zealous fervour, proclaiming it was bad luck for him to see the dress until the day of the wedding. She had also guarded the cloth from the mud and dust with the same energy, for it was as white as a spring cloud.

Toby took no notice of the dress. His eyes were fixed firmly on the woman inside it as she shuffled towards him on slippered feet. The bouquet of flowers in Annie's hands matched the ones pinned in her hair – mostly daisies and daffodils. The bouquet had as its centre a single red rose the size of a man's fist. Maree had approached an American woman named Eileen Guinane with a few shillings to offer for the blooms growing in paraffin tins outside her tent. Mrs Guinane had closed Maree's fingers back over the coins and gladly given the flowers in exchange for an invitation to the wedding. She and her husband, Sam, sat in one of the first-row pews.

Maree struggled to hold back tears. When she followed Toby's stare and turned to see Annie coming down the aisle on Frank's arm the floodgate broke and she let forth a heart-rending sob that set Mrs Guinane off as well. Both women howled miserably. Mrs Guinane passed a hanky to Maree and they sniffled and dabbed together.

Toby had found Sergeant McTavish at Government Camp and invited him to witness the ceremony. The sergeant, dressed in full ceremonial uniform, resplendent with glittering brass buttons, occupied the front pew on the other side of the aisle. Toby had spoken to McTavish earlier and his breath smelled strongly of whisky. He could only hope the good sergeant's influence was not enough to cause Frank to fall off the wagon. After all, only a week had passed since his soon-to-be father-in-law's declaration of sobriety.

Frank guided Annie to Toby's side and squeezed both their shoulders in a fatherly show of affection before stepping away. The priest, Father Connell, waited for the sobbing to reduce to a manageable volume then opened his Bible.

After the short ceremony the wedding party moved outside. Maree opened the tailboard on the wagonette, pulled by a horse borrowed from Blacky Pete, and spread out a luncheon of scones, plum jam, slices of roast lamb and thick slabs of damper. Father Connell brought a steaming kettle of water from his residence beside the church and they stood around the wagonette in the sunshine, eating, drinking tea and congratulating the newlyweds.

Sergeant McTavish pulled a small hip flask from his pocket and offered it around. Toby smiled as Frank placed the palm of his hand over his cup.

'Not for me,' Frank said.

'I would have taken you for a drinking man, Mr Hocking,' McTavish said as he poured a good dram into his own cup.

'Please, call me Frank, Sergeant. Used to be,' he said, winking at Toby, 'but not any more.'

'Wise move. Wish I had your intestinal fortitude, but alas the spirit is weak.'

'I'll take a drop of that, thank you, Sergeant,' Sam Guinane drawled, offering his cup.

The sergeant tipped a generous slug into Sam's cup and turned back to Toby. 'There are a lot of reports coming in about our old nemesis Anderson. It seems the rogue killed a whole station of people east of Kilmore.'

Father Connell let out a gasp. 'May the good Lord protect us from such villains.'

'Indeed, Father,' McTavish said. 'He tried to take the gold escort out of Mount Alexander some months back, but his plans were foiled. Last reports had him robbing travellers along the roads to the diggings, turning up at a homestead every now and then to steal provisions and horses.'

'He should have been hanged on a scaffold by now,' Toby said.

'Back home, we'd have rounded up him and his band. Either that or shot them down where they stood,' Sam said.

McTavish raised an eyebrow. 'It's certainly not for the lack of trying, sir. The patrols go out almost daily, but the fellow has the devil's own luck. And those blacks he's with can hide a trail from our keenest trackers. They just melt away into the bush and turn up a day or two later, miles away from where they were last seen. Still, his luck must surely run out eventually.'

'It would be nice to see the bugger dangling from the end of a rope. Beggin' your pardon, Father.' Toby said. He excused himself from the circle of men and tried to push down the hatred and anger lest it ruin this happy day. Annie saw him approaching and she smiled. The evil was swept away in an instant.

'Are you all right?' she asked, taking his hand.

'I am now,' he responded, giving her hand a squeeze. 'I am now.'

'You get bigger every time I see you,' Toby said as he manoeuvred the wagon into camp.

As she did every Sunday in the five months since Toby had started work at the sawmill, Annie waited expectantly for his arrival. She placed her hands on her swollen belly and smiled up at him. 'He's going to be a big boy.'

'Boy?' Toby applied the brake, climbed off the seat and took Annie in his arms.

'Oh, I'm going to deliver you a son, Mr O'Rourke. Besides, Papa has his heart set on it.'

'Well, let's hope you don't disappoint him, then.'

Annie pointed at the load of timber in the back of the wagon. 'You've done well. Papa and Paddy will be able to get on with the hut.'

'It's only offcuts and bits of odd sizes. Jim's a good bloke to let us have it. He even helped me load it on his wagon.'

Annie took Toby's arm and led him to his place under the tarpaulin. 'If there's anything left of the roast you can take it back to him.'

Toby laughed. 'He'll like that, Annie. He reckons Horrie and me couldn't cook to save ourselves. He loved the cake you baked last Sunday. Horrie, too.'

'Tell him there's more where that came from. Just so long as he lets you keep visiting us.'

'Wild horses couldn't keep me away. Besides, Sundays are my day off. I can do with 'em whatever I want.'

Maree had baked a leg of lamb for Sunday roast. They sat about the campfire and ate heartily, the banter flowing freely.

'There's just about enough timber in that wagon for me to finish the hut,' Frank said, gesturing at the half-finished structure behind the tents.

'Papa is going to build a lean-to on the back for Paddy,' Betty said.

Toby looked over the campfire at his brother. 'Your own room, eh, Pad?

Paddy smiled and got stuck into his roast dinner.

'It'll be a storeroom as well,' Frank said. 'Can't have the boy sleeping rough while we're all in the warm.'

Maree gave a little laugh. 'He's hardly a boy, you daft beggar. By Christmas I reckon he'll be head and shoulders over you.'

'Yeah,' Frank said. 'Paddy's sure shot up over the past months.'

Toby nodded. 'Pa was a big bloke. Paddy takes after him.'

'His strength is growing too. The other day he lugged the ladder all the way from our old claim up to the Eureka lead.' Frank shook his head in wonder at the feat. 'I thought we'd have a hard time managing without you, Toby, but Paddy sure makes up for it.'

'How's the new claim shaping up?' Toby asked.

'A little colour showing every now and then. Some of the old chums tell us the real pay dirt is around forty feet on the Eureka. It'll be a while before we're that deep. If it wasn't for your wages from the sawmill we'd have a hard time making ends meet.'

'Just so long as my wages keep you and Paddy digging. That big nugget is down there somewhere. I just know it.'

When they were finished eating, Toby helped Frank and Paddy unload the timber from the wagon.

'There's enough to finish the hut, lad. But I'm not sure what I'll use to waterproof the roof.' Frank gazed thoughtfully at the pile of timber.

'Pa used sheets of bark on the homestead,' Toby offered. 'You peel them off and open them out, use a couple of heavy rocks to hold them flat while they dry out. Paddy knows how it's done. He'll show you, won't you, Pad?'

Paddy nodded and Frank clamped an arm across his shoulders.

'Thanks, lad. I'm determined my grandchild won't be born in a tent.'

Toby worked in the pit with Horrie and the pair fed logs onto the saw, while Paul and Gary, two labourers Jim had hired, worked at the ramp, ensuring a new log was ready as soon as the last one had been cut into planks.

Hissing Harriet drove the saw blade by means of a leather belt that ran from a flywheel to the blade. While the men worked in the pit, the belt hummed and whipped only inches from their heads. Toby was always conscious of it and never strayed too close while it was operating. Whenever the blade reached a knot in the timber it would jar and send a series of wavelike whip cracks down its length that could take someone's head off if they weren't careful.

They had nearly finished the second log when Toby felt a jerk as he pushed it onto the blade. He eased the pressure, knowing the belt would whip about until the blade built up speed again. Horrie worked on the other side and he gave Toby a knowing look, glancing towards the belt as it writhed about like an angry snake. But this time it did not settle back into a normal rhythm. Like a cannon shot, the belt parted. Toby ducked instinctively and felt the wind fan his face as the belt passed inches from his nose. Horrie wasn't so lucky; the heavy leather belt, six inches wide, slammed into the back of his head and sent him sprawling onto the dirt. Hissing Harriet whined into overdrive now the resistance of the belt and blade were gone. She howled like a demon until Jim jumped into the pit and closed down the main steam valve.

'Are you blokes all right?' Jim shouted, as Hissing Harriet wound down. He pulled the pressure relief, sending a cloud of steam skywards, then went to help Toby with Horrie.

'I'm all right,' Toby said, 'but I think Horrie's out cold.'

They got Horrie into a sitting position. Blood ran from a graze on the back of his head, soaked up by the collar of his shirt. His eyes opened and he looked about dazedly, unsure of where he was. Then his gaze settled on Toby's concerned face. 'Did one of the horses kick me in the head?' he muttered, and lifted a hand to the wound on his scalp.

'Hissing Harriet tried to kill you,' Toby said. 'The drive belt broke.'

'The bitch,' Horrie said, examining the blood on his hand.

Jim went to where the belt had bunched up onto the saw blade. The leather had been slashed and holed by the blade's teeth. 'We won't be doin' too much cutting with this,' he said, throwing the leather down in disgust. 'It'll take me hours to organise a new one. You blokes might as well have the rest of the day off. Looks like we'll be working through this Sunday to make up for lost time.'

Despite his concern for Horrie's injuries, Toby couldn't help but smile. A midweek trip into Ballarat to see Annie. She'd be delighted.

Toby rode Moonlight to the east around Bakery Hill to reach the camp. Here, the tracks and trails wound through old and new mullock heaps. At one pit a group of diggers stood at their windlass puffing on pipes while two armed troopers examined a piece of paper Toby recognised as a gold licence. Further along the diggings a miner called for his mate from the top of a mullock heap, his hands circled about his mouth like a loud hailer.

'Joe! Joe!'

At the Melbourne road he waited for a bullock team hauling an overloaded dray to pass by. He held his breath as he crossed the road through the dust and moved into the diggings on the far side. He had not gone more than twenty yards when a familiar voice hailed him.

'Toby?'

Frank stood at the top of a mullock heap waving his hat in the air.

'I thought it was you.' He slid down the loose gravel. 'What are you doing here in the middle of the week? You haven't quit your job, have you?' There was a hint of hope in Frank's voice.

Toby laughed at the suggestion. 'What? And go back to digging holes in the ground for a living? Not bloody likely. The belt broke, so Jim gave us the rest of the day off.'

'You'll be staying for lunch, then?' Frank asked, and then, without waiting for an answer, 'Annie will be tickled pink.'

Paddy slid down the side of the hill and slapped Toby across the back with a huge arm that almost knocked the wind out of him.

'Good to see you, too.' Toby patted Paddy on the back, raising a small dust cloud. 'Showing any colour?'

Paddy glanced around furtively and cautiously held up his right hand with thumb and forefinger slightly apart.

'Just a little, eh?' Toby whispered, taking the hint. He had forgotten it was taboo to discuss the fortunes of any claim on the open diggings.

'Toby will be joining us for lunch,' Frank explained to Paddy, earning another hearty back slap for Toby.

A shout came echoing up the gully from the direction of the road.

'Joe! Joe!'

'Some poor cove has lost his mate,' Toby said. 'He's been looking for him all around Bakery Hill.'

Frank gave a mirthless laugh under his breath. 'No one's missing, Toby. I don't suppose you happened to see some troopers about on the diggings as you rode over?'

'As a matter of fact I did. Two big buggers were checking licences on the other side of the road.'

'"Joe" is the diggers' signal that troopers are out on a licence hunt. It's a warning to everyone without a licence to stay out of sight.'

'Licence hunt?'

Frank fished about in his pockets, retrieved his pipe and knocked it out on a lump of quartz. 'It's a tactic the gold commissioner is implementing on the governor's orders. Apparently, it's happening on all the diggings in the colony. I got talking to a chap over at Blacky Pete's the other day. He told me there was a riot on the Bendigo diggings when they started doing it there.'

'I'm not surprised,' Toby said. 'Life on the diggings is pretty tough as it is. This kind of thing will only get people riled up.'

'I'll say. There's talk of a meeting to discuss forming a delegation to meet with the governor and—' Before Frank could finish, a voice called from the bend in the track.

'You men! Stand where you are.' Two troopers approached them with carbines unslung and bayonets fixed. They strode over with all the front of government officials going about their duty and pointed at Frank, singling him out as the leader of the trio.

'Your licence, mate?'

Frank slid his unlit pipe back into his pocket. 'It's in my jacket pocket hanging on the windlass handle.'

'And where is that exactly?' the second trooper snapped.

'Exactly twenty feet behind me on the other side of this mullock heap.'

'Don't be smart. We don't like smart-arses, do we, Davey?'

'Well, you did ask for an exact location.' Frank smiled benignly. 'Shall I fetch it for you, Constable?'

'Be quick about it. Stan will go with you to make sure you don't do a runner.'

Frank sauntered off around the mullock heap with the trooper, Stan, close behind. The other trooper turned to Toby.

'You don't look like a digger,' he said, eyeing Toby's clothing.

'I work at the sawmill,' Toby said. 'I'm visiting my father-in-law and brother.'

'Does your employer know you're away from your place of work?' The trooper eyed Toby suspiciously.

'He gave us the day off,' Toby snapped, starting to tire of the trooper's bullying attitude.

The trooper didn't let up. 'This horse? Yours or his?' He jabbed the bayonet towards Moonlight's flank.

'Mine,' Toby blurted, stepping protectively between Moonlight and the needle-sharp bayonet.

'Got a receipt for him?' The trooper smiled into Toby's face. 'I bet you don't have one.'

'No, I don't.'

'So! Stolen, then. Perhaps I should seize him as stolen property.'

'No!' Toby was horrified at the thought of someone trying to take Moonlight away from him. 'I don't have a receipt because he was born on my parents' property. If you don't believe me you can ask Sergeant McTavish. He knows me. He was at our place when I had this horse – almost two years ago.'

'You know McTavish?' The trooper looked unconvinced, but his tone softened somewhat.

At that moment Frank came strolling back along the track with his jacket slung over his shoulder, the licence in his hands and the other trooper close on his heels.

'I'll prove it to you,' Toby told the trooper. 'Frank, what was the name of that police sergeant at my wedding?'

'You should know, Toby. He's more your friend than mine.' Then Frank noticed the way Toby stood protectively between the other trooper and Moonlight. 'What's going on?'

'Just say the sergeant's name please, Frank,' Toby pleaded.

'McTavish. Angus McTavish from Scotland who enjoys a drink more than anything.' Frank's eyes darted from Toby to the trooper, waiting for a sign that he had said the right thing.

The trooper lowered his carbine and took a step back. 'You know Sergeant McTavish?'

'Like I said, he was at my wedding. Known him for years, and he knows that this horse is mine. He'll vouch for me.'

The trooper stepped towards Frank and snatched the licence out of his hands. 'You may be able to prove the horse is yours, but it won't help him any if this licence is out of date.'

'I think you'll find it's all correct, my good fellow. All paid up to the end of the month.' Frank waited patiently while the trooper examined the licence. Unable to find any discrepancy, the constable shoved the licence towards Frank and shouldered his carbine.

'C'mon, Stan.'

The two troopers moved off among the mullock heaps without looking back. A minute later, cries of 'Joe!' began to echo from further along the gully, heralding the troopers' progress.

'Bloody Vandemonians,' Frank spat. 'Six months ago that pair would've been locked up in a penal colony in Van Demon's Land. They get released and come here, straight into the government's employ. What's the gold commissioner thinking, hiring men like that?'

'I guess they take who they can get,' Toby offered, a protective hand on Moonlight.

Frank shook his head as he carefully folded the licence and slipped it back into his pocket.

'We still have an hour or so of work, Toby. Maree is washing dirt down at the creek, but the two girls are at the hut. We'll see you back there at lunchtime.'

Toby found Annie a hundred yards from the hut. She staggered along the track with an armload of firewood.

'What are you doing carrying all that?' he said, and swung from the saddle to relieve her of her burden.

'It's good to see you, too.' Annie frowned at her husband, but welcomed the help. Her belly now protruded a hand's span in front of her, and she waddled a little as she struggled up the incline. 'We were running low on firewood and Betty is feeling too poorly to fetch it herself.' Her voice carried a frosty tone, but she slipped her arm through Toby's for support.

Toby dumped the wood by the fire, took his wife in his arms and kissed her on the mouth. As the kiss progressed she melted her body against his until a cry from the hut forced the couple to separate.

'Whew! That is so yucky. Will you two please stop?' Betty stood in the doorway of the hut, a look of revulsion on her face.

'Hello, Betty.' Toby flashed his most charming smile at her and Betty rushed across for a hug of her own.

'I thought you were supposed to be sick?' Annie said when her sister had let go of her husband.

'I feel better now. Honestly.' Betty didn't look at her sister as she grabbed Toby's hand and led him to his old log seat. 'Sit down, Toby, and I'll make you some tea.'

Toby sat, but made sure there was room for Annie beside him. He removed his jacket and folded it onto the log, then was forced to stand again and hold Annie's arm so she could maintain balance while manoeuvring herself onto the improvised cushion.

'How long before the baby comes?'

Toby asked this question every time he visited. He knew the answer exactly, for he counted the days he was away, but to hear it spoken gave him a deep, paternal pleasure.

Annie winced as she adjusted her weight on the log seat and rearranged her skirts about her legs. 'A month now. Maybe a little less. Mama says that babies almost never come when you expect them.'

'He's an O'Rourke,' Toby offered. 'He has an inbred sense of punctuality.'

'I hope you're right. I don't think I can stand it one day longer than I have to,' Annie said, and burst into tears.

'What's wrong, sweetheart?'

'Is this all there is for us, Toby?' she sobbed into his shoulder as he wrapped his arms about her.

'What do you mean?' He smoothed her hair against her head, holding her as tight as he dared.

'Is this what life is going to be like for us?' Annie gasped out the words between sobs. 'You always working so far away from me? Visiting whenever you can, but always having to leave? I feel that we are stuck like this, Toby. We are never going to be able to leave this wretched place. Never.'

Toby pushed her gently away from him and held her by the shoulders. He used his thumbs to wipe away the tears rolling down her cheeks.

'This is our best chance, sweetheart.' He felt her body stiffen as she fought to stifle the next sob. 'This is our best chance of making enough money to buy our place back. Then we will be together forever.' He tried to smile then, to show her that everything would be all right.

'But, what if we don't, Toby? What if all the gold we ever find is barely enough to fill a tobacco tin? What are we going to do? Every day I see unlucky diggers on the Melbourne road with their heads hung low in defeat. I fear that will be us, leaving this place with our tails between our legs, severely beaten by this—' – she waved a hand as she struggled to find the words she needed – 'this hard land.'

Toby didn't know what to say. In his heart he believed Paddy and Frank would one day find a big deposit of gold. It was going to happen; it was just a matter of time. That was what he was doing working at the mill, buying them time to make that big discovery. But Annie knew this. To say the words to her again would just be repeating himself. She needed more. Annie needed to know that all their hardships, all the long days spent apart were all going to be for something. But he had nothing more to offer. He had only the hope he held in his heart that one day their plans would all fall into place, that they would be a family, living together in the little homestead at Bunyong Creek.

Annie watched him expectantly, waiting for the answer that would dissolve her misery. Suddenly, she gave a little cry of pain and clasped her hands to her bulging belly.

'What is it, Annie? What's wrong?' Toby felt a spear of panic thrusting into his innards. He was about to send Betty scurrying down the hillside in search of her mother, but Annie smiled and took his hand.

'The baby!' she said, all the worry and misery gone from her face. 'The baby is kicking me.'

She placed Toby's hand over her stomach and pressed his fingers into her tight, yet yielding flesh. At first he felt nothing except the warmth of Annie's body against the palm of his hand. Then, something thrust out against Toby's outstretched fingers. The pressure continued, distorting Annie's skin and skirt, moulding it to a shape Toby could feel with his fingers. There was the unmistakable curve of a little heel and the arch of a foot half the length of his ring finger. He could feel and count five tiny toes with the tip of his finger and laughed out loud, keeping his hand tight against his wife's stomach and the tiny shape beneath, revelling in this first contact with his child.

Just as suddenly as it began, the unborn child pulled its foot away and Toby was left with only the feel of Annie's belly against his hand.

'It does that all the time. Usually when I least expect it.' Annie let her hand slip from Toby's, but the smile remained on her face.

'Let's set a date,' Toby said, his hand still on her belly.

'What do you mean?' Annie let the smile slip from her face.

'Let's set a time limit,' Toby expanded. 'A date when we will stop what we are doing here in Ballarat and move on with our lives. Good or bad, we will know when the end is coming. We will have something to look forward to, either way.'

'When?' Annie frowned. 'We have the baby to consider.'

'I know,' Toby said. 'When the baby is here and is big enough and strong enough to travel.'

'Where will we go?'

'I don't know. Home, I hope, but otherwise somewhere where we can be together. That's what you want, isn't it?'

'And Mama and Papa?'

'If they want to. Betty and Paddy, too.' He took a deep breath and held her at arm's length. 'I just want to give you something to hold onto, a hope that one day this will all be over and we will get on with our lives. Think about it. Talk it over with your ma and pa.'

The smile came back to her face and Toby realised he had succeeded. 'I will, Toby,' she whispered. 'As long as we are together. That's all that matters.'

Toby awoke to someone pounding furiously on the door.

'Who the hell is that?' Horrie mumbled from the other side of the hut they shared. 'It's still bloody dark outside.'

Toby swung his feet to the floor and pulled on his boots without bothering with socks. 'I'll see.'

The knocking kept up until he opened the door. Paddy stood in the darkness. Behind him the eastern sky had just begun to pale. It took Toby a moment to realize his brother wore only a long coat over his nightshirt.

'Bloody hell, Paddy. What are you doing here? Is everything all right at the camp?'

Paddy cradled his arms and pretended to rock an infant.

'My God! The baby's here.'

Paddy shook his head and pointed at his belly.

'The baby's coming?'

Paddy nodded, grabbed Toby's arm and pulled him towards the horse yard.

'Hang on, Pad. I have to get dressed. And tell Jim.'

'I heard,' Jim's voice growled from the direction of his hut. He appeared out of the darkness, his braces flapping about his legs. 'Get a move on, lad. Babies don't usually wait for errant fathers, you know.'

'Thanks, Jim. I'll get back as soon as I can.'

Jim waved a dismissive hand. 'Take a couple of days. We'll manage without you.'

Within three minutes Toby was dressed and had Moonlight saddled. The men lined up to wish him well. Horrie was the last to shake his hand.

'Give Annie my best, mate. I hope she and the baby are well.'

'Thanks, Horrie.'

'And if it's a boy you can name him after me,' Horrie added as Toby turned Moonlight for the track and raked the horse's flanks.

Annie lay propped on her parents' bed, several pillows behind her. She was the only one facing the door and smiled as Toby stepped into the hut. Perspiration dampened her dark hair which stuck to her face in dank wisps and curls. Frank held her left hand and Maree her right. Betty fussed about with the linen in a cradle waiting at the foot of the bed. Eileen Guinane poured water into a basin. Annie wore only a nightdress, also soaked in sweat. Her knees were raised and the hem of the dress had ridden up her thighs, but he had no thoughts for modesty as he rushed to the bedside.

'Toby.' Annie released her father's hand and took Toby's. He leaned in and kissed her on the forehead, surprised at the coolness of her skin despite the perspiration.

'I'm here, sweetheart.' He used his free hand to pull a strand of hair out of her eyes. 'I wouldn't miss this for anything in the world.'

Annie smiled. 'I knew you'd make it. Mama said not to be disappointed if you weren't here. But I knew you would be.' She turned to Paddy who stood just inside the door. 'Thank you for fetching him, Paddy. You are the best brother-in-law a girl could hope for.'

Paddy shuffled his feet and looked uncomfortable at the attention. Frank stepped over and rescued him from further embarrassment.

'C'mon, lad,' he said, clapping a hand on Paddy's shoulder and turning him to the door. 'Let's give the women some room to work. There's nothing more we can do.'

They stepped out into the morning air and Frank pulled the door softly shut behind him as Annie let out a low moan. Toby felt her grip tighten on his hand. Her smile was gone, replaced by an agonised grimace. The moan grew to a suppressed scream and Toby looked at Maree and Mrs Guinane, wanting them to do something for his wife. Maree continued to stroke her daughter's hand, smiling benevolently while Mrs Guinane carried the basin of water to the bedside and wiped Annie's brow.

'Closer together now, they are,' Mrs Guinane murmured. 'Not long, child.'

Annie's grip loosened as the contraction passed. The groan petered out and the smile returned to her face. 'Don't look so worried,' she said. 'This started in the middle of the night. I feel like an old hand. It must have been going on for six hours now.'

'Seven,' Maree corrected. 'You are doing wonderfully, my little one.'

'Toby, do you like the cradle Papa made? He has been working on it for weeks,' Annie said.

Toby looked over at the cradle where Betty fussed with the blankets, folding and refolding them as she waited for the baby in unusually quiet anticipation. He could see the quality of workmanship that had gone into the cradle's construction. Each joint was perfectly mated, giving it great strength. The cradle sat atop two polished rockers. Frank had glued felt from an old hat underneath them, ensuring a smooth and silent motion. The headboard had a scroll of ribbon carved into it with a crescent moon and a pattern of stars. Toby recognised the constellation.

Annie noticed where his gaze had settled. 'Our baby will sleep beneath the Southern Cross,' she said. 'He will always be able to find his way.'

'Frank has done a marvellous job,' Toby breathed. He could see the love in the workmanship.

'He gave up his tobacco allowance for four months just to buy the things he needed for that cradle,' Maree said proudly.

He felt Annie's grip tighten again. This time she was unable to suppress the scream as the contraction gripped her and it flew from her throat in a blood-curdling wail.

'Close and strong, they are,' Mrs Guinane said, 'Time menfolk were out of the hut.'

Toby ignored the American woman acting as midwife. He stroked Annie's hand and smiled at her, hoping he was giving her a look of reassurance, for he only felt fear in his heart.

'Nothing more you can do,' Mrs Guinane said, firmer this time, and fixed Toby with a steely gaze. 'Time you waited outside, Tobias. The little one will be with us shortly.'

Toby felt a spark of anger rise within him. Mrs Guinane held his stare and he realised he was up against a temper on a par with his own. Maree broke the stalemate.

'Go now, Toby. I'll send Betty to fetch you when the baby is here. There is no place for a man around the birthing bed.'

Reluctantly, Toby backed towards the door. Annie still held his hand and her fingers slid down his own, prolonging the touch for as long as possible until only the tips of their index fingers remained in contact. Then, that too was broken. Another contraction gripped Annie as he pulled the door open and stepped into the morning light. He had to walk a long way up the hillside before he couldn't hear his wife's screams.

Frank and Paddy had moved the horses up to the yard. They had the saddles off and Paddy was filling the trough with clean water as Toby staggered up to the rails, his mind still back in the hut.

'It's all up to Annie and the little one,' Frank called to him as he carried an armload of fodder to the yard and tossed it over the rail. 'Nothing you can do. When Maree was giving birth to Tom, I think I smoked a quarter pound of tobacco and walked about twelve miles – all in the confines of our kitchen in Hastings. I don't think I was any better when Annie arrived into the world.'

Toby looked across at Frank. His father-in-law stood facing him with a huge grin on his face.

'I just feel so helpless, Frank. There's nothing I can do.'

'You got here in time, lad. That's the best thing you could've done. Annie has asked for nothing but you since she first woke us at midnight. Now that you're here, she can concentrate on bringin' that baby into the world.'

'I – I guess so.'

'C'mon,' Frank beckoned. Let's go and put the billy on. I could do with a hot cuppa.'

Toby lingered at the rail. 'I don't know if I can listen to Annie's screams, Frank. Why don't you fetch the billy and the tea and I'll light a fire up here for—'

'Get your arse down that hill, lad. Annie's screams aren't the only thing you're going to hear. Pretty soon you'll hear the best thing a man can ever hear in his life.'

The trio wandered down the hill and Frank stoked the camp-fire into a blaze while Toby settled himself onto a log. Paddy filled the billy and set the tin mugs along the tailboard of the wagonette while they waited for the water to boil.

A series of groans and screams came from the hut, interspersed with muffled words of encouragement from Maree and Mrs Guinane. Toby sipped at his tea and tried to block out the noise. Frank was telling a little anecdote about the birth of Betty, but Toby was only half listening.

Annie let out a long, loud groan. In his mind, Toby could see every sinew in his wife's neck standing out as she struggled with the Herculean task. Then he heard Mrs Guinane's voice.

'This will be the last one, girl. The baby is crowning. One more big push with the next contraction.'

He could hear Annie panting as if she had just run all the way up from the creek, the air hissing in and out of her lungs. The sounds grew closer together until they merged into another drawn-out groan.

'This is it, girl,' Mrs Guinane shouted. 'Push.'

Annie's groan went on and on. Through it all Toby could hear the words of encouragement offered by Maree and Mrs Guinane. Then a strange thing happened. Annie's groan of agony changed into a peal of laughter. Maree squealed as the laughter died away, but he was unsure if it was with terror or pleasure.

Toby jumped to his feet and turned towards the hut, took two paces and turned for the horse yard. He checked himself and turned back for the hut, determined to enter and find out what was going on. A new noise stopped him.

A very loud and indignant wail penetrated the morning quiet. Toby stood still as he listened. He heard it gurgle and strain as a fresh breath forced its way into unused lungs, and then the wail continued on again, gathering strength with each new breath. It took several seconds before he realised he was listening to the first cries of his child.

'There it is.' Frank jumped to his feet and pumped Toby's arm up and down. 'Congratulations, lad.'

Paddy rushed across and swept his brother into a huge bear hug, lifted him off his feet and swung him about like a rag doll. He only stopped when the door of the hut opened and Betty rushed down the steps.

'It's a boy!' She yelled the words as she sprinted towards Toby. 'It's a boy!'

Paddy placed his brother back on the ground and Betty danced about excitedly.

'It's a boy! It's a boy!' She squealed as her father picked her up in his arms and hugged her. 'Oh, Papa, I have a little nephew.'

'I know, Princess, I know.'

'Is Annie all right? Toby asked.

Before Betty could answer, Maree appeared in the doorway of the hut. She rushed over, embraced Toby and kissed him lightly on the cheek.

'Congratulations, Mr O'Rourke. You have a baby boy. Oh, he's just beautiful.'

'I hope you're saving some of those for me, Mrs Hocking?' Frank asked.

'Certainly, Mr Hocking.' Maree swooped out of Toby's arms and into Frank's. 'We have a grandson. You always wanted a grandson.'

'What about Annie?' Toby asked again.

'She's fine, love,' Maree spoke the words he wanted to hear. 'I have to go back inside and get her cleaned up. I'll call you as soon as you can come in.'

It seemed like hours before Betty appeared in the doorway and beckoned Toby over. When Frank and Paddy went to follow, the girl stood in their path.

'Mrs Guinane says for only Toby to come in. The baby is feeding.'

Frank looked set to protest, but thought better of it. He and Paddy went back to the campfire as Toby stepped into the hut.

Annie was still on the bed, much as he had last seen her. She was still propped up by a collection of pillows behind her head, but now she sat upright and her legs were beneath the covers. Toby noticed that the bedclothes had been changed. These were crisp and white where the others had been sweat-stained and rumpled. Mrs Guinane stepped out through the back door into the little storeroom with the old bedclothes. Toby could see bloodstains showing and felt a pang of concern, but looking back to Annie and the serene smile on her face he knew everything was all right. She held the bundled infant across her chest, one breast exposed through the open bodice of her nightdress as Toby's son suckled hungrily, making greedy little gulping noises. Only the baby's head showed, the skin a blotchy mass of colour ranging from purple to pink. He saw the little nose pushed up against Annie's breast and a gasp escaped his lips.

That nose looks just like mine.

Annie held out a hand to him. He took it and sat on the bed beside her and his son. The baby never broke his rhythm.

'Isn't he the most beautiful thing you've ever seen, Toby?' Annie let go of Toby's hand to stroke the tiny head where a mane of dark hair showed.

'Yes – yes he is.'

The baby finished feeding and turned his head towards his father. Maree had told him some time ago that newborn babies are unable to see anything for many days, but he couldn't help but think his son was studying him with those piercing blue eyes.

'This is your papa.' Annie looked up at Toby. 'Want to hold him?'

'I don't—I wouldn't know how,' Toby stammered.

'Just like me, silly,' Annie said and passed their son to him.

Toby took the infant in his arms and held him like he was the most delicate thing in the world.

'I've been thinking about a name for him,' Annie said once Toby had settled.

'Uh-huh,' Toby muttered, not taking his eyes off his son.

'I thought we could call him Sean, after your father.'

He looked at Annie then. She had a knowing smile on her face and reached out to squeeze his arm. 'I thought it would mean a lot to you.'

'It does, Annie.' Toby nearly choked on the words. Another Sean O'Rourke in the world. His mother and father would have been proud.

His reverie was broken by a loud knocking at the door, followed by Frank's indignant request.

'Can a grandfather see his flamin' grandson yet, or not?'

As the rostered cook for the week, Jim released Toby from his duties an hour early so that he could attend to the evening meal. By the time he heard Hissing Harriet grind to a stop and the relief valve open, he had chops sizzling in the pan and a damper baking in a camp oven. Soon the men wandered over, shaking sawdust from their hair and clothing.

'Smells good, lad,' Jim said as he settled into his usual place.

The men sat around the campfire and Toby dished out their meals. There was no conversation as they ate ravenously, but as they finished and Toby collected the plates, the banter sparked up again.

'I'll bet young Sean's growing,' Paul said between bites of damper.

'Sure is,' Toby said. 'Every Sunday it looks like he's doubled his size.'

'I suppose Annie is busy with him all the time?' Horrie asked. 'Too busy to bake one of her famous cakes?'

'I'll suggest it to her next Sunday, Horrie.'

'That would be wonderful. No offence, mate, but she's a better cook than you.'

Toby laughed. 'None taken. I could do with a bit of Annie's cooking myself.'

They chatted idly into the evening, until Jim produced a bottle of rum and handed around the pannikins.

'A couple of nobblers to bring a good night's sleep,' he suggested, pouring a good dram into his pannikin, before passing the bottle on. When everyone had rum in their cups, he raised a toast.

'To the health of Sean O'Rourke.' And the others followed his example as Toby smiled with fatherly pride. Toasting his son's health had become a nightly ritual at the mill.

'Hello, the camp.'

The voice came out of the darkness. Toby thought he recognised a familiar lilt.

'Come on in,' Jim called and climbed to his feet. The others did the same.

A lone figure on horseback emerged out of the darkness. Sergeant McTavish reined his horse in by the campfire. 'Is this where Toby O'Rourke works?'

'I'm here, Sergeant.' Toby lifted a hand in greeting.

'Thank God.' McTavish swung from his horse. 'Frank gave me rough directions, but I wasn't sure.'

'Frank? Is everything all right in Ballarat?' Toby stepped across and gripped the policeman's arm.

'No—well, yes, everything's all right with your family, Toby. There is trouble on the diggings tonight, though.'

'What's going on?' Jim asked.

'The miners rioted over the outcome of a murder trial and burnt a hotel to the ground.' McTavish noticed the look on Toby's face. 'Don't worry, laddie. Your family are well out of it. I've been tied up with another matter. I thought you might be interested to know I have a man in custody. Tall fellow with a patch over his left eye.'

'That sounds like one of the coves who duffed our cattle,' Toby said. 'He had a friend with little pig eyes and glasses, and only one hand.'

'*Had* a friend is right,' McTavish said. 'The fellow in custody stabbed him over a card game in one of the grog shops. He's dead. Sounds like the fellow you just described. I thought you might want to come and have a look at this bastard. Has to be tonight, though. He's being transported to Melbourne in the morning.'

Scotchy sat chained to a large gum tree at Government Camp along with several other men. Toby recognised him instantly. He had his back to the tree, a heavy chain looped through a set of darbies on his wrists. Toby and McTavish tied their horses to a rail near the gold commissioner's tent, but a constable approached McTavish before they could walk to the tree.

'Super wants to see you, Sarge. Something about the paperwork going to Melbourne tomorrow.'

McTavish gave Toby an apologetic smile. 'I won't be a minute, laddie.' He followed the constable towards a row of tents.

Toby watched McTavish go, then turned his attention back to Scotchy. The duffer hadn't moved and looked like he was asleep, his chin lowered to his chest. Toby knew he should wait for McTavish, but he wanted to confront this man who had caused so much heartache.

Scotchy didn't bother to look up at his approach. Toby wanted to kick him in the ribs and the head and go on kicking until he was a bleeding, dying mess. He swung a booted foot, but aimed for Scotchy's thigh.

Scotchy let out a yelp of pain and glared up at Toby. 'You little bastard. If I wasn't chained up I'd—'

'Did you get a good price for my cattle, Scotchy?'

The duffer studied Toby's face, squinting up at him with his eye. 'Who are you? How do you know my name?'

'You don't remember me, do you, Scotchy?'

Scotchy held Toby's stare for a few more seconds, then shook his head. 'You'll have to refresh my memory.'

'You don't remember me, but I remember you. You and that bastard Dundas tied me and my brother to a tree and ran off with our cattle to the Bendigo Creek diggings.'

Scotchy's eye widened as he made the connection. The briefest hint of a smile played over his face. 'You had a mute brother, didn't you?'

Toby nodded.

'The last time I laid eyes on you, you were hollering all sorts of obscenities at me. That was just before Dundas and me rode away with your herd of scrawny cattle. If I remember rightly, we didn't get too good a price from the butcher at Bendigo. They was too thin, he said. That butcher was more of a thief than us.'

'You did more than just steal a few head of cattle from some boys,' Toby spat at him. 'My brother and me, we lost our home because we couldn't pay back a debt owed against our land.'

Scotchy turned his head away. For a moment Toby thought the duffer was feeling guilt, but realised he was beyond any such emotion. He knew Scotchy would kill a man for the few coins in his pocket and think nothing of leaving his wife and children destitute.

'This man,' Scotchy turned back to Toby, 'the one you owed the debt to. Was he that stocky old fellow with silver hair Dundas and me was chatting to outside the pub?'

'Yes—yes, he was.'

A chuckle escaped Scotchy's lips and he shook his head. 'So that was the old man's plan. He did tell us we would be helping him out with some larger scheme. If I'd known what it was, I would have made the old boy pay double.'

'What do you mean pay double?' Toby shouted. 'What has Henry Pelham got to do with you and Dundas taking our cattle?' Even as he spoke, Toby grasped the whole evil design that had seen him and Paddy lose their home. Henry Pelham had played them like the young fools they were. Eager to please. Eager to gather together a herd and drive it out along the colony's tracks where it would be easy prey for men like Scotchy and Dundas. He had played right into Pelham's hands.

'You all right, laddie?' McTavish had come up behind Toby.

'Tell him.' Toby stabbed a kick at Scotchy's boot. 'Tell him what you just told me.'

Scotchy glared up at the policeman and sneered. 'I got nothin' to say to no one.' He dropped his head to stare at the patch of ground between his legs.

Toby bent and grabbed him by the lapels of his coat.

'Tell him, you thieving bastard. Tell him how Henry Pelham paid you to steal our cattle so he could take our farm.'

Scotchy accepted Toby's rough handling with resigned indifference. 'I don't know what you're talking about.' He looked at Toby and smiled, the skin around his eye crinkling.

Toby brought his fist back, but McTavish pulled him away before he could deliver the punch.

'He's a prisoner of the Crown, laddie. I can't let you beat him up – no matter how much he deserves it.'

'We have to get the truth out of him,' Toby yelled, struggling against the sergeant's grip as he was pulled away.

Behind him, Scotchy chuckled quietly.

S ir Charles Hotham paced up and down the verandah outside his residence at Government House and tugged absentmindedly at his sideburns, as he did when he was agitated. He let out a deep sigh and settled his lean frame into a wicker chair. The sigh was not so much a result of his current predicament, but more a release of his frustration at what might have been.

A naval officer of the old school, Hotham was an ambitious man with a deep-seated dedication to duty – whatever he interpreted that duty to be. He had requested a posting to the Crimea, for that was where the action was. Her Majesty's armed forces needed officers of the highest order, men able to make tough decisions that would ultimately lead to victory. A senior officer who could change the course of a military engagement with a decisive plan could name his own posting, would be the toast of the empire, and have his advancement ensured.

He had requested the Crimea. But it seemed his glory was to be denied him. His superiors had seen fit, instead, to ship him out to this far corner of the empire, as the new Lieutenant Governor of the Colony of Victoria.

The colony itself had been left in a disastrous state by his predecessor. Every branch of the fledgling government was in a state of chaos. Hotham had arrived with strict instructions from the colonial secretary to fix the treasury in Victoria. He had immediately ordered an audit of the department and was astonished to learn that the colony was in debt by almost a million pounds. An unbelievable sum. As if that wasn't bad enough, the treasury still haemorrhaged money at a substantial rate.

The population itself seemed to be in a constant state of protest at the mismanagement of government departments. Miners at Bendigo had rallied and threatened to march on the Government Camp there in protest at the licence fee and the number of Chinese being allowed to flock to the diggings. Hotham was a great believer in strict discipline, and he knew a firm hand was needed when dealing with unruly men.

Now it seemed that the troubles were about to re-emerge on the fields at Ballarat. He had toured there only recently and had been warmly received by the miners. They had expressed their concerns at what they considered an exorbitant licence fee and made pleas for stronger representation in the legislative assembly. Governor FitzRoy in New South Wales had seen fit to lower the monthly licence fee to ten shillings. Surely something similar could be implemented here, they pleaded. He had told them he would see what could be done to address their concerns and the diggers had sent him on his way back to Melbourne with three hearty cheers. Then they had rioted over the result of a murder trial and burnt a building to the ground. When the ringleaders had been arrested and brought to Melbourne for trial, the miners had sent a delegation to him demanding their release. He was the Queen's representative in the colony and the citizens were making demands of him. He would not tolerate it.

All recent despatches from Commissioner Rede at Ballarat carried word of growing unrest. The miners were forming into large and dangerous mobs, calling for changes to government process and taxes. They disguised these treasonous gatherings under the false banner of the Ballarat Reform League, but Hotham could sense the seeds of rebellion taking root among the shafts and mullock heaps of the diggings. It was time a firm hand was used to quell this type of behaviour. Then he could return to the task of sorting out the colony's other problems.

'I'll have the 40th and 12th Regiments march to the diggings at Ballarat as soon as possible,' he mused out loud. 'A show of force is just what is needed. Nothing quiets an unruly mob quicker than a procession of redcoats marching into view with bayonets fixed.'

On Sunday, Toby left for the hut on the diggings before the sun came up. He made his way into Ballarat and onto the Melbourne road before leaving the main thoroughfare and entering one of the side tracks that would eventually climb into the gully where the Hockings were camped. A few men and women made their way along the paths, some in their Sunday finery as they headed for church.

As he rounded the shoulder of the hill, he found his way blocked by a group of men.

'Which way did you come from?' one of them asked. He looked at Toby with red-rimmed eyes and his boots were caked in mud.

'From the sawmill on the western road,' Toby said.

'Did you see anyone with a young girl? She's about fourteen and wearing a blue pinafore. I fear some mongrel has snatched her. We've been out looking since sundown yesterday.' He cast his arm at the six men behind him.

'No, I haven't,' Toby said. 'Where did she go missing from?'

'We live on the edge of Yuille's Swamp,' he said, pointing towards the large body of water to the north of Ballarat. 'She went out to check the eel traps late yesterday and didn't come back.'

'Bloody hell,' Toby said. 'She didn't fall in the water or something?'

The man shook his head. 'Me mates and me have spent all night trudging around the edge of the swamp. When we didn't find her, we thought we'd try the diggings. Someone has to have seen her.'

'Tell you, what,' Toby said. 'I'll fetch my brother and father-in-law from their camp and we'll come give you a hand.'

Toby returned on foot ten minutes later with Frank and Paddy in tow. The man stood by the track with just one other. The rest had gone.

'Me mates have gone to search through the diggings,' he explained. Colin and me thought we'd head back to the swamp and have a look in daylight.'

'Probably the best thing you can do,' Toby said.

'My name's Peter Dunn,' the man said, and shook hands with everyone. 'This is Colin Symes. Thanks for your help. Caroline is just a girl. She's never been away from home before.'

Dunn and Symes led them to the swamp and they followed it to the west. The edge was thick with reeds. The path eventually opened out into a small clearing and Dunn pointed at the water.

'The eel traps are just through there. Caroline comes around here every afternoon and checks them.'

'Let's take a look closer to the water,' Frank said. Symes and Dunn followed him through the reeds.

Paddy wandered about the clearing and studied the ground. There were many footprints. He sat on his haunches to examine a small depression in the mud. Toby moved up beside him.

'What is it, mate?'

Paddy pointed at a small, dainty print made by a bare foot.

'Was Caroline wearing shoes, Mr Dunn?' Toby called in the direction of the water.

'No. She always goes about barefoot.

'Must be hers, Pad,' Toby said, and his brother nodded. 'Let's see if we can find her trail going in and coming back out. Then we'll know she's not in the water.'

They scouted about the clearing. The ground was soft and the prints well formed. After a few minutes it was possible to single out the girl's spoor leading into the clearing from the east. The trail disappeared into the water near the eel traps, and then came back into the clearing.

'She's not in the water,' Toby called to Frank and the others. 'Not in this part of the swamp, anyway.'

The three men came out of the reeds. Paddy herded them away from the spoor to prevent it from being obscured.

'How can you be sure?' Frank asked.

'Her trail is quite clear here,' Toby said. 'She came around the edge of the swamp, went in to the traps and then came back out.'

Dunn looked down at the confusion of prints and scratched the back of his head. 'Where did she go from here, then?'

'It gets a little confusing just here,' Toby said, pointing at a mess of mud and prints. 'But we can't find her bare feet heading back to the east.'

Frank glanced at the impenetrable wall of reeds and scrub on higher ground. 'She didn't go through there. She must have gone further around the swamp.'

'Let's see if we can find her spoor in that direction,' Toby suggested, and they moved off in a loose line, stooped over as they examined the ground.

'Where did you learn to track?' Symes asked as they neared the far end of the clearing.

'Paddy and me used to track down lost cattle on our parents' property up on the Coliban River. We'd hunt down dingos that took an interest in the sheep. Sometimes we'd even track each other when we were playing in the hills. We're no experts, though. An Aborigine tracker could run rings around us.'

'You seem to be doing all right,' Symes said. He was interrupted by Paddy clapping his hands for attention.

'Found something, Pad?'

Paddy pointed at the ground and Toby went to him. 'It's her print all right.'

'Why was she going this way?' Dunn said. 'It doesn't make sense. Our hut is round the other side.'

Toby bent to examine another print nearby. This one was the half-circle of a horse's hoof. 'When you came searching last night, were any of you on horseback?'

'No. We walked from my place around the edge of the swamp,' Dunn said.

Paddy tugged at Toby's sleeve and pointed ahead.

'Yeah, I see 'em, Pad.' More prints led into the distance. 'She was up on the balls of her feet here.'

'What does that mean?' Symes asked.

'My God,' Frank said. 'She was running.'

'Running?' Dunn asked. 'Running from what?'

'My guess would be whoever was on the horse,' Toby said. He followed the prints for a few paces. 'See how the horse's spoor closes with the girl's? He caught up with her here. Her prints just vanish, even though the ground is quite soft. I reckon the cove on the horse pulled her off the ground.'

'I was right,' Dunn said, a look of horror on his face. 'Some bastard has snatched my little girl.'

'We should fetch the police,' Frank said.

'There's no time for that,' Dunn yelled. 'We have to catch the bastard before he hurts her.' He turned to Toby and gripped his arm. 'You can follow the horse. You and your brother can do it. Please, you have to help me.'

'All right.' Toby nodded. 'We'll give it a try.'

The hut sat below a range of low hills to the north-east of Yuille's Swamp, a simple structure of bark and bush timber. A piece of old sacking hung in place of a door. Forty yards from the hut a mullock heap and mineshaft were just visible through the trees. Behind the hut someone had erected a small horse yard by lashing poles to the trunks of saplings. A roan horse stood near the rails, unaware of the men concealed in the bush.

'Are you sure this is the place?' Dunn asked.

'The tracks from the swamp come straight to here,' Toby confirmed.

'I don't see anything,' Frank whispered. 'Maybe they moved on.'

Dunn shook his head. 'Someone lives at this place. They wouldn't leave the horse yarded up like that unless they were close by.'

'He's here,' Toby said. 'In the hut. The girl's here somewhere, too.'

Dunn stood and walked cautiously forward, his musket held low across his hip. The others followed him across the clearing to the hut. A campfire by the doorway had burned down to a bed of white ash. An empty whisky bottle lay beside it. Dunn reached the doorway, pulled the sacking aside and stepped into the gloomy interior. Toby followed him through.

A naked man lay sprawled on a cot, on his back with one arm draped across his face.

Dunn prodded the sleeping figure with the muzzle of his gun.

'Where's my daughter, you bastard?'

The man lifted his arm from his eyes and, for a moment, seemed to have trouble focusing. His gaze found Dunn looming over him, gun in hand, and he pushed himself towards the back wall, skidding across the bed on his bare buttocks.

'Don't shoot,' he whimpered. 'I haven't any money. Take whatever you want, but don't shoot me.'

'We don't want your money,' Dunn screamed. 'Where the hell's my daughter? You lifted her from the track beside the swamp yesterday.'

The naked man tried to push himself back further, but came up hard against the wall. 'There's no woman here. You've got the wrong man. I wasn't anywhere near the swamp yesterday.'

'Bullshit,' Dunn snapped.

'It's the truth, I tell you,' the man whimpered. 'I didn't do nothin' to no girl.'

Toby turned and went past Frank, back out into the sunlight. All around the campfire there was a confusion of footprints, wandering in many different directions. Out of this mess he found a trail moving away from the hut – bare feet, a man's feet – heading in the direction of the mine. Paddy came up beside him and they followed the tracks around the mullock heap to the shaft. Toby leaned over and looked into the shadowy depths. The shaft wasn't deep, about fifteen feet or so. There was enough light to see to the bottom where the crumpled body lay.

A week after Caroline Dunn's murder, the men at the sawmill were sitting about the campfire enjoying an evening nobbler of rum. Paul and Horrie were teaching Toby and Gary how to play rummy, while Jim sat in a camp chair, his back to the fire as he read a copy of the *Argus* newspaper.

'Well, I'll be damned,' he said, twisting to get more firelight on the page.

'What is it, Jim?' Horrie looked up from where he was shuffling the deck of cards.

'That young girl's murder is in the paper. The article runs for nearly a full page. The bastard what did it has been transported to Melbourne.'

'He'll dance the devil's jig at the end of a rope,' Gary said. 'Hangin's too bloody good for him, though.'

Toby remained quiet. He was still having nightmares about the body in the bottom of the mineshaft and just wanted to forget all about the incident. Jim pulled him into the conversation.

'You get a big mention here, Toby. The article credits you with trackin' the mongrel down.'

'It wasn't just me,' Toby said. 'Paddy did a lot of the work as well.' He pointed at the cards in Horrie's hands and tried to change the subject. 'C'mon, we playing or what?'

'Well, the whole colony will know your name now,' Jim said, and turned the page.

'Joe! Joe!'

Along with everyone else at the blacksmith shop on the Gravel Pits, Paddy turned towards the direction of the shouts.

'Digger hunt,' said one of the men waiting in line.

Out across the flats a large group of foot police crossed the diggings. Each carried a musket and the bayonets glinted viciously in the hot sun.

'Look at that, would you?' Another man lifted his hand to shade his eyes. 'There must be thirty of the buggers.'

A line of horsemen materialised out of the heat haze behind the foot police and Paddy realised these were mounted police, ready to chase down any miner who tried to run from the net cast across the flats.

'Bloody hell! They mean business this time.'

Miners climbed from their shafts or left their gold cradles standing in the creek and ran to form a barrier to oppose what in their eyes was a blatant abuse of authority. Paddy and the others at the blacksmith shop ran to join hundreds of men gathered on the flats. They stood shoulder to shoulder across the front of the advancing police. The diggers formed a line near the blacksmith shop, already two and three deep, with more running to join the throng. The foot police came to a halt and eyed the angry diggers.

From the ranks of mounted police an officer urged his horse forward. He stopped behind the line of foot police, drew his sword and pointed it at the diggers as he spoke.

'You men there, have your licences ready for inspection.'

A chuckle came from a few diggers, rising clear above the wind. The laughter was taken up and spread like a bushfire down the line of diggers until they all howled with mirth, some slapping their knees with amateur theatrics.

Beneath his peaked cap, the officer's face turned a vivid scarlet. Paddy realised he was not used to having his instructions treated with such contempt. The horse sensed its rider's anger and wheeled about uncertainly. The officer had to fight to bring it back under control.

'Foot police!' he roared. 'Advance and check their licences. Anyone without a licence is to be taken into custody. We'll see if a day or two chained to the tree at Government Camp won't cool their ardour.'

The foot police started forward, bayonets to the fore. They had not gone three paces when a barrage of stones, sticks and other missiles rained down on them from the assembled diggers. Despite the primitive defence, the barrage continued like a hailstorm until the police, outnumbered by almost six to one, were forced to check their advance and retreat out of range. Several of their number had been knocked senseless and were dragged to safety by their comrades.

The officer trotted his horse up and down the rank of police, a look of consternation on his face at having his men so crudely beaten back.

'We won't show our licences. We won't show our licences.' The cry was taken up like a war chant. The diggers bellowed at the top of their voices and sent the occasional stone flying towards the police to show they were still prepared to meet any assault.

Having had enough of these games, the officer reined in his horse behind the left flank.

'Number one section, prepare to fire. On my order, one round of volley fire over the heads of the miners. Don't aim too high. I want them to feel the wind in their hair. Number one section, fire!'

The left flank of muskets erupted into noise and flame. A cloud of blue smoke hung in the air for a moment, and then was carried on the wind through the mob of diggers. Paddy and some other miners had thrown themselves to the ground, but others remained stoically on their feet. They began taunting the police once more.

'You missed, you trap bastards.'

'Where'd you learn to shoot?'

'Couldn't hit the ground if you tried.'

On the Eureka Lead word passed quickly that the traps were firing on diggers down at the Gravel Pits. Every man dropped whatever he was doing and ran to join the affray. Some, having heard the gunfire, detoured by their tents to retrieve firearms before running to the flats.

Frank smoked a pipe as he waited for Paddy to return with the sharpened pick. He heard the news from a mob of running men and set off to support his mates in the fracas below. A digger running beside him gave a quizzical look and Frank tried to answer between ragged breaths. 'I don't know what's going on, mate, but we better keep with the rest of 'em.'

The Eureka mob reached the Gravel Pits and Frank could see the ranks of police with their bayonets fixed, the mounted constables with pistols in hand. Then he saw red-jacketed reinforcements double-timing down the hill from Government Camp to join the already formidable opposition.

'We need to disperse,' a voice yelled. 'The soldiers will cut us down if given the chance.' Frank recognised the speaker as Peter Lalor, a man who had addressed several meetings to discuss the miners' treatment by government forces.

'Run away?' one of the diggers nearest him asked. 'We need to stand together.'

'And we shall die together,' Lalor yelled into the man's face. 'We aren't prepared for a battle like this, picks and shovels against muskets. Spread the word,' he shouted to all within earshot. The man had a natural gift for leadership and the men looked to him for instruction. 'Tell the diggers to pull back. We shall meet again on Bakery Hill. We need time to prepare, to arm ourselves.'

Frank and the other men ran to their task, spreading Lalor's orders through the crowd of angry miners. But it was happening too slowly. Frank saw that the miners were spread along a front of almost two hundred yards and the yelling and stone throwing had started once more, drowning out voices of reason.

He found Paddy among the crowd and clasped a hand on the young man's shoulder. 'Thank God, Pad. Lalor wants the miners to pull back. We're meeting up on Bakery Hill.' Frank related Lalor's instructions.

Orders were being yelled from the police lines and Frank turned to look. The line of foot police seemed to rise as one and rushed towards the retreating diggers to take into custody those who were not so fleet of foot. He looked about for Paddy and found him three paces away, using an outflung arm to direct what diggers he could towards Bakery Hill.

'C'mon, Pad. Time we were gone from here,' he growled, pushing him along roughly. 'This sort of thing can't keep going on. It's time the men on this diggings did something about it.'

Word spread through the diggings like a scrub fire and the miners hurried in their thousands to an open patch of ground near the bakery, a huge gathering of men who had either witnessed first-hand or had heard of the government's use of unreasonable force during that morning's licence hunt.

Frank and Paddy found themselves near the fore of this angry and vengeful assembly. They had gone back to the hut before coming to the meeting and Paddy carried his musket.

Looking above him, Paddy saw the flag of the Southern Cross, the standard of the diggers, as it fluttered on a makeshift pole, the white stars showing proudly on a field of blue. Four rope stays held the flagpole erect, within which was the stump from which addresses had been made to previous meetings.

Several attempts were made to get the meeting underway, but each person who climbed onto the stump made the mistake of asking for moderation from the diggers and was howled down by the mob before any resolution could be reached. They had been attacked in force and they wanted action. None were prepared to listen to talk of delegations and petitions. But when Peter Lalor climbed onto the stump, the first thing the diggers saw was a pistol clasped firmly in his right hand. He held it above his head for all to see and the rumble of voices died away. Paddy watched as Lalor revolved slowly on the stump with pistol held high.

'Today our rights as free citizens were violated,' Lalor shouted. 'No more!' He shook the pistol above his head.

'No more!' The diggers echoed his words, their voices a blast of sound that echoed among the hills and gullies.

'We have tried the voice of reason,' Lalor continued. 'We have tried petitions and have sent delegations of respectable and honest men to the Governor himself. Still, our rights as free men have been trampled as though they mean nothing.'

'Too right, Pete,' a digger called and the cheer went up. Lalor waited patiently for quiet. Paddy thought he carried a look of solemn regret on his face.

'I propose that if none in government will defend our rights then that duty falls to us. I propose we arm ourselves,' he shouted, raising the pistol once more, 'and form into divisions. That we place these divisions in such a manner that we, the miners of Ballarat, will be able to stand against the tyrants who would see us crushed into the dust.'

A great hurrah went up from the masses. Paddy realised these were the words the diggers had been waiting so long to hear. Here, at last, was a man they could trust to help them stand against unscrupulous officials and petty administrators. Along with the other armed diggers, Paddy raised his sea-service musket and Frank cheered, putting enough energy into his voice for Paddy's share as well.

'Those men willing to stand and fight, I ask now to come forward and enrol. We are lucky enough to have some ex-military men among us and they shall captain the divisions. I would ask you to enrol according to the type of weapon you carry or the type of weapon you are proficient at using.'

Before Lalor finished speaking there was a great rush towards a row of trestle tables where men waited with ink and paper. The diggers jostled each other for position, each wanting to be the first to place his name on a list. Once more Lalor's leadership came to the fore. He soon had the surging crowd organised into orderly queues and proceedings running smoothly.

Because Paddy had the musket, he and Frank joined a line of men wishing to enlist in a rifle brigade. When their turn came to front the table, the digger acting as clerk eyed them curiously.

'I see the lad is armed, mate, but do you have a gun?'

'No,' Frank admitted, 'but Paddy here is mute. He needs me to talk for him.'

'Your son?' the clerk asked.

'Brother of my son-in-law. He's part of my family.'

'Well, this ain't the British bloody Army,' the clerk said with a grin. 'We don't break up families here. What are your names?

'Patrick O'Rourke,' Frank said, clamping a hand on Paddy's shoulder, 'and Francis Hocking.'

The clerk noted their names on one of a bundle of loose sheets of paper. When he was finished he looked up. 'Welcome to the Second Rifle Division. Form up on the left of the flag-pole and await further instructions.' He waved them away.

Paddy walked with Frank to the area the clerk had indicated and fell in with the rest of their divisional comrades. The line wavered a bit and seemed to move about with the mood of the men forming it. Some broke ranks to go to other divisions and talk to their mates. Others attended the stall of a sly grog seller who had the foresight to set up shop at the gathering and capitalise on the huge number of hot and thirsty men. There was no military discipline to this ragtag army of miners, thrown together from men who came from all over the world.

When the last of the diggers had placed his name on one of the lists and wandered off to join his comrades, Peter Lalor climbed back onto the stump.

'Take a knee,' he said, and the diggers dropped as one man. Like the other men, Paddy knelt, removed his hat and held it over his heart. Lalor waited until the noise of their actions had settled, then removed his own hat and tilted his face upwards to the blue and white flag fluttering above him. His voice rang out clear and strong.

'We swear by the Southern Cross to stand truly by each other and defend our rights and our liberties.'

The diggers repeated the oath, word for word, their gaze fixed on the banner above Lalor's head. Paddy echoed the oath in his mind. Despite lacking a voice, he meant every word of it. The flag of the Southern Cross had become their symbol, their declaration to the world that they would fight to defend their rights. Each man made the oath with bared head and hand outstretched to that new flag, and each man carried in his heart the conviction to stand by the words spoken, whatever the cost.

'Divisions form up,' Lalor shouted, and he leaped from the stump. The flag was hauled down and held at the head of a winding column of diggers as they marched in divisions, two abreast, to the Eureka Lead. Here the flag was raised again at the northern end of the lead near the Melbourne road.

While Lalor and the captains retired to a hut to discuss defensive measures, Paddy, Frank and the other men set about constructing a crude stockade wall out of anything they could lay their hands on. Bush poles and split timber slabs were gathered up from all over the diggings and carted up to the Eureka Lead. Carts and drays were seconded to the cause and overturned to form barriers. Where huts were encountered by the men their walls were incorporated in the barricades. One storekeeper returned to his hut to find that it now formed part of the fortifications of what the diggers had begun calling the Eureka Stockade.

A gap of ten or so paces was left in the southern part of the breastwork and two drays were positioned in the opening to act as gates which could be rolled aside if needed. Sentries were posted at these makeshift gates and a series of roving pickets set about patrolling the perimeter.

A blacksmith shop had been enclosed inside the fortifications of the stockade. Paddy watched the sympathetic smithy furiously hammering out crude blades that were then lashed to lengths of bush timber to form pikes. Thus armed, the pikemen began to drill under their divisional captains, marching and wheeling about, shouldering their pikes or grounding them to present a bristling barricade against an imagined cavalry charge.

Late that afternoon the rifle brigades were assembled and some of those without weapons were issued with firearms collected from the mining populace in the name of liberty. Frank found himself in possession of a single-shot 10-bore shotgun that looked as if it had been collecting dirt and dust under some miner's cot for years. It was old and battered, but he felt better for having a weapon in his hands. He immediately set to cleaning and loading the ancient piece, proud to be more than just a supernumerary among the armed men.

A little after four o'clock the Second Rifle Division was called to order by their captain. Paddy and Frank stood together in the front rank, their weapons resting on their shoulders.

'Men, we are desperately short of supplies within the stockade,' the captain began, pacing up and down his line of troops with both hands clasped into the small of his back. 'Mr Lalor has asked that all men not engaged in the actual defence of the stockade at this moment should be sent out to forage for provisions of both a nutritional and military nature.'

He paused and looked at them sternly, raising his voice. 'There is to be no looting. Any storekeeper who provides to our requirements is to be given a promissory note against those goods. Powder and shot are our priorities, gentlemen, then bacon and beef. However, if a kindly publican should offer up a keg or two of the good stuff, who are we to refuse such a kindly gesture?' A murmur of chuckles passed down the ranks, and the captain dismissed them to go about their tasks.

Frank and Paddy made their way out of the stockade and headed towards their camp. Along the way they came across a store and, following orders, Frank ushered Paddy inside and asked the storekeeper for any provisions he could spare in the name of the Ballarat Reform League.

'Take whatever you want,' the storekeeper blurted, eyeing the firearms in Frank and Paddy's hands. He was surprised when the two desperados settled on two forty-pound casks of black powder, some lead bars and shot moulds to make musket balls and a bag of percussion caps. To carry it all they also picked out a wheelbarrow and piled their provisions into it. Frank wrote out a promissory note for all they had taken, including the wheelbarrow, and gave the man a hearty handshake.

'Thank you, sir. Much obliged.'

The storekeeper looked at the note with disdain, but he was happy to see them leave his store.

By this time the sun had lowered onto the western horizon. Everywhere the pair looked there seemed to be parties of armed diggers out foraging for provisions. Frank looked over at Paddy and asked, 'Are you getting hungry, mate?'

Paddy nodded his head and rubbed his stomach. With all that had happened during the day neither of them had eaten since breakfast.

'Did Annie say she was doing dumplings for dinner tonight?'

Paddy nodded, a huge grin on his face. Annie's dumplings, from a recipe obtained from Mrs Guinane, were one of the men's favourite dishes.

'It looks as if we've done our bit for the cause,' Frank said, sweeping his arm over the contents of the barrow. 'There are enough coves out doing the gathering. I don't suppose they will miss us until after dinner time. Come on.'

Maree watched the two men come up the trail to the hut and felt very relieved to see them. All afternoon the diggings had been abuzz with talk of the newly formed diggers' army. While collecting water from the creek she had stopped to talk to a group of women who told her that there was talk of revolution, that the new army planned a raid on Government Camp itself. She did not know what to believe. As Frank and Paddy approached the hut, she ran to confront them.

'Frank, what's going on? Everyone is talking about the diggers forming some kind of militia. They say there's going to be a revolution.' She noticed the shotgun in Frank's hand.

'Where did you get that gun, Frank? You know we can't afford anything like that. Paddy has his gun. We don't need another one.'

'Hush, woman,' Frank said. 'I didn't buy the bloody gun, it was issued to me.'

'Issued? What do you—? Frank, you haven't enlisted in this damned diggers' army, have you? Please tell me you haven't been so stupid.'

Frank shouldered past her and continued to the hut. Paddy gave Maree a smile of apology as he carefully manoeuvred the wheelbarrow around her and followed Frank. They stopped below the step and leaned their weapons against the wall beside the door.

'Francis Hocking and Patrick O'Rourke!' Maree's voice came as a squeal of rage. 'You are not leaving those guns there. What if Betty were to come out? She could hurt herself – or worse.'

Frank looked from the guns to his wife and back again. 'Paddy, take the guns and put them in the storeroom, will you, mate. Make sure the door's bolted so no one wanders in there.'

Paddy moved to obey and Frank took his boots off at the door. 'Did Annie do the dumplings?' he asked. It was a half-hearted attempt to change the subject and Maree saw right through it.

'There are regiments of soldiers and more police on these diggings than can be counted.' Her voice pleading. 'How can a group of miners hope to match the might of an army?'

Frank turned, took his wife's shoulders in his hands and held her motionless in his bear-like grip. He looked down into her eyes and Maree was taken aback by the determination on his face. His voice, when he spoke, was as calm as hers had been.

'I hope we don't have to stand against the soldiers and police, Maree, I really do.' He went to pull her to him, to hug her to his chest, but she hadn't forgiven him and resisted with all her strength.

'But no one will listen to our complaints,' he continued. 'The government and the administrators are grinding us into the dust with their unfair taxes and regulations. Prices on the diggings have tripled since we arrived here and the fee on the gold licence keeps climbing. You've seen how they collect their licence fees – at the point of a bayonet.'

Maree felt the strength go out of her body and Frank sensed it. He pulled her to him and she didn't resist.

'I don't want to lose you, Frank. You or Paddy.' Her voice came as a whisper, the words muffled against his chest. 'You know the government and army will come down hard on anything to do with rebellion.'

'I don't think it will come to that,' Frank said gently. He looked around, and saw his daughters were standing by the big bed. Annie had Sean in her arms and Betty clung to her sister's waist, tears rolling down her cheeks. He held out his arm and they rushed to him.

'Papa, please be careful.' Annie was close to tears herself, fighting hard to control her emotions lest she upset her child.

'I will, petal. I will.'

They ate their evening meal in near silence. When they were finished, Frank kissed his daughters and wife goodbye and hugged his grandson.

'C'mon, Paddy. We had best get back to the stockade with our supplies.'

The girls went to Paddy and hugged him tight.

'Take care,' they chorused, and Paddy blushed openly at the attention.

With firearms slung and Paddy pushing the wheelbarrow of supplies, the men headed down the path that would round the shoulder of the hill and take them out towards the Eureka Lead. It was the path they walked every morning as they went to work the claim and it was the path they came home on every evening. As Maree stood in the doorway and watched the pair disappear into the gathering dusk, her mind raced as she struggled with the realisation that she might never see either of them again. She sighed, turned back into the hut and lifted a lantern from its hook. 'I am just going down to speak to Blacky Pete and ask if I can borrow his buggy.'

'Why, Mama?' Annie looked up from where she was preparing Sean for bed.

'So I can go out to the sawmill in the morning.' She lifted the lantern high and stepped into the darkness. 'Maybe Toby can talk some sense into those two. I know I can't.'

The Warrogah gold escort arrived at the one-building settlement of Stony Creek a little before sunset and made camp some hundred yards from the store. Eight men were employed by the private escort company. The foreman, a swarthy fellow named Jones, set the other guards scrambling about while he watched over them, his carbine hanging loosely in his hand.

'Reece? Be a good fellow and collect as much firewood as you can. Enough to keep the fire burning brightly all night.'

Reece wandered towards the trees by the creek and the foreman turned to the other six men as they erected a tent.

'If anyone needs a piss while standing watch, move away from the tent. The last time somebody pissed on it the damn thing stank for a month.'

With the tent erected and a fire burning, Jones had the horses unhitched and tied to a line behind the camp. He then placed four men around the coach and made an inspection tour. Satisfied everything was in place, he turned and went to the store.

One corner of the ramshackle building had been turned into a pub. Several men stood along the bar and Jones saw they were mostly diggers, on their way from one goldfield to another. Some sat at tables, playing cards or eating a meal prepared by the publican's wife. He paused in the doorway and cast a quick glance about the room before stepping inside. The publican saw him coming and already had a glass on the bar as he fumbled for a bottle of rum.

'Jonesy! Making the run a little early this week, aren't you?'

'Hello, Tim.' Jones took the glass and threw half the contents into his mouth, swished it around and swallowed. 'The Warrogah diggings is a bloody jeweller's shop. They keep pulling the stuff out of the ground. More gold means more escorts. The commissioner doesn't like to have the stuff sitting around.' He turned his back to the bar and cast his eyes over the men in the room. 'Suits me fine. Extra runs means extra pay. I tell you, Tim, working for a private gold escort company is the best move I ever made.'

'The Warrogah diggings is doing well, then?' a grubby little man at the end of the bar asked.

'The proof is sitting in that coach out there, mate. The strongbox has a king's ransom in it. And in a week there'll be another just like it.'

'That so?' The little man stood up straighter. He almost reached Jones' shoulder. 'You just leave it out there all night?'

'It's not left alone,' Jones said. 'Normally, we bivouac for the night in a town with a police post or secure building, but this little place is the only stop on the road to Warrogah. Don't worry, friend. The gold is well guarded.'

'Can we take a look in the strongbox?' one of the others asked. 'I'd love to see all that gold.'

Jones smiled and shook his head. 'Sorry, mate. My men are on orders to shoot anyone who approaches within fifty paces of the coach.' He raised the carbine in his hand. 'They've all got one of these.' He pulled his coat aside to reveal a revolver tucked into his belt. 'And one of these. You'd have your head blown off before you even got close.'

'Another rum, Jonesy?' The publican gestured at the empty glass.

'Nah. One is all I can have, Tim. I really called over to warn your clientele about wandering too close to our camp. Seems I've done that. I'd better be getting back.'

From a corner table Anderson watched the foreman leave. He sat alone with a glass of whisky in front of him, his face partly concealed in the shadows. He listened to the foreman's boots thump across the verandah and down the steps before moving.

Outside, he watched Jones walk away, his bulky frame silhouetted by the large watch fire that cast a wide circle of light about the escort camp. Any normal man would not get within sixty paces of the coach before he was spotted. Anderson waited at the top of the steps, studying the ground around the camp, noting with particular interest how the fire created shadows among tufts of grass and depressions and reminded himself that the Jannjirra warriors were not normal men.

He smiled and went to where his horse was tethered.

Reece changed his grip on his carbine and let out a prolonged yawn. The store had quieted down hours ago and was now in darkness. The dim glow of campfires showed over by the stockyard where a party of diggers had encamped, but nothing moved beyond the circle of light cast by the watch fire.

'Reece, what's the matter?' his friend called from the adjacent corner of the coach.

'I'm busting for a piss.'

'Well, move away from the bloody tent. Jonesy will have a fit if you piss on it.'

'Yeah, yeah,' Reece muttered, and unbuttoned his flies as he moved away from his corner. The fire had burned down and he made a note to throw more wood onto it once he had relieved himself. The ground here was in darkness, just patches of shadow where the tent shielded the ground from the firelight. He walked out about twenty paces, stopped beside a shadowy clump of dry grass, then urinated on the ground. When he'd finished, he began to button his flies, but stopped when he became aware of movement beside him.

The clump of dry grass lifted from the ground and Reece was confronted by a dark face only inches from his own. Something sinister glinted in the feeble light. His panicked gaze flicked towards the knife already in motion.

A little after first light the proprietor of the Stony Creek store and grog shop went out into the dawn and picked up a bucket by the rope handle. He swung it idly as he strolled down to the creek to fetch some water for his morning cup of tea. On his way back to the store he noted the gold escort still encamped beyond the stockyard. The coach stood where it had been the previous evening, the horses still tied to their line.

Funny, Tim thought, *they are usually well and gone by this time.*

He returned to the hut, built a fire in the stone hearth and, once he had it burning satisfactorily, set a billy of water over the flames for his tea.

His wife snored loudly in the bed behind the calico curtain. He wouldn't wake her yet. There were only two travellers in the little bunkroom behind the hut, and they had both drunk more than their fair share of rum before retiring; they wouldn't be wanting their breakfasts for some time. He would let her sleep and enjoy the peace while it lasted. Pouring tea into a mug, he walked out onto the verandah to enjoy a rare moment of solitude.

Strangely, there was still no movement at the gold escort camp. With cup of tea in hand, Tim walked towards the tent. The escort horses whickered softly as he moved past them and he expected at any moment to be challenged by one of the guards. When no challenge came, he moved around the rear of the coach and onto open ground in front of the tent.

Four guards lay in their bedrolls around the now burnt-out campfire, their blankets pulled up over their heads.

'Hadn't you fellas better be on your way?' he called, expecting the guards to leap up and chase him away.

No one stirred.

He moved to the nearest form and gingerly pulled back the blankets. The sight that greeted him made him cry out in alarm. The guard was dead, a deep depression in the top of his skull where he had been struck by some sort of club. The man's eyes were open, fixed wide in fear. The killing stroke had been swift and brutal.

Feeling sick in the stomach, Tim moved around the campfire checking the other bedrolls. Each man had received a killing blow to the head or had his throat cut.

He turned to the tent and pulled the fly open. The bodies of the four remaining guards were piled inside. Flies had found the carnage already and rose in a buzzing cloud that whipped about the storekeeper's head. He threw a hand over his mouth and staggered back, the bile rising in his throat. He came up against the coach and leaned on the open door for support. It was then he realised the vehicle was empty.

The strongbox was gone.

Maree found the sawmill a little after noon, but Toby had gone off with Horrie and a bullock team to drag in a log. Jim Clark fussed about and made her as comfortable as possible on the verandah of his hut as he plied her with one of Paul's camp oven scones and a cup of tea.

'I'm sure he won't be too much longer, Mrs Hocking. They left at first light and are usually back by now.'

'Not to worry, Mr Clark. I don't mean to be a bother, but it is a matter of some urgency.' Maree plucked a few crumbs from her clothing.

'No bother at all, I assure you. I do apologise for the crudeness of our camp. We don't often receive visits from the fairer sex.'

Maree shrugged the apology away. 'I have lived in a tent on the diggings for close to two years, Mr Clark. Your camp far exceeds that.'

'You're too kind,' Jim said. He cocked his head to one side and listened intently as a series of whip cracks drifted out of the trees. He smiled. 'Ah. That sounds like our errant young man at last.'

Maree watched as a bullock team crawled into view from the far side of the clearing. Toby walked beside the lead animal, encouraging the six beasts along by cracking a whip above their backs. Another man walked at the other side with a supple stick he used to turn the bullocks towards the saw pit. The animals dragged a huge log behind them, three feet thick and twenty paces long. When the log was in line with the pit, Toby brought the bullocks to a stop and turned to Jim.

'Fester picked up a splinter in his front hoof.' He used his thumb to point at the lead animal. 'I thought we'd be stuck in the bloody bush all day.'

'Never mind that now, Toby,' Jim said. 'You have a visitor.'

Maree stood. Toby saw her and dropped the whip. 'Maree! What are you doing here? Is everything all right? Where are Annie and Sean?'

'Oh, Toby. I fear there is going to be terrible trouble.'

Toby was unable to go to the stockade that evening. The gold commissioner had put a curfew in place, warning that all lights and campfires should be extinguished within sight of Government Camp. Rumours of a rebel attack were rife, and the soldiers had orders to fire on anyone who approached the perimeter. Knowing that many fingers would be resting on triggers tonight, Maree and Annie prevailed on Toby to wait until first light before venturing out on the diggings. Reluctantly, he agreed, and they ate a meal of cold meat and bread before retiring to bed.

Having heard the diggers were commandeering any horses and firearms they laid eyes on, and not wanting to have either the Lovell or Moonlight taken from him, Toby left them at the hut and walked alone to the Eureka Lead in the growing light of morning.

The extent of the stockade walls surprised him. They enclosed a great deal of ground adjacent to the Melbourne road, about two acres of hilltop with a commanding view of the valley towards Government Camp, a mile away. The fortifications, mostly timber slabs originally intended to line the walls of mineshafts, formed a criss-crossed breastwork that wound around the hillside. In some places fallen trees or piles of quartz stones had been used to fill gaps. On the inside of this makeshift fortification, diggers were busy transforming shepherd holes into rifle pits by piling loose dirt and stones on the outward-facing edges.

As he rounded the edge of the breastwork and approached the gateway, Toby noticed a flag flying from the top of a pole in the centre of the stockade. The diggers' standard waved idly in the breeze above a regiment of pikemen practising their manoeuvres. Other men were grouped around numerous campfires, cooking their breakfast or smoking their first pipe of the day.

Two armed diggers stood at either side of the gateway. The wagons had been rolled aside, leaving the entrance open, but the sentries approached Toby and used their muskets to bar his way forward.

'You don't look like no digger,' the sentry on the left said through a huge black beard as he studied Toby's clothing.

'I used to be,' Toby said. 'I've come to see my father-in-law and brother. I'm told they're part of the Second Rifle Brigade.'

The bearded sentry was unimpressed. 'We'll be needing the password. No one goes in without the password.'

'I don't have a password,' Toby said rather sharply.

'Don't get all hoity with us, mate,' the second sentry snapped and used the barrel of his musket to push Toby back a pace. He was clean-shaven, the skin of his face sunburnt a glowing shade of red. 'We're just doin' our bleedin' job. No one goes in without the password. No exceptions. Government Camp has all sorts of spies about. If you've got genuine business in the stockade then you'll have been told the password.'

'Well, then maybe you could pass a message to them. Frank Hocking and Patrick O'Rourke. Tell them I need to talk to—'

'We aren't your bloody messengers, mate,' the first sentry interrupted. 'We can't go abandoning our post just to deliver your bleedin' regards to whomever, can we, Johnny?'

'No way, mate,' Johnny agreed.

'Well, maybe—Oh, forget it.' Toby turned on his heels and strode away. He stopped by the road and searched within the stockade for a familiar face, someone he could shout a message to, but he dared not approach too close in case one of the sentries thought he was a spy surveying their fortifications and took a shot at him. In the end he gave up. He would just have to hope that Frank and Paddy decided to pay a visit to the hut that day.

He turned and was about to cross the road and head back to the hut when a large contingent of riders came trotting over the crest of the hill. Toby was forced to jump back out of their way or be trampled. The riders were in a loose column of two, about two hundred of them in all, led by a straight-backed man who wore a sabre in a scabbard on his belt. The riders were all civilians, appearing for the most part to be unarmed. Then Toby noticed that each carried a revolver stuck into his belt or worn in a holster at his hip. They spoke freely among themselves as they trotted by and their accents twanged and drawled. Toby had no doubt that the entire procession consisted of Americans.

The head of the column reached the stockade perimeter while the rearguard still passed where he stood. He looked up at the last few men as they trotted past and spotted a familiar hooked nose and moustached face among them.

'Sam?'

The face turned and smiled. Sam Guinane swung his horse out of the file and waved to his companions to continue. 'Hello, Toby O'Rourke. I thought you had given up a prospector's life.'

'True, I have,' Toby said. He stepped up and shook the hand held down towards him. 'It pays the bills for the others to be able to continue digging. I had to do something, Sam. I'm a family man now.'

'Yeah, so I heard. Congratulations.'

'Thanks,' Toby replied. 'So, tell me, Sam, what's all this?' He gestured at the procession of riders, now mostly inside the stockade.

'This, my friend,' Sam said proudly, 'is the Independent California Revolver Brigade.'

'So, you've joined the diggers' army too?'

'Yeah, me and about three hundred of my fellow country-men. We assembled over on the Creswick diggings. What about you? You signed up, have you?'

'No, not me. I came to talk to Paddy and Frank. They're inside the stockade now, but I can't get in there because I don't know the password.'

Sam Guinane looked at the stockade and back to Toby. 'I don't suppose there's any harm in me telling you. After all, you only want to talk to your kin. It's a strange one; I don't understand it at all, but the password is "Vinegar Hill".'

Toby gave a little chuckle under his breath and Sam looked at him quizzically. 'That mean something to you?'

'Yeah, Sam,' Toby admitted. 'Some years ago, a group of Irish convicts revolted against their captors in New South Wales. "Vinegar Hill" was the password used to begin the revolt. I think it stems from the place of a similar revolt in Ireland.'

'How apt,' Sam said. 'Take my arm and swing up behind me. I'll take you into the stockade.' Toby took Sam's offered hand and sprang up onto the rump of the big gelding. 'Old Mason here won't mind the extra weight for a little bit.' He urged the horse towards the stockade gates.

'So, tell me, Toby, this Vinegar Hill? Were the convicts suc-cessful in their revolt?'

'No, they weren't. Those that weren't shot down by the sol-diers were taken prisoner and flogged. The ringleaders were hanged.'

'Yikes! I hope history doesn't repeat itself.'

'Me too,' Toby admitted.

They crossed the road and approached the stockade gateway. The sentries that had confronted Toby earlier were still on duty. They approached the two riders and made to block their way.

'Sam Guinane, Independent California Revolver Brigade,' Sam called down to them, and when they were close enough to be heard without raising his voice he muttered, 'Vinegar Hill.'

On hearing the password the sentries stepped aside to allow them through. The one named Johnny scowled up at Toby when he recognised him perched on the horse behind Sam. Toby gave him a cheeky grin.

Beside the eighty-foot flagpole which bore the Southern Cross sat a blacksmith shop. A little further inside the fortifications stood a rough wooden hut with a canvas roof. Close to the door of the hut a group of men were assembled about a small deal table. Toby noticed that the American who had led the Independent California Revolver Brigade now stood at this table and appeared to be making some kind of report.

'I'll let you down here, Toby,' Sam said. 'You can go and find your kin while I join the others and get Mason fed and watered.

Toby thanked Sam and slid from the horse. He stood for a moment, surveying the scene. There must have been close to a thousand men inside the stockade and he wondered where to begin his search when he felt a mighty slap across the shoulders.

Toby whirled to face his attacker, only to be confronted by the grinning countenance of his brother.

'Paddy! Thank God. Where's Frank? I need to talk to you both.'

Paddy lifted Toby from the ground in a huge bear hug. The barrel of his musket pressed between Toby's shoulder blades and he squirmed uncomfortably until his brother relented and placed him back on the ground.

'Yeah, I'm pleased to see you too, Paddy. Now take me to Frank. We need to talk.'

His brother grabbed him by the shirtsleeve and led him through groups of men. Two ranks of diggers were going through the motion of dry-firing their muskets in volleys, first the kneeling front rank and then the standing second, reloading and doing it all again as they faced an imaginary enemy.

Paddy led him to a shallow shepherd hole, just inside the fortifications. The hole had been converted into a rifle pit with stones placed along the outer edge to offer some protection against incoming fire. Frank sat in the bottom of the hole, his back resting against the side as he puffed on his pipe, a cloud of tobacco smoke in the air.

'Toby!' Frank climbed to his feet. 'What the hell are you doing here?'

'Maree drove out to the mill yesterday to fetch me,' Toby said as he studied the rifle pit. Several pikes lay along the outer edge, ready to be taken up in the event of an attack. He glanced at the shotgun slung across Frank's shoulders.

'She wants you to try and talk Paddy and me out of this business, doesn't she?'

'She's worried sick about you both. Hell, I'm worried sick. If the soldiers come they won't be playing games, you know.' He gestured at the ranks of drilling men. 'In the first volley half those men will be cut down. The rest will be so frightened they will hardly have the sense to reload. Of those that do manage to reload, only a handful will be able to get a shot off before the bayonets are among them.'

'What makes you the expert?' Frank asked around the stem of his pipe.

'Jim Clark was a soldier, Frank. He told me exactly what will happen here if the government forces attack. You don't stand a chance.'

'We won't stand a chance if we all just give up and go back to our tents and our claims,' Frank countered. 'We're here for a reason, Toby. Maybe you've lost touch, but life here is tough, and the unjust laws and actions by those in positions of power only make it tougher. We're not here to make trouble, we're here for a cause. We're here so that life might just get a little better for Annie and Sean and Maree and Betty. You go back to your sawmill, Toby. Leave the real work to us. We're here to see this thing through.' He spat a glob of tobacco-stained spittle into the bottom of the hole, then added, 'We're staying – at least I am. Paddy is his own man. He can make his own choices.'

'Unfair, Frank,' Toby said quietly. 'You know why I'm at the mill, and it's not because I want to be away from Annie or Sean. My work provides you with the funds to go on digging, to keep you, all of you, in food and equipment to keep on going.'

'I know, my boy, I know,' Frank relented. 'But what is the point of being here on the diggings if we can't afford the licence fee or we are being threatened by government thugs with bayonets?'

'But this,' Toby swept his arm to encompass the entire stock-ade, 'this is madness. You can't hope to stand against the might of the British Army.'

'Desperate times call for desperate measures, Toby. Who knows, we may not have to fight. This might just be the kick in the pants the administration needs to sit down and listen to our demands.'

Toby shrugged his shoulders and decided he was not going to win this argument. He turned his attention to Paddy, who stood resolutely at Frank's side. 'What about you, Pad? I don't suppose I can make you come home with me? Frank has said it's your choice.'

Paddy shook his head and pointed to the ground at his feet, signalling his intent to remain inside the stockade.

'Well, I tried,' Toby shrugged resignedly. He had no hope of changing their minds. His brother and father-in-law intended to stand by their convictions. He shook both their hands and climbed out of the pit. 'I'll go and deliver the bad news to Maree and the girls.'

'You're a good man, Toby O'Rourke,' Frank said. He fixed his gaze on Toby's eyes, and Toby remembered that same look on the day he had promised Frank that he would stand by Annie and their unborn baby. 'If something should happen to me, Toby, you'll look after them, won't you? All of them?'

'You know I will, Frank. You don't even have to ask.'

'Then maybe it's better that you're not here with us.'

Frank moved to the edge of the pit and sat down. He lowered his face, but Toby could see moisture in his eyes. 'Try and make them understand, Toby. I know you don't fully understand yourself, but you're a husband and a father. We're here for them.' He turned his face away to study the distant trees.

Toby reached down and grasped his brother's arm. 'Promise me, Pad, if a fight breaks out and things start going bad for you, promise me you'll give up before anything happens to you. Just lie down in your hole or run away or throw your hands up in surrender. Promise me.'

Paddy placed a huge paw over his brother's hand and nodded his head. He held Toby's hand against his arm for a few moments, then let go and backed towards Frank.

Toby turned to walk back to the gateway. Somewhere deep inside him he had a nagging voice telling him to stay; that the only way he could ensure Paddy and Frank's survival was to be there with them. He had almost made his mind up to go back to the hut and fetch the Lovell, to return and enlist in the diggers' army, but then his thoughts turned to Annie, Sean and the others. If all the menfolk were killed, who would look after them? They would find themselves alone in a brutal land, and their only hope of survival would be in becoming servants, taking on a menial job in Melbourne or one of the towns. It was not the life he envisioned for Annie. She would be no man's servant if he could help it. As much as it wounded his pride to walk away from Paddy and Frank, he would do it for Annie and Sean.

As he passed the hut near the flagpole a commotion developed among the men at the table. He heard one man, his voice louder than the others, bring order to the discord.

'We can't possibly stand against such odds, gentlemen. I'm open to suggestions on how we should deal with this new threat.'

Several men tried to speak at once. The first speaker, a brown-haired, clean-shaven digger with a broad Irish accent held up his hand for quiet. Instantly the other men settled and the speaker pointed to one of them. 'What say you, Mr McGill?'

'We simply cannot allow this force to reach the diggings. If such ordnance were to be brought into play we wouldn't stand a chance. I propose we send a party of men out to ambush or waylay the column. It's our only chance.' McGill spoke with an American accent and his tone conveyed the authority of one who had some military background.

Toby noticed Sam Guinane loitering near the side of the hut. The American seemed greatly interested in the discussion taking place. He sidled up to Sam and asked quietly, 'What's going on?'

'That gentleman there is Peter Lalor, the diggers' commander-in-chief,' Sam muttered as he pointed to the clean-shaven Irishman who chaired the meeting. 'He was just paid a visit by an informer from Government Camp who told him the soldiers are moving cannon up from Melbourne.'

'Cannon?'

'Yep, the big stuff. It looks as if the government is taking this little rebellion seriously.'

'The men in this stockade won't stand a chance against cannon fire.'

The nearest Toby had ever come to seeing a cannon fired was the one o'clock signal gun fired by the harbour master in Geelong. He had heard it on several occasions when he had accompanied his father to the sale yards there. He remembered quite vividly the great plume of white smoke and the resounding boom that echoed off the hills, allowing ships' navigators, and everyone else within earshot, to set their chronometers. He had read accounts of the battle of Waterloo and the devastation caused to massed ranks of infantry by batteries of cannon. The accounts had been quite graphic in their description of the carnage, and Toby felt sick to the pit of his stomach as he realised Paddy and Frank might soon be on the receiving end of a deadly barrage. He thought of running back to their rifle pit and pleading with them to come home with him, but he knew it would be to no avail. They were firm in their resolve to remain in the stockade. He would only be wasting his breath.

'Mr Guinane.'

The man Lalor had called McGill was now on his feet and facing where Sam and Toby stood.

'Sir?' Sam straightened his posture as he responded to the hail.

'How well do you know the bushland surrounding the Melbourne road, Mr Guinane?' McGill asked.

'I've only travelled it once, sir. That was when I came here nearly four years ago. I can remember bits and pieces, creek and river crossings, but I forget which part came before the other.'

'See if you can find someone with local knowledge to act as a guide. A detachment of the Independent California Revolver Brigade will be heading out to intercept an artillery column moving up from Melbourne. We can't afford to feel our way. We need to get this right first time. We need a local who knows the lie of the land.'

'Strange you should say that, sir.'

Toby turned and found Sam's stare fixed firmly on him.

'No, Sam. I promised I wouldn't get involved.'

'If you want to help your kin, Toby, this is the best way. If the soldiers get those cannon into position, the men inside this stockade will be cut to pieces.'

'You know the Melbourne road well, sir?' McGill asked.

'I've driven cattle along some sections of it quite a few times,' Toby admitted.

'You sound like the man for the job. What unit are you with?'

'I'm not with any unit, sir. I came to try and talk my father-in-law and brother into coming home.'

'I see,' McGill said simply, the tone of his voice not indicating any sort of judgement. 'Toby is it?'

'Toby O'Rourke, sir.'

'Each man must decide where he stands, Toby. You have made your decision and I respect that. But Mr Guinane is right; if those cannon are allowed to get into position, the battle here will be lost before it even begins. If you have family inside the stockade you will be doing them a great service by helping us.'

'I understand what you are saying, sir. But I promised my wife and her family that I wouldn't get involved in the stockade or any fighting. They are worried out of their minds by the thought of Paddy and Frank being here.'

'A noble sentiment, Mr O'Rourke,' McGill continued. 'But we are simply asking you to assist us by acting as a guide, a scout if you will. The detachment we send out to intercept the column can hardly go galloping off down the middle of the road. All we require of you is to guide them along the back trails to a point of concealment on the road where they can ambush the column. You don't have to be involved in any fighting. And in the end you will be doing your kin and the rest of the men inside the stockade a great service.' McGill paused.

Toby thought fast. What McGill had said was the truth. He did not have to be involved in any fighting. Once he guided the detachment through the scrub to the road, his task would be done. If they succeeded in taking the cannon, then Frank and Paddy would not have to face their wrath. It was the best outcome for all concerned.

'All right, Mr McGill, I'll do it,' Toby said.

'Good choice, sir,' McGill congratulated him. 'Welcome to the Independent California Revolver Brigade.'

'Tobias O'Rourke!'

Annie stood in the centre of the hut with her fists on her hips and her brow furrowed as she fixed her husband with an icy stare. 'You promised me you wouldn't get involved in this stockade nonsense.'

'I'm not involved in the stockade, Annie. Honestly. I'm simply guiding some men through the bush to the Melbourne road.'

'*I* can find the bloody Melbourne road. It runs past not ten minutes' walk from this very hut. Why do they need a guide to find it? A blind man could find it.'

They were alone in the hut. As soon as Toby had arrived back and announced his intentions, Maree had decided to leave them to it, picked up Sean, and ushered Betty out to the campfire to help her prepare lunch.

'We have to stay out of sight. We can't just go galloping off down the road,' he said, echoing McGill's words.

'Why not?'

'Because someone from Government Camp might see us and warn them of our intent.'

'So, you are going off with a bunch of armed men and sneaking around in the bush so the police don't see you? That sounds to me as if you are very much involved.'

Toby hadn't told the women about the cannon. He didn't want to cause them any more concern than they already felt, and had simply told them they were going out to scout for reinforcements being moved up from Melbourne.

'Annie, get your mother back in here. I have to tell you the whole story – and she needs to hear it too. Leave Betty outside with Sean.'

She dropped her fists from her hips and moved to the door.

'Mama, can you come inside for a minute? Betty, keep an eye on Sean out there, there's a good girl.'

She turned back into the hut and waited for her mother to climb the step and enter, shutting the door behind her.

Toby stood with his back to the far wall near the foot of Maree and Frank's bed. He had the Lovell in his hand and the ammunition pouch slung over his shoulder. The women stood motionless by the door, waiting for him to speak, their gazes fixed firmly on him.

'I can't talk Frank and Paddy out of leaving the stockade, as I said,' he began. 'They won't leave. They feel they have some sort of moral duty to the other diggers to stay there and see this thing through, no matter what. What I didn't tell you before, because I didn't want to worry you any more than necessary, is that the military are moving up cannon from Melbourne.'

Maree's hand covered her mouth and she swayed on her feet. Annie moved to her mother's side and helped her down onto the end of the bed.

'This is going to end badly,' Maree said, fighting hard to hold back tears.

'Frank and Paddy won't leave the stockade,' Toby repeated. 'The only way I can think of helping them through this is to help the men who want to stop those cannon from reaching the diggings.' He walked over, placed his hand on Annie's head and stroked it gently. 'I promised I wouldn't get involved in any fighting and I intend to stand by that promise, Annie. I will guide the men through the bush to the road and then my part is done. I can only hope they prevent the cannon from reaching the diggings and being used against the stockade.'

The wall Maree had built up against the emotional turmoil in her heart and mind crumbled. She broke down into a series of sobs, her body shaking. Annie tried to comfort her and held her tight, but the wracking sobs continued. Toby felt ashamed to be witnessing such a moment. He had always seen Maree as a strong woman, capable of withstanding any of the rigours colonial life threw at her. Now, looking down on her as she wept openly against Annie's chest, Toby felt that a little of that firm, strong person had gone forever. Her emotional defences had crumbled, revealing a weakened and defenceless mother and wife, fast running out of the strength to continue.

Annie reached up with a hand and grasped Toby's, pulling it down to her face to kiss his fingers tenderly. She looked up at him with tears in her eyes.

'Go,' she said simply in a hoarse whisper. 'Go and do what you need to do. But come back to me, Toby. Please come back to me.'

T he strongbox was far too cumbersome for a packhorse to carry. The two Jannjirra struggled with it slung between them until they reached the safety of the hills, where Anderson took to the padlock with a hatchet. It took three attempts before the lock finally fell away and they swung the lid open for their first tentative look inside.

The gold was contained in leather pouches tied with string. A slip of paper secured under the strings of each bag had the weight recorded on it. Each pouch contained exactly one troy pound of gold, either in dust or nuggets, and there were one hundred and twenty-eight pouches in all.

Chilbi and Yawong crowded over the strongbox, eager for a look. They held their breath as Anderson untied one of the strings and poured gold dust into the palm of his hand. The orange-yellow flakes of metal caught the sunlight as they tumbled from the pouch, a waterfall of glittering stars. He cast his hand about and the warriors took an involuntary step back. Men had died for this gold. There was powerful magic here.

Anderson poured the dust back into the pouch and retied the string. He then repacked the pouches into two packsaddles. Even if the two Jannjirra could bring themselves to help him, he would not allow them to interfere with the gold. He worked alone, hovering over his task possessively while the warriors looked on from a distance. Anderson led the packhorse himself as they continued towards the mountains.

That night they camped beyond a low ridge within sight of the mountains of the Jannjirra. The death of Tarrat weighed heavily on Chilbi and even the nearness of his tribal grounds could not lift his spirits, for each death brought his people closer to extinction.

Yawong gabbled away like a lubra as he prepared a campfire, and he failed to notice how Warrigal made his sleeping position a little away from them. Chilbi's gaze flicked to the Djarriba, who had the packsaddles positioned under his head, his feet towards the fire. A warrior of the Jannjirra always slept with his head to the campfire, facing out into the bush, for that was where any threat would come from. Chilbi's warrior eye took note of the commanding position Warrigal had over their little encampment – on slightly higher ground and with a huge stringybark at his back. He could sweep the sleeping positions of the two Jannjirra at a single glance.

Chilbi turned his attention to the growing flames, his mind troubled by this strange behaviour. He remembered when he had first encountered the Djarriba on the escarpment of their tribal lands. Any member of another tribe would have been killed instantly for their trespass, but this pale-skinned stranger was different. The elders, Chilbi's father included, had suspected great magic at work. The stranger had been cared for until he returned to health. Instead of being grateful, the stranger had bullied and cajoled the Jannjirra to provide for him, some-times resorting to violence. This had earned him the name of *Warrigal*, the wild dog.

The sickness had come soon after. Warrigal had said this bad magic had been sent by the Djarriba in the lowlands to wipe out the tribe and take their land. He recalled the words of Madagurrie, the old Waddirawong warrior, who had said the Djarriba carry the sickness with them, that they cannot send it on ahead. Had Warrigal brought the sickness with him to the lands of the Jannjirra? Had he cast the evil magic so that the whole tribe had died? He remembered the grip the sickness had on him, the shivering fever and pustules and how only he and his brothers had survived its onslaught. When they were well enough, Warrigal had led them into the lowlands to seek revenge for the sickness.

The Jannjirra were a warlike tribe and had a reputation for raiding those tribes around them. Never had they taken more than they could use, and never had they hurt lubras or children. That was not the Jannjirra way. Warrigal, however, seemed intent on killing anyone who stood in his way – man, woman or child.

Chilbi watched as Warrigal settled down for the night, the revolver resting in his lap, and decided he would need to be watched very closely indeed.

Toby sat astride Moonlight fifteen paces from the twin ruts of the Melbourne road, the Independent California Revolver Brigade spread on either side. Most men were still mounted, but others had become disillusioned with the ambush and now lay in the bracken as they tried to sleep. Above them the canopy was so dense that no starlight penetrated. Even the full moon was reduced to a vague paling of the sky beyond the leaves as it climbed towards its zenith.

'Will they come, do you reckon?' a voice asked from Toby's left.

'What if they've been past already and we didn't hear them?'

'The trail's just there, you goddamn idiot. Cannon being transported make a lot of noise. We would've heard 'em for sure.'

'All right, keep it down,' Sam Guinane growled. 'The patrols will be back soon and we'll have a better idea of what's happening on the road.'

Another hour went by without as much as a solitary digger passing their position.

'Maybe they camped for the night,' Toby suggested. 'No one travels in darkness unless they have to.'

'Well, tomorrow is the Sabbath,' Sam mused. 'Actually today,' he corrected himself, for midnight had come and gone. 'I don't suppose they would attack the stockade on a Sunday. That leaves them a whole extra day to bring the cannon up and get them into redoubts.'

'I hope you're right,' Toby muttered.

They sat on in silence for a while and listened to the sounds of the bush. Nocturnal animals were out and about, scurrying through the bracken. Every so often a wallaby crashed through the undergrowth and startled them back to alertness.

'Riders approaching.'

The word passed down from their left, and moments later Toby heard the unmistakeable rhythm of cantering horses approaching from the east.

'That'll be Sullivan's patrol,' said Sam.

Sullivan and three others had been sent out in the direction of Melbourne with instructions to ride for forty-five minutes and then report back. Sam had given strict instructions that the screen of bracken fern in the ambush site was not to be ridden over and trampled down. The patrol continued along the road for a hundred yards then cut back into the bush and doubled back to Sam and Toby's position.

'Anything, Sully?'

'Nothing, sir,' Sullivan admitted. 'There are a few little camps on the side of the road. Diggers on the move from one goldfield to another. Nothing of a military nature at all. We rode as far as the ridge near the river. In the full moon we could see ten miles further along. I feel confident to report they are not anywhere on that section of road, sir.'

'All right, Sully. Well done, thank you. You can dismount and rest your horses.'

'Maybe they're just slow,' the man on Sam's right said. 'They may be still closer to Melbourne than we thought.'

Sam lifted his hat and rubbed his brow. The night was warm and his face glistened with perspiration. 'Or they are further along than we thought. Let's wait to see what the other patrol reports. We may have missed them while moving into position through the forest.'

Five minutes later the patrol which had been sent off in the direction of Ballarat reported back. With the appearance of the second patrol, Sam sat up in the saddle and looked every bit the army officer as he received the report.

'Nothing, sir. It's as quiet as a church on Monday morn.'

Sam slumped back onto the saddle, perplexed by this strange development.

'I can't understand what's going on. If the information we got at the stockade was good, we should have come across the cannon somewhere on this section of road.'

'*If* the information was good,' someone repeated.

'Why would someone give us bad information?' Toby asked. 'I saw the man at the stockade myself. He looked like a hard-working, honest digger.'

'Maybe that was what he was supposed to look like,' the voice said. 'Maybe he was a – a—'

'—An agent provocateur,' Sam finished for him.

'But what could they hope to achieve by sending us out on a wild goose chase?' Toby ran his eyes up and down the line of men, the answer to his own question already forming in his mind. There were one hundred and fifty men out on the Melbourne road tonight. Men who should have been inside the stockade manning its defences.

'Oh my God!' He felt the cold hand of fear reach into his gut and knot it tight. 'It was a trick to get us out of the stockade. They're going to attack!'

Without waiting for a reply from Sam, Toby spurred Moonlight's flanks mercilessly. The horse sprang forward, vaulted the growth of bracken and tore its way out onto the road.

'I have to warn them. I have to warn Paddy and Frank.'

He heard Sam shout something behind him, but couldn't make out the words, nor did he care. Within three paces he brought Moonlight into a gallop and swung his head to the west, towards Ballarat and the stockade.

Paddy wiped at sleep-deprived eyes and thought his mind was playing tricks on him. Ghost-like shapes moved on the lower slopes, only half seen in the moonlight. Dawn was maybe an hour away. A full moon stood just above the western horizon. Its pale glow lit the spaces between the trees, but darkened the shadows where the ghosts moved. There was something else in the shadows too. He squinted and tried to make it out. It looked like a school of fish reflecting sunlight in the depths. The fish were in a long line that ran across the lower slopes of the hill. A figure moved behind the line and gave it depth. He drew in a sharp breath as he realised he was looking at moonlight as it reflected from the blades of bared bayonets.

These ghosts had teeth.

He would have cried out if he had a voice. His mouth went dry with fear and he shifted the musket into his left hand, then reached down to shake Frank's shoulder. Frank awoke and rubbed sleep from his eyes. He climbed to his feet and rested the shotgun on the edge of the pit.

'What's happening, Pad?'

Paddy pointed through the timbers of the breastwork. The soldiers were a hundred paces away, but advancing towards them with muskets held low and bayonets at the fore.

'Bloody hell!' Frank turned to tell one of the other sentries, but they weren't the only ones to have seen the approaching soldiers. From somewhere up near the blacksmith shop a voice began yelling, 'To arms! To arms! The Camp is attacking!' A stream of oaths rose out of the tents. Men stumbled about in various stages of dress as they hurried to take up defensive positions.

All around him Paddy heard the sounds of muskets being cocked, the ratchet clicks like a chorus of crickets. The sound stilled his panic and he hooked his thumb over the horn of the hammer. His hand was slick with sweat and he carefully dragged the hammer to full cock, then squinted down the sights at the approaching figures.

The ranks were three deep. They stretched around the hillside and were lost from sight beyond the shoulder of the gully. Officers, swords held high, led their men forward. Somewhere, a faint order drifted up the hillside to the waiting defenders. The soldiers halted their advance and an uneasy quiet settled over the scene.

Sweat ran into Paddy's eyes and he blinked furiously to clear it. He didn't dare move a hand from his musket. Beyond the quiet there was a different sound now. He cocked his head and tried to make it out, his brow creased with concentration. The noise came from beyond the hilltop. A fresh wave of fear ran through him as he recognised the rattle and scrape of mounted horses. Lots of them.

Frank had heard it as well. 'Cavalry?' he asked.

'More likely mounted police,' another digger answered. His braces dangled about his legs and his shirt was untucked. He quickly shrugged his shoulders into the braces, hoisted his musket and took up position at the firing line.

'Diggers, steady!'

Paddy recognised the voice of Peter Lalor. Their commander-in-chief stood on a pile of wooden slabs near the blacksmith shop. Lalor had a pistol in his hand and pivoted slowly as he examined the defensive positions of his men.

'Captains, get some pikemen over to the eastern perimeter.' Lalor had seen or heard the horsemen. 'Prepare for a mounted charge in that sector.'

The captains of the pikemen moved to obey and double-timed their divisions across the hillside, pikes held at the ready.

Someone had thrown several timber baulks onto the watch fire and it now flared brightly, illuminating the scene within the stockade. The Southern Cross hung limply in the breezeless air. Men still ran for their positions at the breastwork.

Paddy turned back to the soldiers on the hillside. More orders were given and they advanced once more, closing the distance at a steady gait. A musket barked from somewhere off to his right – the sight of the advancing troops was clearly too much for one digger. An officer marching in the lead fell to the ground and the soldiers stopped, waiting. A voice drifted out of the massed ranks and this time Paddy heard it clearly.

'The Queen's troops have been fired upon. Front rank, prepare to fire!'

Paddy watched the front rank of soldiers drop to their knees and take aim up the hillside. It seemed a hundred muskets were aimed directly at him.

'Get down!' Frank yelled. Paddy felt an arm across his shoulders as he was pulled into the pit.

'Fire!' The roar of muskets came as a single blast. An unbroken line of flashes lit the hillside like lightning in a summer storm. Paddy pressed his face into the rough earthen wall as musket balls swooped over his head like a swarm of angry bees. Pieces of breastwork tore away under the onslaught and rained down on his back. Musket balls ricocheted into the distance or thudded into the dirt. Then the noise rolled away down the gullies and came back in a series of echoes from the bulk of the Black Hills range.

'Diggers!' Lalor's voice from the slabs. 'Return fire!'

Paddy climbed to his feet and took aim through the breastwork. In rifle pits around their defensive perimeter other diggers did the same.

The first rank of soldiers were reloading, ramrods frantically pumping up and down. The second rank stepped through the spaces between their comrades and took up firing positions.

Paddy sighted on a red jacket and squeezed the trigger. The musket jumped in his hands and instantly his vision was obscured by a cloud of smoke. The diggers along the breastwork began firing.

The miners had no hope of matching the well-disciplined shooting of the redcoats. Their return fire rattled out in a cacophony of reports that lasted a full five seconds. Musket smoke hung motionless in the air like morning fog and hid both sides from each other. Burning wads from the muskets had started several small grass fires, adding more smoke to the confusion.

Paddy dropped to his knees to reload. Along the breastwork he could see ramrods rising and plunging in unison. He still felt afraid, but the act of firing that one shot had dissolved its cloying effects. His hands no longer sweated and he deftly worked the ramrod, tamping down the ball. As he returned the rod to the hoops under the barrel his other hand cocked the hammer and placed a cap on the nipple. He was one of the first to finish and stand to the firing line.

The second rank of soldiers fired. Muzzle flashes illuminated the gum trees as the thunder of the second discharge merged with the dying echoes of the first.

Paddy ducked as a ball hit below the pit and spat dirt into his face. He felt the sting of grains of quartz bite into his skin and dropped below the edge of the pit to wipe a hand over his face.

'You all right, young fella?'

He looked up and found Frank's concerned gaze on him. Frank held the unused shotgun in one hand and lifted Paddy's chin to examine his face.

'No harm done.'

Paddy looked at his hand, surprised there was no blood. He shook his head and ran his tongue around his mouth, then spat a glob of dirt onto the ground. Frank placed a fatherly arm on his shoulders.

'Don't get yourself killed, Paddy.'

He shook his head again and Frank patted his shoulder.

'Soon they'll be close enough for me to use this.' He shook the shotgun.

Paddy wondered how long the battle would last once the soldiers had closed to shotgun range. The first two volleys had been swift and deadly. He could hear wounded men screaming from both sides of the firing line. Somewhere up near the horse lines an animal whinnied in panic. Then another noise drowned out the horse and the cries of the wounded.

A bugle call sounded on the hillside below, a rapid but brief succession of brassy notes.

'That means extend to skirmishing order,' the digger beside Paddy said matter-of-factly. 'They're about to charge the stockade.'

Paddy stood to the firing line again, and carefully lifted his head.

The front rank of redcoats took a sidestep and opened their lines. Those behind came forward to fill the gaps. Here and there a body lay on the ground, some moving and some still. An officer pointed up the hillside with his sword and the bugle rang out again. A great roar went up from the soldiers and they broke into a run.

'Get ready, Pad. Here they come.'

Paddy watched in horror as the soldiers rushed forward. They yelled screams of rage as they came, a hundred different war cries, muskets held low, bayonets a bristling line of cold steel coming to feast on human flesh.

Muskets fired from inside the stockade and redcoats fell at random, but the gaps were closed up and the soldiers came on without check.

Paddy took aim at a soldier and fired. When the gunsmoke cleared he could see the man lying face down on the ground, but others swept past him as they continued the charge. They were close enough now to see features on their faces. A walrus-moustached redcoat ran straight at him, his shako tilted forward and hatred gleaming in his eyes. Only twenty paces separated the soldiers from the breastwork. Not enough time to reload before the redcoats would be among them.

A pitiful few shots answered the charge as the soldiers reached the breastwork. Frank fired his shotgun at a group of soldiers tearing defensive slabs from the ground. One soldier fell, but the others continued their work until a gap had been made and the redcoats poured into the stockade.

Paddy watched the soldiers coming at him and knew the battle was lost. There were too many of them for the diggers to beat back. Toby's words came to him as he stood with a useless musket in his hands and soldiers running at him, screaming like banshees.

'Give up or lie down in your hole, Paddy.'

At a rifle pit twenty paces to Paddy's right the diggers rose to meet the charge and were instantly cut down by bayonets. One digger threw his hands up in surrender, but the soldier opposing him lunged forward with his musket. The gory tip of the bayonet emerged between the man's shoulder blades and he sank to his knees. The soldier placed a booted foot on his chest and worked his bayonet free.

So much for surrender.

The digger beside Paddy leaped to his feet. 'C'mon! We have to fall back. We need to regroup on higher ground.'

He climbed from the hole and made a mad dash towards the blacksmith shop.

Frank slapped Paddy on the shoulder. 'Let's go!' He pointed at the retreating digger.

They climbed from the pit and ran for the shop. Muskets fired in random explosions of noise and Paddy ducked instinctively as a ball whistled past his ear. The digger running ahead of him threw his arms out and his musket clattered into the dust as he fell headlong to the ground. Paddy and Frank couldn't stop to help; to do so would be suicide. They leaped the dying digger and kept their heads low as they crossed the open ground below the blacksmith shop. Paddy expected at any moment to feel the slap of a musket ball between his shoulder blades. His breath sawed in his throat and, beside him, he could hear Frank wheezing, almost spent. He reached out, took Frank's elbow and urged him over the last few yards.

Frank slumped against the side of the blacksmith shop and doubled over as he struggled for air. Paddy's breath came hard, but he recovered quickly. All about him he could see more diggers running in from the rifle pits. One of the rifle brigade captains stood by the forge, directing men into new defensive positions.

'Get that cart turned over. Close the gaps. We won't have long.' The captain's face was the colour of beetroot. A musket ball had grazed his upper arm and blood soaked into the sleeve. The man seemed oblivious to his wound as he set the few defenders to work.

Paddy went to a handcart, squatted on his haunches and took hold of the axle. With a grunt of effort, he straightened his legs and the cart toppled sideways. Two diggers helped him drag it against the wall of the blacksmith shop, then they closed the gap between the cart and forge with wooden crates. Beyond the forge more diggers used timber and stones, bags of horse feed – anything that might offer some protection against the soldiers.

'Where's Peter Lalor?' Frank's voice. He had recovered enough to help his comrades and dragged a supply box towards the new perimeter.

'Hit in the arm,' someone yelled. 'The first bloody volley. He was being taken care of the last I saw.'

The barricade was little more than a haphazard wall of wood and stone, boxes and bales of hay. 'That'll have to do,' the captain yelled. 'Everyone into position.'

In his haste to help build the barricade, Paddy had forgotten to reload his musket. He looked about and found a pitchfork lying near the forge. It was better than nothing, so he picked it up and stood to the barricade.

In the ruddy glow of dawn he could see across the dusty ground of the stockade to where the soldiers reassembled in preparation for the final assault. It only took moments for them to ready themselves, their front facing the blacksmith shop, a wall of crimson jackets and deadly steel. Then an order was shouted and the crimson wave surged forward, coming to engulf the last of the rebels.

'Here they come!' the captain shouted unnecessarily. 'Fire!'

A few muskets banged at the red wave roaring towards them, a pitiful popping noise that hardly drowned out the battle cries of the charging soldiers. Paddy saw one or two fall to the ground, but the others came on. He adjusted his grip on the pitchfork and waited for the wave to break over the top of them, his heart racing and blood singing in his ears.

The soldiers reached the barricade and the diggers stood to meet them. Miners fought back with the tools of their trade, picks and shovels against the cold steel of the bayonet. Frank used the barrel of his empty shotgun to deflect a bayonet thrust and brought the butt around in the same motion, catching a young soldier under the jaw and sending him flying into the trooper beside him.

Another soldier climbed the crude defences in front of Paddy, lowered his bayonet and prepared for the thrust. Paddy lunged forward as hard as he could and ran the pitchfork through the soldier's shoulder. The trooper screamed and tried to fall back, but the pitchfork stuck in his flesh. The pair danced with each other at the ends of the six-foot pole, the soldier screaming in agony the whole time. Horrified, Paddy let go of the handle and the soldier backed away through his comrades, dragging the pitchfork with him. Then he was lost from sight as more soldiers closed in.

Frantically, Paddy searched for another weapon – a pick, a spade, anything he could arm himself with – but there was nothing in reach. The redcoats crashed over the barricade and diggers screamed as the bayonets cut into them. Paddy and Frank were forced backwards under the onslaught, but they only managed a few paces before their backs came up against the wall of the blacksmith shop.

Frank stood ten feet from Paddy. He had managed to get hold of a soldier's carbine and was using the bayonet to keep three troopers at bay, beating them back with savage thrusts at their throats. The soldiers backed away and for a brief moment Paddy thought Frank had fought them off. Then he saw the real reason why the troopers were opening the ground between themselves and Frank.

Mounted police had broken through the eastern side of the stockade and were using the momentum of their horses to break down any pockets of resistance. One of these horsemen saw Frank outside the blacksmith shop and charged towards him, sword held at the ready. Paddy watched the rider clear a pile of boxes in a graceful leap, but Frank failed to see this threat bearing down on him as he fought off the soldiers.

The mounted officer passed Frank on the right, giving his sword arm a clear swing, the classic backhanded, downward slash of the cavalryman.

Paddy tried to shout a warning. His breath rushed up his windpipe and his mouth worked to call Frank's name. Instantly, the fire flared in his head. He tried to ignore it, to fight through it. It was Frank's only hope. A guttural groan increased in volume to something that might be audible, even over the din of battle, but the pain in his head burst into flames of agony. His vision starred and Paddy almost passed out as the warning shout died in his throat.

The mounted trooper brought his sword down and Paddy heard the blade hiss through the air. The speed of the swing blurred the motion into a bright arc of gleaming steel. The arc reached Frank's left shoulder near his neck and continued down at an angle, severing muscle and artery as it went. For a moment the two were locked together, Frank and the policeman, joined by the blade, one end held firmly in a hand and the other embedded deep into vital organs. Then the policeman's horse carried him onwards and he levered the hilt of the sword upwards in much the same way as a woodcutter releases his axe from a stubborn piece of red gum. It came away from Frank's flesh with a sickening squelch.

Frank kept his feet, a look of utter surprise on his face. He staggered a few steps as a bright fountain of blood jetted from the gaping wound and splashed into the dusty earth of the Eureka Stockade. Then he fell over backwards and hit the ground hard.

Paddy ran to Frank's side.

A horrible gurgling noise came from the gaping wound. Paddy took Frank's hand and squeezed it. His eyes opened and flicked towards him, glazed and unseeing at first, but brightening as he recognised the young man leaning over him. Paddy felt a return of the pressure through his fingers and Frank's mouth opened to speak, but it was full of bright blood that dribbled down his face with each gurgling breath. Their eyes remained locked together and Paddy felt the pressure of Frank's fingers increase, tightening painfully. Then the hand went limp.

Paddy lifted Frank's hand to his chest and held it tight. The tears came freely and silently, running down his face and falling onto the blood-soaked shirt of the man who had been a father to him for the past two years.

His grieving was cut short as rough hands dragged him to his feet and clamped a set of darbies around his wrists.

'You're under arrest for high treason.' The policeman pushed him towards a group of prisoners who were under guard by redcoats. Paddy went willingly, his grief for Frank having dissolved any fight left in him.

In the light of the new day he could see soldiers and police scouring the tents and huts. He lifted his head to the flagpole where a trooper rapidly worked the halyard. The Southern Cross came down the pole and the trooper cut it free. He waved it high above his head as if it were the prize belt of a championship fight.

The diggers were beaten.

The stockade was crowded with soldiers and police, but they paid little attention to Toby as he rode up to the ruined fortifications. Many civilians were already at the scene.

The bare flagpole pointed at a blue sky like a bony finger. Some wounded miners still lay within the breastwork and were being attended by a man Toby recognised as one of the diggings' doctors. The hut which had stood near the flagpole was now a smouldering ruin and most of the tents inside the perimeter had been burned or slashed to ribbons. All this, Toby took in at a single glance. It was the group of wagons near the back of the stockade that drew his attention.

The dead were lined up in a long row and lay shoulder to shoulder on bloodstained scraps of canvas or calico scavenged from the remaining tents. Soldiers were loading the bodies, one by one, onto the wagons.

Toby dismounted and walked to the line of bodies. The dead had their faces uncovered and the flies were already at work. A little terrier dog sat on one body, howling pitifully for its master. A soldier chased the dog off and his mates helped him lift the corpse into the wagon. As soon as their backs were turned the little dog leaped into the wagon and continued its howling lament.

The soldiers ignored Toby as he approached the line of corpses that stretched along the hillside and past the remains of the blacksmith shop. He found Frank's body near the far end. It was the patches on the elbows of the red chequered shirt that caught his eye. Maree had stitched those patches when Toby visited the camp one Sunday, her neat, tight cross-stitch as recognisable as if she had signed her name beside each repair. The massive wound in Frank's shoulder still oozed blood that pooled in the dirt.

'Oh God, no,' Toby whispered. Flies crawled across Frank's bloodstained face. He would have shooed them away, but there were more bodies in the line and he moved on, the dread of finding Paddy's mutilated corpse building in his stomach. When he reached the last body he was shaking so much he had to will his legs to take each apprehensive step. There was no sign of Paddy among the dead lying on the ground and he went back to the wagon the soldiers were loading and climbed up on the spokes of the rear wheel to peer inside.

Paddy wasn't there.

'Is this the first load of bodies?' he asked the group of soldiers.

One of the soldiers had a corpse by the ankles as his mate struggled with the wrists. They swung the body back and forth a couple of times to build momentum and let it sail into the air to land in the wagon with a thud. The soldier looked up at Toby as he dusted off his hands.

'It's the first one, all right. Looks as if we'll be making a couple of trips.'

Reassured, Toby jumped from the wagon and hurried to where the wounded were being treated. The diggers lay on the ground they had defended and waited for the doctor's ministrations. Those that could sit up did so, but a contingent of soldiers and police stood close by. Wounded or not, they were prisoners of the Crown. A soldier moved to cut Toby off and usher him away, but a familiar voice rang out from among the group of policemen.

'Toby? What the hell are you doing up here, laddie?' McTavish strode towards him with his hand outstretched in greeting and the soldier, who had been about to send Toby away, shrugged his shoulders and returned to stand with his comrades.

Toby let the sergeant take his hand and pump his arm up and down as if it were a piece of rope. 'Hello, Angus,' he said. 'I'm looking for my brother. Have you seen him?'

'He was here?' McTavish asked, a look of incredulity on his face.

'Frank, too,' Toby admitted. 'I tried to talk them out of it, but they wouldn't listen.'

'I've no' seen either of 'em, laddie, and I was here from the start.' He let go of Toby's hand. 'Lots of prisoners were taken to Government Camp. Maybe they're among them.'

'I know where Frank is,' Toby said quietly.

'Really, where—?' McTavish stopped himself as Toby turned towards the line of bodies.

They stood in silence for a moment and watched the soldiers load the dead. Two of them had another digger slung between them by the wrists and ankles and were making their way to the back of the wagon. The horses could smell blood and were restless. The wagon jostled backwards and forwards until another soldier went to the offside horse and tried to settle it.

'Can I take him home, Angus? Can I take Frank home with me?'

'All the bodies are to be taken to the Camp,' McTavish said. 'Commissioner's orders.' He turned to look at Toby. 'As soon as his body can be released I'll get word to you, laddie. And I'll find out about your brother as well. I wouldn't worry about him. He's not with those poor men,' he said, gesturing at the wagon, 'and if he's not with the wounded being treated here, then he was either taken prisoner or was one of the lucky ones who escaped. Either way, you can't do much good here. Go home, Toby. You won't be welcome up at the Camp. Go home. They will need you there.'

Toby nodded and headed back to where he had tied Moonlight. As he walked, he heard the sergeant's voice behind him, haranguing the soldiers loading the wagon.

'Can ye no' show a little respect for the dead, ye heavy-handed bastards. For Christ's sake!'

Toby made his way down to the creek and followed it upstream to the gully below the hut. People rushed towards the stockade now that word of the battle had filtered out. Several women tried to question him as he picked his way past, but he pretended not to hear them. Soldiers still skulked among the tents and some were herding little groups of prisoners in the direction of the Camp. Toby made no effort to avoid them. If they were to arrest him and cart him off to the lock-up he would look upon it as a blessing, for he had no stomach for the onerous task awaiting him at the hut.

The women were all outside as he rode up the gully. They recognised him and rushed down the path, skirts held high, yelling questions as they ran.

'We heard the shooting. Is Papa all right?'

'Did you see them, Toby?'

'Have you been to the stockade?'

'Did you see Paddy and Frank?'

Toby swung out of the saddle and stood among them. His wife, mother and sister-in-law grabbed at his clothing and tugged at his sleeve as they implored him to answer their questions. He could hear Sean wailing in his crib.

Since leaving the stockade Toby had searched his mind for the right words, but there were no words he could use that would lessen their pain. What were the right words to tell a woman that her husband would not be coming home ever again? How do you tell two daughters that their father is lying dead in the dust of the stockade? Toby was dumbstruck, but in the end his silence said it all for him.

Maree stopped her questions and stepped back, a hand clutched to her mouth. Toby had been trying hard not to look at any of them, but his eyes found Maree's across three feet of space and, in that single glance, she had her answer.

He watched his mother-in-law fall to the ground, her skirts billowing out about her as she collapsed.

'Not my Frankie!' Maree beat at the ground with her fists. 'Please, God! Not my Frankie!'

Annie stooped to her mother and held her. Maree tried to fight her off, turning her fists against her daughter as Annie embraced her. Betty ran screaming towards the hut.

'Toby?'

Annie held a hand to him. He took her fingers into his palm. Her face was wet with tears and her hair had worked loose from its bun and hung in her eyes.

'Paddy?'

Even through her grief for her father, Annie was thinking of him. Frank had not been the only one at the stockade.

'I don't know. Under arrest, I think. McTavish is looking out for him. He wasn't at the stockade when I got there.'

'Did you—?' Toby knew what she wanted to ask.

'I saw him at the stockade, sweetheart. They're taking his body to the Camp.'

Annie nodded and untangled herself from her mother's arms. She stood and inclined her head to where Maree sobbed uncontrollably.

'We should take her inside.'

Toby stooped and lifted Maree in his arms. As he carried her into the hut, he realised that everyone in this simple structure had become his sole responsibility. The magnitude of it pressed down on him as he remembered the promise he had made to Frank, and he hoped like hell he was man enough for the task.

C hilders hurried through the main hall of Government House towards the Lieutenant Governor's private rooms. He carried a dispatch from the Gold Commissioner at the Warrogah diggings and, having read the message himself, decided the Governor would want to be apprised of it immediately, rather than wait for Monday.

He knew the Governor and his wife were readying themselves for church. The carriage stood waiting at the front of the house. Childers had informed the driver there was likely to be a delay. The Governor would want to deal with the problem the message conveyed before he left.

He knocked at the heavy door closing off the Governor's private rooms and waited. Footsteps approached the door from the other side and moments later it was opened by the Governor's personal servant, an owl-faced man in his fifties who gave Childers a look that said: 'What do you want?'

'I need to speak to the Governor please, Pritchard.' He had been about to add, 'On a matter of some urgency,' but the mere fact he was asking for the Governor on a Sunday morning should convey, even to Pritchard, the importance of his visit.

Pritchard gave a slight nod and opened the door for Childers to enter. He stepped through the doorway and found himself in a sitting room. Several other doors led further into the house and Pritchard made for one of these. The military man in Childers would not allow him to be seated when his superior entered the room. He opted to stand by the high window, hands clasped firmly into the small of his back while he waited.

'Ah, Childers.' Hotham strode into the room. He wore a dress uniform and a frown on his face. 'You have some news for me?'

'Nothing from Ballarat, sir,' Childers said. 'I have not long ago received an urgent dispatch from Commissioner Blair up on the Warrogah diggings.' He produced the message from behind his back and offered it to Hotham. 'It is a rather disturbing report, sir.'

'More disturbing than the miners banding together and starting a rebellion?' Hotham raised an eyebrow as he took the message.

Childers watched his superior's expression as Hotham squinted down at Blair's small, tight script. He saw the Governor's eyes widen and knew he was reading the part where Blair reported the deaths of the entire gold escort party and the loss of the shipment. When the Governor's expression changed to a scowl he knew he was reading where the local police had deduced that the perpetrator of this heinous crime was the bushranger known as Warrigal Anderson and his band of savages.

'It would seem our old nemesis is at it again, sir,' Childers offered.

Hotham let his hands fall to his sides. He turned to the window and stared out into the well-manicured grounds. The only sound in the room was the governor's breathing.

'How long have you been in the colony, Childers?' The governor spoke without turning to face him.

'I am proud to say I have completed nearly two terms, sir: five years in New South Wales and another four here.'

Hotham fell silent again, but this time he tapped the dispatch against his leg. Finally, he turned back to the room. 'Have you spent much time out in the forest country? What do they call it here – the bush?'

'A little, sir. I was stationed at Windsor in the 'forties. We made quite a few forays into the hills west of the settlement to search out convict bolters.'

'Did you catch them?'

'Most of them, sir. Some didn't last in the bush and gave themselves up readily. Others, the stubborn ones, died in the deep ravines and gullies of the Blue Mountains and left us only their bones to find. Some we never found at all.'

'You have had some experience in the bush, then, chasing down bolters?'

A knot of panic tightened in Childers's stomach. Was the governor going to send *him* out to chase down Anderson?

'A—a little, yes, sir. But I was one of many soldiers. We had help from native trackers, local settlers – bushmen with knowledge of the land.'

'Tell me, Childers,' the Governor said, holding up the dispatch. 'In your opinion as a chaser of convict bolters, why can't we catch this scoundrel?'

Childers relaxed a little. Hotham was only examining the ground from which Childers was to offer his opinion – an opinion the Governor now waited for expectantly.

'By your line of questions, I suspect you already have an understanding of why the man is so hard to catch, sir.'

'Let me hear it from you, Childers. Humour me.'

'Well, sir, he knows the bush. He knows it very well. I have heard stories that this Anderson fellow spent a few years living with the natives he now uses as his henchmen. The Aborigines are a mysterious lot, sir. The ones I worked with at Windsor seemed to have some sort of affinity for the country they were born into, a sort of ownership that works both ways. They consider themselves to be part of the land, belonging to it just as much as it belongs to them. Aborigines know the land better than we know our own wives' faces, sir. Not just the hills and valleys and geological features. They know its secrets. I have seen an Aborigine walk five steps into the bush and disappear from sight as if he never existed. I have followed a tracker through the dense forests on the western side of the Nepean River for two days and emerged in the exact place on the banks of the river we needed to be. A tremendous feat of navigation.'

'Are you suggesting some sort of magic?' Hotham inquired, raising a suspicious eyebrow.

Childers shook his head. 'No, not magic, sir. They have a knowledge and understanding of the world they live in that we can't even begin to comprehend. This Anderson fellow has that knowledge, or at least he has access to it. If we were chasing him through the streets of London or the English country-side we would stand an excellent chance of running him to ground, but in the Australian bush I'm afraid he has a formi-dable advantage.'

'So, are you telling me this Anderson fellow cannot be brought to justice?'

'Not with the current methods we are using, Your Excel-lency.'

'But what of the native trackers? Surely they can hunt down their own?'

'They probably can, sir. But there are places in the moun-tains this Anderson runs to that spooks most of them. The police have tried several times to mount an expedition, but the trackers quickly lose interest when they realise where they are going. There may be one or two native policemen who might be willing to try – one from a remote part of the colony perhaps who isn't subject to the taboo of entering a sacred place.'

'But if a white man had this – what did you call it? – this knowl-edge of the bush, then he might stand a chance of success?'

'Better than the average Englishman, yes, sir.'

Hotham lifted his head and bellowed, 'Pritchard!' A moment later the servant appeared in the doorway.

'Your Excellency?'

'Be a good fellow, Pritchard, and fetch that copy of the *Argus* I asked you to keep for me.'

'Very good, sir.' Pritchard slunk back through the doorway and returned a few moments later carrying a folded newspaper in front of him as if it were a tray of drinks. He offered the paper to the governor.

Hotham opened the paper and flicked through several pages until he found what he was looking for.

'Here, Childers, in this article there is mention of a bushman who helped to track down some vile creature in very rugged country. Where was it?' Hotham squinted as he scanned the article. 'Why do they always have to make the print so fine— Ah! Here it is, this fellow O'Rourke. He seems to have some knowledge and understanding of the bush and the ways of the natives. If you can believe the article, he has certainly shown his willingness to bring offenders to justice.'

The governor offered the paper to Childers. He took it and quickly read the section of print over which his superior's finger hovered.

'Ah yes, sir,' Childers nodded. 'If the story is true, then this man O'Rourke is certainly the type we need.'

'Get him, Childers.'

'Sir?'

'I want you to procure his services in the name of the Queen. Offer him the reward money if he will help us. I believe it is quite a sum.'

'A thousand pounds if I recall correctly, sir.'

'He can name his own terms, damn it. Just get him. If not him, then someone like him.'

'I shall draft a dispatch for the commissioner in Ballarat immediately, sir. With luck I can have it out on tomorrow morning's coach.'

'No, not a dispatch, Childers, not tomorrow. You can leave immediately. Go personally and speak to this fellow O'Rourke. With the rebellion at Ballarat they will be distracted. Go yourself and see what you can do. I can cope without you for a few days.'

'Yes, sir. Can I keep this?' Childers waved the newspaper. 'It might provide me with some clues on how to find the fellow.'

'Yes, yes. Now, get moving, man,' the governor snapped, impatient for action now that a course had been decided on.

'Damn it! We shall have missed the ten o'clock service now.'

Toby could not bring himself to look at the rough-sawn timber coffin and he cast his gaze about the graveyard. The Ballarat cemetery had not been untouched by the gold rush. A few shafts and mullock heaps were scattered among burial mounds and crosses. A great number of those mounds were small in size. This observation made him conscious of the little life he held in one arm and he increased the pressure protectively.

There were many new graves dotted about. The Eureka Stockade had given the funeral businesses of Ballarat a roaring trade over the past few days. As they approached the cemetery there had been two services underway. The Camp had only released the bodies of the fallen to family yesterday, and the heat made it all the more necessary for a quick burial.

Annie stood at Toby's side. His free arm was about her waist, and he could feel the little tremors that shook her body as she cried. Maree sat on the far side of Annie. Father Connell had kindly produced a camp chair for the widow, and Maree endured the ceremony with a stoic quiet. A black veil covered her face and Toby could not tell if she was crying. She had not spoken more than five words since Frank's death.

Betty stood beside her mother, a small wreath of flowers clutched in her hand. She had roamed the countryside for hours to find enough blooms for it. She sobbed quietly and dabbed at her eyes every now and then with a handkerchief.

Paddy stood opposite Toby, his gaze fixed firmly on the rectangular hole in the ground. He had turned up at the hut yesterday evening and gone straight to his bunk in the little storeroom without acknowledging anyone. Toby had learned from Father Connell that most of the diggers being held at the Camp lock-up had been released. Only a handful of men were being held over in custody, awaiting transport to Melbourne on charges of treason. Toby wondered how much the decision to release the diggers had been based on the sheer numbers held. It must have been a nightmare dealing with all the miners who had been marched in chains to the Camp. Whatever the reason, he was glad to have his brother back home in one piece.

A man in military uniform stood in the shade of a gum tree quietly watching the service. Gold braid showed brightly on the man's shoulders and the peak of his hat, which was tucked respectfully under his left arm. The Gold Commissioner himself did not wear a uniform of such flash and finery and Toby supposed this fellow was a man of considerably high rank.

'And so we commit the body of Francis Hocking to the earth—' Father Connell intoned. He continued in that high voice, developed to carry to the far corners of large churches. Toby turned his attention back to the ceremony and, when it finally concluded, helped Annie escort Maree to the borrowed cart.

'You girls head on home,' he said to Annie, and handed her up into the cart. 'Paddy and I will be along after we've finished here.' To save money no gravediggers had been employed. Toby and Paddy had dug the grave that morning and they would be the ones to fill it in. Two shovels stood ready at the pile of fresh earth.

Toby waited until the cart moved off, and then walked back to the graveside. He thanked Father Connell for the service and tried to slip a handful of shillings to the clergyman as they shook hands, but Father Connell would not have it.

'I consider it an honour to perform the service for such a fine chap. To accept payment would only sour the occasion further.' He pushed the coins back into Toby's hand and pulled his hat onto his head. 'Now, if you will excuse me, young man, I have three more services to conduct before day's end.' He tipped his hat in farewell, collected his camp chair and strode away through the cemetery.

Toby went to the shovels and handed one to Paddy. Together they piled dirt into the grave. When it was half full Toby stopped for a breather and wiped the sweat from his brow. He looked over towards the big gum tree. The officer still stood watching them.

'I wonder what he wants, Pad?' Toby gestured towards their spectator.

Paddy paused long enough to take a quick glance, shrugged his shoulders and turned back to the task at hand. When they were finished, the burial mound stood a foot out of the ground. Toby packed the dirt down tightly with the back of his shovel while Paddy collected lumps of quartz to mark the perimeter.

'As good a grave as any,' Toby said, and Paddy nodded his agreement. A polite cough came from behind them, and he turned to see the officer standing a few paces away.

'Do I have the pleasure of addressing Mr Tobias O'Rourke?' the man asked. The gold braid glistened even brighter now the man stood in sunlight. His stovepipe hat was coal-black and the trousers crisp and clean with razor-sharp creases. They looked as if they had just come from the tailor's. This was not a man who lived or conducted business on the diggings.

Toby nodded and the man said, 'Allow me introduce myself. My name is Childers and I am aide to the Governor.'

'Of—of the colony?'

'Yes, that's the fellow. Sir Charles Hotham, Lieutenant Governor of the Colony of Victoria.' Childers studied the two astonished faces before him.

'Is there somewhere we can talk?'

Toby was reluctant to take Childers to the hut. Maree and the girls might see him as representative of the forces responsible for Frank's death, but in the end it was his only choice. Anti-government sentiment ran high on the diggings, and he felt Childers's chances were better at the hut than anywhere else in Ballarat, despite the cool reception he might receive.

He needn't have worried. Maree pulled herself together long enough to make morning tea and even managed to reheat some scones which she served up with butter and jam. Annie found a half-decent saddle blanket to spread on one of the log seats so that Childers's immaculate trousers might be spared some of the dust and grime. The Governor's aide sipped tea and ate scones as he outlined the reason for his visit.

'So you see, Mr O'Rourke, the Governor is convinced it will take a person knowledgeable in the bush – a person such as yourself – to hunt down this Anderson fellow.' He brushed crumbs from his tunic jacket as he spoke.

Toby looked into the embers of the fire and listened to the *tink-tink* of the cooling camp oven. He was aware of Paddy's eyes boring into him from across the fire and Annie, who had been in the process of tidying up the crockery, stood stock-still as she waited for Toby's next words.

'I didn't find the man who murdered Caroline Dunn on my own, Mr Childers. I was part of a larger group. The *Argus* played up the story of my bushman skills somewhat.'

'I see.' Childers looked crestfallen. 'The Governor has rather pinned his hopes on you.'

'I would think the Governor has other things to worry about.'

'Yes,' Childers said. 'There is a substantial reward,' he added quickly. 'It would all be yours. I believe it is in the vicinity of one thousand pounds.'

Toby was unable to hold back the gasp of surprise that escaped his lips. 'As much as that?'

'The Governor has allowed me to go as high as twelve hundred,' Childers pressed on. 'He is very keen to resolve this matter.'

'I'll bet he is,' Toby said. 'The gold the escort was carrying must have been worth quite a sum?'

'Several thousands of pounds,' Childers admitted. 'There might even be part proceeds in the gold's value if it is recovered. However, I am unable to commit to anything definite as the gold escort was conducted by a private company. I should think their insurer would be glad to see it returned. Their reward alone might even exceed the bounty on our friend Anderson.'

A jumble of thoughts ran through Toby's head. Here he sat, two years after his parents' murders, and the Governor wanted him to help track down the man responsible. The memory of that fateful day was still strong in his mind and probably would be for the rest of his life. He could still smell the rancid breath as Anderson pulled him to his feet by the shirt front and grunted in his face. *'Don't be fool enough to follow me, boy.'* How Toby wished he could go back to that day. He would load the Lovell, saddle Moonlight and ride out after Anderson. That was what he should have done. But then he lifted his eyes to Paddy and remembered his brother's wound. He could not have left Paddy like that and chased after Anderson. He'd needed to stay and care for his brother.

But maybe, just maybe, it wasn't too late.

'Can I have a little time to talk with my brother and wife, Mr Childers?'

'Certainly, sir. Take as long as you need, but remember, I am due to depart on tomorrow morning's coach.' Childers made to stand, but Toby waved him back into his seat.

'Please stay, Mr Childers. I'll have an answer for you before you leave our camp.'

Toby gestured to Annie and Paddy, and they walked up the hillside towards the horse yard.

'You didn't mention that this is the man who murdered your parents,' Annie said, as soon as they were out of earshot.

'Childers didn't mention it either,' Toby replied. 'I don't think he knows – or remembers. Anderson has killed quite a few people since then.'

'Why didn't you tell him?'

Toby shook his head. 'There is no need. Besides, if he thinks I've got a personal stake in hunting down Anderson, then he may expect me to do it for nothing.'

Annie drew in a sharp breath. 'You're not seriously considering doing this, are you, Toby?'

'What else are we going to do, Annie? Your father is gone. Paddy can't work the claim on his own. If we're going to stay here, I'll have to give up work at the mill and come back to help him. We'd just be scratching about in the dirt like we've been doing for the past two years – with nothing to show for it.'

Annie lowered her chin to her chest and he could see tears welling in her eyes. He knew he'd hurt her talking about Frank's death in such a way.

'We could all go to some cattle run. There is plenty of work for everyone there.' Annie lifted her face, defiant again.

'It wouldn't be our place, Annie.' He took her shoulders in his hands and shook her gently. 'Don't you see, I want more than that for you? I want you to be able to stand on the verandah of our own home. I want you to be the lady of the household, not answering to anyone. I want a place we can pass down to Sean and any other children, knowing we've left them something special, something we've put our hearts into and they can see it every time they open their eyes – they can see what we built for them with our own hands and our hearts.' He let her go and turned to face up the hillside. 'We'll never have that working for someone else.'

'I'm scared I'll lose you. I've already lost Papa.' Annie stood her ground, tears rolling down her face.

He could hear the fear in her voice and couldn't stand it. Taking her into his arms, he pulled her tight against his chest.

'You won't lose me, sweetheart. If I can't do this thing then I'll turn around and ride home. If I succeed, all well and good, but if not we'll all move away from here.'

'All right,' Annie said, her voice muffled. 'But you make sure you come back to me, please, Toby.'

Toby looked to where Paddy stood by the path. Their eyes met and he could see the determination in them. His brother was no longer the frightened boy who had crawled under the table.

'What do you say, Pad? We gonna chase down this cove or what?'

Paddy gave a sharp nod.

'Let's go and tell Childers.'

A few more scones were gone from the plate and several crumbs had reappeared on the aide's tunic. He looked up expectantly as the trio approached.

'You have yourself a deal, Mr Childers,' Toby announced. 'I do, however, have a few minor stipulations.'

'I see.' Childers's look of elation changed to one of suspicion. 'What are these stipulations?'

'Firstly,' Toby held up his right index finger, 'my brother will come with me. He's a skilled bushman like myself. You will, in effect, be getting two for the price of one.'

'Of course,' Childers said, clapping his hands. 'You can take whomever you like with you. What else?'

Toby raised another digit.

'Since neither of us will be here to work, I feel we should each draw a wage of four shillings a day, with a period of five weeks paid in advance to my wife.' He looked over at Paddy and received a nod. 'Both lots to be paid to my wife before we depart,' Toby confirmed.

Childers face carried a look of astonishment. 'So, in effect, two for the price of three. I can make no guarantees, Mr O'Rourke. The governor is allowing me a little leeway on this venture. I am sure something can be arranged, though. What else?' Childers eyed the two raised digits on Toby's hand suspiciously.

'Angus McTavish, the mounted police sergeant is to accompany us, along with the native tracker Barraworn. Some extra constables might also be needed if things come down to a fight.'

'Agreed,' Childers announced. 'Is that all?'

'Provisions and extra mounts for the expedition are to be provided from government stores.' Toby had been about to hold up another finger, but decided it was unnecessary. He lowered his hand to his side.

'One other thing,' Toby added, and Childers frowned. Toby ignored the look and went on. 'There's a cove being held in the Melbourne Gaol. A cattle duffer called Scotchy.'

'What about him?' Childers's look changed to one of puzzlement.

'He robbed me and my brother of some cattle two years ago. We planned to sell those cattle to pay off a debt against our land. When we couldn't pay, the man we owed the money to took our farm.'

'I don't see what this has to do with the task at hand, Mr O'Rourke.'

Toby sat opposite Childers so that their eyes were on the same level. 'Scotchy said the man we owed money to, Henry Pelham, hired him to steal our cattle so that he could take our land.'

'What would you like me to do, Mr O'Rourke?'

'I couldn't get him to admit it to anyone that mattered, and I couldn't get anyone to listen without proof.'

'The burden of proof is an onerous one, sir, but cornerstone to our rights as British subjects.'

Toby felt his anger flare and fought to suppress it. He had heard enough of 'burden of proof' and 'direct evidence'.

'I just want someone to listen to me, sir. I want someone to look into the matter and not shrug it off as the rantings of some boy.'

Childers looked into his eyes. He must have come to some decision, for he stood and said, 'I'll see what I can do about having the matter looked into. Is there anything else, sir?'

Toby shook his head.

'I'll have the Gold Commissioner here in Ballarat prepare everything you need for the expedition,' Childers said. 'Anything and anyone at his disposal will be made available to you. When can you leave?'

'As soon as everyone is ready,' Toby said. 'Tomorrow if it all happens quickly enough.'

'I shall see to it myself, Mr O'Rourke.'

A nderson never once gave up the lead rope of the pack-horse, even though it made for difficult riding through the bush and up along the spur to the escarpment. He could have tied the rope to his saddle, but couldn't bring himself to give up that contact with the gold in the packsaddles. The best he could do was change hands every so often to rest the strain on his arm.

His mount was content to follow along behind the horses of the two Jannjirra and he let it have its head as he thought about what lay ahead of him. They hadn't left a single member of the escort party alive, but he supposed their bodies had been discovered soon after daybreak when they failed to break camp. The killings alone would bring many soldiers and mounted police to the area. Every traveller on the colony's roads would be under heavy scrutiny, especially one travelling in company with natives. He glanced back at the packhorse and the bulging packsaddles and knew he couldn't risk trying to move through the settled areas, even in the bush and along back trails, not for a while.

Tilting his head back, he looked up at the heights of the escarpment, now looming over them. He would rest up in the tribal lands of the Jannjirra. As far as he knew, he was the only white man who had ever been up there. No one else had discovered the narrow defile that enabled the final climb past the cliffs and onto the heights. It had been nearly eight years since he had made his way up this very spur, cold, wet and on the point of starvation, wondering if the soldiers were still chasing him or had given up weeks ago and left the bush to deal with him.

He lowered his eyes to the backs of Chilbi and Yawong. Soon, he would have them dismount and move back along their spoor, erasing all trace of its existence. After that, their usefulness was done. They would not let him ride off alone with the gold and he couldn't allow himself to be seen with them once he returned to the settled areas. That would raise too much suspicion. It would be best if they remained in their tribal lands. His hand drifted to the grip of his revolver.

Days later, as the sun hung low in the west, the trio made camp among a scree of boulders, a circular enclosure only accessible through a cleft between two gigantic stones. The gang had used this place a few times before. It was sacred ground to the two Jannjirra, and many of the sheltered areas were covered in rock paintings of scenes from their mythology.

'Brush all traces of dirt from your feet,' Chilbi warned at the entrance. 'Carry no dirt into this place. The ground beyond must remain pure.'

He and Yawong carefully scrubbed at the soles of their feet. Anderson, the only one wearing boots, stamped his feet a couple of times and made a cursory examination. 'Clean as a whistle,' he said.

Chilbi gestured at the weapons. 'These are touched by evil. Our ancestors will be angry for bringing them into a sacred place.' He and Yawong gathered the firearms, spears and war clubs and stacked them to one side of the entrance. He pointed at the revolver in Anderson's belt. 'Your Djarriba weapon. Put it with the others.'

'No,' Anderson said, gripping the revolver. 'I think I'll keep this with me.'

'You have no respect for the evil in your weapon.'

'Oh, I have plenty of respect for the evil in this weapon,' Anderson said, grinning.

'The Djarriba gold,' Chilbi pointed at the packsaddles. 'Men have died for it. It is tainted with bad magic. We should leave it outside.'

'More men will die if it is touched.' The grin slid from Anderson's face. He stooped into the low entrance, dragging the packsaddles behind him.

Beyond the boulders a cliff rose towards the sky, and a deep overhang sheltered an ancient campsite, the roof blackened by generations of fires. On the far wall someone long ago had painted a likeness of the Rainbow Serpent, the creator of all life, its long coils winding about hand stencils and stick figures.

'How long will we stay here, Warrigal?' Yawong asked.

'I know you want to be on the tribal grounds of your ancestors. You can stay here forever.'

'Will we not return to the lands of the Djarriba? Will we not continue to take our revenge for the sickness?'

Anderson smiled and patted the packsaddles. 'The war is over, my friend. We have hurt the Djarriba deeply for sending the sickness to us.'

Chilbi shrugged and turned away. Anderson watched him go, his mind deep in thought. He flicked his gaze to the packsaddles and back to the two Aborigines, his hand still on the revolver.

C hilbi's father walked out of the mists of his sleeping mind and paused at the limit of his vision. The elder was dressed in a kangaroo-skin cloak, his face painted in the ceremonial markings of the Jannjirra. He carried no weapons, for this was a sacred place and not to be tainted with evil or the instruments of death.

'Greetings, my son.' Barramat held up his hand.

'Greetings, Father.'

Chilbi felt a deep yearning in his soul – a regret for things that were lost and would never be again. His father looked fit and strong, every bit the warrior and elder of the tribe that Chilbi remembered, not the coughing form covered in pustules in the last days of his father's life when the Djarriba sickness came for him.

'I miss you, Chilbi.'

'I miss you too, Father. One day we will be together in the spirit world.'

'That time is far away. You have a duty to perform before you join your ancestors. You will be the guardian of all that is sacred. The ceremonies that appease the spirits of our people will be yours alone to complete.'

'These things I will do, Father.'

Barramat turned towards something beyond the ether, a look of fear distorting his features. 'You must prepare yourself, my son. The evil is coming.'

'What do you ask of me, Father?'

The figure of his father retreated beyond the firelight, beyond the vision of Chilbi's mind.

'Please, Father. Don't leave me.' But only Barramat's booming voice came out of the shadowed distance of the dream.

'Wake up, Chilbi,' the voice said. 'You are the last of the Jannjirra people. Wake up and *run*!'

Chilbi sat up, his eyes wide open and pulse racing. Someone stood above him and he drew a breath of superstitious fear.

Yawong leaned over him, a silhouette against the stars, his head turned to face another figure that approached out of the darkness.

Warrigal stepped carefully towards them and pulled the revolver from his belt.

Chilbi rolled to his feet, eyes on the pistol swinging towards him.

Warrigal paused and braced for the shot.

'Run, Chilbi, run,' Yawong screamed and lunged through the air. He pushed Chilbi aside as the revolver fired. The muzzle flash lit the darkness. Yawong took the ball in the chest and fell.

Chilbi ran. He angled towards the rocks as he heard the revolver cock for a second shot, and threw himself headlong onto the ground as Warrigal fired. Something hot and hard tore across his thigh. He felt the skin open as the ball ripped across muscle. Using his momentum, he tucked himself into a ball and rolled to his feet. The pain in his leg was excruciating as he limped hard and fast for the entrance.

Somewhere behind him he heard Yawong cry out, then the sound of another gunshot.

He emerged from the boulders and paused beside the pile of weapons. His spear lay where he had left it and he hefted it in his right hand. Twenty paces away the horses stood tethered to a line and Chilbi sneered at the animals that were so precious to Warrigal. With a grunt of exertion and anger he let the spear fly. It whispered through the air and hit the packhorse behind the shoulder. The fire-hardened point pierced the animal's ribs and cut deep. The horse let out a terrified scream of surprise and collapsed on its side.

The other horses panicked at the dying bellows of their comrade. They kicked and whinnied as they fought to break away. Chilbi pulled the spear from the dying horse and turned to the animal beside it. This time he found the animal's heart. The horse fell to the ground, kicked twice and lay still. He retrieved the spear and moved towards the last two animals. When all the horses were dead, he pulled his spear free and limped into the night.

Anderson reloaded the revolver and stooped to the entrance. He couldn't see more than a few paces, but a pale patch of darkness showed where the passage opened to the outside. He could hear the horses screaming and thrashing about. The Jannjirra had left their weapons on the outside and he knew Chilbi would be armed, if not with a musket then with a spear, a more frightening proposition. If the young Aborigine came for him, it would be fast, silent and fatal.

He kept his back to the rock as he approached the starlight. In the gloom he could see that all the horses were on the ground. One animal still kicked feebly, but the screaming had died away.

Chilbi had worked fast.

There was no sign of the Aborigine, but that did not mean Chilbi wasn't out there in the darkness, waiting with the spear. He cursed softly under his breath and retreated into the campsite. With Chilbi still alive, he would need to leave. If he remained here, he was as good as dead. The young warrior would take revenge for the killing of his brother. Anderson's only hope lay in getting away. The Aborigine had been hit in the leg, of that he was sure. By dawn the wound would be hurting, the limb stiffening. He could only hope the warrior was wounded badly enough to prevent him from giving chase.

He returned to the packsaddles and cursed as he looked down at them. A fortune in gold lay at his feet and he had no horse to carry it out of the mountains. At the campfire he found a pair of saddlebags among the equipment and spent the next few minutes loading pouches of gold dust into them. When he was finished, he stood and hefted the saddlebags onto his shoulder to test the weight. Not too light that he was wasting valuable space; not too heavy that he would never make it out of the mountains on foot. He had shoved forty pouches into the saddlebags, twenty in each. There was no room for more.

With the saddlebags loaded, Anderson gathered rocks from within the arena and packed them over the gold and valuables he couldn't take with him. The chance of anyone wandering into the camp before he was able to return with a horse was pretty remote, but he felt better for having hidden the gold. By the time he was finished, the eastern sky had begun to tinge with the promise of daybreak.

Chilbi stood on the ridge above the camp, his back to a large gum tree to break his silhouette against the skyline. He watched Anderson walk into the bush with a pair of saddlebags draped over his shoulder and a flour bag in his hand. The Djarriba headed into the north. This direction surprised him. He had expected the bushranger to make his way south, towards the settlements of his own kind.

His father's words still haunted him. He could hear the whisper echoing in his mind, as if the elder had planted the words deep into his soul so that he would never forget them.

'*You are the last of the Jannjirra people. Run!*'

The loneliness welled up and rushed to engulf him. From this height he could see into the camp. Yawong's body lay where he had fallen. He truly was the last of his people, and his blood ran cold with the thought of it.

Warrigal reached the edge of the bush and stopped to survey the hills, his free hand wandering to the revolver tucked in his belt.

He knows I'm out here, Chilbi thought. *He knows I will come for him.*

He waited until Warrigal was gone from sight then climbed down from the ridge. The wound in his leg oozed watery blood, the muscle aching. He knew he shouldn't waste time. He needed to catch up with Warrigal while he still had the strength, but a sense of longing drove him towards the camp.

As he crouched into the narrow passage, he shivered. Normally Chilbi marvelled at the paintings lining the narrow passageway, but today they held no wonder for him. The people who had painted them were no more.

He dragged Yawong's body under an overhang of the inner wall and gathered up small boulders and stones, piling them so the bush creatures couldn't get at the remains of his brother.

The campfire still smouldered and in its ashes he found the charred remains of every musket, spear and club. Everything had been burned, including the food bags. He found the pile of stones where Warrigal had buried the gold, but would not allow himself to be tainted with its bad magic by touching it.

Going back through the entrance, he stood for a moment over Warrigal's tracks. Then, without looking back, he shouldered his spear and followed the spoor into the trees.

Cells stretched into the distance, each with a heavy door and peephole built at eye height so the gaolers could inspect the inmates. The roof was supported by iron beams, which were in turn supported by an intricate pattern of braces and crosspieces. Despite the gaol being at maximum capacity, Childers could hear his own footsteps echoing back to him through an eerie quiet.

'The prisoners aren't allowed to speak, sir,' the warder said, guessing Childers's thoughts. The man's voice was barely above a whisper, but it carried clearly and would have been audible to someone standing on the opposite gantry. 'In fact, they aren't even allowed to see each other. We put hoods on their heads when they're moved about. Keeps 'em docile like, sir.'

Childers inclined his head to show he had heard the man's words. He had no desire for conversation. In fact, he had no desire to be in this depressing building at all. It was only his sense of duty and a promise he had made to a fresh-faced young man on the Ballarat diggings that gave him reason to be here at all. He would look into young O'Rourke's allegations. He felt he owed the fellow that much. Then he would leave and hurry to where the air was pure and fresh and smelled of gum leaves.

The warder stopped outside a cell near the end of the wing. Here, the gantry expanded into a wide landing with a trapdoor built into the middle. A hangman's noose hung from a beam above the trapdoor, perfectly still in the unmoving air, the rope sprouting coarse fibres along its length like the bristles on a dog's back.

'Here we are, sir,' the warder said. He looked through the peephole. 'Prisoner, step to the rear of the cell and face the wall,' he growled through the grate. The warder waited, eyes pressed to the opening. Childers heard soft noises of movement from within the cell, then the warder stepped back and unlocked the door.

The cell was about eight feet deep and five wide. A narrow sleeping mat occupied half the floor area. A bucket sat just inside the door, giving off a foul odour. Childers used his foot to push the bucket out through the doorway and onto the gantry, conscious of the look he received from the warder. He ignored the gaoler and turned his attention to the tall figure in prison clothing facing the wall at the rear of the cell.

'You may turn around,' Childers said.

The man turned and fixed him with a stare from a solitary blue eye. The other eye socket was covered with a patch. His face seemed rather sallow, probably as a result of being denied sunlight for some time, Childers thought. The eye swept over him, taking in the gold braid and air of officialdom in one casual sweep. Almost immediately the man's face adopted a look of contempt.

'My name is Childers. I am aide to the Governor. You are Jonathon Bowmore, I presume?'

The prisoner gave an almost imperceptible nod.

'For God's sake, speak up, man. If I am to circumvent the hangman's desire to stretch your neck, then we must speak with each other.'

The eye blinked. 'You're here to help me?'

'Maybe not directly,' Childers admitted. 'However, the matter we discuss may warrant a stay of execution while some formalities are sorted out. They could go on for years.' Childers clasped his hands into the small of his back. 'Now, am I addressing Jonathon Bowmore or not?'

The prisoner nodded again, a definite movement of the head. 'People call me Scotchy,' he said.

'I wish to discuss with you the matter of some cattle you stole during the summer of 1852.'

Scotchy remained unmoving. Childers saw the eye study him again, roving up and down his uniform as he tried to fathom why the Governor was concerning himself with stolen cattle. 'What about it?' he finally responded.

'You did not act on your own initiative, did you?'

'What do you mean?'

Childers smiled. 'What I mean, dear chap, is that you did not come up with the idea of stealing the cattle of your own volition. Someone put you up to it,' he expanded, on seeing the puzzled look on the man's face.

'Is this really going to help me? With the hangman, I mean.'

'My good fellow, if another investigation were to be opened it may prevent the hangman from getting at your neck for some considerable time.'

Scotchy nodded. 'Some toff come and asked us to steal some cattle from a couple of brats.'

'Did he say why he wanted you to do this?'

'He didn't,' Scotchy said, shaking his head. 'But the lad who hired us for the droving job was screaming something about losing their land if they lost the cattle. If I'd known what the toff was goin' to get out of it I would've held out for more than twenty pounds, believe me.'

Childers nodded. 'I see. I don't suppose the gentleman who put you up to this task gave you his name?'

'No names were needed so long as money changed hands. We didn't give him ours and he didn't give us his.'

Childers didn't need a name. It appeared young O'Rourke was telling the truth. This thief and his friend were paid to steal the cattle from him. The only person who stood to gain anything from the situation would have been the fellow the boys owed money to.

'Thank you,' Childers said. 'You have been most helpful. He turned and stepped through the doorway. 'Good day.'

'What about helping me with the hangman,' Scotchy yelled. He tried to follow Childers, but the warder blocked his path and used the tip of a baton to push Scotchy back through the doorway.

'Oh, I'll help you with the hangman,' Childers called over his shoulder. 'I'll have him replace that rope. It looks terribly frayed. I'd hate it to snap and botch the job.' He stepped out for the stairs to the ground floor. From behind him came the sound of the baton striking flesh.

A t Government House Childers found a clerk sitting at a desk in an outer office.

'Do you have any idea where a place called Bunyong Creek is, Wilder?'

'Bun-yong Creek?' The clerk enunciated each syllable as he tapped the desk with a pen. 'Never heard of it, sir.'

Childers reached over and patted the man's shoulder. 'Be a good fellow and find out where it is for me. I have to speak to the Governor about a grave injustice.' He stepped back and moved towards the door. 'What sort of mood is he in?'

'I wouldn't call it a good one, sir,' the clerk said. 'It never is these days.'

T his is where we lost the bastard after he shot your folks.' McTavish gestured at the ground around them. 'Other patrols since have tracked him to this area. Some have even gone higher.' He lifted his face to the blue-tinged heights. 'None have ever picked up his trail.'

Toby studied the heights above them and scratched at the growth of beard on his face. The six-man party were eight days out of Ballarat and he hadn't shaved since leaving the hut on the diggings the morning after Childers's visit. The ridge appeared to be a natural ramp that climbed to the rim, but from where he sat his mount, he could see that the final climb would not be an easy one for horses. Tumbledown boulders littered the edge, looking for all the world like the battlements of an ancient castle.

'It's obvious they went up there,' he said. 'There must be some place where a horse can get through.'

They spent the morning climbing the ridge and at midday reached a screen of rocks and boulders that appeared impassable. 'Let's dismount and scout around on foot,' Toby suggested. 'Anderson got horses up there somehow.'

Leaving the horses tethered, they split into two groups, each setting off in a different direction to explore the barrier. Toby and Paddy, accompanied by a constable named Gatwick, went to the right, while McTavish, Barraworn and a second constable named Sloan headed to their left.

For an hour or more they crossed rocky and steep ground, but the line of boulders appeared unbroken. Toby moved further downslope and tried to study the lay of the land with the eye of a horseman. The ground was open enough close to the rocks, maybe not for a mounted man, but certainly for a horse being led on foot.

'I don't see any way up there. Not from this place, anyway,' Gatwick said, his moustache twitching as he spoke. The constable still wore his blue tunic and his face gleamed with perspiration.

'And yet they got up there,' Toby reminded him. 'They wouldn't climb the ridge to a dead end. There has to be a way.'

They walked back up to the boulders and continued searching, exploring the spaces between the huge natural monoliths. Late in the afternoon, Toby was about to give up and suggest they head back to find the rest of the party when he heard Paddy clapping his hands for attention. He looked in the direction of the noise, but his brother was nowhere in sight.

'Pad? Where are you? Have you found something?'

The clapping continued, more urgent than before. Toby and Gatwick moved along the wall of rock until they came to a large bush that had taken root in one of the fissures.

'Paddy?' He listened for the clapping. It seemed to come from behind the bush and Toby pushed it aside to find Paddy crouched in a narrow passage no more than four feet wide.

'You think this is it, Pad?' Toby asked sceptically. They had followed similar gaps in the boulders only to be confronted by a dead end.

Paddy nodded and pointed at the ground. Toby followed the direction of his finger and saw the hoof print of a horse, perfectly formed in damp earth.

'This has to be it,' Toby said. 'Well done, Pad. Let's go and find McTavish and the others.'

It took half a day to negotiate the narrow passage leading onto the escarpment. The footing was treacherous, and Toby had each rider dismount and lead his horse up the incline, one careful step at a time, their animals' flanks barely squeezing through the press of rock. The two packhorses needed to be unloaded and led up the same way, the supplies divided up among the men and hauled to the top before being reloaded.

The country beyond the escarpment was sparsely treed. Anderson's natives had not used anti-tracking after clearing the passage and the spoor was plain to see. Toby was tempted to ride as fast as possible until McTavish reminded him they could now consider themselves in enemy territory and needed to be alert. Gatwick and Sloan each led a packhorse and McTavish moved them into the middle of the group. He gave Barraworn instructions to follow the spoor and Toby and Paddy followed behind the tracker.

'If we are ambushed by Anderson or the natives, we should rally on the packhorses. Then we can decide the best action to take,' McTavish advised. To Toby's ear he didn't sound too convincing.

Each man ensured his gun was loaded, with a cap on the nipple. Gatwick and Sloan even went as far as carrying their carbines in one hand while they rode, but soon tired of this as they negotiated twists and turns. It wasn't long before they followed the example of the others and left their weapons in the scabbards.

At noon they reined in beside a cluster of rounded boulders and ate johnnycakes washed down with gulps of water from their canteens.

'We need to find a creek and water the horses,' Toby muttered to Barraworn. The tracker nodded and led the party along a twisting game path towards a distant rise. Twenty minutes later they found a narrow stream cascading down the hillside.

'How the hell does he do it?' Gatwick said as he filled his canteen while his horse drank thirstily.

'He can smell it,' Sloan explained.

'Maybe his horse could smell it. He just loosed his rein and let the horse follow its nose to water.'

'No,' Sloan insisted, 'I saw him flaring his nostrils. He could smell it himself all right.'

While the horses drank their fill, Toby took Paddy and Barraworn to scout along the creek bank. If this stream was the only water for some miles, the natives who lived up on the plateau must use it as well, he reasoned. Carrying their muskets, they followed the little creek downstream, looking for any sign of human habitation. They walked in the water, for the scrub on either bank was too thick. Barraworn took the lead, his shaggy mane of black hair flicking from side to side as he searched. After ten minutes of sloshing along, the tracker stopped and squatted on his haunches.

Toby moved up to Barraworn's shoulder and squatted beside him. 'What is it?' he whispered.

Barraworn pointed to a break in the scrub on the left bank. Here the ground had been packed flat and hard by the passage of many feet over the years. Only human feet could flatten the dirt in such a manner. Animals would have left the bank churned to mud.

'This place here where lubras come down for water, boss.'

'Let's follow the path back into the bush,' Toby said. 'See where it leads.'

Barraworn stood and moved cautiously onto the bank. On the far side of the clearing a track led away through shadowy scrub. He cocked his carbine and moved onto it, Toby and Paddy close behind.

The track followed the bank of the creek. Every now and then an offshoot snuck away towards the sound of water hidden behind dense bush. These showed only the marks of wombats and marsupial rats. They stayed with the main path which eventually turned away from the creek towards a stand of tall gum trees. Barraworn paused and waited for Toby to come up beside him.

'Old gunyahs, boss.' Barraworn pointed into the trees with his chin.

Toby could see nothing unusual beneath the trees. Barraworn must have sensed his puzzlement. The tracker pointed again with the barrel of his carbine.

'One there, boss.' The barrel stabbed towards a pile of fallen branches that looked as if a bonfire had been prepared some time ago and never lit. 'Another there.' Again, the carbine pointed at a similar pile of dead branches and sticks.

Toby suddenly realised what he was looking at. The gunyahs had lost their leafy protection against the elements, leaving only a skeletal framework of sticks. As the realisation struck him, he could see more dilapidated structures scattered through the trees.

He waved Barraworn forward and the trio moved out into the trees. This campsite had obviously been a favourite for the semi-nomadic Aborigines. Well-worn paths twisted through the trees in every direction, the earth packed hard and flat by the passage of many feet, so that, even now, Mother Nature had not completely reclaimed what had once been hers.

Barraworn led them along a broad pathway to a space between the boles of two gum trees where he stooped and picked up a piece of charred wood.

'Campfire, boss. Long time ago,' he explained, unnecessarily. The blackened stick had a furry coating of moss on one side. Many small bones lay scattered on the ground. Toby recognised the femur of a wallaby and the skull of a possum discarded in the grass.

'Let's get back to the others,' he said. 'We'll bring them here.'

'**Y**ou wanted to find an Aborigine camp, Angus,' Toby said, pointing at the tumbledown structures when they returned. 'Doesn't look like it's been used for a couple of years.'

McTavish swung from his horse and strode between the old gunyahs. He stooped to look into one gloomy interior, then another. Finally, he turned back to Toby and the others.

'This fellow Anderson escaped from a convict work party some years ago. He was chased as far as the escarpment before the soldiers gave up.' He walked back to his horse and took the reins. 'Every now and then a settler would report seeing a white man among a group of natives, but no one was sure. No one wanted to come up here and look for a convict bolter. This tribe remained out of contact for a long time. I suppose they looked after Anderson, fed him and so on. The poor buggers were unaware of the evil they were harbouring.'

'But what happened to the Aborigines?' Sloan asked.

'I don't know, laddie. They may have gone down to the settled areas, as a lot of tribes do. Maybe they went deeper into the bush. By all accounts this mob was a pretty reclusive lot. But I'll bet a week's pay these are the same Aborigines Anderson found.'

Toby looked at Paddy and shifted the Lovell in his hands. He could sense Anderson's malevolent presence, somewhere out there in the bush. He said, 'We can camp here tonight. Tomorrow we'll follow the tracks into the interior.'

To continue north into high and wild country on foot would be suicide. Starvation and death awaited in that direction. He had deliberately travelled north to take him away from any pursuit that may have tracked him to the edge of the escarpment, but Anderson knew if he stood any chance of making it out of the mountains, he would now need to head west, to the fertile river valleys where settlers lived. If he could reach a settlement or road, he could steal a couple of horses and come back for the rest of the gold.

The saddlebags were slung over his shoulder, and they thumped against his chest and back as he picked his way through the trees. The revolver was tucked into his belt and he carried a small calico bag containing spare powder and shot, a roll of banknotes and a few pounds of flour. It wasn't much, he knew, but with a little luck he would soon be out of these cursed hills and able to spend a little of the money or gold dust on a meal at an inn or homestead – or use his gun to get what he wanted.

Late that afternoon, he trudged up to the edge of the plateau and looked down into a broad river valley. Some twenty miles away, light reflected off water. There was a large river down there and, judging by the high country to the east, it must be flowing into the west, towards the settled areas. If he could reach it, he could follow it to civilisation. The country between the river and where he stood was covered with thick forest, and the valley wall dropped away steeply, plunging a half-mile or more to where the glittering water lay.

Two days, maybe three and I'll reach the river.

He shifted the saddlebags onto his other shoulder and started forward.

B arraworn paused beside a wall of boulders and eyed the markings on one of the great stones. All that morning he had led the party into the north, his keen eyes picking out small features which reassured him they were on the right track. Here and there he found the remains of campfires or trees which had been stripped of their bark to make the carrying bowls Aboriginal women use to collect food. He could see rocks that bore marks where tools and spears had been sharpened. To him the countryside had the same look an abandoned town or village might have to a white man, and the beginnings of superstitious dread were creeping into his mind.

'What is it, Barraworn?' McTavish asked, as he reined in beside the tracker.

Barraworn turned to the sergeant, his eyes wide with terror. 'This place, bad *yamma*, boss.' He cast his gaze over crude paintings of figures, the outlines of hands stencilled beneath the overhang of a huge boulder where they were protected from the weather. 'This the place where spirits live.'

'What's the problem?' Toby asked as he came up beside them.

'He says there is bad magic in this place. Evil spirits live here,' McTavish said. 'The laddie's scared to hell.'

Toby studied the rock paintings and then looked into the terrified eyes of Barraworn. 'All right, matey,' he said. 'You go and scout around to see if there are any recent tracks leading away from here. Don't come too close if you don't want to.'

Relieved, Barraworn urged his mount away from the boulders. He gave them a wide berth as he circled around to cast for recent spoor.

Toby swung from the saddle. He passed Moonlight's reins to Sloan then pulled the Lovell from its scabbard. McTavish did the same and they moved cautiously along the natural wall of boulders. They had not gone far when the warbling call of a magpie caught Toby's attention. He looked to where Barraworn sat his mount, fifty paces out into the bush. The tracker made the warbling call again and pointed back towards the boulders.

Toby and McTavish moved along the base of the boulders until they were in line with the direction Barraworn had indicated. Four dead horses lay beside the rocks, all tied to a tether. The mountain dingos had been at work, the sides of the dead animals torn open.

'What the hell do you suppose happened here, laddie?' McTavish asked, his eyes sweeping the ridge above the boulders.

'They don't look like gunshot wounds,' Toby said, eyeing one of the dead horses. 'These animals were killed by spear.'

There were human footprints around the horses, made by bare feet, and something else which made the skin prickle on the back of Toby's neck.

Another footprint lay in the dust. Unlike the others, this print had been made by a booted foot, the impression perfectly clear. Toby squatted and tentatively traced its outline with a fingertip. The man who had killed his parents had stood on this very spot not too long ago. He felt a hollowness in the pit of his stomach. Was it fear, or something else? In his mind he was outside the homestead at Bunyong Creek, his shirtfront in the grip of a dark stranger who had just gunned down his mother and father.

'Don't be fool enough to follow me, boy!'

Beside that print he found another and another. They retreated into a gap in the boulders and he stooped to follow them through.

'Careful,' McTavish cautioned. 'There could be anything in there, laddie.'

Toby cocked the Lovell and stepped into the opening. The walls were covered with many rock paintings: animals, birds and men formed by dots or childlike lines, some looking so fresh it seemed they had only been painted yesterday. Seven paces carried him through and he found himself standing on the edge of a natural amphitheatre. The far wall was a cliff face. Boulders stretched away at either hand, the ground covered with small rocks and tufts of spindly mountain grass. Here and there trees had gained purchase in gaps between boulders, their growth stunted and malformed by their precarious position.

McTavish stood beside Toby. 'Looks as if they've gone, laddie,' he said, glancing into the shadowy interior of the overhang.

'Yes, but how long ago were they here? We should get Barraworn in here to have a look. He can tell us when they left.'

'You've got no chance of getting him anywhere near this place. Did you see his eyes when he spotted those paintings on the rocks?' McTavish said, then, without waiting for an answer, 'Don't worry, he'll find the freshest set of tracks leading away, and those will be the ones we'll follow. We're close to the bastard now.'

Toby went to the remains of a campfire and placed his hand on the grey ashes.

Stone cold.

McTavish moved up beside him. 'Like I said, laddie, they're gone.' The sergeant sniffed at the air. 'What's that smell?'

A smell of putrefaction came from somewhere close by. 'Maybe from the dead horses. No, the breeze is blowing the wrong way.'

'Seems to be coming from over here,' McTavish said. He crossed to an overhang of rock in which many stones had been piled up. 'Yes, it's definitely strongest here.' The sergeant stooped and pulled a few rocks away, then jumped back.

'My God!'

Toby thought the sergeant had flushed a snake from beneath the stones, but as he moved closer, he could see what had caught McTavish off guard. A human hand protruded from beneath the pile of rocks, the hand of an Aborigine.

'Is this a burial ground or something?' McTavish asked.

'I don't know,' Toby replied. 'Let's dig a little deeper and see what we find.'

They shifted more rocks from beneath the overhang. The smell of death became overpowering and brought a cloud of flies buzzing about, but they worked on in silence.

'A young buck,' McTavish said, once the makeshift grave had been revealed. He stepped back to where the air was a little sweeter.

'He was shot,' Toby said, studying the wounds.

'But why? And look at the clothing – a strange mix of civilised and native garb. This fellow has spent some time down among the settlements.'

'Do you suppose he was part of Anderson's gang?'

'Certainly looks that way to me,' McTavish replied. 'It would seem our friend did not want to share the proceeds from the gold robbery. There's nothing more we can learn here, laddie. Let's cover him back up and see what trails Barraworn has found for us.'

They piled stones back over the body and it occurred to Toby that this was hard work. 'Anderson didn't shoot all of his men,' he mused aloud.

'What makes you say that?'

'He's not the type to gun down a man and then take the time to cover the body so that dingos can't get at him.'

'I see what you mean. We may have an ally out in the bush looking to do our job for us.'

'Maybe,' Toby said. 'But we must remember we are the strangers in this place. The survivor of this slaughter may not be too pleased to see us here.'

They finished covering the body and, as they moved back to the entrance, Toby found another pile of stones in a narrow crevice. 'Another body, do you suppose?'

'I don't know, laddie. Let's take a quick look.'

Once more they shifted away stones.

'Two packsaddles,' Toby said when they had removed enough to see what lay beneath. He clambered over rocks to untie one of the flaps and examine the contents.

'Bloody hell!'

A gold watch on an expensive-looking chain rolled out of the pack and onto the ground. Toby thrust his hand inside and brought out several rings, a few gold sovereigns and about thirty-five pounds worth of banknotes.

'What is it, laddie?'

Toby thrust the contents under the policeman's nose. McTavish eyed the small fortune, his bushy eyebrows raised in surprise. Toby's hand contained the equivalent of two years' pay.

'These two packsaddles are full of more of this,' Toby said.

'Anderson's ill-gotten gains. Too heavy for him to haul out of here without horses.' McTavish lifted the other flap and riffled through the contents. He tossed several leather pouches to Toby.

'From the escort gold?'

'Some of it, I think. A few of these contain coins,' Toby said. 'There are a few with jewellery in them, but most have nuggets and gold dust.'

'Then he still has some of the escort gold with him. Whatever he thought he could carry out of here.'

'Unless he's hidden that somewhere else. Not putting all his eggs in one basket so to speak,' Toby mused. 'Maybe he's coming back with new horses to collect the lot.'

'That's possible, laddie,'

'What are we going to do with it all?'

'It's far too bulky to take with us,' McTavish said. 'Let's cover it back up. We can come back for it later. Right now we need to travel as fast as possible.'

Sloan, Gatwick and Paddy were standing by their horses near the opening when Toby and McTavish emerged. Gatwick was smoking a pipe and looked rather concerned.

'That bloody tracker of yours will not come anywhere near this damned place, Sergeant, and I can't say as I blame him. It gives me the creeps, it does.'

'Not to worry, Constable,' McTavish gave him a cheery smile. 'We'll be moving on as soon as he gives us a direction to go in. Where is the good fellow, by the way?'

Sloan pointed to a distant shape in the trees. 'Over there. He won't come any closer than that. Says there are evil spirits at work.'

'Yes,' McTavish said, as he took the reins of his horse. 'We have seen their work inside.' He swung up onto the back of his horse, leaving Sloan with a puzzled look on his face.

They rode over to where Barraworn sat his horse a respectful distance from the boulders.

'What have you found for us?' the sergeant asked.

'White fella go this way, boss,' Barraworn said. 'Maybe two, maybe three days ago. Black fella follow along behind.'

'So it would seem your theory about a survivor is correct.'
McTavish tipped his hat at Toby.

'Survivor?' Gatwick asked.

'I'll fill you in as we ride, Constable,' McTavish answered.
Then to Barraworn he said, 'Lead on, Macduff.'

A t sunset Anderson found a place to hide among some
rocks where the ground was hard and stony and he
knew his trail couldn't be followed. He dared not light
a fire. Late that afternoon, he had stumbled across a small
spring and had spent a little time mixing water with his meagre supply of flour to make up a dough which he had then
eaten raw. It was bland and tasteless, but had mostly stilled his
hunger pangs.

He backed into a gap between two large rocks and made
himself as comfortable as possible, propped facing the opening. Attack, if it came, could only be from that one direction,
and he drew the revolver from his belt and placed it ready for
use on his lap. Satisfied he had done all he could, he fell into a
fitful sleep.

At dawn, he crept carefully from his sleeping place. The
valley was still shrouded in darkness, but the heights on the
far side were beginning to lighten as the first tentative rays
of sunrise played against them. Behind him, the mountainous
interior loomed. To the west, a band of high cloud stretched
from horizon to misty horizon, too thin to promise rain.

Anderson placed his revolver into his belt, hefted his calico
bag and the precious saddlebags over his shoulder, and set off
once more along the edge of the escarpment. The line of cliffs
stretched on and on, an unclimbable barrier. No wonder the
Jannjirra had remained isolated for so long, he thought. But the

line of cliffs was not continuous. About two miles away a spur descended into the valley, reaching almost to the river.

His spirits lifted as he realised this might be a way off the escarpment at last. Adjusting the saddlebags on his shoulder, he moved on.

Following the spoor wasn't easy. There was no trail left by horses, and the bushranger seemed to be employing anti-tracking techniques as he travelled, making use of every patch of rocky ground or watercourse to mask evidence of his passage. Often Barraworn was forced to dismount and cast back and forth hundreds of yards to the left and right until he regained the trail and they could follow on. At one place the trail entered a creek and they lost time searching for the place where Anderson had left the water.

'Do you suppose he knows we're onto him?' Sloan asked, as he and Toby searched the creek downstream from where Anderson's trail entered the water.

'I don't think so,' Toby answered, without looking up. He studied a patch of reeds at the water's edge, looking for a snapped or bent stem that might indicate Anderson had come this way. 'He can't know we're up here. I think he's trying to put off whoever speared those horses.'

Sloan opened his mouth to ask another question, but before he could speak a low whistle came from upstream.

'C'mon,' Toby said, splashing water in his haste, 'Barraworn has found something.'

They returned to the horses and rode up the creek to where the rest of the party waited. Barraworn squatted in reeds beside the far bank, shaking his dark, scraggly head as he examined the ground.

'You found something?' Toby asked.

'Yes, boss,' Barraworn nodded. 'One fella, same one at horses, he got white fella boots on. Another fella, him black fella, boss. Follow along-a white fella, but him hurt. Use a spear to help him walk.'

He pointed to several little plug marks in the dirt and the story that the tracks told became clear. Bare footprints led across the soft earth beside the creek, and beside each left print was a corresponding depression made by the end of a walking stick or spear that the person was using like a crutch.

'It seems the fellow who killed the horses is injured, but has not given up the chase,' McTavish said.

'Yes, but what will he do when he realises we're up here? Will he allow us to keep after Anderson or will he try and stop us?' Toby responded.

'Surely he will see we are after the same thing,' Gatwick said. 'We all want to catch up with Anderson.'

'He may not see it that way, laddie,' McTavish responded. 'To him, any stranger may be the enemy. We are in his tribal lands uninvited after all.'

'But he's hurt,' Toby said, 'and he's making no effort to conceal his tracks. He'll lead us straight to Anderson if he's able to keep up. We can overtake him and keep well out of his way. Once we're past him he won't be able to get near us.'

They moved off once more with Barraworn in the lead. Toby's words proved true; the native's tracks were far easier to follow than Anderson's. He began to wonder if the injured Aboriginal might lose interest in the chase and lead them away from their quarry, but each time he questioned Barraworn about Anderson's spoor, the tracker was able to point out the bushranger's trail beside that of the native.

S unset found them on the edge of the escarpment. Paddy looked into the valley, a sea of shadow, a bottomless void sucking at the riders as they traversed the rim. A cool breeze came out of the north-east and he pulled his jacket from the bedroll behind him and shrugged it on, trying to ease a little of the stiffness from his back and legs at the same time. He could not remember having ever spent so much time on horseback. They had taken eight days just to reach the plateau and another five to cross it, riding from first to last light. No cattle drive or muster had ever taken that long, not without a break here and there. As he looked at the wild country to the north he supposed they would be another three to four weeks in the bush.

At the head of the party, Barraworn dismounted and led them to a patch of rocky ground. He paused every few seconds to study a seemingly inconspicuous piece of earth or rock. Finally, he stopped outside a narrow opening between two boulders and looked back at the others.

'White fella, him sleep here last night.'

Toby nodded. 'Be too dark to follow soon. I suggest we rest up here for the night. We're not far behind the bastard now. No fire, no smoking in the open. If you feel the urge to light a pipe, make sure you're screened by the boulders.'

Wearily, the men swung from their mounts and began to make camp. Paddy removed Patch's bridle and examined the horse's gums.

'Bit-sore?' Toby asked, as he led Moonlight to where they were positioning the horse line. Paddy nodded and Toby took hold of Patch's head so he could see for himself.

'Just a hint. See how it looks in the morning. You may have to ride on a halter for a day or two.'

Paddy grimaced. With a halter a rider had only a fraction of the control of a bridle. But he would do what was necessary to prevent further injury to his horse.

'You and I have last watch tonight, Pad,' Toby said over his shoulder as he moved away. 'Eat something and get your head down – and don't forget to un-prime your musket before you curl up in your blankets with it.'

Paddy nodded to show he understood. He let go of the horse's mouth and moved to where his musket sat in its scabbard, the hammer uncocked and resting on the percussion cap. He yawned as he pulled the weapon from the scabbard. In his tiredness he forgot that his right hand was still covered in saliva from the horse's mouth. He curled his wet thumb over the hammer and pulled it back. The hammer had almost reached the half-cocked position when his thumb lost its grip. The musket discharged in a brilliant muzzle flash that lit the campsite. Luckily for Paddy, he had the weapon pointed at the ground, but he felt the bottoms of his legs blasted with dirt as the ball struck somewhere under Patch's belly. The horse reared in protest and Paddy only just caught the lead rope in time to prevent him bolting away into the darkness.

Men swore and whirled about as they looked for the direction of this unseen attack. McTavish drew his pistol and dropped into cover behind some rocks. Gatwick struggled to pull his carbine from its scabbard, dancing in a circle with his panicking horse, while Sloan and Barraworn had their weapons up and pointing uncertainly into the darkness.

'Are we under attack?' McTavish carefully lifted his head.

Toby noticed the smoking musket in Paddy's hand as his brother fought to calm the frightened horse. 'It's all right. There's no attack. Paddy's musket went off.'

'Bloody hell,' Gatwick roared. 'You frightened two years off my life, young fella.'

Out in the valley, echoes boomed off cliffs like a peal of distant thunder. The sound rolled on and on for miles until it dissipated into the darkness. McTavish got to his feet and uncocked his pistol. 'That was unfortunate. If Anderson didn't know we were after him, he does now.'

Paddy finally got Patch under control and stroked the animal's neck. He kept his eyes steadfastly on the horse, for he had no desire to see the anger in Toby's eyes.

Before the confusion of echoes muddled any chance of singling out the original sound, Anderson realised the gunshot had come from the escarpment above him. He was halfway down the spur with the river only a few miles away. Tomorrow he would reach it and follow it back into the settled districts. But, with the dying echoes still rumbling down the valley, his mind worked in other directions.

He was certain Chilbi had not fired that shot. He hadn't left the native with any firearms or even a single pinch of gunpowder. The shot had come from someone else. There were white men up on the plateau, and white men meant horses. If he was able to steal a horse from them, he could go back and retrieve the gold.

Whoever was up on the escarpment would be making camp for the night, waiting for first light before attempting the descent. He considered climbing back onto the plateau and setting up an ambush, but it had been a long and tiring day just climbing down to where he was. There was no way he could reach the rim before sunrise. The men up there must be chasing him. There was no other reason for them being there. Somehow a pursuit party had picked up his trail and followed him into the mountains of the Jannjirra.

If they are chasing me, they will catch up tomorrow. Then we shall see if I can't get my hands on a horse or two.

hrough crisp, clear air, Toby could see the silvery surface of a river as it snaked through the valley. In several places the waters were disrupted by a white bar where the river tumbled through rapids. Wild forest continued unbroken on either bank, a dense blanket of green that stretched as far as the eye could see. The far wall of the valley was capped by two hundred feet of sheer cliff face, the rock taking on an orange hue in the dawn light. Ahead of him, a spur dropped steeply, a tree and boulder-strewn ramp that would eventually take them down to the river.

McTavish twisted nervously in his saddle, eyeing the shadows in the surrounding bush. They were all nervous since Paddy's blunder with the musket last night. Finally, the sergeant's gaze settled on Barraworn where he squatted on the ground.

'Well?'

Barraworn's fingertips traced the outline of a boot print in the soil.

'White fella come this way, boss.'

'What about the other one?' Toby asked.

The tracker frowned and moved back and forth across the spoor, searching for any sign of the Aborigine following Anderson.

'No black fella tracks here, boss. Plenty up there,' he added pointing back towards the top of the escarpment. 'I can go back up and track him from there.'

'No. Stay with the white fella tracks. He's the one we want.'

Even as he spoke, Toby could not help but let his gaze search the surrounding bush. It was disconcerting to know that the Aborigine may now be behind them. But there was nothing to be done about it. They could waste hours trying to find out where he'd gone. Their time would be better spent following Anderson, especially now he knew they were up here. He looked to where Paddy sat forlornly at the tail end of their little column. His brother had stayed out of the way when they broke camp that morning. He knew Paddy was embarrassed and hurting following the discharge of the musket, but there was nothing he could do about it now.

Let him ride at the back of the line for a day or two, he thought. *He'll get over it.*

With Barraworn in the lead, they continued towards the river. In places the going was steep and difficult, the horses forced to squat on their haunches, slipping and sliding on loose scree. In others the slope was densely wooded and barricaded by tumbledown boulders, forcing a long traverse to find a way through. They continued without a break until well into the afternoon. When the ground began to level, Toby could hear the murmur of cascading water. Ten minutes later he glimpsed the river through the trees, no more than seventy paces away and some forty feet below.

The bush was so dense and low that they were forced to dismount and lead their horses the last twenty paces through a tangle of scrub. Finally, they stood above the rushing waters, the bank close to twenty feet high. Barraworn turned downstream along Anderson's spoor, and the rest of the party followed on foot, leading their mounts.

Toby stopped and let McTavish come up beside him. 'Once we find a way down to the water, we'll rest up for a bit, let the horses drink their fill. God knows they deserve it.'

McTavish nodded and moved on past Toby, who waited to relay his instructions to Gatwick and Sloan. The policemen both gave a smile at the welcome news and kept moving, leaving Toby to wait for Paddy. The path remained empty for the next few minutes and he began to worry that something had happened to his brother. He was about to head back along their trail when he glimpsed Paddy a hundred yards along the riverbank, examining the inside of Patch's mouth.

'He'll have to put a halter on that horse,' Toby said under his breath.

Paddy finished his examination and began to follow along, leading Patch on a loose rein.

I can't wait forever, Toby decided. *He'll just have to catch up once we find a way down to the river.* He turned and headed off, leading Moonlight back towards the rest of the party.

From below the edge of the riverbank, Anderson watched the black tracker lead his horse downstream. His guess had been correct; they were looking for somewhere to get down to the water so the horses could drink. Earlier that morning he had found the nearest place was a quarter-mile further along where the bank had collapsed onto a narrow strip of sand. Anderson had laid his spoor for them to follow, then doubled back deep in the bush and crossed to this hiding place, careful not to leave any sign that would alert the tracker.

His plan was simple enough: he would wait beside the trail until the last horseman came level with him and then spring his ambush, kill the man and take the horse. He would then head upstream and look for a place to cross the river and lie up where any pursuers would be easy targets in the open, should they try and follow.

The black tracker moved past and he adjusted the heavy saddlebags onto his shoulder. Their weight would be a hindrance, but he dared not put them down. Once he moved, there would be no stopping.

Almost a minute passed before the second horseman drew level on the riverbank above him. He had chosen a place where he could see for fifty or more paces along the game trail and the third man was just coming into view upstream of his position. The man above him wore a police uniform with sergeant's chevrons on the sleeve. The police sergeant stopped almost level and turned to look back behind him. Anderson heard him curse and then the sergeant continued on his way. The next two men wore police uniforms also. They were closer together than the first pair and talked quietly to each other as they led their mounts. These two led a packhorse each, and Anderson eyed the bulging packs hungrily.

For one brief moment of despair he thought the fourth man was the last of his pursuers. The trail upstream remained devoid of any more men and the two policemen were far too close together to allow him any chance of success. As he watched them pass, he cursed his rotten luck. Then the fifth man and horse materialised out of the shadows along the riverbank.

Anderson let the policemen pass and studied the approaching horseman. He was far enough behind the others to allow his plan to work. The man was young and dressed in civilian clothes. Perhaps from a nearby cattle run, employed as a guide into the mountains? Someone who had a little knowledge of the lie of the land? Whatever the reason for the young man's presence in the police party, he'd found his victim and cocked his revolver, glad of the rumbling water behind him that would mask any sound of his movements when the moment came.

The man approached with reins draped lazily over one shoulder, his face shadowed by many days of beard. He carried a musket in his right hand and Anderson eyed the weapon wantonly. It was just the sort of long arm he would need to shoot down any pursuers that tried to cross the river behind him. His gaze drifted to the horse following behind its master like a faithful dog, finely muscled and well proportioned, a mount that looked as if it could run well in rough bush, with the stamina to carry its rider far. Anderson could hardly believe his luck.

He stood from his position and took one look back down the riverbank. The trail remained clear of any other men. With the revolver held in front of him he stepped out of the bush. Man and horse both continued on their way, unaware of the danger behind them.

Paddy slipped the bridle from Patch's head and pulled a halter on in its place. Unless he took steps now, he could injure the horse. When he caught up with the others, he would swap Patch for one of the packhorses and rest the animal's mouth from the troublesome bit. Although Patch would follow happily along behind moonlight and he could ride on the halter if need be, if the ground became tricky, he would need to have more control over his mount than the halter could offer.

He slung the bridle over his shoulder and took up the lead rope, tugging it urgently as he stepped out. He had no desire to annoy the others further, following his unfortunate incident with the musket.

As he walked, he looked down at the river some twenty feet below. The water ran wide and deep, the bank severely under-cut and impassable. Ahead he could hear a thundering rush as the river cascaded over a bar of rocks. The narrow game trail stretched ahead. Paddy urged Patch along and they entered a sunlit clearing. He pulled his hat low over his eyes and could see his brother about to lead Moonlight into the bush at the far side of the clearing. Toby was only a hundred yards ahead of him now. He had made up his lost time.

A shape appeared out of dense bush above the riverbank. At first Paddy thought it was a kangaroo, a big eastern grey that had been trapped against the steep bank by the appearance of men and horses and was now making a bolt for higher ground, but he paused in mid-stride as he realised this was no kangaroo. He watched as the man lifted a pistol and started down Moonlight's flank. He was a big man and a full, unkempt beard obscured his face, but Paddy knew he had seen this man before.

Anderson.

Undetected by Toby, the bushranger closed to within three paces and aimed the revolver at the back of his head. In the next moment the man who had murdered Paddy's parents would take his brother from him.

His musket was still in its scabbard and would take too long to retrieve. Paddy filled his lungs to shout a warning and instantly the pain flared in the side of his head. Any noise he made died in the back of his throat, little more than a rasping hiss.

Anderson closed to a pace from Toby, the pistol almost touching the back of his head. Paddy drew another breath and opened his mouth. As he let the air rush through his throat, he felt the blinding agony tighten its grip on his mind. He managed to tense his throat muscles, to tighten his neglected vocal chords to a point where they might make some kind of noise, but the throbbing flared into a blinding pulse of agony. Stars swam in his vision and he felt the tension go out of his throat as his voice was taken from him and that horrible hiss began.

His eyes wide with terror, the air still running up his windpipe, he felt a deep anger that filled him with the strength only a wild rage can summon. As the anger gripped him, Paddy took control of it and turned it inwards, into the shadowy recesses of his mind where the pain dwelled. The malignant force was powerless to resist.

With this new-found strength of will, Paddy tensed his vocal chords. His breath ran hard through his throat and his voice boomed out loud along the riverbank.

'Toby, look out!'

Toby spun around at the warning. He had no time to look for the owner of that strangely familiar voice, for he was immediately confronted by a pistol only inches from his face, the muzzle appearing as large as a cave and the knuckle of the finger through the trigger guard beginning to whiten as it took up the tension. Instinctively, he threw up his arm and knocked the pistol aside as it discharged. A blast of heat from the muzzle singed his face. The ball passed a quarter of an inch from his ear, his eardrum almost rupturing at the roar of noise.

Anderson's thumb curled over the hammer and the cylinder rotated as he cocked for a second shot. The Lovell was in Toby's right hand, but there was no time to bring the heavy weapon up. He let it clatter to the ground, grabbed Anderson's gun arm and lifted it high. The revolver fired again and the ball shot harmlessly into the sky.

'You little bastard.'

Anderson's face was so close that Toby could smell his putrid breath. The dark eyes were filled with rage.

Holding Anderson's arm high, Toby pivoted on the balls of his feet and pushed his hip into Anderson's side. The bushranger realised the futility of trying to use his pistol and let it drop. At the same time he brought his other arm around Toby's front, reaching for his throat, his fingers clawing as he tried to get a death grip on the younger man's neck.

Moonlight reared and plunged, his reins gripped in Toby's hand. The horse came down on the struggling men, driving them apart. Toby let go of the reins and Moonlight galloped for the nearby bush, leaving them to fight it out.

Anderson stooped and snatched up the revolver. Shouting came from down the riverbank as Gatwick and Sloan appeared, running fast with their carbines at the ready. Sloan fired, still at full run, and the ball whispered between Toby and Anderson.

Toby threw himself to the ground as the bushranger faced the policemen and fired three shots in quick succession. Gatwick went over backwards and Sloan stumbled, hit in the leg. Anderson steadied himself for a killing shot at the limping constable, but Toby launched himself from the ground. He hit Anderson's arm as the pistol fired and the shot went wide.

Anderson dropped the empty pistol and advanced on Toby like a bear. He let the pair of saddlebags slide down his arm, caught them in his hand and brought them up in a backhanded swing that caught Toby in the chest. He sprawled backwards into the scrub at the edge of the riverbank and Anderson moved in for another blow.

Rolling to his feet, Toby rushed at the bigger man. They came together with a jarring thump, like a sack of wheat hitting a wagon load bed, jostling crazily as each tried to get a hold on the other. He felt hands clawing at his throat and arched his back to stay out of reach.

Somewhere in the distance someone was yelling. The others had heard the gunshots and were coming. Out of the corner of his eye he could see Paddy running towards them, musket in hand. All he had to do was hold Anderson for thirty seconds and his brother would be here to help him.

Anderson gave up trying to get at Toby's throat and used his size and reach to envelop him in a powerful bear hug. Toby was helpless with his arms pinned to his sides and the breath being squeezed out of him. He threw his head back and slammed his forehead into Anderson's chin as hard as he could. The bush-ranger cried out and staggered sideways. Toby kicked as hard as he could, landing blow after blow on Anderson's shins, but the bushranger seemed impervious to the pain.

His head tingled as he approached the limit of consciousness. In those last few seconds he panicked and kicked downwards with all his strength, trying to push himself away from Anderson. The bushranger was unprepared for the move. He staggered a few paces with Toby in his arms, twisting back and forth in a macabre dance. The pressure on Toby's chest relaxed a little and he bent his knees for another thrust at the ground. This time his kick found no purchase.

Anderson's eyes were only inches from Toby's and he saw them widen with surprise as the bushranger realised they were on the brink of the riverbank.

As he went over backwards in Anderson's arms, Toby heard his name called by that familiar voice. In the brief moment before he hit the water, he realised it was Paddy. Then the water closed about them, muting all sound. Toby felt himself tumbling as they were swept downstream.

His shoulder brushed against something smooth and hard, the stones of the riverbed. Ice-cold water numbed his senses. One of his boots was snatched from his foot, sucked away by fast-moving water. Anderson let him go then. Toby felt the arms release him as his eyes adjusted to the murky depths of the river. A vague shadow passed in front of him as Anderson struggled for the surface, trying to drag the heavy saddlebags with him. Then all thoughts of Anderson were pushed from Toby's mind as he fought for survival.

He kicked and pulled for the surface as hard as he could. Aching for air, his vision waned to a pale curtain as unconsciousness loomed. His head broke through into sunshine and he drew in two quick breaths as the current spun him about and he saw Paddy running along the riverbank above him. The current carried him up against a submerged tree trunk and he was swept underwater. Slimy wood grazed along the back of his head, then he struggled for the surface again. This time he was able to take several breaths, but the water picked up speed as it squeezed between boulders. Rocks and trees rushed by in a blur and he was tumbled and pummelled, slammed backwards into a partly submerged boulder and the wind was driven from his lungs.

Toby felt the last of his strength going. His arms were weighed down, as if by lead, each stroke a laboured agony.

Then, just as quickly as it had started, the cascades ended, and he found himself in calmer water. His foot touched bottom and he pushed upwards, gulping at the air, filling his aching lungs.

Exhausted, he half swam, half waded for the nearby bank. Coughing, he struggled onto a sandy spit and crawled until he could go no further. He lay there panting and retching up river water, spitting it onto the sand.

A shadow moved in front of him and he looked up. Anderson came towards him, water dripping from his clothing and hair.

He was bleeding from a gash in his forehead and his shirt was torn open across his chest. The saddlebags were gone. He held a rock the size of a loaf of bread in his hands as he staggered towards Toby.

'I lost my gold.'

Anderson's voice was little more than a rasp, but it carried a menace that made Toby shiver with something more than cold.

'Because of you I lost my gold. It's out there somewhere.' He pointed at the river with his chin. 'It's gone.'

Anderson took another step and Toby wanted to tell him of all the things he had lost, of the heartache and grief he'd had to endure because of Anderson. But there was no time for such words. Anderson raised the rock above his head and Toby could only stare at the instrument of his own demise, too exhausted to try and evade the blow. He waited for death, watching with a strange detachment as the rock rose to full stretch and the muscles in Anderson's arms bulged as he prepared to put every ounce of strength into the blow.

The bushranger gave a little grunt as something appeared in the middle of his chest. Anderson looked down at where a pointed piece of wood projected a foot from his body, a look of utter surprise on his face. Blood trickled from the wound and he staggered, twisting sideways. It was then that Toby saw the shaft of the spear in Anderson's back, eight feet of it, still quivering from the impact.

The colour drained from Anderson's face and his lips trembled. Blood frothed onto his beard as his breath bubbled. Toby watched the mouth work, trying to form words as the bushranger fell to his knees. The long spear prevented him from going over backwards. He let go of the rock and it thudded harmlessly into the sand, fingers clutching at the crude point of the spear, his eyes flicking from side to side, finally settling on Toby. This time he found the last vestige of strength and breath to utter one final word as he collapsed sideways onto the sand.

'Chilbi!'

At the far end of the sand spit stood a solitary figure, a young Aboriginal man wearing a kangaroo-skin cloak.

Toby tried to climb to his feet. The movement stirred the Aboriginal into motion and he turned and limped towards the scrub above the riverbank. At the edge of the trees he paused to glance back at the two men on the sand, one dead and one alive. Then he stepped into the shadows of the bush and was gone.

Toby had never seen a structure as grand as Government House. He and Paddy gaped in awe as they strode towards a pair of huge doors set back on a wide verandah. A batman swung the doors open and ushered them into a reception hall where Childers stood waiting across an expanse of blue carpet.

'Ah! Toby and Patrick. You're early. That's good. The Governor abhors poor punctuality.'

They were left with no time to admire their ornate surroundings as Childers led them through a set of doors at the back of the hall and into an outer office.

'I'll just check His Excellency is ready.'

He went to a set of large doors at the rear of the office, knocked discreetly and pushed one open.

'Tobias and Patrick O'Rourke, Your Excellency.'

A voice called from the room beyond. 'Show them through, man.'

Lieutenant Governor Sir Charles Hotham sat behind a huge desk. Sunlight showed through a pair of high windows and splashed across the carpet, illuminating the governor's gaunt features. Despite a head full of dark hair, his beard was wispy and sparse. Hotham had a thin frame. Only the gold-braided epaulettes on the shoulders of his naval uniform served to give his body any breadth. A sword in a glittering scabbard hung from a stand beside the desk. When he stood, the Governor was tall, offsetting his slender frame.

'Gentlemen, I am so pleased to meet you.'

'A pleasure, Your Excellency,' Toby said, remembering how Childers had addressed the governor.

Hotham smiled. 'I have read the excellent report prepared by Sergeant McTavish. It seems you had quite an adventure out in the mountains. And a fruitful one, too.'

'Yes, sir—uh, Your Excellency,' Toby stammered.

'Yes, quite,' the governor said. 'I shan't keep you long. I'm sure you're anxious to return to your family in Ballarat. I only wanted a brief opportunity to thank you both personally. The good Lord knows my short term as governor of this colony has not been an easy one. You gentlemen have given me a bright note I can include in one of my despatches.'

'Thank you, Your Excellency,' Toby said, getting a feel for rolling the title off his tongue.

'Yes, well—' The governor returned to his chair, seemingly thankful to be off his feet. 'I have approved the payment of the reward as posted. You gentlemen possess quite a bit of wealth now. I hope you intend to spend it wisely?' He gave Childers a little look, just a brief flash of his eyes.

'Yes, sir—I mean, Your Excellency,' Toby said. 'I would like to arrange for half the reward money to go to the widow of Constable Gatwick. I wanted to divide it up equally between all members of the pursuit party, but Mr Childers tells me police officers are not entitled to reward money.'

'A noble gesture, young man,' the governor nodded approvingly. 'Childers will make the necessary arrangements. Still, six hundred pounds is a considerable sum.'

'We have plans to set our family up on some land,' Toby explained.

'Yes, quite. Land, eh? Always a good investment for the future.' He settled back into the chair. 'Childers will formalise the reward payment with you. You have the heartfelt thanks of a colony held in the grip of terror by a ruthless man.' He waved a gesture of dismissal and lowered his eyes to the documents on his desk. 'Good day, gentlemen.'

'Thank you, Your Excellency.' Toby said. He and Paddy turned for the door Childers was swinging wide to facilitate their exit.

'Just one thing, Mr O'Rourke.' The Governor's voice stopped Toby at the threshold. 'I hate to ask, but it needs to be said. I don't suppose we shall be seeing you spending large quantities of gold dust over the next months?'

Toby felt his temper flare. Was the lieutenant governor of the Colony of Victoria accusing him of being a thief? A harsh rebuke began to rise in his throat. Then his eyes settled on the frail-looking man behind the desk, his sorrowful gaze fixed on Toby, almost apologetic for having asked the question.

'The gold shipment Anderson had in the saddlebags is at the bottom of a river in the mountains, Your Excellency.' Toby strained to keep his voice even. 'I believe Sergeant McTavish is returning to the mountains to retrieve the other gold and valuables we discovered.'

A thin smile played at the governor's lips. Toby realised his angry reaction to the question had given the Governor his answer. 'Quite right, young man. Quite right.' And Childers pulled the door closed.

Childers led them through several doors and they found themselves in a sitting room.

'Please, have a seat, boys. I shall have a clerk draft the necessary documents and then you can be on your way.

They sat for twenty minutes or more, then Childers returned with a sheaf of documents in hand. He handed one to Toby.

'Here you are, sir,' he said. 'This document authorises the treasury to release to you a sum of six hundred pounds.'

Toby reached carefully for the document in Childers's hand. He half expected to see the sheet of paper vanish or burst into flames before his eyes. Here it was, finally, after scratching about in the dirt of Ballarat to find their fortune, after enduring such tragedy and loss that no one should be expected to endure. Toby's fingers clasped the paper. He felt the coarse weave. He could smell the ink. It was real. Here, in his hands, was the means of their going home. He offered the document to Paddy, but his brother just sat silent and motionless. Childers interrupted the quiet.

'I have another document here,' the aide said.

Reluctantly, Toby lifted his eyes.

'This document,' Childers said flatly, 'overturns the ruling of a certain magistrate with regards to the surrender of land in the district of Bunyong Creek to one Henry Pelham.'

The words drifted past Toby as if they meant nothing. He blinked at the aide several times. 'You mean—'

'Your land has been returned to you, Toby. You and your brother. The governor has overturned the magistrate's ruling.'

'So all we have to do is pay what's owing to Pelham? We don't have to convince him to sell it—?' Toby's voice trailed away as Childers shook his head.

'You don't understand, Toby. I paid Henry Pelham a visit myself. He was most accommodating when he realised his little ruse had been dragged into the light. You don't owe him anything. Pelham was most anxious to avoid prosecution over the incident. In exchange for the return of the land – debt free and with all improvements intact – he will avoid a costly prosecution and possibly a lengthy gaol term. Once he knew that rogue Scotchy had given him up, he relented quite quickly. It was most improper of me to offer him immunity, but you boys don't want to be tied down in lengthy legal proceedings. You want to take your family home.'

'We can go home? We don't owe Pelham a thing?' Paddy asked.

'Not a brass razoo. The reward money is yours to do with whatever you like.'

The brothers locked eyes on each other and Paddy let out a whoop of triumph. Not to be outdone, Toby gave a whoop of his own, louder than Paddy's. His voice was in practice. They were still whooping and cheering as they crossed the lawn towards the gates by the road.

C hilbi went down to the wattle grove beside the creek and selected several branches no thicker than his little finger. These he took back up to the cave below the cliffs, where he had a small fire burning. Sitting by the fire, he chewed the end of each stick, separating the fibres to make paintbrushes. When he was satisfied with his creations, he took them deeper into the cave. The walls were covered with many murals and hand stencils, paintings of animals and spirits, stories of the history of the Jannjirra people.

Squatting beside several wooden bowls of paint, Chilbi continued with his labour of love. The mural on which he worked showed a pale stranger arriving in the midst of his people. The stranger was welcomed and treated as one of the tribe. As the story progressed across the rock, the Djarriba used their magic to infect the people with a great sickness, and everyone died except for three young brothers and the pale stranger. The survivors, led by the pale one, descended into the lands of the Djarriba and took revenge for the sickness. The warriors killed many Djarriba, but one by one they were killed off. Now, only one warrior remains, one last survivor of the people, and this is his mark.

Chilbi picked up a bowl of white paint and tipped it into his mouth. He sloshed it about for a few moments, mixing it with his saliva until he was happy with the consistency. Then he drew a deep breath through his nose and placed his right hand against the rock at the end of the mural. Paint erupted from his mouth in a fine mist, plastering the back of his hand and the rock around it. When he lifted his hand away, its outline remained there on the rock, picked out in white.

His story had ended.

Later, Chilbi wandered to the edge of the escarpment and looked out across the valley. Here and there, lights twinkled in the lowlands, the Djarriba settlements that grew closer to his tribal homeland with each passing season. One day they would reach the escarpment, and Chilbi wondered what would happen to the rock paintings and the sacred places when they did. Would they erase all sign of the Jannjirra people? When Chilbi was gone, would there be anything left to tell of their existence?

He still pondered these questions as he limped back to the campfire. The season was changing, and tomorrow he would move camp to be near the sacred burial grounds where he had other duties to perform. He turned his head in that direction and felt the yearning in his soul, an unmistakable urge drawing him towards the mountains where the remains of his people lay.

The spirits of his ancestors were calling him home.

T he day had started out cloudy and grey, but by late afternoon the sullen overcast drifted into the east, carried away by the breeze. The sun chased the chill from the air and the women removed their woollen shawls and draped them over the back of the seat.

Sitting astride Moonlight, Toby turned to the wagonette and smiled. Annie smiled back at him. She sat in the middle of the wide seat with the reins in her hand, her mother and sister on either side. She had folded a burlap bag under her bottom to cushion the jolts which the tired old springs beneath the seat were unable to cope with.

Beside Annie, Maree held Sean. Her face still showed dark shadows of grief and heartbreak. Toby knew she cried every night. Sometimes her daughters cried with her, huddled together in a wailing embrace beside the campfire, but mostly she cried alone in the darkness when she thought no one could hear.

Paddy rode beside the wagonette on Patch. Despite having found his voice, he remained a man of few words, but Toby was glad for each and every rationed sentence that came from his brother's mouth.

'Where's the homestead, Toby? How far? Will we be able to see it soon?' Betty was all but standing in the seat as she looked about. Toby didn't answer her; he simply pointed ahead to where the trees opened up and the ground rose into a long spur of ridge line. There, on a natural shelf of flat ground that overlooked the valley, sat the homestead.

'Oh, Toby!' Tears of joy ran down Annie's cheeks. 'It's beautiful, just as you described it.'

The slip rails were wide open. Toby smiled at this last little act of defiance on the part of Henry Pelham. Annie steered the wagonette through the gap and he stopped to dismount and push them closed, but Paddy slipped to the ground and seized the first rail before he could kick his foot out of the stirrup.

'I've got it, mate.'

Toby smiled at the sound of his brother's voice, each word a marvel to his ears.

Paddy pushed both rails closed and looked up at his brother. 'Just the way Pa likes it. Closed good and tight,' he added to

Toby's delight. Then he remounted and they trotted up beside the wagonette.

'We are now on O'Rourke land,' Toby told them. 'Welcome to your new home, ladies.'

A cheer went up from the three women and they clapped their hands with such delight and gusto that the horse flicked its ears with annoyance. Sean squealed his protest at the noise.

They climbed the track to the homestead and reined in below the verandah. Betty was so excited she sprang to the ground the instant the wagonette stopped and ran to the open door to peer inquisitively inside. Pelham had closed nothing behind him.

It was just as Toby remembered: the rough-sawn planks, the verandah and walls of split timber, a roof of bark sheets held in place by a latticework of bush poles.

He offered his hand to Maree and she took it and stepped down, taking in her surroundings. Annie stepped to the edge of the wagonette and he used both hands to lift her down, pulling her close and kissing her as her feet touched the soil. Their soil. Then he took her hand, led her up the steps, across the verandah and through into the kitchen.

The cast iron stove sat cold, and no pots or other utensils hung from the hooks along the mantle. Everything was gone, even the table under which Paddy had crawled on that fatal day long ago. Toby didn't care. He could get a new table, new chairs, new everything. He pushed the door open to his parents' bedroom. It was bare of everything except the faded curtains his mother had sewn. The big bed was gone.

He stepped back into the kitchen and went to the lean-to room at the back of the house. Both beds were still there. The homemade mattresses were soiled and sagging from the weight of the stockmen who had occupied them, the supporting ropes desperately in need of tightening.

They withdrew back into the kitchen to find Maree stooped in front of the stove as she examined the firebox.

'I've sent Betty to collect some firewood,' she said. 'We may have to boil water in the billy until we find the kettle, but we won't starve or go cold with this beauty fired up.' Then she smiled. Toby thought it the first genuine smile Maree had given since Frank's death and it chased weeks of grieving off her face in an instant.

'Toby? Come and give me a hand to unload, will you?' Paddy called from beside the wagonette.

They toiled until late in the afternoon, unloading and placing their belongings in the homestead. When they had finished only one item remained on the floor of the wagonette load bed, a mysterious crate which Toby had arrived back in camp with before they left Ballarat. No amount of questions could get him to divulge the contents of that crate.

Paddy went to unhitch the horse and lead it into the yard, but Toby stopped him. 'Leave it in the traces for a little while longer, Pad. We've still got one more important job to do before it gets dark.' And he patted the crate.

With a little urging, he managed to get everyone back onto the wagonette. He took the driver's seat beside Annie and whipped the horse into motion, steering the wagonette around the horse yard and up along the ridge. As they climbed higher, he and Paddy pointed out places of interest to the others.

'That's the pond where we shoot ducks,' Paddy said.

Toby looked down at the little body of water that had been the driving force behind Henry Pelham's greed. The pond was fringed with green grass and, even after a long summer, fairly brimmed with clean water. Soon, he and Paddy would head down to Geelong and buy a mob of cattle to begin breeding another herd.

They reached the crest of the ridge and Toby swung the vehicle in a wide circle to face back down the slope. He reined the horse to a stop, applied the brake and then set about getting everyone down.

Taking Sean in his arms, he walked away from the wagonette a little. 'This is where your Grandma and Grandpa are buried, Sean.' The piece of ground to which he gestured was indistinguishable from the rest of the ridge. A few pieces of quartz lay strewn among grass tussocks.

Paddy went to the far end of the stones and picked up two pieces of wood. They were nailed together.

'That's the cross we made for Ma and Pa's grave,' Toby said, and bent to replace the stones which had been kicked out of place by wandering cattle. Then he and Paddy went to the wagonette, lowered the tailgate and used two planks of wood to slide the heavy container onto the ground. Toby handed Paddy a nail iron and his brother set about prying the lid off, working his way carefully around the outside.

'It's a beauty', Paddy whispered when the lid came away. His fingers traced the outline of each letter chiselled into a polished granite headstone.

Toby retrieved two spades from the wagonette and they spent the next half-hour digging the headstone into the ground, ensuring the earth was packed tight around it. Finally, they were finished, and the brothers stood back to admire their handiwork.

Toby felt he had kept the promise he'd made on this very spot. He had brought a family back to the place that had been so important to his mother and father. His father had always said that this was a family place and a place like this needed a family to make it thrive and prosper the way it ought to.

Well, Pa, he thought, *there's a family here again, an O'Rourke family. I know you'd be proud.*

The dark was growing and the stars coming out as Toby and Patrick O'Rourke got everyone loaded back onto the wagonette. Toby urged the horse into motion then slipped his arm behind Annie's back.

'Look!' Annie pointed into the night sky above the homestead where a bright firmament of stars shone. 'That's the Southern Cross.' Her hand instantly traced the outline, found the Pointers and dropped to the horizon. 'South,' she said.

'Yes,' Toby answered, noting that Annie's finger pointed at the homestead. 'The Southern Cross is showing us the way home.'

Acknowledgements

There are many people who have offered their generous assistance on the path to bring *Blood in the Dust* to publication. If I have forgotten anyone, please forgive me.

To Lorraine Archibald and Cathy Couzner, who helped with the development of the early drafts of this novel, you are both angels. Thank you very much. To Jo Hamlet, Jackie Cavill and the members of the Donnybrook Writers' Group, your words of encouragement will never be forgotten. To Wilbur and Niso Smith, their foundation and Georgina Brown, I can't thank you enough for the wonderful opportunity you have presented me. To Kevin Conroy Scott and my agent, Charlotte Colwill, thank you so much for taking a chance on a writer from the other side of the world. To Kate Parkin and my editor, Claire Johnson-Creek, at Zaffre, thank you for all your hard work. To Rachel Capps and Rob Munro, my online writer friends whom I have never met in person, thank you for picking me up and dusting me off whenever I needed it. To my ex-Air Force and firefighter friends who have read my work, offered advice and spurred me along, thanks guys. To my mother and father, who have always believed in me, I love you both. Finally, I'd like to thank my family; Michael, for becoming my I.T. guy, and Rhonda, my wife, for enduring the ups and downs of living with a writer. I know that at times it's not easy. Thank you, sweetheart.

B.S.

Want to read
NEW BOOKS
before anyone else?

Like getting
FREE BOOKS?

Enjoy sharing your
OPINIONS?

Discover

READERS FIRST
Read. Love. Share.

Sign up today to win your first free book:
readersfirst.co.uk